WHEN THE WILLOW BREAKS

Paul R Grindrod

Copyright © 2013 Paul R Grindrod
All rights reserved.

ISBN: 1484157176
ISBN 13: 9781484157176

CHAPTER 1
Saturday 5th December 2009 (Morning)

It's Too Darn Hot

The first Saturday in December at the southernmost tip of Africa was hot, dry and windless and Richard (a fully paid up Hydrophobic) had; in an attempt to ease the throbbing pain of his hang-over, started his day splashing and thrashing inaptly in the tepid waters of the swimming pool. Learning to swim, ride a horse and knit being just three things that remained on his ever growing sixty two year old 'to do list'. By ten o'clock the sun's rays were so hot that the option of staying in the open became impossible and moving to the shade of the patio eased himself into the yellow striped fabric of his sun lounger. Reaching for a second bottle of sparkling water he unscrewed the cap and taking a long cool drink re-capped the bottle and pressed it to his aching temple and cursed the so called expertise of the weathermen. Weathermen who like politicians, estate agents, lawyers and second hand car salesmen, seemed unconcerned by the untruths, falsehood and lies they pedalled daily to their eager and gullible audiences. On his darker days, days that seemed to increase (daily!) Richard would include priests, vicars, rabbi and imam. "Liars all." he cursed as he looked up at the clear blue sky. For today the weatherman prediction of brisk south-easterly winds had been wrong (there was no wind). His promise of a thirty percent chance of rain was false (there was no rain). And worst of all his assertion that temperatures would remain in the low twenties was untrue, for the temperature had soared up into the high thirties, leaving the land and its unsuspecting people to bake under bright cloudless skies. Now no longer able to cope with the rising heat Richard picked up his towel and moving to the air conditioned cool of the house went to lie on his bed.

As evening approached and the shadows began to lengthen Richard was awoken to the sound of a thousand sprinkler systems as they 'putt putted' their song of salvation and rolling off his bed he moved slowly to the window. Above him the skies were still clear and bright promising (threatening?) another hot day on the morrow. But for now he was happy as along with the rest of a grateful population he sent up his prayer of thanks to God, to Allah and to 'goodness' for a safe passage through the day. As the light began to fade men, against all logic began to light fires. Fires that heralded the ritual of the 'braai vleis', the cooking of red meat over open fires whist consuming large amounts of lager, red wine and brandy. Richard offered no argument to this unwritten law as encouraged by a half dozen of his male friends he placed another Rhodesian blackthorn log onto an already brightly burning pyre and then watched with primitive wonderment as the bright sparks rose like glowing imps into the night sky. As the night grew steadily darker the more staid of the women began to move indoors to gossip and prepare salads (salads that would remain untouched by their men folk) whilst men in their ego and alcohol filled drunkenness began to dance the 'Gumboot'. The dance, a corruption of an old Zulu war dance performed by Wellington boot clad Zulus on the gold fields of Johannesburg, and involving much clapping of hands and lifting of legs usually, when performed by white men, resulted in at least one of the participants falling backwards into the swimming pool or onto the open fire. This mayhem continued late into the night when just before midnight (or was it just after) and having emptied far too many glasses of red wine (or was it bottles) Richard made one final and lecherous attempt to bed his PA, but failing made his weary and lonely way to bed.

CHAPTER 2
Sunday 6th December 2009 (Early Morning)

Sleepless Nights

Even with his 'French doors' wide open and the ceiling fan slowly turning Richard's bedroom had remained hot and his sleep disturbed. Disturbed by the heat of the night, his drunken state and the thin cotton sheet that wound itself around his bare legs. His tormented plight was not helped by the massed chorus of cicada beetles that sang noisily outside the window nor by the single mosquito that 'zeeeeed' lazily around his head. But in truth it was not the heat, sheet, beetle or mosquito that kept Richard from sleep but his thoughts, worries and dreams (if in fact one can compartmentalise the three concepts of thought, worry and dream). Alone in the darkness he listened and waited as the mosquito's drone grew steadily louder and nearer. Then came the attack, the pain and blessed relief as he brought his hand down against the side of his face, the force of the blow not only taking the life of the mosquito but caused Richard's ears to ring and hum. Quietly he lay as he continued listening for any signs of a renewed attack. He heard nothing, save the sound of his own breathing and the distant call of guinea fowl and rolling onto his front he sank his face into the softness of his pillow and closed his eyes. 'Level' (a horizontal palindrome) were Richard's last rational thoughts as once more he drifted into his own pointless and private world of thoughts, worries and dreams.

For Richard morning came early and noisily with the south east wind (promised yesterday) blowing wildly through the tree tops and tugging angrily at the fabric of his window blinds causing them to rap unrhythmically against his window pane. Half awake he turned in his bed and felt for the comfort of his wife's body, a sad smile forming at the corners of his mouth as he remembered that she wasn't there and that she wouldn't be there. Pulling a cool pillow to his chest (a poor substitute for the warmth of a female body!) he closed his eyes and fell into a long and peaceful asleep. He didn't move again until the early morning sun had begun to warm the polished boards of his bedroom floor. Rolling onto his back he opened his still tired eyes, pushed himself upright, stared up at the slowly turning blades of the ceiling fan and tried to recapture the pieces of his dream. It was a dream that had taken him back to England and to his 'little ones'. He could remember clearly playing cricket in the back garden and laughing as William hit the ball into the old Sycamore for the third time. He also remembered the boy's mother calling them for lunch and the three of them running as they shouted their challenge of *'Last man in is a sissy.'* Sadly he was unable to retrieve any other highlights from wherever it is that old dreams are stored and turning he looked red eyed at the bright numbers of his alarm clock. It was a clock that scolded his slovenly behaviour and yelled at him to get up, but still resisting the call to rise he pulled the cotton sheet to his chin and closed his eyes. Another hour had passed before Richard finally roused himself to wakefulness and leaning precariously out of his crumpled bed he picked the fallen pillows from the floor and propped them behind his head. Then, with his mouth tasting like the bottom of a bird cage and his head throbbing he lifted the crumpled sheet from his legs and swung them to the floor. Padding tip-toed he crossed to the balcony where he lowered his heavy head onto the coolness of the wrought iron balustrade and squeezed his eyes tightly closed. Relieved by the metal's cool comfort he lifted his head and took a long slow breath of the morning air, the aroma of warm pine, dry earth, jasmine and wood smoke sending a heady cocktail of smells to his already overloaded senses. Lowering his head once more to balustrade's metal he took a few moments to collect his thoughts. Sighing heavily he shaded his eyes from the now rapidly rising sun and looked out across the wide valley. In the distance the ancient bougainvillea of a neighbouring wine farm drooped lazily over bright lime washed boundary walls and the even older gnarled vines held their ever ripening hopes for another prosperous year. Lowering his gaze he looked down to the pool where Gabriella stood drying herself on an over sized towel. For several minutes he stood silently watching (ogling) as she see-sawed the towel across her shoulders and back and then bending began to pat dry her long tanned legs. Then rapping the towel turban-like around her head she moved towards a sun lounger and eased her body onto its striped fabric. Realising that he had perhaps lingered (ogled) a little longer than was polite Richard turned and walked quietly to his bathroom beginning what was colloquially known by the males of the family as the three S's, that is to shower, shave and empty his bowels. Returning to his bedroom and feeling a little less 'night before' Richard dressed, ran a stiff wire brush through his short grey hair and then happy with his appearance made his way downstairs to the kitchen. Normally, that is to say on weekdays, Richard, being conscious of his waist line and his increasing number of tooth fillings, tried to forgo the luxury of sugar. But this was the weekend and so taking a blue and white striped mug from its hook he dropped in a tea bag and reached into the cupboard for a blue and white striped sugar bowl. As he did so his mind, as it was want to do more and more these days, took him back through the years. How well he remembered the long past week-ends when with his second son John he would go joyfully and boyfully off to Blackpool and book into a semi decent boarding house. On these trips father and son would follow a number of set rules. Rule number one was that there was to be no talking before ten in the morning. Rule number two was to have a full English breakfast in a 'greasy spoon café'. Their third ritual, having lined their stomachs with grease and caffeine, was to 'down' their first pints of Guinness and hopefully down them before one o'clock. The rest of their day would be spent drinking and watching rugby on wide screen TV. As they watched a steadily growing number of 'Hen Parties' would file through the bars. For some reason many of the inebriated young ladies (particularly the Welsh girls) found this father and son relationship 'lovely' and would bring their scantily clad bodies over to where father and son sat. Richard, his hearing and eyes sigh not being as good as they used to be, had to lean closely so that he could hear and see the young ladies clearly. Being gentlemen neither father nor son ever touched a one of those lovely girls and that was a truth and then as darkness began to fall they would make their way (alone) to an Italian restaurant where they would eat pizza, drink red wine and chat with the waitresses. On those trips Richard's dreams were full of the wonderfully erotic long legs and white teeth of nubile females. Those had been good days, days when John had been freer to spend time with his 'old man'. Yes they had good times, good times indeed. Roused from his reverie by the strident ringing of the kitchen telephone Richard put down the sugar spoon and in a less then jovial mood picking up the cordless instrument and spoke. "Two six zero five."

"Richard?" a gentle and subdued North Yorkshire accent enquired.

"Walter?" Richard queried somewhat redundantly, for the voice was well known to him.

"It is." came the Yorkshire man's reply to which Richard, knowing that Walter had never been much of a conversationalist or a man to 'wear his heart on his sleeve, moved to the kitchen table and pulling out a chair sat down and with the tip of his index finger began to align the salt pot with its pepper pot mate. For many years Richard and Walter had worked together, first in the Health Service and later in Private practice. The two men had got on well, but both being somewhat introvert, their relationship had gone no further. There had been no after work drinks and little sharing of family happenings. In the April of 2006 Walter's wife had been diagnosed with terminal cancer and Walter, no longer able to cope with the 'trivial problems' of other people or people in general (including Richard and his attempts to help) had left the practice. Sadly in the September of the same year Barbara had lost her battle and Walter had descended into deep and lasting depression and the pair had not spoken for over two years. Now Richard, not really wanting to go down the road of regret, recrimination or melancholy asked Walter how he was.

"I'm missing Barbara like hell." Walter told him and then in a brighter tone added 'that it was time he moved on'. An awkward silence followed as Richard racked his brain for the words to meet both his and Walter's needs, the silence so long that Walter, thinking that the line had been disconnected began to tap anxiously at the centre button of his telephone. Roused from his reverie by the clicking in his ear Richard uttered an 'Hello' and a 'Sorry' and Walter, unsure if the 'sorry' was intended as a mark of regret for his missing Barbara or for the extended silence informed Richard that he was thinking of making a trip to Cape Town. "You're coming to see me?" Richard asked in surprise and then turned as the sound of the kitchen door opening paused the conversation. Placing the tip of his finger on his lips he smiled up at his advancing P.A and mouthing a silent 'Good morning' returned to the conversation.

"Yes if that's okay." the waiting Walter queried, his tone once more tentative.

"Sure it's okay." Richard reassured as the curious Gabriella tapped him on the shoulder.

"Any idea when?" he questioned as he raised his hand somewhat impatiently to the equally impatient Gabriella who mouthed a silent 'Who is it?'

"I believe that the best months to visit are January or February." Walter continued unaware of the skirmishing at the other end of the line. "When it's not too hot or cold?" he questioned.

"Good choice *Walter*." Richard said emphasising Walter's name for Gabriella's benefit. Nodding her understanding Gabriella then moved to the table and sat down. "Any dates in mind?" Richard continued as he watched Gabriella pick up his newly aligned salt cellar and start to inspect its blue and white stripes.

"Not as yet." the waiting and obviously relieved Walter answered. "But I'll visit the travel agents in the morning and then get back to you."

"Okay and great." Richard told him "and I look forward to seeing you soon Walter, take care." Then, thinking that his conversation with the usual taciturn Walter was over, Richard smiled across at Gabriella, who for no apparent reason was tapping pepper onto the palm of her upturned hand, and whispered "You okay?" Smiling back she told him she was fine.

"Thanks Richard and it's been good talking to you, oh and Happy Birthday." the now chatty Walter continued, "Is it fifty four or fifty five?" How Walter knew or had remembered his birthdate Richard didn't know. As far as he could remember he had never in the past received a card from Walter and he certainly had no idea of Walter's date of birth or for that matter his age. "Well thanks Walter, that's very kind of you." a grinning Richard told him. "And believe it or not I'm sixty two today, but" he quickly added "I don't feel it."

"And you probably don't look it." Walter told him and then keeping to their new 'let's support each other' script promised to telephone again when he had a better idea of his travel dates. "Oh and give my regards to Gabriella." he added and then rang off. For a short time Richard sat holding the 'purring' telephone in his hand then getting to his feet he replaced the hand set and moved once more towards the work tops and tentatively tapped the hot kettle with the palm.

"How was he?" Gabriella asked as turning in her seat she got up and moved to stand beside her boss.

"He sounded okay," Richard told her as he clicked down the kettle's switch "but he's still missing Barbara like hell." "Oh the poor man," Gabriella suggested and reaching across her boss she removed the lid from the blue and white striped bread bin and taking out a white sliced loaf squeezed it. "Life can be so shit." she added then Gabriella, ever compassionate but ever practical informed Richard that the bread was a bit off. "But it should be okay for toast. Want some?" she asked.

"And life can be good." Richard countered as the sensual aroma of his P.A.'s scent filled his nostrils forcing him once more to suppress the unwanted feelings of desire (lust) and yearning. "We just have get things into perspective " he announced as he spooned coffee into the cup "and roll with the punches."

"Oh yes, says mister in control."

"And what's wrong with being in control, pray tell?" Richard asked his tone holding more than a hint of displeasure. Over the years Richard Blackwood had developed (drifted into) a number of conversational genre. The first was his professional genre, a style of conversation that revealed itself as a calm almost calculating way of talking. It was a way of addressing distressed clients that not only put them at their ease, but also opened their minds to new ideas. The second genre had been with him since childhood. This was his 'chatter box' mode and was used when he was either in a good mood or under a lot of emotional pressure. His third mood was to sulk and when in 'sulk mood' he would either remain silent (his record being three days) or like now subject his listener to such negativity that giving up and giving in to his childish annoyance they would walk away leaving Richard to his very hollow victory. It had to be said that on most occasions Richard was well aware of the mood he adopted and sadly on most occasions he was unable (unwilling?) to do anything about it.

"Oh nothing, but." Gabriella told him.

"But what Gabi?" Richard persisted peevishly.

"Oh nothing and if you're going to be grumpy why don't we just forget it?" she told him crossly. "I just thought that the man had gone through a couple of rough years and deserved a little sympathy."

"I think you mean empathy." Richard corrected smugly.

"Okay empathy." Gabriella conceded "So, is he coming to see us or not?" On the face of it was a fairly simple and honest question, but Richard in his tired and grumpy mood continued with his negativity.

"Yes." he told her irritably. Now annoyed by what she saw as his rude prevaricating Gabriella turned to face him. "Come on, Richard grow up." she snapped "When?" Sadly her admonishment went unheeded as the obstinate Richard, continued with his stubborn and childish game. Taking two slices of bread from the packet Richard inspected them and dropped them into the toaster. Again Gabriella asked then question 'when' and again the question reminded unanswered as Richard moved to the fridge and took out a jar of 'Fine cut Marmalade' and waved it in Gabriella's general direction.

"Want some?" he asked. With her patience at breaking point and yet knowing from experience that at times like these politeness was the best policy, Gabriella told him 'No thanks, just butter' placing her hand on his shirt sleeve.

"Come on Richard." she smiled primly "When?" Whether Richard had grown tired of his little game or he was not yet tired of living (for he knew well the limits of Gabriella patience) he turned and smiled back at her.

"I think he said he would be coming in early January." he said and then Gabriella, pleased with her victory took her hand from his sleeve and slipping immediately into her 'I'm in charge' mode placed plates and coffee mugs on a tray.

"Perhaps when Walter arrives," Gabriella suggested the boot (slipper?) now firmly on her foot "you could take some time off and show him around."

"Now why hadn't I thought of that?" a sarcastic Richard asked.

Because mister," Gabriella countered even more sarcastically "you have me to do your thinking for you." And Richard, knowing from experience that any form of fight back was hopeless, sat silently watching as toast, coffee and marmalade were brought to the table.

The couple's conversation over breakfast was at first subdued, but by degrees it drifted back into companionable civility and by the time breakfast pots were washed and put away their usual calm had been restored. Wiping her hands on the tea towel Gabriella folded it and hanging it neatly on the oven door she crossed to the dresser. Opening the bottom right hand drawer she took out six white envelopes and a small red box. Handing them to her boss she wished him a 'Happy birthday'. Laying his cards on the table Richard sat down and began, somewhat self consciously to turn the box in his hands. "Thanks Gabi," he told her "and sorry about my antics of last night. I think I may have crossed a line."

"You did and what line would that be?"

"The line that says we mustn't..."

"Mustn't what have a good time on your birthday boss?" Gabriella laughed "Well if you must know I'm flattered that you chose me to flirt with and I'm even more flattered that you can remember what happened." Relieved and happy with the reply Richard pushed back his chair, placed his hands on Gabriella's shoulders and returned her kiss. "You're a star O'Brian." he told, "but I think you know that O'Brian don't you?"

Gabriella O'Brian was indeed a 'star'. Born in the southern half of Ireland to an Irish father and an Italian mother her mixed ancestry seemed to give her an easy and carefree charm. She was a tall woman standing five foot eight in her stockinged feet. Her thick black hair was worn shoulder length.

It was true that she had a few 'laughter lines' at the corner of her green eyes, but to Richard's mind that only added extra character to her otherwise clear complexion, a complexion that belied her fifty years. Yes Gabriella was indeed a good looking woman. Richard had always struggled to find the right words to describe Gabriella to his friends and had never done better than 'dependable' and 'funny'. The pair had first met over five years ago when a kind and wise friend had advised her to visit Richard's UK therapy practice following the horrific injuries her husband had received in a road traffic accident. When Michael died Gabriella's world had fallen apart and Richard using Cognitive Therapy had helped her to understand and to deal with the loss in her life. Later she had joined his practice as his PA. If truth were known it had been Gabriella's organisational skills that had been instrumental in the rapid growth of Richard's U.K. practice and it was Gabriella who had put her weight behind the idea of setting up the Cape Town operation. Now Richard, happy with the ease of his escape from last night's indiscretions, held up the red packet and boyishly asked if he could open it now. "Certainly not," Gabriella told him as she re-asserted her authority "cards first and then boxes." and so dutifully placing the box in his trouser pocket Richard began to examine the hand writing on each of the envelopes in front of him.

"A yacht on the high seas, I bet this is from my mother." he guessed as he flipped the card open. He was correct. "And this picture of leggy young women is definitely from Steven and Katie" he said as again he opened the card to confirm what he already knew. "That's two out of two Gabi" he boasted.

"Oh really?" an impressed Gabriella told him, but unwilling to manipulate Richard's inflating ego she drew her eye brows together and asked what came before a fall. "A garden scene, this must be from my little sister." Richard continued ignoring her challenge. "And this red sports car that will be young James."

"Okay mister clever clogs, but there are still two cards left" Gabriella told him but Richard, convinced that he was equal to the challenge just smiled and turned the penultimate card in his hands. "Well this one is definitely from you Gabi." he announced triumphantly "There's no mistaking your scrawl." and taking the card from its envelope he began to read.

'Happy Birthday and May the Lord Bless You Always' the printed verse told him and underneath in Gabriella's clear hand was written *'To a dear friend and a fine man. Thank you for being you and for everything you have done and all you mean to me. Strive to be happy, Love Gabriella.'* Telling her 'thank you' and that he would indeed strive to be happy Richard leant forward and once more kissed her cheek. To Richard the thought of having to strive for happiness was something new. Like all people he had had his share of disappointments. As a young boy he remembered asking for a guitar but being given a ukulele banjo. *'A ukulele only has four strings.'* his father had said. *'It will be much easier for you to get your small hands around the neck.'* And as a teenager he remembered asking for a saxophone and receiving a clarinet. To Richard's these well remembered disappointments had helped to mould him into the man he was today and now, as he thought again of those birthdays past, of their excitement and their disappointments he moved slowly to the lounge. One by one he placed the cards on the mantle shelf much as his mother had done, her husband's card on the far left followed by her children and then friends and neighbours. So it was that with his mother's card on the left Richard worked down the line with Steven's next to it. Then (as his mother had done as a reminder to her wayward and forgetful children) he left a gap before placing Steven's card and then the cards from his two sisters. Gabriella's card he placed, with a slight feeling of awkwardness on the far right. Continuing to hold the final and unopened envelope in his left hand, which he knew would be from his sons William and James, boys that he loved so dearly, yet in his heart how he wished the card could be from Grace or from his number two son John. For some seconds Gabriella stood watching, unwilling to break into Richard's sad reflections and then, unable to stand his pain any longer, asked with forced excitement "Aren't you going to open it?" Resignedly Richard slid his finger under the flap. "It's from William, it's his writing Gabi." he told her as he ripped at the envelope flipped and taking out the card began to read. *'There goes another year and here comes another wrinkle.'* he read. *'Love you Dad from William and James*

XX X. Carefully placing the card on the shelf Richard stood back and stared quietly at the gaps, gaps where John and Grace's cards should have been, gaps that seemed to shout their own messages of pain, regret and failure. "Come on Richard, let it out." Gabriella said as she moved to his side and in her compassion touched his hand. "You'll be okay; it's just that you've had a few rough months. Being away from the family can't be easy." Oblivious to her presence Richard, a man who gave such a believable show of being calm and detached, this Behavioural Therapist who ably guided his clients through the most difficult and heart breaking situations, continued to stare at the gaps between the cards. Gaps that seemed to mirror the voids and emptiness of his life. Gaps that cancelled out all the love and affection embodied in the six joyful cards before him. "Richard." The voice came to him from far way. "Richard." Gabriella repeated then as if waking from a deep sleep Richard turned.

"I'm fine Gabi." he said and then, as he looked into her anxious and troubled face, his tears began to fall.

"Oh Richard I'm so sorry," she told him "come on let it out." Then as his sorrow built and her sympathy (empathy) grew Gabriella, against all the rules of their relationship took his face in her hands and kissed him. It was a kiss born of compassion and respect, but a kiss that was destined to happen, a kiss that spoke of their mutual longing. This was not their first kiss that had happened very early in their relationship when passions had been running high, passions that had almost wrecked their friendship and Richard's marriage.

CHAPTER 3
Sunday 6th December 2009 (Midday)

Number One Son

Richard stood and watched as the double garage doors slid silently up and over. On trips to see Steven it was always a bonus and an aid to his drinking, if Gabriella drove. Unfortunately this ever wise ever vigilant P.A. was on to that little trick and even before the hopeful words 'shall we take your car or mine' were out of his mouth Gabriella was pushing her sun glasses to the top of her head and suggesting that they take the Audi. Richard fully understood Gabriella's motives for they both knew that whenever he and Steven got together they tended to drink too much, and of late Richard's drinking too much was becoming something of a norm. "Mine it is then." he conceded as he stepped forward and with no attempt to hide his disappointment opened the passenger door. At one time Richard's 'old fashioned' way of opening doors for 'ladies' had not been welcomed by the 'I'm more than able to open my own doors thank you very much' Gabriella. But now, as she swung her long legs into the car's foot well she adjusted her skirt, clicked her seat belt into place and smiling up him. "Thank you my man." she told him as like some kind of old retainer he stepped forward and gently closed her door and walking round the vehicle climbed behind the wheel.

Although the afternoon sun was high and its rays hot the trip from Richard's home in the leafy district of Rondebosch to that of the even leafier district of Kirstenbosch the air felt pleasantly cool. As they travelled high and arching trees sent their sweet smelling scent of pine, oak and sycamore through the car's open sunroof and windows. Closing her eyes against the dancing brightness of the high canopy; and Richard's good humoured and unremitting chatter, Gabriella moved her seat backwards and reclined her body down into soft black leather. Just what it was about the final six inches of a woman's legs that brought out the primitive in men Richard didn't know nor at that moment did he care, for as the black cotton dress rose upward so too did his eye brows and the contents of his trousers. Oh yes Gabriella O'Brian was indeed a beautiful, sensuous and desirable woman. "It's no wonder I'm having difficulty understanding this relationship young lady!" Richard told himself as his P.A. once more shifted in her seat. "Just who are you Gabi, friend, colleague or lover?" Had Richard's words been spoken aloud Gabriella's answer would have undoubtedly been 'Who do you want me to be Richard?' but the words were not spoken out loud and so with her eyes still closed Gabriella's lips parted into the briefest of a smile. "You just keep those beady little eyes on the road ahead Blackwood" she told him and doing as he was told Richard turned his eyes to the road ahead. The rest of the journey continued in silence.

The gates to the secure housing complex were high, heavy, ornate and closed. Stopping the Audi Richard waited for the bored, lounging and unsmiling security guard to amble out of the sanctuary of the gate house and smiling up Richard handed his Photo Pass into the guard's huge black hands. After cursory checks the guard handed the pass back and then bent to make a long and thorough assessment of the driver's still lounging passenger. Seemingly happy with his assessment (although there were no outward signs of joy) the gates were opened and Richard giving his nod of thanks, a nod that was returned with no more the briefest of white toothed grins, slipped the car into first gear and moved off. Moving slowly he made his way between lush green lawns and manicured multi- coloured flower beds towards the large and detached house that was Stephen's home. Parking the car under a high and ivy covered 'lapa' he pushing open his door and stepped out into the cool shade where he was immediately met by a tall and green jacketed African. With a slight bow the man wished Richard a 'Good morning' and then moving towards the passenger bowed again and then with a ramrod straight back opened Gabriella's door. Accepting the

African's offered hand Gabriella swung her legs out of the car and stood, straightened the seams of her skirt and smiled up, thanked him wished him a 'good morning'. The voice that answered her was deep, smooth and rich in the consonants of the Zulu tongue. "Good morning Madam," the voice rolled "I trust you are well."

"Oh very well thank you Jacob." Gabriella told him "and you?" Whether it was Gabriella's fascination with the deep and brassy bass of Jacob's voice or Jacob's pleasure with the soft Irish- Italian lilt of Gabriella's was unclear, but both seemed be attracted to the other. It was not an outwardly sexual attraction, although given a different time and place who could tell what may have happened? No this was an attraction of warm mutual liking, of having met before in another life, met in a different time and place! "I'm very well thank you madam." Jacob told her as he gently closed the car door and then turned to face her. Ever since their first meeting the liberal Gabriella had had difficulty with Jacob's use of the word 'madam'. For one she was not his madam, or for that matter anyone else's madam, and two the word madam only seemed to emphasis the cultural and racial gap between them. It was a gap that she didn't agree with and a gap she didn't want. So on their first meeting she had asked Jacob to please call her by her given name of Gabriella. It was a request he had acquiesced to, but on her second visit his use of the word had returned. Again Gabriella had asked him to please call her by her given name and again Jacob had, with difficulty used it. After that visit Richard had to his cost tried to explain that having to use Gabriella's name had caused Jacob some embarrassment "Cultural and racial difference still run deep Gabi in this country." he had told. It was a statement she didn't like or agree with and she told him so, but later and after careful thought she had bowed to what was in fact Jacob's wish.

"And how are Precious and the children?" Gabriella continued.

"They are also well..." Jacob told her as they began to walk towards the house. "Thank you for asking..." Whether or not Richard noticed the double omission of the 'madam' word Gabriella certainly did and turning she held out her hand to Jacob's straight and solemn frame. "No thank you Jacob."

she told him. "No, thank you Gabriella." the proud African whispered. "And God bless you."

With her heels 'click clacking' on the white marbled floor Gabriella followed Richard through the high Redwood front doors and into a wide and antique lined hallway. On all sides flower arrangements bloomed, their heady aroma mingling with the fresh scent of recently polished furniture. Ahead a wide and ornate stair case wound gently upwards and mid-way up (or down) and with his back towards them stood Richard's first born son. On hearing Gabriella's clicking approach Steven turned and with outstretched hand descended the staircase to meet them.

"Mornin' father." he beamed as he slipping effortlessly into the flat Lancashire vowels, "And Gabi?" he added as he nodded towards Richard's P.A. and taking his father's hand he squeezed it. Responding happily to his son's Lancastrian drawl Richard threw his arms around Steven's waist and lifted him off his feet.

"Eye lad, en thanks fert invite" he smiled as he spun his son in a wide arch and then lowered him slowly to the ground. Safely back on terra firma a grimacing Steven arched his back and then to the ruinous sound of bones clicking against each other he rotated his neck several times. "Bin 'ere long?" he asked "I didn't 'ear you arrive."

"That's because son," Richard explained as he put his arm around his son's waist "I'm silent, but deadly."

"Silent and deadly, now that sounds like one of your farts dad." Steven said laughing at the old family joke.

"You think so?" Richard grinned as he glanced conspiratorially over his shoulder at Gabriella, "Well let me tell you something...compared to some people I'm no more than a farting novice." To Gabriella, who was well versed in the wired and wonderful banter of the Blackwood males, the statement drew no more than an aloof 'Oh yes?' but to Steven's girlfriend it was an affront not only to Gabriella but the whole of womankind. Dressed in a white shirt (probably one of Steven's) tailored blue jeans and a pair of black slip on shoes Katie moved slowly down the staircase. She had first met Steven on one of his visits to the Grand West casino where she worked as a croupier.

It was a job she enjoyed and continued to enjoy despite Steven's efforts to persuade her to take a job that didn't place her under the lecherous gaze of so many other men. But now with her tanned face framed by her short black hair and a look of genuine pleasure on her face she smiled down at the advancing Richard.

"We ladies" she said as he took Richard's hand "do not fart,"

"Oh no, so what happens to young ladies farts?"

"Well sir if you must know a fart fairy comes in the middle of the night and takes them away."

"Ah how quaint." Richard told her as he bent to kiss her hand "but not particularly believable."

"So you have a better explanation?" she asked. Richard had not.

"So mister," she added having won the argument "just how old will you be this time?"

"How old do you think I'll be Katie?" Richard asked as he foolishly selected a number well below sixty.

"Mmm now let me think, somewhere between forty and death?" Katie offered and then smiled broadly she bent and kissed him gently on his cheek. It had not been the answer Richard had hoped for and so placing his hands on her shoulders he sighed loudly and then thanked her for her encouragement. "Still at least you're looking young and lovely today." he told her truthfully.

"What only today!" the pedantic Katie moaned as she moved her lips into an exaggerated pout.

"No not only today my dear," Richard smiled as he corrected himself "today and always." This last tacky and reprehensible comment proved far too much for Steven, who calling his father 'a 'randy dog' suggested that he 'chat up his own bird', took his father's arm and led him towards his study.

As the two men walked down the hallway Steven was conscious of the conversation he had had with Katie earlier in the day, a conversation where Katie had expressed her concern about his father's relationship with Gabriella.

"You know Steven," she had said, "I don't think Gabriella knows that Richard and Grace are separated"

"Oh come Katie, Gabriella's not stupid of course she knows.'" Steven had told her impatient as always with any criticism of his father.

"Okay we'll see," Katie had persisted, "but I'm concerned about both Gabriella's and your dad's happiness."

"Look Katie I don't think Grace will ever take dad back and we both know that Gabriella is spending all her time at work, or hanging around the house with dad. They might as well be together."

"Okay, but have a word with him Steven... just to please me, I don't want to see anyone hurt."

"But is it any of our business Katie," Steven had asked. "They're both grownups you know."

"Please Steven."

"Okay but no promises. If the moment comes I'll pry."

"Not pry, take an interest. Please."

"Okay," Richard had repeated, "And meanwhile you can interrogate Gabriella. What a party this is going to be. Now where did I leave those thumb screws?"

CHAPTER 4
Sunday 6th December 2009(Afternoon)

Girl Talk

Unzipping her soft leather handbag Gabriella placed it on the breakfast bar and began to delve into its depths. One by one she placed object of various colours and shapes into a pile until that pile no longer able to maintain its shape spun and rolled across the counter's marble surface. Unperturbed by the noise and clatter of falling make-up, scissors, nailfiles, keys, coins, pens and other assorted treasures Gabriella bent and picking up the fallen items placed them back in her bag. The task of retrieval complete she placed her hand once more into the bag's cavernous depths and removing a golden cylinder turned to Katie. "This is a fabulous kitchen." she admired as she eased the cherry pink lipstick upward and began to smooth it the across her lips.

"It is nice isn't it." Katie agreed. "Steven has such good taste don't you think?" she agreed "Coffee or wine?" she asked.

"No contest Katie." Gabriella laughed as she returned her lipstick to the dark abyss of her bag. "If Jacob is doing the driving I'll do the drinking."

"Wine it is then." Katie approved as she crossed the kitchen and opened one of the many oak cabinets. "Steven's got some really nice wines." she smiled as she surveyed the array of bottles in front of her. "Come on Gabriella let's treat ourselves." and taking a down a bottle of '86 Chardonnay she placed it on a tray. Collecting two large and long stemmed crystal glasses she placed them next to the bottle and then with her ever present packet of cigarettes she picked up the tray and walked out to the garden. Above her the sky was clear blue and cloudless. "Sun or shade?" she asked as she placed the tray on an old looking, but obviously new wrought iron table.

"I think the sun for me, but only for a short time," she added "a lady can never be too careful about her complexion can she?"

"She cannot." Katie agreed as she once more picked up the drinks tray and moving further into the garden placed it on a low table eased herself down onto the thick yellow and white striped cushions of a sun-lounger. "So Gabi come on and tell me how you are?" she asked as she poured two generous measures of the white liquid and handed one to Gabriella.

"I'm fine."

"That's good to hear Gabi" Katie nodded and taking a cigarette tapped the end against the packet "because sometimes I worry about you."

"No I'm fine really Katie and but, well …" she hesitated.

"Go on." Katie encouraged as she put the cigarette to her mouth.

"No it's nothing and I really shouldn't complain, but."

"But?"

"But sometimes life can feel so empty."

"Empty?" Katie echoed as she picked up her lighter and flicked the flint.

"Oh it's nothing Katie and I know it's silly." Although the women had known each other for only a short time their relationship was developing into a trusting one. "But," Gabriella continued. "I still miss Michael so much. He was such a wonderful man and I seemed to have had him for such a short time." Unsure of how to respond Katie put the flame of her lighter to the cigarette and taking a long and cancer causing drag blew, as if to save Gabriella the same fate, the smoke into the air.

"Look Gabi I'm not sure if I should ask this question …?" she started.

"You can ask me what you like Katie." Gabriella smiled as she lifted her glass and saluted her friend. "I don't want to have secrets from you. Apart from Richard you're my only really close friend. Cheers."

"Cheers Gabi." Katie said as she absently returning the salute. "Look,"

"Yes?"

"Well I don't want to cause you any distress, but do you think you will ever marry again?"

"What a strange question Katie why do you ask? No man could ever replace Michael and I have Richard for company. Nice wine, thanks."

"Yes it is nice Gabi," Katie said as she emptied her second glass of the expensive Chardonnay "but Richard can't have been much company for the last few weeks I would have thought."

"Not good company Katie?" Gabriella asked, suddenly unsure where the conversation was going. "What do you mean not good company, I don't understand."

"You do know, don't you...?" Katie stalled.

"Know what Katie?" Gabriella asked suddenly unsure where the conversation was going.

"Well... that Richard has left Grace."

Slowly Gabriella placed her glass onto the table. "Where ever did you get that idea from Katie?" she asked. "Richard phones Grace every night and if she hadn't wanted to spend Christmas in England with her mother and family she and the boys would have come out here."

"No Gabriella." Katie said refilling her glasses. "He split up with Grace just before you came out. I just knew he hadn't told you." Again Katie took a long draw on her cigarette. "I told Steven you didn't know."

"Bloody hell Katie I think you've got that wrong, I would have known." Gabriella continued. "Richard couldn't hide something like that from me."

""I'm sorry Gabi and guess it's none of my business, but I think you'd better ask him. I know he has this 'thing' for you and from what I've heard always has. Now I need more wine." and getting to her feet Katie turned and walked briskly back towards the house. "But," she called over her shoulder. "I thought you ought to know."

Pushing back her own chair Gabriella got to her feet. "Just what are you saying Katie?" she called as she followed her friend back towards the house.

"Oh come on Gabi." Katie sighed as she lifted another bottle of wine from the rack.

"No you come on Katie." Gabriella pleaded as she placed a firm hand on her friend's shoulder. "And please will you just stand still for a moment." With practiced skill Katie removed the foil wrapper from the wine bottle's neck and removing the cork flipped it expertly into the bin.

"Okay Gabi," she said as she poured new wine into new glasses and handed one to her friend. "You just sit down and calm yourself. Have a sip of this. I think you're going to need it."

"Katie, just tell me what you're getting at then perhaps I'll be able to calm down"

"Look Gabi you're not making this easy." Katie said as she turned back towards the garden.

"Not making what easy Katie?"

"Well your relationship with Richard of course."

"What about my relationship with Richard?" Gabriella asked as once more she took her seat at the patio table. "I agree that Richard gives me most of what I need. He's solid and dependable and he offers me companionship. He was with me in the dark days when Michael was ill you know and helped to pull me through when Michael died."

"And love Gabriella what about love?"

"Love Katie, what do you mean?"

"I guess being closer is what I mean."

"Closer?" Gabriella repeated crossly.

"Yes closer Gabi more committed."

"More committed Katie. In no way am I ready for more *commitment* as you call it."

"Oh really is that so?" Katie questioned as once more she refilled her glass.

"Really and if this splitting up with Grace is true, and I don't believe it is, but if it is, well how did you know?"

"Look Gabi Richard and Steven talk and then Steven talks to me, but listen Gabi I don't want Richard or Steven to know about our conversation. You won't drop me in it will you?"

"Well Katie if you don't want trouble perhaps you shouldn't gossip and to answer your question, no as you so poetically put it, I won't drop you in it, but what about Steven?" Gabriella asked "does Steven think Richard and Grace will get back together?"

"I asked him that Gabi and Steven said he didn't know. He never really got on with Grace and blamed her for the breakup of his parent's marriage."

"And do you think Steven wants to see his dad and Grace split up?"

"No, I don't think so. Steven's not usually a vindictive man."

"God Katie what a mess and you know what Katie." Gabriella said as she stood up and walked to the pool's edge. "You would like Grace, she's one of us."

"One of us, what does that mean?" Katie asked as she followed her friend to the water's edge.

"Well Grace is a strong woman." Gabriella explained. "She's a woman who hates injustice of any kind. She believes in fairness and loyalty. I think that's why she finds Richard so aggravating at times."

"Richard aggravating, how do you mean?" Katie asked.

"Oh you know in the way men can be, thoughtless, unreliable, and childish."

"Is that how you saw Michael?"

"At times yes and Steven?"

"Steven can be pig headed when he sets his mind on something. He just can't seem to let things go. He forgets what time it is. It's always 'in a minute' or 'I'm just doing this or that'. He can drive me mad. It's one of those I can't live with him and I can't live without him situations. In the end he's just a little boy in a man's body. Bless him."

"Gee Katie," Gabriella sighed as she watched her friend drain yet another glass of wine. "I wish we hadn't had this conversation."

"Yes, me too and I'm really sorry Gabi." Katie agreed as she took out another cigarette and tapped it against the packet. "I didn't mean to upset you. I was just thinking about your happiness and please remember" she added as she flicked her lighter into life "that you're still a young and beautiful woman. And yes you're right, Richard is a good friend. And yes, he will be there for you as long as you need him. But just be more aware that Richard is a man." she grinned as she drew in the white smoke "and men can be real bastards. Believe me; I've known a few in my time."

CHAPTER 5
Sunday 6th December 2009 (Mid Afternoon)

Man Talk

Leaving the girls to do whatever it is women do when they get together (probably gossip was Richard's guess) he followed Steven down the corridor to the study where he settled himself into the deep comfort of leather chair.

"So son how's business?" he asked raising his hand to accept the offered libation,

"It's booming dad." Steven told him as he lifted his whiskey glass in salute. "The money's just pouring in, so much so that I'm thinking of setting up a trust fund."

"Really?" his father questioned "Who for?" he asked.

"I think you mean for whom dad!" the ever pedantic Steven corrected with a smiled.

"Okay whom..." Richard conceded and then, as if to lock the word into his memory banks he mouthed it several time. "Whom," he repeated "Whom." And then changing the subject asked what Steven's partners thought about the idea?"

"Michael Bennet is right behind me," Steven informed him "but Charles the tight wad is far less enthusiastic."

"Charles Ascot Chisholm" his father scoffed, "Of all the people I've ever met that man really winds me up, the money grabbing bastard, if I had my way..."

"Yes dad I think I get the message ..." Steven grinned, "But as a therapist shouldn't you be a little more tolerant?"

"Tolerant with Ascot Chisholm you must be joking?" his dad countered, "God with a name like that you'd think he'd be loaded."

"Oh he's loaded alright dad and he intends to stay that way. But then hasn't that always been the way of the world, the rich get rich and the poor get poorer?"

"Oh true son." Richard agreed. "So who... sorry whom were you thinking of as beneficiaries?"

"I thought something like the Big Issue dad." Steven suggested as he put down his drink and reached for the cigar box and clicked open the cedar lid. "They seem such a great organisation, want one?"

"A Big Issue?" his dad joked and then holding up his hand told his son 'no thanks'. "I've done three months without them and it would be a pity to break my record."

"Well done dad I'm proud of you." Richard's first born told him and then suddenly unsure if he had recently told his father of his love and pride added "But you knew that, didn't you?"

"Oh yes son, I know." his father laughed "but it's always good to hear it again."

Closing his eyes Steven drew on his King Edward. "Sure you won't have one dad." he asked as he blew the grey smoke towards the ceiling. "It is your birthday." Leaning forward Richard lifted a cigar from the box and turning it between his fingers inhaled its sweet aromatic scent and then placed back in the box.

"No thanks son." he said as he sat back into the soft leather of the chair and watched as the grey smoke of Steven's cigar drifted ghost like across ceiling. Its aroma reminding him of all the good times he had spent with Steven, whiskey glass in one hand and a good cigar in the other. For several minutes the two men sat silently and contentedly, each lost in their own world of thoughts and wishes.

"Katie and I were talking earlier." Steven's said at last as he bit hard into the bullet Katie had given him.

"Oh yes." Richard questioned as he bit into his own bullet. "And what were you talking about?"

"Oh it was nothing really. We were just wondering when you're going to make an honest woman of Gabriella?" Richard's response was brisk and pointed.

"Hell Steven where did that question come from?" he asked as he placed his glass on the side table and turned to face his son.

"Oh nowhere dad," his son lied. "It's just that Katie and I were talking this morning."

"Talking," Richard exploded, "gossiping more likely young man." he cursed, "Don't you two have anything better to talk about than an aging man and his secretary?"

"Now father," his son told him "it's you who is making the relationship sound sordid."

"No Steven," Richard fumed "I'm just giving Katie the spice she's looking for anyway," he added "you may have forgotten, but I am still married to Grace and as the line goes, he lied, Gabriella is just a friend and colleague."

"Just a friend dad, I don't think so?" Steven told him unbelieving, "She's much more than that."

"Oh is she?" Richard questioned "and what makes you think that?" he asked and immediately wished he hadn't.

"Well you must be shagging her you old dog." Steven explained and then wished he hadn't and his father in a mixture of anger, embarrassment and disbelief got to his feet and moved to the window.

"Now young man," he said as he turned to face his son, "you just listen to me. For one, I object to your language, and for two you can believe me or believe me not, but I have never laid a finger on that woman." he lied for a second time. "Yes she's a very special lady and I enjoy her company, but nothing else Steven. Grace is my soul mate and I'll wait until she is ready to forgive me. Now, end of conversation, Okay?"

"Okay," Steven conceded, still unconvinced.

"You okay?" Richard asked four hours later he sat beside Gabriella in the Audi.

"Tired," she told him "but I guess the day was interesting for both of us."

"Interesting is a word." Richard agreed as Joseph eased the car around the twisting lanes of Constantia.

""Did you get the third degree from Katie?"

"Just a bit and you?" she asked.

"Oh yes just as bit." Richard smiled as Gabriella's weary and nodding head came to rest against his shoulder.

Once home Richard went to make coffee and brought them into the lounge. In his head he knew that this was not the time or place to try talking to Gabriella about the morning's events or of his conversation with Steven. Both he and Gabriella were tired and he for one had had far too much to drink and so when the words came they came out all wrong. To Gabriella's credit she listened politely but then the emotions of the day proved too much for her and sobbing loudly she pushed Richard aside and made her way upstairs to her bed.

"Well old chap Richard told himself ruefully as he made his way down to the office "that could have gone better." But Sunday night were Skype nights, and time for him to call his little boys in England and so standing at his desk he clicked on his computer and went to pour a glass of whisky. "So mister?" he asked himself as he waited for the machine to warm up. "To woo or not to woo that is the question. And my friend," he added "if you're going to woo then who to woo?" The silliness of rhyme bringing a sudden smile to his lips he took long and throat burning swig of whiskey and then turned as the computer's urgent buzzing announced that the William Blackwood was on line.

CHAPTER 6
Sunday 6th December 2009(Evening)

Love in the Afternoon

For six and a half days a week Duncan Chadwick worked in the family business; a business that had been set up by his great grandfather in the early 1900's. Over the years the business had seen its ups and downs, two world wars and too many recessions had all helped or hindered the firm's development and now as Christmas approached Duncan pondered his wisdom in employing a second sales assistant. Bicycles, it would seem were not as popular with the latest batch of computers using and Xbox playing morons. Still Duncan thought as he rolled down the shop shutters and mounted his newly acquired twenty six gear drop handle bar racing cycle, he and his mother were comfortable and wanted for nothing. Yes Duncan's life was full, for if he wasn't busy at work or sitting at home with his invalid mother he would be indulging in his greatest passion of cycling. Today however Duncan would be foregoing the delights of an eighty mile Trans- Pennine cycle ride and taking one of his ladies out for a spin. Duncan, it has to be said, was not a particularly good looking man, but for some reason his athletic frame and his wry sense of humour did seem to attract the fairer sex and so, for the second time in a week Duncan Chadwick guided his green Ford Mondeo (circa 1998) through the sun lit lanes of his native Lancashire. As he travelled he sang; his bass-baritone voice complimenting Freddie Mercury as he headed towards the climax of 'Bohemian Rhapsody'. Duncan knew the words and the road well and was soon making a right hand turn into his chosen and secluded spot. Parking the car as far away from the road as possible he switched off the engine then turning to his left he bent and kissed the woman sitting next to him. In no way was it a passionate kiss but it was enough to rouse the woman into action and reclining the Mondeo's seat backwards she lifted her skirt. Duncan's second kiss was more passionate as he fumbled impatiently with the small buttons of the women's white cotton blouse. Murmuring softly the woman offered no resistance as Duncan's rough strong hands found their way onto her thigh, her murmuring turning to moans of pleasure as she grasped his erect and unsheathed penis. And then he was inside her, her wet and waiting vagina sending waves of pleasure up and causing her eyes to close and her mouth to open with sighs of joy. Sadly Duncan Chadwick was not a particularly attentive lover, if he had been he would; as he raced huffing and grunting to his urgent climax, have heard the four words that fell unbidden from the woman's lips. "Yes Richard, please more." she pleaded as the damp and dying member was taken from her. Nor were the words heard by Richard Blackwood as he sat quietly beside his P.A. as they made their way home from his sixty second birthday party.

CHAPTER 7
Monday 7th December 2009(Morning)

Upset

Having checked his diary the night before Richard knew that there were only two appointments requiring his attention, the first at eleven o'clock would be at the offices in Cape Town and the second a home visit to Shirley Marchant in Table View. Whenever possible Richard preferred to see his clients in their home environment for it was here that he found them to be more relaxed which in turn helped him to put their lives and needs into context. Dressed in what he thought of as his therapy outfit of dark trousers, short sleeved shirt and black shoes he stood in front of the mirror. Buttoning down his shirt collar he ran a brush though his hair and then made his way downstairs to the kitchen where he found Nellie his housekeeper tidying already tidy drawers. Turning at his approach she smiled and flicking down the switch on the already warm kettle opened the tea caddy and removed one of the perforated bags.

"Not having one Nellie?" he queried although he already knew the answer, for Nellie Christian was of the 'old school'.

"No thank you master." she told him as she placed the tea bag in a mug "I've just had some." The fact the Nellie, couldn't, wouldn't or shouldn't share a cup of tea with her 'boss' still caused Richard some irritation (embarrassment) but her use of the word 'master' really struck hard. The word causing him such deep seated discomfort and awkwardness that he didn't know what to do or say to make it better, for himself or Nellie

At one point in South Africa's history Nellie would have been cast as a Cape Coloured. In the bad old days her parents would have taken the pencil test. It was a test where the authorities pushed a pencil into a black person's hair. If the pencil stayed in your hair you were classified as black, if the pencil fell out you were classified coloured. Families were split by this cruel and simple test, their futures decided by a pencil. And so in those often brutal days a child would go to live with the parent with hair of the same density. Nellie's father had passed the test and she had grown up as a 'coloured'. As such she would be a little more privileged than the children of black parents. "Are you sure you won't have some tea?" Richard asked as he watched Nellie pour boiling water onto his tea bag. Her answer remained the same and so, in the kitchen in the suburbs of Cape Town the remnants of colonialism and apartheid lived on.

With his mug of tea in hand Richard made his way to the lounge and sat down at the piano. For some time he had been trying to master his latest challenge, 'Angel Eyes' and so turning the pages of the music book he began to play. Struck again by the way the baby grand responded to his 'ham fisted' attempts to play jazz he battled for half an hour with the first eight bars and then finally admitted defeat and moved on to the slightly easier Streisand hit 'The Way We Were'. His hour of 'me' time at an end and without much progress being made Richard forced himself away from what had become one of his greatest pleasures and prepared for work.

Richard's journey into work was agreeable enough, the post rush hour traffic always being lighter, and for Richard anything that helped to make the day less stressful was always a bonus. Not that his working day caused him any undue distress, Richard enjoyed his work, so much so that he often had difficulty in actually calling it work. Today however, as he steered the Audi into its reserved and secure parking bay, his mind was full of trepidation. It was not an anxiety born of any client based issues, oh no, for Richard clients offered few new challenges. No this was a far more menacing threat, this was Gabriella O'Brian. Lifting his brief case from the boot of his car and with his opening lines of an apology forming in his brain he walked slowly, very slowly towards the office building. Stepping out of the lift he strolled with an unfelt nonchalance down the brightly lit corridor to the suite marked Emotional Solutions and paused. Then pushing open the door wished his receptionist a 'Good morning' and made his way to Gabriella's office where he loitered like a school boy awaiting his head master's displeasure. If he could have found some reason to be elsewhere, anywhere at that moment, he would most surely have chosen to be there, but there was nowhere to run and so taking his courage in both hands he pushed open the door. For some moments he stood and watched as his P.A. finished her phone call and then switching on his brightest smile he stepped forward.

"Good morning Gabi..." he beamed to a stony silence.

"Like a coffee?" he offered to the sound of turning papers. "Gabi?" he questioned as he moved further into the room (into the lion's den) still no reply. "Come on Gabi let me get you a coffee?" he offered.

"No thank you Richard I'm fine thanks."

"Sure?"

"I'm sure thanks."

"Got much on today?"

"Mostly accounts."

"And?" he queried.

"And?" she parried.

"And?" he persisted.

"And," she relented, "I have a meeting with Harry Spears. We're doing a presentation later in the month. "Remember?" she said accusingly as she looked up from her pretend world of work.

"Yes Gabriella I remember." he told her triumphantly and pushing her 'out- tray' to one side he sat down on the edge of her desk. "Somerset West at nine o'clock on the twentieth, right?" he questioned.

"Yes that's very good Mr Blackwood." Gabriella conceded unable any longer to continue her negativity. "Harry has great hopes that you'll work your magic and inspire his people to greater independence and efficiency."

"No problem Gabi." her boss crowed "not with you at my side." he slimmed.

"Bastard." she told him.

"Granted." he conceded, "Now I have to see a new referral at eleven."
"Yes."
"And then I'm off to see Mrs Marchant in Table View."
"Yes?"
"And I just wondered if you fancy bunking off for lunch?" he offered.
"Nice thought," she told him "but I'm a bit busy."
"Come on Gabi...we only live once." he coerced.

"Indeed we do Richard." his P.A. conceded and with a little more passion than a decision to have lunch merited. Getting up from the desk Richard crossed to the window and looked down on the street below. He knew he had to talk to Gabriella about the events of the weekend and about his ham fisted attempt to reassure her about their relationship but, if truth were known he felt confused and he was pretty damn sure she felt the same. In all the time Richard had known Gabriella he had never had any secrets from her, either in his business or private life. He had shared with her the ups and downs of his marriage, much as men do when in the pub with their mates and now he realised that his failure to tell her of his split with Grace had been a mistake. But, would Gabriella really want to hear that he still loved his wife and still wanted to be with her, he thought not. No if Richard were honest what he really wanted was the status quo, the best of both worlds, both Gabi and Grace but and that was a ridiculous idea wasn't it? And so the idea was dismissed but not before an involuntary smile had flickered across his lips and the words *If only* had flashed across his brain.

"Look Gabi about..." he said as he turned from the window, but that was as far as he got as Gabriella rising from her desk crossed the room and stood beside him.

"No Richard" she told him "what we did was wrong, but I'm not sorry and I'm not sorry because life is too short. I've known you and loved you for a long time..." and then she paused placed her hand on his shoulder. "I'm in a new country Richard" she continued "and I intend to make a new start and I'd like to make that new start with you." The silence that followed told its own story, no words were needed but still they came as Richard turn to face his friend, lover and confident.

"Gabi" he began again and again he stalled.

"Yes Richard?" she encouraged.

"I do love you Gabi." he whispered. "You know that don't you but..." Knowing what was coming Gabriella took her hand from his shoulder moved silently back to her desk.

"But Grace..." he began, he got now further.

"No Richard." she told him "We've been through this already and I'm not interested. Grace is lovely woman and..." But now it was Gabriella's turn to stall as she fought for the words and the will to continue. "Oh what the hell" she cursed "I love you and I want to be with you okay. But I can't, and I won't wait forever." Her words were spoken with such love and determination that they left Richard in no doubt whatsoever about her determination and her resolve. "So Mr Blackwood," she said as she moved back to his side, their previous conversation, if not forgotten then most certainly closed. "Mrs Marchant, do you still want me to come with you?" For some moments Richard stood and silently looked down at the street below. In his heart he knew that he loved his wife more than anything in the world, but Grace's actions over the last six months had left him feeling unsure. And Gabriella! Well with Gabriella there had been an instant chemistry from their first meeting, but the thought of leaving Grace and his boys, well it filled him with shame and dread. Fantasy was one thing, he knew that, but adultery and the abandonment of his young sons was quite another thing. But now Gabriella was drawing a line in their relationship. If he wanted to be with her he would have to commit myself fully and that *would* mean leaving Grace and the boys. Yes it would seem that the ball was clearly in Richard's court and for the first time in a long time he would have to make a decision and make it on his own.

"Richard..." Gabriella's voice came for far away, beckoning him back to the here and now, to the business of the day. "Richard" she asked "are you okay?"

"Yes, sorry, what?" he faltered as he turned from the window.

"Mrs Marchant Richard, do you want me to come with you?"

"If you like Gabi," he told her "although I think I'll be safe with Mrs Marchant, but on the other hand" he smiled "a chaperone may be wise?"

"Oh Richard, you haven't been leading more ladies up the garden path have you?" Gabriella smiled as if the earlier conversation hadn't taken place.

"No not me," Richard told her as he lifted his shoulders in sad resignation "but some women do seem to find me attractive you know."

"Ah yes and those would be the blind ladies I expect." Gabriella told him and then she laughed.

"Blind, deaf or one legged, "Richard told her with sad irony. "I like them all."

"Then I'd best come with you." she grinned and taking his arm she gently squeezed it. "We wouldn't want you breaking too many hearts" she suggested and then she looked deep into his eyes and with her own hard earned and well deserved irony added two words. "Would we?" she asked.

"Any calls Rachel?" Richard asked as he walked slowly and thoughtfully into reception.

"It's Monday Richard. There've been plenty of calls, but nothing for you." his receptionist smiled as looked up at the sound of his approach. In no mood for cheery banter Richard thanked her and then in the hope of finding a little peace and quiet made his way to his office.

"Good morning boss, I was just looking for a missing file." his most troubled and troublesome colleague beamed as he pushed open the door. With sinking heart Richard returned her greeting and then watched in disbelief as folding her legs she eased herself to the floor. "Daniels." she explained flipping open a folder, "I must have put it on the wrong pile.

"Oh," Richard discouraged as a pair of pink and white woollen tights rose from the darkness of his colleague's long black skirt. Amy Nell was a single lady in her early forties and a lady who Richard, if he were ever asked, would probably have described her as plain. But a lady, he would also have been quick to add, made the best of what she had. Amy's long black hair showed no signs of greying and her makeup was used with care. From Afrikaans stock she had lived the early part of her life on a beef farm in the Orange Free State and at five foot eight inches tall was solidly build but not Richard thought, overweight. Today Amy was dressed smartly and as usual in black from top to toe, apart from her socks.

"Busy?" Richard asked the need to be hospitable locked into his psyche.

"As always Richard, you know I don't like to be idle. Would you like coffee?" she asked half rising from her squatting.

"No thanks." Richard told her as he averted his wondering eyes from the increasing span of bright woollen underwear. "I have a client due at eleven. So how are things with you?" he asked.

"I'm fine really Richard," she told him, "but I've just had Mr Devlin in and I'm not sure where he's taking me. Some of the things he tells me are a bit scary."

"Best tell me more Amy," Richard offered as he looked involuntarily down at his watch "but I'm a bit pushed for time."

"I'll be brief." Any told him as she too checked her own time piece. "It's just that he's been telling me about his time on the border with the army and I'm not sure what is truth, what comes from a vivid imagination or maybe from his paranoia.

"Perhaps he just likes to talk? Richard suggested as he moved towards the door. "But keep me informed and if you ever want to discuss the case just come and find me, okay?" then he turned. "When's your next supervision Amy?" he asked his hand on the door handle."

"Later this week and yes I'll keep you posted."

"Otherwise " Richard questioned and regretted the question even before it had left his lips.

"You know me Richard." Amy told him with a smile "I can make anything into a problem."

"Oh don't I know it?" Richard agreed as he threw her a knowing smile. "Make a problem, ask for a solution and then do your own thing."

"It all helps to keep you on your toes boss and it helps me to gain some attention." And then with head bowed Amy Nell returned to her notes.

Back at reception he picked up a pile of new referrals and opening the first began to read. *'Mrs Sharpe came to me three months ago saying that her mother....* Rubbing the back of his neck he placed the papers back on the desk. Richard's attempts to live a normal life, whilst living a lie were now beginning to take their toll. His chickens were coming home to roost.

CHAPTER 8
Monday 7th December 2009 (Mid Morning)

Give me Patients

"Good morning Mr Blackwood." The woman, probably in her late forties was tall, slim and wearing a dark orange turtle neck sweater. It was a sweater that to Richard's debauched and appreciative mind was probably a size too small. Her skirt, also dark orange clung tightly to her shapely thighs and to Richard's roaming and licentious eyes, was just a little too short. Her tights, also dark orange, flowed flawlessly up and curved seamlessly down to her dark orange high heeled shoes. Uncrossing her long legs the woman stood and moving seductively forward took Richard's hand and control of the conversation. "Good morning." she repeated breathlessly "I'm Elizabeth Taylor and this," she said indicating the six foot four mass of humanity standing silently standing beside her "is my son Raymond. He's a little shy" she panted her hand still in Richard's "and doesn't go out much. I blame his father he was such a..." Gently extricating his hand from Ms. Taylor's tender embrace Richard tilted his head upward and smiled.

"It's a pleasure to meet you Ms. Taylor..." he began.

"Elizabeth please." the effervescent lady sparkled as she held up her manicured hand.

"Yes Elizabeth," Richard echoed pulling his eyes from the ladies heaving chest "and you Mr Taylor, how are you?" Mr Taylor made no reply, or he made no reply until his mother's elbow had connected with the roundness of his ample stomach. Then standing with head bowed as if in shame or disgrace and with a dark patch of sweat growing under the arm pits of his once blue Eton shirt, Raymond Taylor told Richard that 'he was fine' and offered his hand. Taking the large, damp hand in his Richard thanked his new client for coming in and then fighting the urge to wipe his now damp hand down the seat of his trousers turned to his right. "Would you like to follow me?" he asked indicating an old and half frosted glass door behind him. Raymond Taylor, head still bowed, stayed where he was. Not however his vivacious and vociferous mother who collecting her designer handbag from the chair beside her advanced purposefully and resolutely toward the door. She didn't reach it as smiling apologetically Richard placed his hand protectively on the door handle. "I'm sorry Elizabeth," he explained gloomily "but it is a rule of our practice that new clients are always seen on their own. I'm sure you understand." he added doubtfully. Elizabeth did not understand nor did she want to understand for this was a lady who had spent most of her life getting nothing but her own way.

"But Raymond" she suggested threateningly "would want me to come with him. Wouldn't you Raymond?" she bullied. For some minutes no one spoke and then Richard, who had spent the last five years vying and sparing with much greater adversaries than Elizabeth Taylor smiled benignly.

"I'm sorry Elizabeth, but those are the rules. Now..." he said turning to the ever alert Rachael "could you get Ms Taylor some tea?" and without waiting for either woman to answer guided his new client from the room.

Silently and slowly the two men walked down the wide and highly polished corridor until Richard, selecting the second room on his right stood to one side and allowed Raymond to enter. Like all the rooms in the Emotional Solutions suite room two was furnished to Richard's own personal, if somewhat chaotic style. The wooden desk although highly polished held the signs of age with stains of both water and ink marking its surface. The three brocade armchairs didn't quite match and the coffee table had a decided list to port. Against the far wall an old sideboard, looking as if it had come from an old deceased aunt's estate, held a bowl of fresh fruit and on the floor the pastel rug, once vibrant had faded into an undeterminably mix of brown and yellow. On the walls were a mixture of landscape paintings and photographs showing scenes of the UK and Africa. Snow covered Cumbrian

Mountains contrasting with the arid deserts and lush wine lands of Namibia Cape. Moving to the coffee table he bent and picking up a newly filled water jug waved it nonchalantly in the air.

"Like some?" he asked. Raymond declined.

"Sure?" Richard checked.

"N-no, yes, n-no I'm f-fine?" his flustered guest stuttered before uttering what was to become his mantra, "Sorry" he said.

"No worries." Richard reassured as he poured the cool liquid into his glass. "Shall we make a start?" Unhearing and repeating his 'sorry' Raymond had moved to the window.

"It's j-just… my mother" he explained as he looked out across the city, "she's just used to p-people doing what she tells them."

"Is she?" Richard questioned as he picked up his water and moved to stand beside his client.

"Yes s-sir," Raymond confirmed as he looked first to his left and then to his right.

"Including you?" Richard asked pointing his glass up the wide avenue.

"I guess so M-Mr Blackwood." Raymond conceded as he followed Richard's gaze up towards the station and beyond. "B-but she means well?" he added as he dropped his eye to the street below and then to his highly polished size fifteen Ferragamo Chelsea boots.

"Yes I'm sure she does Raymond." Richard admitted as he turned his back on the view and moved from the window. "Shall we make a start?" he asked holding out his hand to indicate the choice of seating available. Following Richard's suggestion Raymond moved to the centre of the room and then settled uncomfortably onto the sofa's edge.

"I'm s-sorry," he repeated as he studied the watercolours on the wall in front of him "but do you think I could have some water?" Then, continuing what for Raymond was something of a speech he admitted that he felt nervous. "P-people make me nervous" he added, "I'm sorry." Admitting that he often felt the same Richard moved towards the coffee table and after pouring water into a glass and placing it in front to his client sat down.

"If I sit here Mr Taylor" he explained as he opened his file "you'll be able to see what I'm writing, it that okay?" Agreeing that it was indeed 'okay' and having finally found his tongue Raymond bravely asked if Richard would call him Ray.

"Mister Taylor sounds so formal." he clarified as his cheeks coloured in embarrassment and his shirt front took on a darker hue.

"No problem Ray." Richard told him. "I know this is not easy for you, so if you'll call me Richard we can make a start. Now first things first do you think you could tell me how you are feeling today, say on a scale of one to ten." Telling Richard that he was okay and felt quite comfortable Raymond crossed his long legs and settled nonchalantly and nervously back into the sofa.

"So can we say that you're what, a five or a six?" Richard queried. Agreeing that six was fine Raymond leant forward and against all odds asked 'why?'

"I'm glad you asked that Ray." Richard said both pleased and surprised at his new client's boldness, "If we mark your score today" said pointing at the paper work in front of him "then mark it again the next time you come we'll be able to see if you're feeling any better or worse. It just helps us see if we're making any progress." Agreeing that keeping a score seemed like a good idea Raymond turned to face his therapist and smiled for the first time.

"I think I'm going to enjoy our meetings." he admitted and picking up his glass took a long sip of water. Returning Raymond's smile Richard thanked him.

"It's good to get feedback Ray," Richard told him as he took another piece of paper from the file "Now do you think you could me to make a list of all the things that stops you being happy."

"Not including my mother?" the now more relaxed Raymond asked as he flashed a conspiratorial smile at his therapist.

"Include your mother if she stops you being happy Ray." Richard smile noncommittally "remember, it's your list and it's your life we're talking about."

"No I was only joking Mr... Richard, my mum's okay really, she just wants to keep me safe."

"And do you feel unsafe Ray?"

"I know I'm nervous about going out."

"And do you know why?"

"I guess I don't have much confidence and I'm frightened of looking silly. I'm frightened of people picking on me."

"And do they pick on you?" Richard asked as he placed the file on the cushion beside him and turned the better to see his client's face and reactions.

"Some boys threw fruit at me."

"When was that Ray?" Richard asked as his voice slowed and dropped a decibel.

"About... I don't know...maybe two years ago?"

"And was that the first time you felt silly or felt picked on?"

"No the first time I remember feeling that way was on my second day at nursery school. We were told that we could take our favourite toy to school. My mum didn't have much money in those days and when I showed the class my toy they all laughed because it was old and shabby."

"And that was how long ago Ray?" Richard questioned although he already knew the answer.

"Twenty seven years ago Richard, silly isn't it?" his client confessed.

"No Ray," Richard said his contradiction carefully balanced. "Perhaps it was cruel, but silly no. Our emotions are very important things you know." And then sensing that their relationship was now strong enough for him to challenge further he asked if Raymond knew what happiness was, although again he thought that he already knew the answer.

"I don't think I've ever been happy Richard." Raymond told him, his tone matter of fact and emotionless. "In fact I'm sure I've never been happy. What is happiness Mr Blackwood." he asked, his voice for the first time holding a slight tremble.

"Happiness Ray?" Richard echoed as he fought for time and an answer. "Happiness?" he repeated "Happiness is a state of mind, or so the books tell us." And then still at a loss for an answer he asked his client what he thought happiness was.

"Is it not being sad?" Raymond asked, his voice mirroring the word.

"I guess." Richard told him changing tack "so what makes you sad Ray?"
"Everything, I don't go out, I don't have any friends, I'm Thirty Six and I still live with my mother, I guess I'm just a waste of time and perhaps don't belong here."

"Oh no Ray you belong here as much as anyone else, I tell you what will you help me fill in another paper?" Richard asked unhappy at the direction he had led the conversation and without waiting for answer reached for Raymond's file and removing the 'Dysfunction Thinking Sheet' began to lead Raymond through the fifteen questions.

Fifteen minutes later Richard clicked his pen closed and placed the completed papers on the table in front. "You've said true to a number of those questions Ray" he pointed out as he picked up his glass "and this makes me wonder about you always wanting to please others and about your fear of getting things wrong. Do you think you set yourself high standards?"

"Oh I have to Mr...Richard" Raymond stuttered as once more his head and his voice dropped to their earlier sad and matter of fact tones. "My mother doesn't like me if I get things wrong."

"Doesn't like you or the things you do Ray, there's a big difference you know." Richard explained as he raised his glass in salute to his client and sipped. "Do you love your mother Ray?" he asked his own tone now matter of fact.

"I should love my mother shouldn't I?" Raymond asked somewhat perplexed and then following Richard's lead reached for his glass and began to examine its contents.

"Gee Ray should is a big word and not one I particularly like." Richard admitted and then he paused. "You do know that as a human being you have rights don't you?"

"Rights Richard?" the increasingly uncertain Raymond questioned as he placed his still full glass on the table. "Rights what do you mean?" Placing his own glass on the table Richard removing two sheets of papers from the file and handed them to his client. "As you will see Raymond" he added as he eased himself into the sofa "it tells you that you have rights. A right to be happy, a right to make decisions that affect you and a right to change your mind." Then crossing his legs he placed his hands behind his head and waited as Raymond slowly examined each line of print.

"My mother's a lawyer you know." Raymond explained as he turned to the second of the typed sheets "And she told me never to rush when I'm reading any documents. It seems a bit silly when you trust someone, doesn't it, but..."

"You take your time young man," Richard told him as he slipped unconsciously into the less formal form of address. "We've still got plenty of time" he added as he glanced quickly at his watch, a watch that told him that in reality he had only fifteen of the forty five minutes of the session remaining. Ten minutes later a still and even more perplexed Raymond thanked his therapist and handed him the papers.

"No Ray you keep them." Richard told him. "Take them with you and if you get a quiet minute read them again. Then, when you come back and see me, we'll be able to discuss them, it that okay?" he checked.

"Yes okay" an unconvinced Raymond said as he folded the papers in half and slid them into his shirt pocket.

"Now Ray our time is up," Richard said as he clicked his pen closed as if to emphasis the ending of the session "but before you go I'd like to thank you."

"Thank me Richard, what for?" an even more bemused Raymond asked as he pushed his huge frame upwards. "Thank you for your patience and your honesty." Richard told him. "I know it's not easy sitting there and answering my questions. So thank you. Now let's go and book you another appointment."

As they entered the reception area the two men were met by a less then calm Elizabeth Taylor who, getting to her feet moved towards her son, took his hand and asked him if he was alright. Telling his mother that he was fine Raymond then informed her that Richard had asked him to come back and see him again. Elizabeth made no reply, but turning held out her hand and thanked him for his time. Telling her that it was his pleasure Richard handed Raymond his new appointment card and then steered mother and son towards the door and the lift. "I'll see you next week Ray." he called as the lift door closed. He had liked Raymond and would be making him a priority although he had real doubts whether Elizabeth Taylor would be allowing her son to keep the next appointment.

Walking in silence mother and son crossed to the car park where Elizabeth after opening the passenger door for her son walked round the car and climbed behind the steering wheel. It was not until they had reached the Bloubergstrand exit of the N1 that either of them spoke and it was Raymond who broke the silence. "Mummy!" he said quietly and without looking at his parent. At first his mother didn't answer but continued to stare at the road ahead and then in a rare expression of affection she removed her hand from the steering wheel and patted her son's knee.

"Not now my baby" she said softly, "mommy is driving."

CHAPTER 9
Monday 7th December 2009(Noon)

Shirley Marchant

Standing by the window Richard watched as Raymond and his mother left the building then returning to his office began to write up his notes. He had almost completed the task when Gabriella put her head around the door and asked if he was ready for lunch. He was.

"I'll be right there." he told her as he moved the computer's mouse to File and Save and then shut down the machine.

It was another beautiful summer's day in Cape Town and although the temperature had reached a midday high of forty three degrees some relief was provided by the brisk south easterly wind that blew in from the ocean. With his mood lifted by the weather, his positive session with Ray and an attractive woman on his arm Richard crossed to the busy Heerengracht intersection and towards the shady plaza of the 'i' Café'. Selecting an outside a table he smiled as he watched other diners collecting their jackets and leaving, probably for a long and boring afternoon in air conditioned offices. It was a thought that lifted his mood even further, even though he knew that at some point of the day he would have to have a very difficult conversation with Gabriella. But for the moment he removed his jacket and hung it on the back of one of the stylish black and chrome chairs.

"So how was your morning Gabi?" he quizzed as he watched his P.A. place her handbag protectively at her feet and pick up a menu.

"It was good thanks." she told him over the top of the white laminate sheet. "And yours?"

"Also good Gabi, I saw our new client Raymond Taylor. He seemed like a nice guy but has got himself tied up in that old triangle of victim, persecutor and rescuer."

"And which is he pray tell." Gabriella questioned as she bent and lifted her recently deposited handbag onto her lap flipping it open to remove her lipstick.

"Oh he's definitely the victim Gabi." Richard enlightened as he turned to scan the now emptying cafe for signs of service. He saw none.

"Oh I know that feeling Richard," Gabi smiled ruefully as she unscrewed the top of the golden cylinder "but a victim of whom?"

"Of his mother my dear, quite definitely his mother. Richard informed her as she began to apply the crimson gloss to her lips. "It's nice colour Gabi, it suits you." he told her as with growing fascination he watched her move her now soft and glossy lips against each other.

"And you deduce all that from one session?" she asked as a tall green shirted waiter arrived and after flashing them what appeared to be a genuine smile asked if they would like to order. Returning her lipstick to her handbag and her handbag to the floor Gabriella suggested that the waiter give them five more minutes, then picking up the menu suggested that Richard would have Raymond sorted in four or five sessions.

"Oh I don't see why not." Richard told her as the waiting waiter opened his pad in anticipation of drinks order.

"A glass of light white wine for me please." she told him and then glancing briefly in Richard's direction added a glass of Windhoek light to the order. Sixty minutes later and with lunch over the pair set off once more through the early afternoon sunshine. "Shall we take yours or mine?" Richard queried as he walked hopefully towards Gabriella's red Mini and then stood pointedly by the passage door. Protesting that Richard hadn't driven her anywhere in the last few weeks Gabriella pressed the button on her control fob and climbed behind the wheel. "But Gabi," Richard protested his hand on the door handle and his whinging voice sounding like that of a wronged and affronted teenager "I drove on Sunday, don't you remember." he asked.

"Okay, yes but only one way." Gabriella pointed out her own voice taking on the tone of an annoyed and exasperated parent. "Don't *you* remember?" then and without waiting for a reply and seemingly happy with her partial victory she leaned across the car and pushed open the door.

Taking the N1 highway out of Town Gabriella steered the Mini passed the docks and then took the left turn to Table View. On they travelled with only the hum of rubber on asphalt and constant murmur of the KFM radio station to break the silence until they reached the Bloubergstrand junction where Richard turning in his seat told Gabriella that before hitting the big time Steven had owned a house in Table View and had then, for no apparent reason, asked her if she had ever been to The Blue Peter. Indicating and turning right she told him she'd heard of it. "But," she added "I haven't been there yet." the yet sounding to Richard clearly and unmistakably like a threat. "Then we must make a plan my dear, now it's right here and the house is...."

"On the left Richard, yes I know."

Pulling the car to the curb Gabriella switched of the engine and then turned to look at her boss. It was a look that suggested to Richard that some deep and meaningful conversation was about to be start and so lifting his eyebrows in a way that said 'Not now and this was definitely not the time or the place for a deep and meaningful conversation' he turned to face her.

"Oh it's nothing Richard." she told him unconvincingly. Knowing her as he did Richard didn't believe her, although he would have dearly loved to and so he unzipped his bag and took out his notes from the previous Marchant session and waited.

"Are you sure?" he asked in a tone that he hoped would point her to the right answer.

"Yes sorry Richard it can wait." she told him, again unconvincingly.

"Sure?" he asked pushing his luck.

"Yes I'm sure; now tell me about this case." With some relief and it has to be said some regret Richard looked at the front cover of the file he knew so well.

"This is quite a sad case Gabi." he started. "Mrs M has a son who she thinks is into drugs, and who she knows drinks heavily. His girl friend is a slut, Mrs Marchant's words not mine and her mother didn't want her, Mrs Marchant not the girlfriend." he clarified. "Her husband used to beat her and she tells me she was close to her father but he died when she was quite young."

"Gee Richard..." Gabriella started to say.

"Wait Gabi," Richard told her holding up his hand, "there's more."

"There is...."

"Yes," he continued, "her neighbours are rude and noisy. She has an illness that is slowly killing her and to cap it all she feels stuck and wants to move but has no energy."

"The poor women," Gabriella finally managed to say, her concerns clear and understated. "Do you think you can help her?"

"Of course *we* can help her, that's if she wants to be helped." Richard told her somewhat impatiently.

"Meaning what?" Gabriella asked surprised at Richard's harshness.

"Meaning Gabi, that what we need to do is to get her to look at her 'Needs' and not her 'Problems'. That's if," he added "the things she put on her 'Problems List' are *'her'* problems and not her son's. He is thirty years old for god's sake."

"But I'm sure she only wants what's best for him." Gabriella protested.

"Yes Gabi I'm sure too and wouldn't it be nice if we had a magic wand and could control and change other people's lives as we wanted, but we can't Gabriella, can we?"

"No we can't Richard, but ..."

"But nothing Gabriella," Richard told her the irritation in his voice clear. "Shirley Marchant has to learn like the rest of us."

"And what lesson is that Richard?"

"That we just have to get on with life." and then he smiled and gently touching her arm. "Come on old girl," he grinned "let's go and change lives."

Leading the way across the wide grass verge Richard pressed the call button on the security gate and waited. "Yes." the terse reply finally came "who is it?"

"Mrs Marchant good afternoon this is Mr Blackwood from Emotional Solu…" he began but got no further as the high and solid metal gate slowly swung open. Following the sound of barking dogs the pair followed the winding garden path up to the front door where they stopped, waited, debated and then waited some more.

"Shall I knock?" Richard questioned as the snarling of probably a very large pack of vicious animals increased and the even more frightening sound of a women's voice yelling 'Get down. Get down you naughty boys, get down.' filled the air.

"Best not." Was Gabriella's advice as the sound of doors slamming followed then calm descended and the door opened.

"Ah Mr Blackwood please come in." Shirley Marchant said as she stood to one side to let him pass. "And I see you have…." she stalled as the unmistakable and unwanted odour of unwashed dog reached Richard's delicate nose.

"O'Brian, Gabriella O'Brian." Gabriella rescued as she held out her hand.

"Oh yes of course O'Brian." came the less than welcoming reply then taking Gabriella's manicured hand into her own long, cold and bony appendage Shirley Marchant wished her welcome and turned to greet Richard.

"Thank you for coming out to see me Mr Blackwood," she smiled "I do find travelling so difficult these days." A tall slim woman, slim to a point of looking physically unwell Shirley Marchant was just fifty seven years old. Amazingly only seven years older than the gorgeous Gabriella and just five years younger than he was. Today, as on most days, she was wearing a bright full length yellow print dress and her green shoes were slip-on. Shirley Marchant's hair was grey and shoulder length, her face was long and pale and her small eyes held a yellow pallor, a further sign if more evidence were needed, of her ill health. 'Hell life can be hard' it was a fact and one that Richard hoped he hadn't spoken out loud.

"Come through to the garden." the ailing Mrs. Marchant offered as she hobbled her way through the cluttered kitchen and out into the garden "I've made us some tea and a chocolate cake. Do you like chocolate cake Mr

Blackwood?" she asked as once more she failed to acknowledge Gabriella's existence.

"Indeed I do." Richard answered as he dutifully followed his tray carrying host to the table and sitting down politely accepted the extra large slice of cake she offered.

"And you Miss...." she asked as she plated a lesser piece of cake and handed it to the decidedly irritated Gabriella.

"It's O'Brian Mrs. Marchant." Gabriella prompted for a second time "Gabriella O'Brian."

"Indeed it is." came Mrs Marchant's indifferent reply "O'Brian, tea Richard?" Watching the souring exchange with growing unease Richard nodded his head in assent, dabbed crumbs from the side of his mouth and suggested that they make a start.

'So Mrs Marchant" he asked as he flipped open her file "perhaps you'd humour me by answering the wellbeing question again. It just helps us to assess how much progress we are making."

"Yes of course Mr Blackwood." his client told him as she handed him his tea cup "You want a number between one and ten, it that right?" Nodding again Richard took the cup and placed it in front of him.

"That's right." he nodded as he spooned sugar into his cup and stirred.

I'd say I was about a five."

"So," Richard asked as he smiled at Gabriella's empty cup "would you say that makes your cup half empty or half full?" Unsmiling Shirley Marchant told him that her cup was less than half full.

"Life has not been kind." she added her voice breaking at the remembering. "I've had a lot of problems with my husband and my son, well...

"Indeed," Richard said as if on cue. "Life can be very cruel but," he added keeping to the 'Therapy' script "perhaps you could tell me of one or maybe two positives that have happened since I last saw you?"

"Positives Richard, positives, let me see?" his client pondered "Well... I would say a positive is that I'm still here, but I'm not sure if that would be a true."

"You don't want to be here Shirley?" Richard asked concerned that his client maybe hinting at suicide.

"Sometimes life is too hard Richard, but" she said picking up on his concerns. "I'm not suicidal, you don't have to worry."

"I'm pleased to hear it." Richard encouraged. Coroner's courts were very low on his list of places to visit before he died and if truth were known he wasn't that keen on visiting them even after death. "And negatives?" he asked "Could we list any negatives since I was last here?"

"Ah now that's much easier Mr Blackwood." Shirley Marchant told him with some relish "I'd put my son and his new girl friend on a list of negatives. She's only after his money, but he can't see it. He's such a silly boy."

"Yes I think you told me last time Mrs. Marchant." Richard interposed gently. Visiting Mrs Marchant's son's silliness was another place that he didn't particularly want to visit at that moment in time. "So," he prompted "would you like us to use today's session to look at that problem or perhaps one of the other problems we listed on my first visit?"

"Can we talk about my son please? He's all I've got and I don't want to lose him."

"No certainly not." Richard agreed unhappily. "But we do need to be clear about the problem we want to solve. Do you remember how we do that?" he questioned.

"I do Richard. It's about changing problems into needs, but how we do that?"

"Now that's why we're here Mrs Marchant." Richard smiled "So, shall we make a start?"

Sadly the forty five minutes session passed without much progress being made. Shirley Marchant seemed happy to just talk, which left Richard in something of an ethical dilemma. To take people's money for just listening was not what his practice was about. To help people to change their lives was his aim and forte, but how to move the case forward, this was the skills of therapy and so after extended goodbyes Richard followed Gabriella out of the house and into the car.

"That was another good session and another happy customer Mr Blackwood." Gabriella beamed as she slid behind the steering wheel. "Although I don't think she was too pleased that I turned up. I think she fancies you."

"Now watch that paranoia Miss O'Brian." Richard grinned "but seriously Gabi," he added "I'm really not sure that our role is to make people happy."

"It isn't?" she asked perplexed.

"No Gabi our role is to help people think clearly and if clear thinking makes them happy then well and good, but do people want to think clearly? Maybe for the Marchant's of this world confusion and unhappiness are better than fact? Now let's head back to the City."

"Oh do we have to go back Richard?" Gabriella asked as she turned towards him and lowering her eye brows as if to give him the clue what the answer was adding that it was such a lovely day.

"But if we set off now Gabi." Richard suggested weakly "we'll miss the rush hour traffic."

"And if we go back now Richard *I'll* miss the Blue Peter."

The journey from Table View to Bloubergstrand took less than ten minutes and after parking the car at the rear of the hotel they walked down the access road towards the beach. Following Gabriella Richard crossed the road and walked out onto the sands. From where he stood he had a clear view of Table Mountain with the ever present line of ships riding at anchor and awaiting their turn to enter the harbour at Cape Town. Beyond the ship and in the distance was the infamous Robben Island.

"Gosh Richard look at that view it's amazing." Gabriella said as childlike she jumped up and down and pointed at a view that she had only seen on post cards. For several minutes she continued to stand and stare and then removing her shoes she began to move towards the water. "Come on." she called towards a hesitant Richard. Running into a cold ocean in his 'therapy suit' was not something he had planned for his afternoon and given the choice he would have much preferred to sit under one of the bright umbrellas on the Blue Peter's veranda. But, not wanting to spoil 'her' moment he bent and unlacing his shoes removed his socks and pushing them into his trouser pocket began to walk towards the water.

"Come on Richard." Gabriella called again as she playfully leapt the gently rolling waves. Then, as could have been predicted, she let out a squeal of delight and shock as a high rogue wave sent it's spray shooting upwards darkening the hem of her cotton skirt. Any other day, or so he told himself, Richard would have been happy to lose his inhibitions and run into the surf, run as he had with his younger sons, but.... 'But what?' he questioned and rolling up his trousers he walked carefully into the ocean. Even though Richard knew the water would be chilly its icy coldness took him by surprise and he soon found himself lifting one foot after the other in order to avoid its freezing bite. Shouting her challenge of 'Come on softy' Gabriella turned and walked back towards him. Then taking his hand she began to lead him into deeper water. As their hands touched something moved from Richard's subconscious into the here and now. Something inexplicable and something wrong. It was guilt. Yes he had slept with and made love to this woman a number of times but he had never felt this depth of wrongdoing and disloyalty. Dropping her hand Richard began to wade out of the water.

"What's the matter Richard?" Gabriella called after him her surprise and shock clear in her tone. "Richard?" she repeated "Richard?" Still moving away Richard turned and looked back.

"I'm sorry Gabi." he told her "but I just can't."

"Can't what Richard?" she asked.

"I can't do this Gabi." he told her his words almost an apology. "I can't do this, holding hands. You should be…"

"Grace?" she asked finishing his sentence for him.

"Yes Grace. If there was no Grace in my life I'd be happy to…" and again he was unable to continue.

"But there is a Grace Richard." Gabriella told him gently as again she held out her hands to him. Then recognising his continuing distress she placed them behind her back. "Oh come on Richard." she encouraged "and I promise not to bite." Unable to look at his friend, his colleague and lover Richard stood and looked out to sea. Looking past the line of ships and Robben

Island Richard's mind took him back across the water, across the six thousand miles of ocean to England and to his wife. There he saw Grace, her face framed by her hair and her green eyes shining. Then the first tears came, starting in the corner of his eye they rolled slowly down his cheek and then his shoulders lifted and from his body escaped great sighs of despair.

"Grace." he whispered, "Grace. I'm so sorry." Once again Gabriella moved forward and once more she held back.

"Come on my friend." she said as she smiled what she hoped would be a smile of reassurance. Then she turned and walked away.

"Please come and sit Richard." she begged as she sat down and scooping up the grains of golden sand let them run through her fingers. "Come and tell me about Grace, just as I told you about Michael all those years ago."

Moving to sit beside her Richard's words at first came hesitantly, then more quickly as waves of sadness and remorse flowed from his body. He told her of his selfishness and stupidity. Of how he had tried to bully Grace and when that hadn't succeeded how he had used their boys to try and blackmail her into letting him have his own way. Then how when all else had failed he had fallen back on anger and threats. "And then," he said. "And then I left her."

"I know Richard and I'm so sorry."

"How long have you known Gabi?" he asked not really surprised by her revelation, for it seemed that Gabriella O'Brian knew most things.

"That doesn't matter Richard." she told him quietly. "Just talk to me." And so pulling his knees to his chest Richard sat and gazed out to the far distance and to the hazy sun as it sank ever lower towards that mighty ocean. Then Gabi, sensing that the moment was right gently put her hand onto his. As she did so he made no attempt to pull away or prevent the touching. Nor did he try to remove the hand once it was resting on his own, but almost subconsciously, as if to a secret and silent rhythm, he began to pat the slender hand of his friend, colleague and lover.

"Richard" Gabriella's words were almost in a whisper. "Close your eyes and make a wish." Doing as he was told Richard closed his eyes and wished.

"I wish, I wish," he said, "I wish that it was Grace who was sitting here with me now." Then realising what he had just said he turned to look at Gabriella. "I'm sorry Gabi I didn't..."

"Its fine Richard" she told him "if you can't be honest with a friend..."

"And your wish Gabriella?" he asked.

"Oh I wish I was sat here with Michael." she told him

"I know, I know." he sighed. Then getting to his feet he bent and taking her hands in his pulled her to her feet and placed his arm around her waist. "Come on old girl" told her with more joy than he felt "and you can buy me supper."

CHAPTER 10
Tuesday 8th December 2009 (Morning)

Dream and Nightmares

Richard had slept fitfully his dreams full of confused and erotic dreams of Grace. Dreams of Grace walking towards him through calm seas wearing the white dressing gown she had 'borrowed' from the Lodore Falls Hotel in Keswick. As she walked the gown slipped from her shoulders revealing her strong neck and firm breasts, her long slender fingers sliding down the zip of her favourite blue jeans. Then he was lying in their bed in England, his arms wrapped around her soft warm body, her nakedness moulded to the contours of his own. Then suddenly Grace was gone and he found himself walking towards the beckoning arms of Gabriella, as they embraced he again found himself in the arms of his beloved Grace. Together they danced a slow and sensual dance whilst above them white gulls dived and dipped and in the distance the steady shrill sound of a siren wailed it's urgent scream. Turning in his sleep Richard reached for his wife, she was not there and pulling his pillow to his chest he slept and dreamt on. "Richard!" the voice came to him clearly its tone urgent and demanding, "wake up, we're late." Rousing himself into wakefulness Richard Blackwood blinked an unbelieving eye at the alarm clock and returning his dreams to their own weird and illusory world he pushed himself upright and uttering his first words of the day ' oh shit' he swung his legs to the floor. Fifteen minutes later showered, dressed and grateful for the buttered toast Gabriella had prepared for him he walked slowly toward the Audi and slumped wearily into the passenger seat. "Sleep well Richard?" his bright and bushy tailed P.A. asked as she slipped the car into gear and moved swiftly down the drive towards the rush hour traffic.

"Not really. And you?" Richard asked more in politeness than interest as he brushed stray bread crumbs from the crotch of his trousers and winding down the car window took a long deep breath of the morning air.

"Oh like a log," the unperturbed Gabriella told him. "It must have been all that sea air. We must do it again sometime."

"We must?" an unconvinced Richard questioned as he looked dubiously at his second slice of toast, took a bite and consigned the remainder of his breakfast to its plastic container. On the pair travelled, Richard with eyes tightly closed bravely fighting the waves of nausea that threatened to overwhelm him and Gabriella silently praying that if the inevitable happened it would happen outside the car. Then opening his eyes Richard spoke informing Gabriella that he felt dreadful and asked if she had any pain killers. Suggesting that she may have some in her handbag Gabriella nodded to the back seat and Richard, closing his eyes against the movement of the car, turned and grasping the bag pulled it over the seat and offered it to his driver.

"No Richard I'm driving." he was told and clicking the clasp open he looked hesitantly into the aroma filled bag's pockets and pouches.

"You do know that my mother told me never to go in a ladies handbag don't you Gabi." he protested as he gazed into dark chaos of the bag.

"Why?" his companion wanted to know. It was a question that Richard couldn't answer other than to say that he didn't know.

"But," he admitted as he placed his hand into the depths of the bag "I have been tempted to look but never have. Now," he asked as he surveyed the bags myriad packets and tubes "where would one keep pain-killers?"

"Oh just rummage man." an increasingly inpatient Gabriella told him "they're in a blue packet."

"So is everything else Gabi." he told her as blushing involuntary he lifted out packet of tampons from the bag and smiled ruefully. "So that's why mother told me not to delve in ladies handbags." he grimaced as Gabriella grabbing the bag from him placed her own hand in the bag and without having to look produced and handed him a packet of paracetamol. Then tossing the bag on the seat behind her she then began to slow for the dirty brown Toyota 'bakkie' that moved slowly in front of her. Checking her rear view mirror she flicking down her indicator arm and pulled out to overtake. As they drew level the half a dozen black workers on the back of the pickup looked across and smiled. Lifting his thumb in greeting Richard smiled back and as he did so the loud blast of a car horn broke the silence and wiped the smiles from eight faces. "Now where the hell did that come from?" Gabriella asked, her comments aimed as much to herself as anyone else and then. "Okay, okay I see you." as another loud blast rent the air. Putting her foot to the floor Gabriella accelerated passed the Toyota then pushing up the Audi's indictor arm pulled carefully into the left hand lane. Away shot the black 4x4 its driver blasting his horn and gesticulating with two fingers of his left hand. To which a rarely rattled Gabriella found herself yelling "And you pal!" to the rapidly disappearing 4x4's spare wheel.

The parched and sandy soil at the motorways edge had now begun to give way to grass, short dry and brown at first but then turning to longer and greener hues at they neared the town. Taking the Somerset West exit Gabriella began to slow for the red traffic light.

"So Richard, what do we know about Pamela James?" Gabriella asked as she rolled slowly forward and waited for the lights to change.

"Well she's married with two small children." Richard told her.

"No it can't be!" Gabriella argued as she looked to his right checking the traffic flow.

"It is." Richard protested as Gabriella timing her approach perfectly dropped the Audi into second gear and turned left, her skill and determination leaving the driver of the black Range Rover 4x4 searching for gears.

"Ah and beautifully done my girl." Richard beamed as he grasped the reason for her dissention and voiced his appreciation as she slid the Audi effortlessly through the gears leaving the bullying 4x4 in her rear view mirror. "Now we go right at the lights Gabi and the road we want should be on our left." he encouraged as they slowed for the next set of red lights and stopped. Lowering her window Gabriella smiled sweetly up into the scowling face of the driver in the next lane and then slipping the Audi into first gear moved off. Sadly for the 4x4 driver she only travelled a few yards before she stopped (at the still red light). Mr 4x4 however who was not going to let 'any bloody Audi driving hussy' get one over on him had slammed his vehicle into first gear and raced off through the still red light and had almost hit a blue and white car coming in the opposite direction. As red light turned to green Gabriella, keeping her eyes to the front and her face unsmiling moved slowly past the two parked cars. In the rear view mirror she could see the door of the second car open and the blue trouser leg and the shiny black shoes of a traffic officer step onto the pavement. Then a half a mile further down the road she turned left, stopped, checked the address on the paper in front of her and opening her own car door stepped out into the warm sunshine.

CHAPTER 11
Tuesday 8th December 2009 (Mid Morning)

Pamela James

The home of Pamela James was a pretty single storey building set on a quiet tree lined street, the walls of the house were covered in a warm mass of Bougainville and sweet smelling Jasmine and beneath the Jasmine bloomed flower beds in the diverse colours of pansies, begonia and geranium. A fine mist hung in the air as the sprinkler system performed its daily task of trying to keep the front lawn looking fresh and green. The door to number twenty one stood open and as Richard placed his hand on the white 'picket gate' the first drops of cooling water began to stain the sleeves of his new blue shirt.

"I'm right behind you Gabi." he smiled as he stepped back and held the gate open for his P.A. to pass through. Gabriella stayed put and sensing that some act of chivalry was expected on his part Richard pushed open the gate and walked in a quick and undignified manner to the front door. Reaching the veranda he stopped once more and called out a hopeful 'Hello'. As he spoke a small child put its head around the door. 'Hello young man' Richard smile as he knelt to place himself at the same height as the infant. His actions however resulted in nothing more than the child dissolving into loud cries of 'Mummy mummy' and Richard retreating to the wet safety of the veranda. From inside the house he could hear the sound of a female voice begin her reassuring call of 'It's alright my little one mummy's coming' and true to her word, mummy appeared at the front door. "There there," she calmed as she bent to pick the child up and then seeing a strange man on her step asked if she could help'. Smiling through the damp mist Richard took a step forward. "Mrs James?" he asked hopefully and was relieved to hear that indeed the lady of the house was Mrs James and that a slow dawning was beginning to spread across her face. "Mr Blackwood?" she questioned and then explained that she hadn't expected Richard until ten. Subconsciously and with cold water beginning to dampen his shirt and skin Richard look down at his watch and the dial that told him it was already ten fifteen and then kindly suggested that if his visit was not convenient he could come back later. Happily he was told to 'come on in' and then at the realisation that the sprinkler system was still pumping out its life giving spray and that Richard was 'All wet' Pamela James turned to the house and began to shout. "Lee, Lee." she called "Lee turn off the water." And so as the watery mist began to die Richard turned to the waiting Gabriella, nodded and followed Pamela James into the house.

    The interior of house, in contrast to the garden, was a scene of chaos. Large pieces of wooden furniture were surrounded by the clutter of child rearing. Toys, prams, carry cots, bottle warmers, play mats and newspapers littered the floor. Pointing to nowhere in particular Mrs James then asked Richard if he would like to sit and then almost as an afterthought suggested that she get him a towel. Brushing water from his arm Richard declined the offer and telling his hostess that 'he was fine' asked if he could introduce his colleague Gabriella O'Brian.

    "Oh yes hello Miss O'Brian." Pamela James smiled, her use of the title 'Miss' making Richard wonder what she had seen to make her assume Gabriella was a single lady. Then moving towards the kitchen Pamela asked her visitors if they would like some tea. Clearing away some of the debris from a deep cushioned arm chair Richard took out a thin brown manila file and removing the top from his black biro waited for his client to return. Normally when asked if he would like tea Richard would either say no (tea making was such a waste of time) or he would offer to help with the preparation. Preparing tea with another person could be a great 'ice breaker but, today Pamela had not allowed him to make either choice and so he sat and waited impatiently aware that somewhere a small child was probably watching him.

"Have you lived here long Mrs James?" Richard asked when his client finally returned.

"Just three years Mr Blackwood" Pamela told him as she placed the blue and white striped mug in front of him. "We moved here from Johannesburg when my husband lost his job" she explained as she took her seat opposite him and began to bounce her young daughter Jade, (Richard's earlier guess at the child's gender proving incorrect) on her knee. "My parents live in Somerset West. They've been such a big help. I think you know my mother's sister." And then she paused as if she expected Richard to know everyones mother's sister. "Mrs Marchant...?" she finally said. "She lives in Table View."

"Ah yes Shirley Marchant." Richard smiled with some relief as he pondered the thought that he may know everyones mother's sister after all. "Oh yes I know Shirley well." he grinned, relieved that an awkward moment had passed.

"It was Shirley that suggested we contact you Mr Blackwood, it's my husband,"

"Okay Mrs James." Richard nodded, pleased that an opening to the session had been provided. "So can I ask you a few questions before we talk about your husband?" he asked and then paused as he waited for Pamela James to provide her husband's name.

"Yes of course Mr Blackwood, but you need to know that Lee is in the garden." Pamela confided "He knows that you're here but he doesn't want to talk to you."

"That's fine." Richard conceded "But," he cautioned "I will have to talk to him at some point. Now ..." and for a second time he paused and waited for Pamela James to invite him to use her first name. He didn't have long to wait for as if on cue his client lowered the now bored Jade to the floor and asked him to call her Pamela "or better sill." she added with a conspiratorial smile "Pam. All my friends do." Thanking her Richard in turn asked her to 'please call him Richard' and then waited as the now braver Jade scrambled up onto Gabriella's knee and sat watching as he removed a sheet of paper from his file and placed it on his knee. "Now Pam," he began "I have a sheet of paper here that asks how you are feeling and it asks me to write down a score of one to ten, so Pam." he said as he looked across at his client, "How are you feeling at this point of your life?" The effects of Richard's words were immediate as Pam reached into her pocket and pulling out a well used tissue dabbed her eyes. "I'm sorry Mr Black...Richard." she sobbed apologetically it's just that..." and then she stopped. Tears were nothing new to the experienced Richard, even so to sit and watch a young and attractive woman weep at such a mundane question touched his heart and forced him to close his eyes against his own tears. Then collecting and hardening his emotions he spoke.

"That's Okay Pam." he told her. "I always think tears are better out that in. Now tell me what was it that made you cry?"

"Oh I don't know Richard," she told him untruthfully "I guess I'm just feeling sorry for myself. It's been a hard few months."

"Been a hard few *months* Pam?" Richard questioned as he leant forward for effect and repeated Pamela's words back to her. "Only months?" he repeated.

"No I'm sorry Richard," his client replied truthfully "it hasn't been a few months it's been two maybe three years."

"Yes and a very hard three years I would guess Pam." Richard prompted gently "So let me take you back to my first question. How are you feeling today on a score of one to ten?"

"Can I say a minus Richard." his client smiled through her sniffles.

"You can say what you want Pam." Richard told her "This is your time and no one else's. Do you want me to write minus one?" he asked.

"No." she smiled. "Mark me as plus one Richard, I may need room to sink lower." and then she laughed before adding "Only kidding." It was a statement that Richard didn't really believe but held his counsel before adding the 'if nothing else happens that morning he had seen Pamela laugh and he had seen Pamela cry'.

"Not bad for a mornings work eh Gabriella?" he confided with a smile.

"Not bad at all Richard." Gabriella agreed as Jade climbed down from her knee and went to the waiting arms of her mother who smiling across at her therapist told him that she thought that he was going to be good for her."

and then Pamela James was serious again. "Tell me Richard do you think you'll be able to help Lee?"

"I'm sure we can." Richard told her emphasising the 'we' and then returning to the 'script' informed her that they had about twenty minutes left. "So," he suggested "let's see if we can make a list of everything that stops you being happy." again Richard's emphasised the one word 'we'.

"Well Mr Blackwood that seemed to go well." Gabriella said as she pointed the car into the midmorning traffic "That poor woman, men can be such..." She got no further as Richard smiling across at her suggested that she mind her language. "What I was going to say." his P.A. protested "was that men can be such delicate souls."

"Ah indeed they can." Richard agreed. "But I'll reserve judgement on Mr Lee James. Did you see him loitering by the kitchen window? He didn't want to join us, but was interested enough to listen to what we were saying."

"I don't see anything wrong with that Richard." Gabriella argued "I think I'd be curious if my partner was discussing me with a stranger."

"To be curious is okay Gabi," Richard told her "but I fear our Mr James may have crossed a line and entered his own strange world of paranoia."

"That's quite a leap Richard," Gabriella questioned "just how do you get from Mr James being curious to his being paranoid and without even seeing him."

"In my defence Gabriella" Richard protested "I only said he 'may' have crossed the line, but if you look at the things we listed on Pamela's 'Problem Sheet', things that her husband is or is not doing what have we got?" and then he paused as he waited for Gabriella's answer.

"Sorry Richard I thought that was a rhetorical question." his P.A. told him "But I guess we have his curiosity or mistrust, but that's only a matter of degree isn't it?"

"It is Gabriella." Richard agreed "and taken on its own is no real evidence at all. But what else did Pamela tell us?

"Well that he tends to keep himself to himself. He doesn't talk to her and when he does they argue, but surely lots of couples go through a stage of not getting on. Its normal isn't it?

"It is Gabi," Richard admitted "but what other words did she use to describe him?"

"It's in the notes Richard," Gabriella offered "but I think she said he was suspicious and insecure."

"That's right Gabi and anxious and frightened. She used all those words and even a cursory look in a medical dictionary would confirm that paranoia is a distinct possibility." Richard told her.

"So Richard, if you believe that Mr James is paranoid shouldn't you do something about it. Think about Pamela's safety."

"But we are doing something we're offering to talk to him. The alternative to that is drugs therapy or a psychiatric hospital or both and for how long? No Gabi I'm sure the paranoia is there, but I don't think we need to panic just yet."

"But what about Pamela she has needs too?" Gabriella protested. Smiling Richard asked if Gabriella had been reading his books again.

"I may have." she told him.

"Which?" Richard questioned.

"Perhaps some Ellis and maybe some Beck and Eysenck."

"Oh very good, tell me more." Richard encouraged.

"Abraham Maslow, who says by the way, that we all have basic needs and if those needs aren't met we're in trouble."

"Tell me more."

"Well Pamela is fed and clothed and she has somewhere warm to sleep and I guess she's loved."

"Go on."

"But there's no self esteem and without self esteem where are we?"

"Struggling?" Richard suggested.

"That's right?" Gabriella confirmed. "So I did I read Maslow correctly?"

"You did young lady and well done. And now as a reward I'm going to let you take the lead with our new client."

"But Richard I'm not qualified..." Gabriella protested.

"Not qualified?" Richard asked "Not qualified for what Miss. O'Brian... listening?"

As Gabriella was pointing the Audi towards their second appointment of the day Lee James was making his angry way back into the family home. "So the good Dr Strangelove and his glamorous assistant have gone have they." he sneered. "And when are they sending the van to take me away Pamela? Oh sorry, please call me Pam Mr Blackwood, all my friends do. What friends are these Pam?" he mocked, "I haven't seen a friend around these parts for a long time."

"Please don't Lee." Pamela pleaded "Mr Blackwood only wants to help."

"Help who. I don't need any help." her husband mocked "What I need is for you and your dammed interfering bloody family to leave me alone."

"Oh Lee listen to me please, I'm sure if you would just talk to Richard he would be able to..."

"Richard is it, what happened to Dr Blacklove. Fancy him do you. I don't know why you don't bloody go to him. See if he can put up with your whinging. Now I'm going out, I need a drink."

"Oh Lee please don't." Pamela James pleaded once more, but her words were spoken to a slamming door. Lee James had gone and he wouldn't be back for quite some time.

CHAPTER 12
Tuesday 8th December 2009 (Early Afternoon)

Patricia Morgan

Patricia Morgan stood on the balcony of her penthouse flat and watched in silence as the Audi manoeuvred off the main road and into one of the many parking bays that lined the sea front in the quiet and mainly Afrikaans speaking town of The Strand. At sixty three years old she was still an attractive woman, her clear complexion and smart clothes belying the years she had spent in the drab mining towns of South Wales and later in the still drab but more prosperous mining towns of Southern Africa. With increasing curiosity she watched as a rather short man (probably in his early sixties) climbed out of the car and turning towards the ocean stretch and then take a long deep breath of sea air. Her interest was further aroused by the tall elegant woman (probably in her early fifties) who pushed open the driver's door, stood, straightened the seams of her expensive skirt and moved to stand beside her companion. Then sliding her arms into the sleeves of her smart black jacket turned and looked up at the high rise block. As she did so Patricia Morgan stepped back from the balconies' edge and walking back into the coolness of her flat crossed to the kitchen and flicked down the switch of her state of the art kettle and waited.

"Okay Gabriella." Richard encouraged as they entered the gleaming chrome and gold lift. "You've watched me do this a hundred times so just relax and enjoy." Smiling a confident but unconvincing smile Gabriella reassured him that 'she was okay' and that 'anything he could do she could do better'. It was a bold statement but one that Richard could find no argument with and so stepping back to let her lead the way he wished her 'good luck' and invited her to 'break a leg'.

"Mr Blackwood?" Patricia Morgan smiled as she opened the door to her flat and without waiting for his reply thanked him for coming and informed him that Dr Morkel had spoken highly of him.

"My pleasure Mrs Morgan," Richard smiled as he took her hand in his."It's always nice to get out of the office and a trip to the sea side is a real bonus. Now can I introduce Mrs O'Brian? Gabriella will be conducting the first part of the interview." Stepping forward Gabriella held out her hand. "It's lovely to meet you." she smiled as she took Mrs. Morgan's manicured hand in her own. At the meeting of manicured hands a instant and lasting bond was formed, it was a bond that would soon bare rich fruit. Leading the way into her large and modern lounge Patricia Morgan poured tea and Gabriella, after explaining the rules of confidentiality placed her china cup on the coffee table and asked her client if she would rate her present well being on a scale of 1-10.

"Oh how interesting my dear." an interested Mrs Morgan informed her "I would think somewhere between six and seven." and lifting a plate of Garibaldis from the coffee table she offered them to Richard who smiling his appreciation thanked her and then settled back into the comfort of the deep red leather arm chair.

"So Mrs Morgan" Gabriella began once more. "We can start to list any problems that impact on your well being?" and then looking across at Richard quickly added. "That's therapy speak for anything that stops you being happy"

"Now what a good question," Mrs Morgan said "Why don't you call me Pat"

The rest of the session had passed without difficulty with Mrs Morgan, obviously warming to the task of therapy and enjoying the attention of this bright and obviously experienced practitioner, had asked Gabriella to please call her Pat. "And I'll call you Gabriella, if that's alright with you dear?" she had said before explaining that she had concerns for her eldest daughter whose husband was working away from home and how she thought that her grandson was missing his father. She had then gone on to talk about her annoyance with her younger daughter who was always asking for money and her son who lived in England and wouldn't talk to her. Then she had talked about her new boyfriend who she really loved but was afraid that he was only after her money. After thirty minutes Gabriella had looked across at Richard who had quietly tapped the face of his watch indicating that the session should be brought to a close. With some sadness Gabriella had brought the session to a close telling her client what a pleasure it had been to visit her and asking if she would like her to come back. Patricia had of course been more than happy to agree to Gabriella's suggestion and as the lift doors had begun to close she moved forward to kiss 'her therapist' on the cheek. Moving back into her apartment Patricia had made her way quickly out onto the balcony where she had stood waving as Gabriella had reversed the Audi backed onto the main road and made her way up Beach Road towards Cape Town.

"So Miss O'Brian how was it for you?" Richard asked as they bounced their way over the beach fronts myriad traffic calming hump.

"It was great Richard." Gabriella told him excitedly. "And thanks for letting me do it, I never thought it would be so easy." Then she checked herself. "I did do okay didn't I?" she asked.

"Indeed you did Gabi." Richard smile as the next speed hump lifted him into the air. "I knew you would or I wouldn't have let you try. But we'll have to keep it quiet from the rest of team until we can get you booked onto a course. You'll need to get yourself a qualification if you're going to practice full time."

"But don't you think I a bit old for college and studying?" she asked.

"One is never too old Gabi." Richard told her "and I can always use another therapist." Suddenly Richard Blackwood found himself in a good mood. "So tell me," he asked as the next speed bump loomed ahead "what are you going to do with Mrs Patricia Morgan?"

Arriving at the office Gabriella made her way to the kitchen to warm soup whilst Richard, still in buoyant mood went to prepare for the monthly team meeting and realising that the meeting was due to start in fifteen minutes made a mental note to telephone Grace then made his way to the main office. Finding the team already waiting he wished them a "Good afternoon." and taking the cup of soup Gabriella offered sat down at the head of the table.

"So Richard," his newest team member asked as he took his seat "Did you have a good morning?" Christopher Winston Smythe was a pleasant enough young man, a man who to Richard's mind had worked hard to find his place within the team. Sometimes however, Chris's attempts to please his boss could drift into what some Richard and some of the other team members, particularly Amy saw as 'toadyism'. Telling Chris that he was fine Richard turned to Gabriella and somewhat redundantly asked if she had copies of the agenda?" Still in an upbeat mood and grinning smugly Gabriella tapped the sheath of papers in front of her and beaming her 'don't be silly smile' began to pass them round the table. Thanking her Richard took a sip of his soup, mushroom not his favourite and one by one began to scan the faces surrounding him.

"Chris if you please." he instructed as his eyes came to rest on his newest and youngest member of his team. Nodding, almost bowing his acquiescence, Chris turned to the first the pages of the ten page document and then coughed nervously. At thirty eight years old Christopher Smyth would, in another place and time, have been what Richard would have called a 'toff'. Today however less polite words were used to describe such a man. Today the dapper Chris wore a pair of pale blue slacks. His shirt was cream, with top button unfastened and his cotton jacket white with a pale blue handkerchief in the breast pocket. To complete the ensemble Chris wore on his sockless feet, a pair of light brown suede slip on shoes. It was indeed a look that wouldn't have looked out of place in the halls of academia, or perhaps on a television chat show host. Clearing his throat and in clear Queens English Chris announced that there were ten items on the agenda and then he paused.

"If I could have your attention," he demanded his tone over the top and authoritarian "then perhaps we can make a start." It was no secret that Richard was looking for a new team leader to replace Scarlet who would soon be leaving to have her first child. Nor was it a secret that Richard was using these meetings to assess the strengths and weaknesses of any possible candidates. Amy and Chris had on several occasions clashed as they attempted to score points from each other. It was a contest which made the meetings interesting but at times very exasperating. The only other contender for the job was Gideon, a mainly Afrikaans speaker who at times struggled with the English language, and sadly for Gideon, English was the main language of Richard's client practice.

"Item one." he began as unable to cope with his colleagues' looks of shock and amusement he looked down at the papers in front of him. "Item one," he repeated "is to look at the possibility of taking our work into schools." and raising his head he turned to Gabriella. "Do you have an update?" he asked.

"We do Chris." she told him.

"And?" he asked a little too sharply, it was a mistake and he should have known it, the rest of the team did.

"It's from the governors of a private girls' school Chris." Gabriella told him, her tone now cool and disappointed. "They were particularly interested in ideas for their boarders. Amy and Scarlet are due to revisit the school in three weeks time."

"And is there any particular reason why Scarlet and Amy are leading on this one?" Chris asked his attitude still superior and abrasive.

"Girls school, female therapist Chris!" Amy Nell pointed out and scored herself five points in her 'get one over on Chris scale'.

"Really, I would have thought a male perspective would have proved useful." a wounded Chris asked, his annoyances at Amy's interruption clear to everyone.

"Nothing has been decided yet Chris." an equally annoyed Gabriella explained as her eyebrows knitted and her right index finger began to tap quietly in the table top. "Would you be interested in giving the girls the benefit of your skills and knowledge?" she questioned.

"Well I'm sure that I could help them in their relationships with boyfriends and brothers". Chris pointed out as he mentally scored himself five points in his 'get one over on Amy scale.

"And you'd know all about boyfriends." a venomous Amy smirked scoring herself another seven points as the sound of manicured nail on wooden surface began growing louder and more rapid.

"That's a good point Chris." team leader Scarlet cut in "and no more of that Amy if you please." she added before turning to Richard and asking what he thought.

"Well," an amused and diplomatic Richard replied as he took another unhappy sip of his soup "I think it all depends on what the school governors want don't you?" and placing his mug on the table pushed it away from him.

"So are we saying that Amy and Scarlet will continue with negotiations and come back to us in a week or so?" Chris asked as he turned once more to his agenda.

"Well that's obvious, don't you think Richard?" a mischievous Amy asked as the sound of rapidly tapping finger nails increased and Richard, covering his face with his hands slowly closed his eyes.

The rest of Richard's afternoon passed quickly and at four forty five Gabriella came to tell him that she was going home and to ask him what he would like for his evening meal.

"I'm easy lass." he told her as he closed the last of his files.

"I'll do a curry if you fancy." she offered.

"That would be good Gabi, do we have wine?"

"Wine and curry?" she questioned.

"Okay, I'll get some lager." he offered.

"Go for it." she told him. "See you at seven?" At five thirty Rachael came to tell him that she was leaving and to ask if he would 'do' the lights and alarm and then for the first time in a long time Richard sat alone in his office. It had been an interesting and eventful day. Gabriella's obvious skill with Mrs Morgan had pleased him, so much so that he though she may well be the solution to the Chris and Amy situation. Sadly Gideon's lack of English would be a problem if he were to appoint him as team leader, "I guess," he told himself "only time would tell and getting up he walked slowly through to reception. He knew that at some point he would have to phone Grace, but for all his communication skills he was unable to think of an opening for the positive conversation he wanted to have with her. Moving from room to room he checked that windows were closed and that lights were switched off and as he walked he rehearsed in his head the conversation he would have with Grace. 'Hello Grace' the very word Grace excited him, "but then what?" he asked himself. Would she be dismissive and ask him what he wanted. And what if William or James answered? Returning to his office he told himself to 'just do it' and picking up the telephone he dialled Grace's number. Alone in the silent office he waited as the telephone signal travelled the six thousand miles down the line to England and to his home. Then the telephone began to ring and he could picture the scene, the telephone ringing once, twice as the boys played on their Xbox whilst Grace made their tea. Three rings, four and Grace would be drying her hands in anticipation of her mother's evening call. Five rings, six and then his own voice telling him that he was sorry that he unable to take the call and to please leave a message and he would get back to him. "Damn" he cursed he hadn't expected or planned for this. Silently he sat with the phone to his ear. "Grace its Richard." he finally said, the nervousness in his voice clear. "I'll ring you again tomorrow. I love you, good night." and returning the receiver to the handset he cursed once more his lack of foresight. 'Bugger, bugger, bugger' he cursed and then picking up the receiver he re-dialled.

"Hello Grace this is Richard," he said with more confidence than he felt. "How are you, and the boys? If you get a moment will you ring me please?" then replacing the hand set he got to his feet and switching off lights as he went left the office.

CHAPTER 13
Wednesday 9th December 2009 (Morning)

An Inspector Calls

The following day Richard woke early, showered, dressed and made his way down stairs. His first appointment was not until ten thirty which gave him plenty of time to relax. Retuning the radio to KFM he moved to the sink and refilled the kettle and switched it on, then moving to the breakfast table he sat and poured milk on his Bran Flakes. From the radio came the unmistakable voice of Elvis Presley singing *'I was an oak now I'm a willow now I can bend'* he sang, *'and here I'll stay until it's time for me to go'*. As the song ended the ever cheerful presenter broke in to announce the news.

"The headlines, government economists are reporting that the country is continuing to move towards recession and now some breaking news. Reports are coming in that the Chief Executive Officer of Euro –Cape Partnerships Mr Steven Blackwood has...;" the sound of boiling water prevented Richard hearing the rest of the piece and getting up he walked quickly to the dresser and turned up the radio. "And the headlines again; Government economist's report that the country continues to move towards recession and some breaking news; the Chief Executive Officer of Euro –Cape Partnerships Mr Steven Blackwood has been abducted from his home in Kirstenbosch." With a nauseating panic rising in his stomach and his knees feeling as if they could no longer hold his weight Richard reached for the table and lowered his heavy body into one of the pine chairs. Suddenly he felt very cold, afraid and tired. Sinking his head into his hands he tried to gather his thoughts and to find some logic in the illogical. And then his training from past years kicked in, it was training that he had used many times with angry and aggressive patients. 'Slow down Richard,' his inner voice told him. 'Calm down, you are not an emergency service, calm down' and getting to his feet he walked purposefully towards the stairs.

"Gabi awake up?" he called as he started to climb "Gabi, Gabi wake up." Hearing no reply he moved towards her bedroom door, to forbidden ground. "Gabriella." he shouted as he knocked on her cedar wood door and then waited. Again he knocked, this time louder, but again no reply came and pushing open the door he stepped inside. Suddenly the sweet smell of cedar wood changed to the sensual scent of Gabriella. It was the aroma of fresh warm apples and something else, something that was neither sweet nor bitter, a distinctly sleepy bedroom fragrance, a fragrance that would remain on her pillows long after she had left her bed.

"Gabriella wake up, Steven's been kidnapped." he called as he moved into the room. From the shower he could hear the sound of Gabriella's singing. *'You don't have to say you love me'* she sang, her voice strong and melodic above the sound of hissing water. *'Just be close at hand.'*

"Bugger" he cursed as he moved further into the room to where the shower room door stood slightly open, a sweet scented mist filling the air. Standing for some seconds Richard debated his options and then and for some unknown and bizarre reason, for he had already seen, held and made love to Gabriella's naked body, he turned round and entered the shower backwards.

"Gabriella." he pleaded. "Gabriella, Steven's been kidnapped."

"'You don't have to stay forever.'" she sang and then she saw him. "My god Richard." she screamed. "What the hell are you doing?"

"Steven's been kidnapped." Richard repeated.

"He's what?" Gabriella asked as she slid the shower cubical door open and put out her a bronzed arm.

"Steven's been..."

"Yes I heard." She told him "Now pass me my towel." and suddenly she was in charge. "Okay you go and make some coffee" she ordered "and I'll be right down."

Standing in the kitchen telephone in hand Richard dialled the number for Steven's home. "Hello this is Detective Boyd."

"Let me speak to Katie."

"I'm sorry sir." the ultra calm voice replied "she is not available."

"I must speak with her," Richard demanded his voice beginning to rise.

"I'm sorry sir I cannot help you." the officer replied with quiet authority.

"Listen…" Then Gabriella's hand was on his.

"It's okay Richard." she said taking the telephone from him. "Thanks, yes." he heard her say and then "Yes I'll tell him." and then she put down the telephone and turned to him.

"A car will pick us up in ten minutes."

With lights flashing the blue and white police car cut through the rush hour traffic, the twenty minute journey to Steven's home taking us just ten. Making her way into the lounge Gabriella crossed to where Katie was being comforted by a uniformed female police officer.

"Katie?" she questioned as she drew her friend to her breast. "Any news?"

"Hello Gabi thanks for coming, was the traffic bad?" the tear stained Katie asked as she took a step backwards and lowering her head wiped the tears from her eyes.

"The usual," Gabriella informed her as she led her towards the sofa. "But never mind the silly traffic Katie," she continued as she began to stroke Katie's cold and trembling hands "how are you?"

"Oh I'm fine Gabi I'm just waiting for news."

Standing in the door way Richard heard the word fine and immediately thought just how wrong it was for the situation, for he felt anything but fine, it was not only Katie's partner that was missing but his son, but said nothing as Katie rising from the sofa asked if they would like some coffee. Leaving Richard to his own thoughts the two women moved to the kitchen and fifteen minutes later returned, both tear stained and with a tray containing four mugs.

"So what happened?" Richard asked as he took the steaming mug from the tray.

"I don't know Richard." Katie told him as she moved once more to the sofa and placing the tray on the coffee table sat down. "I was still in bed. Steven came up to say good bye then I heard a car on the drive, someone shouting and then gun ..."

"It's okay," Gabriella soothed as once more Katie dissolved into a flood of tears. "Come on have your coffee before it goes cold."

"Ms Benjamin?"

"Yes?" Katie asked as she turned to look as a tall and prematurely balding man strode into the room.

"Could I have a word? I'm inspector Kevin Dorrington and", he said nodding towards a blond and attractive female. "This is Sergeant Megan Boyd."

"Yes inspector?" Katie repeated and placing her coffee mug on the table got unsteadily to her feet.

"I'm not sure that Ms Benjamin is in any state to be interviewed at the moment sir." the blond sergeant suggested as Katie sank once more onto the sofa.

"No perhaps not Sergeant?" Dorrington agreed. "So Mr Blackwood, would you mind."

"Yes, no, certainly." an unusually hesitant Richard offered as he too placed his mug on the coffee table. "How can I help?"

"Alone, if you don't mind sir?" the inspector insisted.

"Yes of course inspector, Katie?" he asked but receiving no answer he held up his hand and leading the way to Steven's office asked if the inspector would like coffee.

"No thank you sir." he was told brusquely "I have some bad guys to catch." and suddenly and for some unknown reason Richard felt that the inspector was including him in his list of 'bad guys.'

"This is a nice house Mr Blackwood" the inspector said as he settled himself into one of Steven's deep and comfortable club chairs took out his note book and crossed his legs. "Does your son own it?" he asked.

"Yes why?" a bewildered Richard questioned.

"Are you and your son close Mr Blackwood?"

"Yes inspector very, but where is all this taking us?" he asked.

"This interview Mr Blackwood has to do with the abduction of your son, Mister Steven Simon Blackwood." he said and then looking down at his notes added "on Wednesday 9th of December 2009."

"Yes inspector, but how can I help?"

"Well sir whoever took your son was either very clever or very stupid."

"Yes." Richard encouraged.

"Well sir, your son was taken from his own home and in day light."

"Yes...?"

"And whoever took your son must have been very confident that he or they wouldn't be seen."

"And..?" Richard asked as somewhat confused he began to scratch his cheek.

"And Mr. Blackwood" the inspector continued "they were either very lucky or they knew the layout of the house and the movements of the people in the house."

"And" Richard repeated.

"And we have" Dorrington said looking across at his partner, " several suspects, many of whom bear the surname Blackwood and yes Mr Blackwood you are on our list."

"I am?" Richard asked incredulously.

"Yes sir and other suspects include Ms Katie Benjamin and Mr Joseph Insignias one of your son's staff. As we speak I have officers trying to track down your other son John who is allegedly on safari in Botswana. We have already interviewed your ex wife and my colleagues in the UK will be speaking to your wife and sons."

"But why look at a Blackwood?"

"Because sir you may or may not know but, your son is a very wealthy man and he was just about to change his will and set up a trust fund to help the homeless, but you knew that of course didn't sir?"

"Yes Steven had mentioned it." Richard admitted.

"Mentioned it sir? Weren't you upset at the prospect of losing over ten million Rand?"

"Steven didn't talk about numbers inspector." A long silence followed and then the inspector spoke again. "We don't know the whereabouts of Mister Joseph Insignias but we will find him."

"And just what makes you think one of Steven's own family would want to abduct him inspector?" an increasingly annoyed Richard asked.

"Facts sir and not only abduct, but kill."

"Oh inspector that's just plain ridiculous." Richard laughed. "What about all the other people who would want to kidnap Steven for his money, for a ransom?"

"Do you have a ransom note sir?" the inspector asked.

"No of course not, do you." Richard asked.

"I'm not at liberty to say sir."

"Then I'll take that as a no." Richard told him.

"Take it as you please sir. Now where were you this morning between four and seven o'clock?" Detective Kevin Dorrington's questioning got no further as a young and obviously nervous uniformed officer came into the study, the bad news he had to impart written clearly upon his face. Crossing the room he bent and whispered urgently into the inspectors his ear then crossing the room left the two men alone.

"Well sir." the inspector said as clearing his throat he suggested that they rejoin Ms Benjamin. What followed would stay etched in Richard's memory for a long, long time as entering the lounge once more the inspector again cleared his throat and announced that he was sorry.

"Yes inspector?" Katie asked as she got unsteadily to her feet and looked up into the stranger's face her eyes searching for any sign of hope or optimism and then in a voice that was barely audible she repeated the one word. "Yes."

"I'm so sorry," the inspector began "but we've located Mr Blackwood's car. His body was found ..." Dorrington's next words were lost as Katie let out a sound the like of which Richard had never heard before. It was an animal-like shriek of pain, a cry of distress and despair.

"I'm sorry." The inspector repeated as he turned to leave the room. His leaving, or so he told himself, was to allow the family time to grieve alone but, in truth his leaving was the result of his own feelings of inadequacy. Many officers felt the same whenever they had to give families bad news, for although they had all attended courses that dealt with such matters Kevin Dorrington's view was that no amount of training he got would ever prepare him for the act of blowing apart the life of another human being. Standing alone Richard watched as Gabriella crossed the floor to where Katie stood shaking. Gently taking her hand she once more guided her to the sofa where clasping her knees to her chest Katie Benjamin buried her head deep into the folds Gabriella's skirts. Silently the two women wept, Katie for her recent loss and Gabriella for the grief of all those years ago. Grief that like Katie's was all consuming. And Richard, feeling like a spectator and unable to offer anything to the tragedy unfolding before his eyes moved towards the door and passing through closed it quietly behind him. Only then did he feel his own tears began to build and closing his eyes he tried to form a dam with his lids. It was a pointless exercise as suddenly the familiar shudder of loss and grief hit him. Hit him in his head, hit him in his stomach and hit him in his heart. And then the watery flood gates opened.

CHAPTER 14
Wednesday 9th December 2009 (Evening)

Kidnapped

Steven Blackwood was not a man known to panic and when he finally woke drugged and bruised his first thought was to escape. In his late teens and in need of a challenge he had spent three months on an officer training course with the British army. As part of his training he had been dragged from his bed in the dead of night, blindfolded and dumped in the middle of the English country side. It was an experience that he had not enjoyed and had been instrumental in his turning down a commission. Now as he lay in the darkness with his head aching and hands tied in front of him he remembered again the words of his staff sergeant. "Your first duty Mr Blackwood sir is to escape," he had been told "and to do that mister you will need to use your head and your five senses." Streven's first sense, his sense of sight told him little except that it was dark. His sense of touch told him he was sitting on dry and dusty straw. His sense of smell confirming the above adding the dry acid stench of chicken shit, whilst the sickly taste of hot and confined chickens that filled his mouth completed the sensory cocktail. Pushing himself to his knees he engaged his fifth sense and listened. He heard nothing but the movement of small animal's, (chickens possibly, but probably rats) and the rapid beating of his own heart. His assessments complete he got to his feet and staring into the darkness waited for his eyes to adjust to the darkness. Eventually in the distance he was able to see if not light then a brighter shade of darkness and moving slowly he inched his way towards it. After several falls and cuts he reached the source of light and easing the corner of a rusted corrugated iron sheet from a window frame he looked out. Above him the moon was high in a clear sky. To his left and not more than a hundred metres away he could see the dark shape of tall pines moving in the breeze and to his right, well he couldn't believe his luck. Only two weeks earlier Steven and his father had passed the very same edifice. Yes, they had passed it in the daylight and on their way to play golf but now the 'gods' who took care of the needy had doubled their bounty and illuminated it. The Taal Monument (A monument to the Afrikaans language) stood on the hillside not more than three or four miles away. Moving away from the window Steven stood still and listened. Again he heard nothing, but sniffing the dusty air he realised that the smell of fresh air had grown stronger. Once more he began to move, cautiously following the walls of the building towards fresh air. Several minutes later he found himself in front of two high doors. The bottom of the doors had over the years been worn away leaving a three inch gap at their base, it was a gap wide enough to let fresh air flow in but far too narrow to afford Steven any meaningful view of the world outside. Leaned his back against the doors to test their strength he realised that his route to freedom lay elsewhere and sliding to the floor he closed his eyes. Sometime later he was awoken by the sound of a vehicle slowly bumping its way up a rutted track. As it moved the beam from its head lights danced in the air until finally come to rest on the gap under the barn doors and illuminating for the first time the interior of Steven's prison.

CHAPTER 15
Thursday 10th December 2009(Afternoon)

When Sorry is the Hardest Word

"I'm so sorry." Dorrington said again. "It was a stupid mistake to make. I had assumed my colleagues had done their job properly"

"Inspector I don't know whether to hit you or hug you." Richard told him as they walked through the mortuary door and out into the bright sunshine. The shame-faced Dorrington didn't answer, his anger and embarrassment apparently still too raw. He had first informed Richard of Steven's death and had then added insult to injury by asking him to go with him to identify Steven's body.

"Heads will roll Dr Blackwood." he said, his awkwardness elevating Richard through the ranks of academia. "Heads will most certainly roll."

"And I would bloody hope so." Richard told him his own anger rising again. "You come to me and in your total fucking incompetence and inform me of the death of a son and without bothering to checking your facts? God man I thought that the detective arm of the South African police force was a cut above the bloody bribe taking rest, but apparently."

"I'm sorry sir I can only apologise once more sir." Dorrington said as he followed the rapidly striding Richard to his car. "Would you like me to inform Ms Benjamin of the..."

"Cock up inspector?" Richard growled as he clicked the Audi's remote and yanked open the driver's door.

"Yes sir," the inspector told him "and I'm sorry.

""Yes inspector so you say, but you can leave the informing to me, I'd much rather you spent your time trying to find my son."

"Yes sir and thank you. And let me assure you that heads will roll and arses, if you will pardon the language, will be kicked."

"Kick away inspector," Richard told him without humour "and please phone if you have any news."

"Certainly sir I'll be in touch as soon as I hear anything." Dorrington confirmed as he turned and walked toward his sergeant, "Good bye sir and thank you for your understanding." he called over his shoulder and then more quietly "Shit Boyd in the car I need a drink."

"So he didn't take it well sir?" Dorrington's sergeant asked as she slipped the car into first gear and moved off.

"Yes Boyd I guess you could say that and he's going to be even more pissed off when he learns that kidnappers usually kill their victims within a week of taking them."

CHAPTER 16
Monday 14th December 2009 (Morning)

Depression and Drinking

Richard was well aware of the statistics surrounding kidnappings and when there was no news of Steven the next day or for the rest of the week he began to lose hope. Whatever it was that controlled his feelings and emotions had now begun to shut down. It was as if someone had rolled down a giant emotional shutter, a shutter that would lock out the cruel world of pain and prevent any intruders breaking into his delicate emotional vault.

On the day that Steven had been taken Richard had gone back to the house alone. Gabriella had decided to stay with Katie and now he sat alone in the lounge as he had done for the last six long days. Pouring himself a glass of Jack Daniels he sipped it slowly and pondered once more his sad and empty life. Richard's next glass of 'Jack' was a double and it slid down rather more quickly as he began to dig more deeply into his life. As with the previous six days he didn't bother to measure his third glass, the effects of his melancholy and the whiskey having taken control of his inhibitions. Richard drank into the night, drinking until the newly opened bottle was empty and he had made serious inroads into a second. At that point he fell asleep his chair

CHAPTER 17
Tuesday 15th January 2009 (Morning)

I Drink to Remember

The next morning when Nellie came into work she found Richard still asleep in his chair and failing to wake him telephoned Gabriella. Gabriella had then dialled Richard's number waking him from an agonised and fitful sleep.
"How are you Richard?"

"I was fine until someone woke me up." She was told before the telephone was slammed down. She rang again in the afternoon but unable to get a reply decided to call round at the house where she found Richard asleep in the lounge with three empty bottles of Jack Daniels at his side. Trying the gentle approached and getting no response she bent to check that her boss was still breathing then, satisfied that he was still alive she took his shoulder and with increasing vigour began to shake him.

"Richard, Richard." she called but failing to get a response she braced herself and slapped his face. It was slap that did little other than to cause Richard to groan quietly and to briefly open his eyes. Renewing her shaking and shouting Gabriella finally managed to get Richard to respond, she wished she hadn't as Richard sat up, opened his eyes and leaning forward asked her 'what the hell she was doing?' and then dropped his head into his hands.

"I was about to ask you the same question mister. " Gabriella told him angrily as he lurched forward, and putting his hands over his mouth attempted to prevent the tidal wave of warm vomit escaping. He failed, the thick brown fluid shooting out between his fingers and covering the carpet, his trousers and the front of Gabriella's blouse with warm dampness. "Oh shit Richard, you dirty bugger." she yelled as another wave of brown vomit spewed from his mouth and onto the carpet. Then leaning back in his chair he closed his eyes and utter the two words 'I'm sorry'.

"Sorry, sorry? Never mind sorry get yourself upstairs to the bathroom man." Gabriella shrieked as she took his warm and sticky arm and pulled him to his feet.

"Sorry Gabi …" was the best that Richard could manage in terms of an apology as he staggered against the supporting frame of his P.A.

"Never mind the sorry, who's going to clean this lot," she told him and then a little more gently added. "Come on then, let's get you changed and into bed. Even in his drunken state Richard could not resist.

"I thought you'd never ask." he smirked drunkenly and then wished he hadn't.

"Look you can do this on your own if you want Richard," Gabriella warned him sternly, "Or" she added "you can behave and get on with it."

With a great deal of assistance Richard made his way upstairs and into the bathroom where the ever faithful Gabriella helped him to undress, shower and get into his bed.

"Thanks Gabi." Richard told her as she moved to collect his soiled clothing from the floor and then away and above the call of duty or friendship, went to make a start on cleaning the lounge carpet.

CHAPTER 18
Friday 18th December 2009 (Morning)

Bodies Found

Richard slept the whole of Wednesday and Thursday. On the Friday, although he had no idea of the time or the day, he made his unsteady way downstairs and into the kitchen. The phone on the wall was ringing but he chose to ignore it. He wasn't feeling particularly hungry but opened a few cupboards to see if there was anything he fancied. As he did so the telephone rang again. Picking it up he yelled a "Yes what?" into the mouth piece.

"Mr Blackwood?" a cheery asked "it's Detective Dorrington and I need to talk to you."

"Have you found Steven?" Richard asked, his hope cutting though his depression.

"Well...." the inspector began.

"Well no?" Richard cursed as he crashed the phone back on its cradle and then for good measure added a frustrated "You fucking fool." Continuing his search for sustenance Richard was again unable to find anything he 'fancied', he did however find another bottle of Jack Daniels. Opening it he took a sip and then with bottle and unwashed glass in hand he made his way back upstairs and into bed.

Kevin Dorrington's need to speak to Richard has been four fold. Firstly he wanted to tell him that a ransom note had been delivered to Steven's office in Cape Town. Secondly, that the body that had been found in the boot of Richard's car had been identified as one Mr Michael Bennet, one of Steven's wealthy partners who had homes in England, Cape Town and Paarl. Enquiries had been made at his all his properties but without learning very much about the life and times of what appeared to be a secretive, almost reclusive Englishman. Thirdly he had wanted to ask Richard if any of the names on his ever growing list of suspects meant anything to him. The names on the list included a Mr Charles Ascot Chisholm and a Miss Priscilla Dwangu a croupier at the Grand West casino. Finally Dorrington had wanted to inform Richard that the body of Mr. Joseph Insignias had been recovered from the sea off Table Bay and that the cause of his death had *not* been drowning.

"Oh bloody hell Boyd." Dorrington moaned after he had put the phone down. "If the trail is this cold after only a week what's it going to be like in a month?"

"Very cold sir?" his sergeant had offered and immediately wished she hadn't as the glowering Dorrington told her that she was very funny and to get her coat.

CHAPTER 19
Thursday 24th December 2009 (Afternoon)

Christmas Eve

"Yes I know that it's Christmas Eve." Dorrington said as he stood with his sergeant on the deep shag pile carpet of Charles Ascot Chisholm's Cape Town office. "But I need to ask you some questions about the ransom note you received. "Have you touched it sir?"

"Yes I have."

"But didn't I tell you that you if you received a note you weren't to touch it sir?"

"Did you inspector? I don't remember."

"Do you have the note here sir?" Dorrington continued.

"I do." Charles Chisholm said as he took a white handkerchief from his pocket and wiped it across his large and perspiring forehead. Then lifting the telephone he tapped the one key and spoke. "Carol would you bring me the ransom note please?" he asked and replacing the handset he pushed his heavy frame out of his chair and moved to the window.

"Just how many people have you allowed to handle the letter sir?" Kevin Dorrington asked, his annoyance now beginning to show.

"Why inspector?" Chisholm asked without turning.

"Why...?" Dorrington asked, the words 'you great fat idiot' not very far from his lips, "because sir it may contain some forensic evidence. By now the letter will be so mauled we won't be able to... Oh never mind." he conceded as the door open and the hips swinging Chisholm's well dressed and expensively perfumed PA 'cat walked' across the room.

"The ransom note sir." she said as she aimed her smile and oozing sexuality at the inspector. Both smile and oozing missed their target as Kevin Dorrington thanked her and then took the letter from her.

"And you would be?" he asked.

"Westerman, Carol Westerman." The less than PA answered and with chin in the air she turned to leave.

"Just a moment Miss..." Dorrington questioned, his 'on demand' memory loss doing little to enhance Carol's ego or self-worth. "Would you mind going with Sergeant Boyd please? I think you may be able to help us with our enquiries."

Half an hour later Dorrington and Boyd made their way back to the car. "Well sergeant?" Dorrington asked.

"Well sir if you ask me, he's as bent as a five cent note and I'll bet my pension to a pair slippers that he's pushing something white, powdery and illegal up his nose!"

"And" Dorrington smirked "he's probably pushing something white and wrinkly up his PA as well. What a shit."

"Indeed sir," Boyd agreed "But it's a good job we don't have to lock up every shit or the streets would empty."

"That's a bit jaundiced for a Christmas eve sergeant." Dorrington smiled. "Now you'd best get yourself home and try and relax for a couple of days."

"And you sir?"

"Wife and kids time Boyd." Dorrington smile as he got climbed out of the car and moved towards his home and then he turn. "Oh shit Boyd" he cursed "I haven't got Beth a present."

CHAPTER 20
Thursday 24th December 2009 (Evening)

Sometimes I Feel Like a Motherless Child

Gabriella had telephoned Richard twice during the day to ask if he needed anything. The first time she rang he told her *'No thanks'* the second time he was less polite and her told to *'Just fuck off and leave him alone'*, not the kindest or wisest thing he had ever done as Gabriella worried about his state of mind decided to pay him a visit. Finding him in a state of unkempt exhaustion she offered to get him a doctor.

"A doctor?" he questioned angrily "No I don't want a fucking doctor so just piss off and leave me alone." Not one to be easily thwarted Gabriella had persisted.

"Come on Richard," she pleaded, "Please let me help."

"Gabi I don't want a doctor and I don't want you, I want my son back so please just go away and leave me alone." Hiding her hurt and conceding a partial defeat Gabriella told him 'Okay 'and that she would see him in the morning. Ungraciously Richard again told her that she needn't bother and to 'Just leave him alone' which reluctantly she did.

Waiting until he heard the front door close Richard brought his whiskey glass to his lips, drained the last of its contents, flung the glass against the wall and made his way back to bed. Richard's self-pity and despair had now reached a far greater depth than he would have ever thought possible. He didn't want a doctor nor, he told himself did he want Gabriella 'the fucking stupid bitch'. What he wanted was his son, Grace and his mother and bending his head as if in prayer his began to cry.

"Mother help me please." he wept and then in his sadness the words from one of his favourite operas began to sound in his head and he began to sing, his voice weak and trembling. "Sometimes I feel like a motherless child, sometimes I feel like a motherless child, sometimes I feel like a motherless child long way from home." and then his sobbing stopped and he was still.

"Oh Grace. I'm so sorry." he said, but his calmness was short lived and again he began to tremble, great waves of loss and grief hammering at his body, hammering at his mind, hammering and hammering until all strength and reason were gone and then he slept.

Waking in darkness Richard made his way to the bathroom to empty his bladder, the yellow fluid stinging and burning as it splashed noisily against the porcelain and down his leg. "Shit." he cursed in disgust as he brushed the offensive liquid from his trousers. Crossing to the sink he rinsed his hands and after splashing cold water onto his face he looked into the mirror. "Shit." he repeated at the red and puffy image that looked back at him and then, smiling a sad and pathetic smile, he turned and picking up his bottle of Jack made his way back to bed.

CHAPTER 21
Friday 25th December 2009 (Morning)

Is There Anyone There?

Christmas Day came and Richard deciding to contact his sons picked up the telephone and dialled his UK number and waited. 'Please leave a message' the answer phone told him, he hung up. His next call was to his second son John. The two men hadn't spoken since Richard's break up with Grace when Richard had thought that John would be a good and loyal son and take his side against the unreasonable Grace, but he had been wrong. John was made of more noble stuff than that and knowing that Richard was in the wrong had tried to persuade his father to think again. Unhappy with his son's disloyalty the two men had argued. Push came to shove and Richard no longer a physical match for John had ended up sitting undignified and angry on his backside. Richard had then stormed off and although John had on a number of occasions tried to mend their relationship Richard, being his usual bloody minded self had ignored all attempts at reconciliation. Frustrated and upset John had taken his wife and Richard's first grandson back to Africa to live his dream and set up a safari business in Botswana. Impatiently Richard listened as his call travelled the six thousand miles to Southern Africa and then John's phone began to ring and a voice he didn't recognise told him to 'Please leave his name and number and we will get back to you'. Leaving a message asking John if he would ring him back Richard put down the hand set and made his way downstairs to the office. Picking up the notes that he had been preparing for a seminar Richard tried to focus his tired eyes on the typed script but failing started to search for one of the many pairs of spectacles that were scattered strategically around the house. Eventually finding a pair on Gabriella's desk he returned to his own work space, sat down and began to read.

"What a load of shit." he laughed out loud as he turned to the second page. "What a load of bollocks." and then in anger and despair he threw the pile of papers high into the air. "Bollocks, pure bollocks." he ranted and sheets of A4 drifted passed his head and turning his back on the chaos made his way to the lounge.

"Damn and blast." he cursed as he opened the drinks cupboard and found that he had finished the last bottle of Jack. Gloomily Richard looked at the array of bottles in front of him, amongst them Brandy, Calvados and Rum then for some bizarre reason he picked up a bottle of Southern Comfort and clutching it by the neck he made his sad way up the stairs and into bed.

CHAPTER 22
Friday 1st January 2010(Morning)

Time to Pull One's Self Together

Richard's Christmas came and went without his involvement in any of the festive activities. He received cards from Gabriella and from his little boys but there was no news of Steven nor did he hear anything from John or Grace. Gabriella had visited him on the twenty sixth and brought him a Christmas present and one from Katie and the team but he had nothing to give her in return. She had tried to console him by telling him that the New Year would bring a new start but Richard's mood had continued to be negative.
"A new year - what bloody good is a new year to me," he had ranted. "Turn back the bloody clocks if you want, let time stand still if you must, do anything but don't make me face a new fucking year." Pleading she had told him that they were all suffering and that they had to believe and hope.
"You believe what you want," Richard had told her angrily, "But don't you come here telling me of hope and bloody peace and that time will heal. I don't want to heal, what is there to heal for? So just leave me alone, just fuck off and leave me alone."
Richard's self-imposed isolation continued until the twenty eighth when Gabriella brought a doctor to see him, but refusing his help and telling him that he could 'fuck off as well'. The good doctor had however seen it all before and told Richard that if he didn't talk to him he would see to it that he was admitted to a psychiatric ward. Believing the doctor's words to be true Richard talked to him for half an hour and then agreed to see him again the next day 'with a colleague from psychiatry'. He then walked with the doctor

to the front door, but before the medic was off the drive Richard was asking Gabriella if she would get hold of Rose Freeman. Rose, a psychotherapist who worked in competition with Richard's therapy practice was a lady for whom Richard had a great deal respect.

"If," he told Gabriella "I'm going to let anyone help me it's going to be someone I know and trust and not some pill pushing psychiatrist"

"Well that sounds like the best idea you've had in a little while" Gabriella told him "I would have suggested myself but," she added with a smile "I knew you'd do it in your own time eventually." Knowing that the 'eventually' was a reprimand and one he probably deserved he let it pass and instead asked Gabriella how she was coping.

"I'm okay Richard," she confided "but a little tired, it's been a hard few weeks."

"And my little boys Gabi, have you heard from them," and then the realisation hit him "Oh god I didn't even remember to send them their Christmas presents." Moving to his side Gabriella laid her hand on his.

"Don't worry," she told him "some kind soul will have sent Xbox games and probably cards to your mother and family." Then sighing Richard took her hand and began to gentle stoke it.

"Oh thanks Gabriella." he told her "Just what would I do without you?

"And who said it was me," she asked with a smile and removing her hand told him that it had been a pleasure. Thanking her again Richard then asked how Katie was.'

"She's bearing up and trying to keep busy, which reminds me, Detective Dorrington has been trying to get hold of you.

"Oh god," Richard sighed again and closing his eyes as if in anguish asked what the inspector wanted.

"I guess he just wants to update you." Gabriella told him "And when you speak to him please don't be rude." and pausing for effect added "Again."

""Yes well." Richard began to say but seeing the look in his P.A.'s face thought better of it and instead repeated that he was sorry and that he had let everyone down "Not just you Gabi but Katie and my boys." Taking his hand Gabriella told him that now was not the time for regrets and recriminations. "What happened has happened" she said "we all coped as best we could. Your son is missing, if you'd just shrugged it off then I really would have been worried. Now do you have Inspector Dorrington's number?" Confirming that he had the number Richard once more apologised.

"Oh will you stop it with the sorry," she told him gently. "You'd have done the same for me or any of the team. "Now," she added as she moved towards the door "you just get yourself better okay?"

"Sure." Richard told her and then his tone almost pleading he spoke her name.

"Yes?" she said turning.

"When are you planning to come home?" he asked. Returning to his side Gabriella leant forward and gently kissed his cheek.

"I'm not sure Richard. Let's see how Katie gets on next week and then..." her sentence remained unfinished as again she moved towards the door. "I'm sorry Richard." she said "But I must get going."

That evening Walter telephoned from England. "How's it going Richard?" he asked the note of concern clear in his voice.

"I'm fine Walter fine." Richard lied "It's good to hear from you."

"And you my friend." Walter told him and then "Look Richard Gabriella phoned me to tell me about Steven. I would have phoned earlier but she said not to." and then he paused "I'm sorry." he said, "Would you like me to postpone my trip?" The pause that followed told Walter that the answer was 'yes' but Richard's answer came back 'No'.

"That's the last thing I want to happen Walter." Richard told him, his anxiety rising at the thought of having to entertain even a good friend like Walter. "You just get yourself here as soon as you can. I need all the friends I can get."

"Sure?" Walter asked.'

"Sure." Richard told.

"Gee that's a relief." Walter sighed "I've got a flight booked for Monday."

"Really, that's good" Richard bluffed, "will you let Gabriella have your flight number and we'll meet you at the airport?"

"Will do mister, so I'll see you on Monday Richard?"

"Indeed Walter and well done. See you on Monday bye." Slowly Richard recradled the hand set and then lifting it again dialled Gabriella's number. "Walter's arriving on Monday." he told her, although she already knew. "And he'll phone you with details okay? Oh and Gabi did you manage to contact Rose?"

"Yes," she told him "but she won't be able to see you for a week. She's a very busy woman you know."

"Oh I know that" Richard moaned "busy taking my clients."

Replacing the phone Richard pulled his exhausted body up the stairs and turning on the shower stepped into the cascading water. Throwing back his head he lifted his arms as if in praise to the 'god' of hot water and then stood letting the healing waters flow over his aching body. For healing was what he needed, healing not just of his body but also his mind. Reaching for the shampoo he poured the cold liquid into his hand. "Step one," he told himself as he rubbed the blue liquid into his scalp "was to name the problem and step two was to change the problem into a need." Taking the scented soap from the dish he began to wash. "Then my friend all you have to do is meet the need, simple." he said and then bracing himself for the shock that was to come he counted 3-2-1and then turned the control dial from 'red' to 'blue. Suddenly the joy of warmth turned to the skin stinging pain of cold. Lingering for as long as he could Richard then stepped backwards and wrapping a warm towel around his waist he walked back to his bedroom.

"Okay pal so what's your need?' he asked himself as he looked into the bedroom mirror. The lines around his eyes were few, but the strain of the last few weeks had left dark triangles around their corners and his lower lids had sagged making him look old and tired. Tugging at the bags beneath eyes Richard smiled, the action of smiling transforming his face and for a brief moment removing all the signs of fatigue. Then pulling on his dressing gown he walked over to the window. Outside the night was calm and above him the bright moon shone in the clear sky.

"Well," he told himself. "'It would seem that you're in a far worse state than most of your clients." and then he smiled. "At least they can come to you for help." Making his way back to the mirror Richard looked again at his tired face. "I think old chap." he declared out loud "that its time this nonsense ended." and as he did so an involuntary smile flickered once more across his lips. "Gee Blackwood" he told himself "you're a funny little man but I do like you."

CHAPTER 23
Sunday 3rd January 2010 (Evening)

Escape

Having returned home on the Saturday Gabriella now sat with Richard as he pleaded with her to set he alarm clock.

"But Walter's flight is only due at nine and it's only an hour to the airport." she reasoned

"Yes but we'll need to double that amount of time in the rush hour and then add another half hour to park and walk to the terminal and then we'll be only just in time." he told her and so bowing to his 'superior knowledge?' she got up and made her way to bed. At eleven thirty the telephone rang rousing Richard from his Mozart induced sleep. Cursing as he hit his shin against coffee table he picked up the phone and listened.

"Do you want me to come now?" he asked. "Yes okay I'll see you tomorrow. Yes great." he added and then "Yes I'll see you tomorrow good night and sleep well. Yes I bet you will. Bye." Then for the second time in less than a month Richard made his way up the stairs and turned right.

"Gabriella," he called "Gabriella, wake up." When no reply came he moved once more towards her room and towards forbidden ground and knocked loudly on her door. "Gabriella, Gabriella." he shouted again "Gabriella Steven's home."

The food the two men had brought Steven on his twenty second day of captivity was again tasteless, but it was plentiful and he was grateful to have his hands freed from the ropes that bound him and for the water to wash down the taste of cheap sausages. Both of Steven's captors were big, black and belligerent. From the start of his imprisonment they had made it clear that there would be no nonsense and when Steven had started to disagree with them they had beaten him savagely, breaking his nose and causing bruising to his back and legs. Following his initial beating they had left him to his own devices and although his surroundings remained dark he was now better able to find his way around and try to devise some means of escape. Today lady luck would finally come to his aid.

"Eat more quickly." the lead and slightly drunker captor snapped as he picked up Steven's half eaten meal and walked towards the still open barn door. "Now get some sleep and maybe tomorrow," he sneered, "we can all go home." Once more in his world of half light Steven listened as the bakkie rattled its way down the track. Getting quickly to his feet he picked up the hay fork that had almost impaled him on his third night of captivity and ran hands free to the wooden ladder that led to the hay loft. Climbing the ladder was difficult and painful but reaching the top he moved as quickly as his aching body would let him and crossing the rough boards made his way to the far end of the loft. Using the hay fork he levered the corrugated sheet from the window and kicked out the rotting frame. Then he waited and listened. The noise of the falling window frame had been loud but when no one came to investigate he climbed through the gap and hanging from his finger tips dropped. Not sure how long it would be before his captors realised their mistake in not retying his bonds, he began to run bending low to make a smaller target should they return. He ran hard towards the trees and stopped to regain his breath. Then throwing caution to the wind he fled down the rutted track and fifteen minutes and two miles later he reached the road, the rest was relatively easy. Thumbing a lift from two slightly drunk golfers on their way home from the Pearl Valley golf course he was dropped at the police station in Paarl where he explained the situation. He then telephoned Katie and by eleven o'clock Steven Blackwood was safely home.

CHAPTER 24
Monday 4th January 2010 (Morning)

Walter Wilson

Walter Wilson was due to fly in from England and true to her word Gabriella was ready and waiting when Richard came downstairs showered, shaved and feeling more like his old self.

"I'd forgotten how well you scrub up." she told him as he pulled out a kitchen chair and sat down.

"It's certainly been a while," Richard agreed "Let's just hope I've turned the corner." and then, his face breaking into joyful grin he asked her what time they were visiting Steven.

"If Walter's on time and he's not too tired we should be there by eleven, excited?" she asked. Richard didn't need to answer, his beaming smile being worth more than a thousand words.

The journey to the airport took a little time, as Gabriella had predicted, a little over half an hour and by seven thirty Richard and Gabriella were stood looking up at the arrivals board, as Gabriella had predicted an hour and a half early. In other circumstances she would have taken great pleasure in giving Richard a dose of 'I told you so.' but she resisted accepting instead Richard's offer to buy her breakfast as a moral victory. As they ate they discussed the hectic events of the night before. Richard had wanted to go to Steven as soon as he heard the news of his return and it had taken all Gabriella's powers of persuasion to convince him that Steven would be exhausted and want to sleep. With their breakfast finished the pair wondered across to the arrivals hall where they were eventually rewarded by the sight of Walter emerging from the twilight world of 'baggage claim'. Walter Wilson was not a tall man, standing a little over five foot six inches tall and slim, very slim, his thinness at times making him look decidedly unwell. In fact Walter Wilson was a keen jogger and cross country runner who had won the district cup for the over fifties for the last three years. Today he was dressed casually in slacks and a light weight cotton jacket, the pale blue of his eyes matching his jacket perfectly. His white hair, which he wore pushed back from his face, was a little longer than Richard's which again seemed to emphasise his thinness and pointed features. A quiet and thoughtful man Walter spoke rarely but when he did it was with a gentle North Yorkshire accent. Lifting his hand in greeting Richard moved forward and taking Walter's hand he shook it firmly and then throwing his arms around his friend's shoulders hugged him. It was a show of affection that took Richard, Gabriella and Walter by surprise.

"Walter my friend," he beamed as his bemused friend took a protective step backwards "it's good to see you."

"And you Richard. How are you?" Walter asked his voice full of caution and concern.

"I'm fine." Richard told him with a sombre face. "But the last few weeks have been hell." and then with his voice and features sliding effortlessly into cheerfulness he told Walter that Steven's was home. "And you're here" he added "so all is well."

"Steven's home?" Walter echoed, "How, when...?" Grinning Richard told him that it was a long story and that they'd be seeing Steven later and he could asked him himself.

"Now," he asked "how was your trip?" Nodding towards an old couple as they grumbled and groaned their way towards the exit Water explained that his trip had been long, cramped and boring. "The food was poor, I got little sleep and there were too many rude people." he said as he again looked in the direction of the still whinging pensioners.

"So you're a fan of air travel?" Gabriella suggested brightly.

"However did you guess?" Walter moaned, his smile indicating his appreciation of irony.

"Oh it was just something you said." she told him the warmth of her smile making Richard feel like a spectator.

"Airports are such strange places Gabi." Walter asserted as he placed his hand on her shoulder. "Hospitals are there to try and make people better. Hotels are there to pamper the weary. Factories make things and homes offer security, but airports?"

"Airports my man are horrible and no more that a means to an end." Richard informed him as he lifted Walter's overnight bag onto his shoulder adjusted the strap.

"Unless", the ever bright Gabriella suggested. "You're meeting a good friend and then they're …"

"Still hell Gabriella," Walter told her "but then they become a necessary evil?" and slipping his arm through hers they began to follow the whinging couple towards the exit. "And how are you Gabriella," he asked as Richard, now feeling like a stranger watched them walk away. "You're looking well." Walter continued as they saunter slowly after the trolley pushing, chattering throng.

"Thank you Walter," she told him and then very uncharacteristically for the normally brave and stoic Gabriella she admitted that she tired. "It's been an awful few weeks for everyone." she told him and stopping she turned and waited for the approaching Richard to catch them up. "Sorry Richard, need a push?" she offered as the bag carrying, trolley pushing Richard came to a halt beside her.

"No," he told her as he again adjusted the strap of Walter's overnight bag. "You go on and collect the car, I'll wait for you by the door." Gabriella needed no second bidding. She had spent the last month supporting and at times pandering to the needs of both Richard and Katie. It was a task that she didn't actually object to but, enough was enough and to be in the company of this attentive man, if only for a few minutes was, well it was refreshing and so taking Walter's arm she set off to claim the car. Although Gabriella had known Walter for less time then Richard she had always got on well with him. There was something about his quiet thoughtfulness that in Gabriella's eyes placed him above most, perhaps all the men she knew.

"How's Richard been?" the ever thoughtful Walter asked as he fed money into the ticket machine.

"Oh," Gabriella whispered as she looked around to check that her boss was not in ear shot "I've been really worried about him Walter. When Steven was taken he just seemed to give up. It was a reaction that I hadn't expected from him and it really threw me."

"Fear Gabi" Walter confided gloomily "it affects us all differently. I've known people set up shrines to their loved ones, people who stop their clocks and stop their own lives. "But," he added optimistically "Richard has recovered quickly if already able to get out and about."

"Today is his first time away from the house Walter," Gabriella corrected "and he's still very delicate." Hearing the catch in Gabriella's throat Walter turned and for a second time he placed his hands on her shoulders. It was a simple act, not a particularly sexual act but, as they stood there in the midst of the hustle and bustle of the airport something warm and intimate passed between them.

"He's a lucky man to have you Gabi." he told her.

"And I'm lucky to have him Walter." Gabriella agreed "he saved me when Michael died you know?" she told him as if some kind of explanation were needed.

"Yes I know," Walter told her "and we'll sort him out, you'll see."

Taking the N2 highway Gabriella steered the Audi onto the N3 and passed the hospital and university.

"I never expected it to be like this Gabi." he said for the fourth time as they left the highway and entered the leafy lanes of Rondebosch.

"So what did you expect?" she asked "Prides of lions and elephants roaming the streets?"

"No not exactly," he told her "but this is so modern and clean." Speaking for the first time since leaving the airport Richard leaned forward and resting his arms on the back of Walter's seat told him that he knew what he meant.

"Most Europeans," he said wisely "only seem to hear about the troubles in South Africa. And" he added "they think that the beautiful Cape and the bustling Johannesburg are next door to each other and not a thousand miles apart."

"Pretty much like the American's." Walter added not wanting to be outdone in the Wisdom stakes, "Did you know that many of them think that London and England are the same place. And you'd be surprised how many of them have never heard of Yorkshire."

"Never heard of where?" Richard asked grinning.

"Oh very funny Richard," the partisan Walter told him "especially coming from a Lancastrian."

"Well at least the Yanks have heard of Henry VIII and Elizabeth I, both of whom you will remember were 'red rose' and thus Lancastrian monarchs."

"And they also know about Richard of York..."

"Who you will also remember 'gave battle in vain." Richard gloated as Gabriella drew the Audi to a halt outside the high, heavy and ornate iron gates of Steven's home.

"Boys, boys please." she pleaded as she waited for the security guard to check her pass.

"Is there much trouble here?" Walter asked as he surveyed heavy gates and security guards something he had only seen at the entrance of stately homes and the approach to Downing Street.

"Very little," Gabriella informed him as the heavy gates slide open. "People see to their own security. Private guards and high walls seem to keep most undesirables away." The slipping the Audi into first gear she steered the car slowly up the wide drive to a shady carport where Richard stepped out of the car and into the arms of his first born son.

"Hello dad what's new?" Steven asked his voice stronger than Richard had expected but his broken nose making it sound as if it had travelled some distance down a hose pipe.

"Oh nothing much," Richard told him "my eldest son is home safe and I'm so..." and then he swallowed hard in his effort to hold back the tears.

"Steady old man, there are females present." Steven joked as he handed his father a clean white handkerchief.

"Sorry," Richard apologised as he took the handkerchief and pretending to blow into it handed it back. "Kidnappers usually top their prey after three days you know." he said, his voice breaking with emotion. "I really thought I'd lost you son."

"What, top a Blackwood?" Steven told him "Never, now let's have some coffee."

"He looked well considering." Walter suggested as half an hour later he lifted his damp shirt from his back and settled himself into the coolness of the air conditioned Audi.

"Yes thank god." Richard agreed as he wiped the sweat from the back of his neck. "Now Gabi home and don't spare the horses."

Richard's home 'Seven Oaks' had been built in the mid nineteen thirties in the style of a columned Georgian mansion. Set in its own grounds it boasted wide French doors, and bay windows with flower beds, mainly roses beneath. The eastern end of the house had been planted with Ivy that all these years later was still trying to fulfil its primeval instincts and reach the sun. Today however its efforts were being thwarted by a short black man in yellow wellington boots who swayed precariously at the top of an old wooden ladder.

"Morning boss." he called as the car came to a rest and Richard climbed from the back seat. Closing his door Richard turned and waved, he wished he hadn't as placing one precarious foot on a upper floor window sill the man swayed and waved back.

"Morning Boss" the seventy year old called again at which point Richard, closing his eyes shouting his warning of "Be careful young man." and leading the way indoors left the snip happy Colin to his task. The interior of the house, as one would expect from a house of that period and type boasted a plethora of dark wooden beams, high and gleaming chandeliers and statue filled plaster niches. Standing at the foot of a wide and ornate staircase Richard explained the builder of the house had been a fanatic of the board game Cluedo. "That corridor" he said pointing to his left" runs for some thirty yards and then turns right. If you follow that corridor it will take you right and right again until you find yourself back where you started. There are all sorts of rooms leading off it, library, billiard room, my study, an office and best of all a cosy little 'Den' as the Americans call it."

"So where's Miss Scarlet?" Walter asked then and grinned in anticipation.

"Oh she was killed in the library with a knife - the butler did it you know." Richard smiled and picking up Walter's suitcases led the way up oak staircase. Ten broad treads he stopped on a wide landing and looked up. "What do you think?" he asked as the enormous stuffed head of a water buffalo looked sadly down at them. "Big fella Walter don't you think?" Richard questioned

"He is," an impressed Walter told him "and he looks rather cross."

"I think you'd be cross if someone put a bullet in your ass and hung you on a wall." Richard laughed, probably his first for some time.

"I guess so." Walter conceded "But he's a good looking fella and well hung."

"Who's well hung Richard?" Gabriella asked from the foot of the stairs.

"The buffalo Gabi." Walter told her innocently and then blushed as the context of the 'well hung' hit him.

"Come on old man you've had a long trip" Richard told him as he picked up the suitcase and then turning to Gabriella told her that they'd be down in ten minutes. Moving to his left Walter then began to climb, he didn't get very far.

"No Walter," Richard called after him "Ladies go to the left and Gentlemen go to the right."

"Really?" Walter asked in surprise. "And what happens if a gentleman goes to the left?"

"If a gentleman went left Walter" Richard told him "he wouldn't be a gentleman." Accepting but not understanding Walter followed Richard to the room prepared for him where he unpacked showered and twenty minutes later joined Gabriella in the lounge.

"Do you play?" he asked as he moved towards the baby grand piano and lifting the lid began to tap out the favourite 'Chopsticks'. Smiling at his ham fisted attempt at musicianship she told him 'No' and then mischievously asked. "Do you?" Moaning at her unkindness he told her 'No' and closing the lid went to sit beside her.

"But I've wanted to learn for a long time," he added "what about Richard does he play?"

"Oh he's pretty good," Gabriella told him "but sadly he hasn't played much of late."

"Steven?" Walter suggested.

"Steven." Gabriella confirmed "he really did think he's lost him you know. God I remember when I lost Michael, my life just fell apart. Losing someone so close is..." and then she stopped a sad smile forming on her lips.

"I'm sorry Walter" she said as she gently touched his arm. "How are you managing without Barbara?"

"Oh I have good days and bad Gabi." he told her and then in an attempt to change the subject he walked to the window. "This is a lovely house." he said.

"Yes it's very beautiful Walter and you're welcome to stay as long as you want." Smiling up at her Walter thanked her.

"Gosh Gabi life can be hard." he said as he sadly shook his head "

"Indeed it can Walter," Gabriella agreed and that's why we have friends." and taking his arm she led him outside.

"Do you have family in England Walter?" she asked.

"Just my two boys and Emma," he told her "most are on Barbara's side of the family so I don't see much of them now."

"And the children?" she asked.

"I don't see much of the boys, they have their own lives and families. Emma visits me most weekends now that she's out of the army. I don't think you met the kids, did you?"

"No" she said as again she took his arm "and I'm not sure how well I know you Walter, you were always so busy, but now that we have some time lets change that."

"I'd like that Gabi" Walter told her as he put his arm around her waist and gently squeezed and then realising what he had done he removed it.

"We tend to spend a lot of time out here Walter." Gabriella told him as aware of his unease she led him past the pool and towards the B.B.Q. area. Walter's show of physical affection had surprised and pleased her. She had always found him to be a kind and caring man, but in all the years they had worked together she had never known him to touch her. "Richard likes to eat outside or 'Braai', as the locals call it." and suddenly Gabriella found herself chattering away like a school girl meeting a film star.

CHAPTER 25
Tuesday 13th January 2010 (Early Evening)

Panama Jack

It had been a week since Walter's arrival and after finishing work early Gabriella informed the men that she had booked a table and would be taking them out for a meal in the city.

"Initially," she said as she as she accepted the glass of red wine Richard offered her "The meal was going to be a welcome to Walter to South Africa but, with Steven's safe return to us a triple celebration, a welcome to South Africa for Walter, a welcome home to Steven and a welcome out of depression for Richard so," she ordered "Get yourselves scrubbed up and please don't keep a lady waiting!"

'Panama Jack's' restaurant was situated in the working area of Cape Town docks, it's isolated spot making Walter wonder if he would be safe from knife attack or from being 'press ganged' by some bearded parrot carrying pirates. As this was to be a triple celebration Gabriella had decided that she was going to spare no expense and so the three ate well, the wine flowed freely and within the hour Richard was on his feet proposing a toast to his eldest son.

"Come on let's celebrate the return of my big boy." he said as he lifted his fifth or sixth, glass of red wine to his lips.

"To Steven and Katie," Gabriella echoed. "Here's to a very fine couple."

"And here's to Richard and Gabriella, two very fine people and good friends." Walter added.

"And here's to us and to life, to love and the future." Richard called as he waved his glass at the assembled diners although in truth he couldn't help wondering if his life had really taken a more positive turn. With some trepidation he realised that he was putting an awful lot of trust in Rose Freeman. *'If Rose fails to help,'* his negative side told him. 'Then you will surely be lost.' But for moment the wine had put him in a positive mood and so he continued to drink.

"This is a great place Walter." he slurred "It reminds me of the good old days in England. Remember the Chinese we used to go to for our team meeting. Now what was it called?"

"It was the Sun Dragon." Gabriella told him without thinking. "Remember how April always tried to avoid coming, always having an excuse about being too busy."

"Which reminds me Gabi," Richard said as he lifted his glass in salute to his friends. "You seem to be keeping yourself to yourself these days, was it something I said?"

"No it's not that Richard, I've just been busy." she told him.

"That's what April used to say." Walter laughed, this consumption of wine causing him to lag behind in the conversation.

"Doing anything in particular? Richard asked.

"No just this and that, you know?" Gabriella told him.

"No I don't know Gabriella." Richard said a little too bluntly. "Just what are you doing?" It was a question too many.

"Hell Richard." she told him crossly "What is this, the third degree?"

"No Gabi," he said "it's just that Walter and I were talking and...."

"Well as flattered as I am that you two hero's should find my life of interest I don't see why I should have to answer to you for my every movement. I'm a free woman after all, aren't I Richard?" she added pointedly.

"Sure, sure Gabi," Richard replied suddenly flustered. "It's just that...well okay Gabi fair cop, we just wondered if you'd got yourself a fella."

"And if I have?" she asked.

"Oh nothing..." he told her innocently then unable to stop himself he asked "Have you?"

"Yes Richard and yes Walter I've met someone." Even though Richard had prepared himself for the answer he still felt his resentment stir.

"Who?" he asked.

"Oh Richard," Gabriella told him in exasperation. "His name is Adam and he works at the university. I've known him for some time and he asked me for a drink okay?"

"Yes of course it's okay Gabi." Richard lied "So what does Adam do at this university?" he asked.

"He's over here doing research into Homelessness." Gabriella told him calmly.

"Well that should keep him busy for a few years."

"No he goes back home soon. His funding is just about up."

"Good." Richard hissed and then hearing the venom in his voice he back tracked. "I'm sorry Gabi, what I meant to say was that it's good that you met him before he returned home."

"Oh Richard its fine," Gabriella smiled "I know you just want me to be safe and happy."

"Ah Richard" the now very drunk Walter slurred "you two sound just like father and daughter and it's so hard when your little girl grows up and leaves home isn't it Richard."

"And who said I was going anywhere?" Gabriella wanted to know.

"So it's not serious?" Richard questioned the relief in his voice clear to everyone and grinning mischievously Gabriella told him that one month was not a great deal of time in which to be making decisions about her future "So" she asked "Is it okay with you if I wait and see dad?" By some unspoken agreement the subject dropped and ten minutes later the trio left the restaurant calling their thanks to their yawning waiter and anyone else who would listen.

The three travelled home in silence each lost in their own private thoughts, thoughts about life and about love and about their futures. Richard's own ponderings were mostly about Gabriella, a woman who seemed to have everything a man could ever want. Why then he asked myself don't I make a move and tell her how I feel about her. His answer came quickly; *'Because you fool'* he told himself, *'you will lose Grace and possibly Gabriella forever.'* Walter's answer to the same question was far less complicated, it was his love for his dead wife that held him back, but he wondered, for how long.

CHAPTER 26
Wednesday 14th January 2010 (Late Evening)

I love you Richard

On reaching home Walter and Gabriella went through to the lounge to talk whilst Richard making his unsteady way to the kitchen switched on the percolator, prepared the coffee tray and with elbows on table placed his weary head in his hands. Although the evening had been pleasant enough Gabriella's revelation about Adam had thrown him. Not that he begrudged her a life outside work but the thought there was another man in her life was, 'Well what was it?' he asked. Roused from his deliberations by the hiss and rumble of the coffee maker he got to his feet and with tray in hand returned to the others. With conversation between the three lacking any direction or interest Gabriella stretched and getting to her feet told the men that she was 'off to bed'.

"Fancy a brandy?" Richard asked as he settled himself deeper into his arm chair.

"Why not?" Walter agreed as he struggled to his feet and yawned loudly. "One more won't do any harm. No you stay where you are." he suggested to the motionless Richard "I'll get them."

"Thanks pal but I'm not too sure about it not doing any harm, I've drunk more in the last few months than I ever have." Richard challenged and placing his feet on the coffee table, crossed his legs and putting his hands behind his head closed his eyes. "But never mind eh" he grinned inanely as Walter crossed to the drinks cupboard and poured two large brandies "In for a penny in for a pound, what do you say?" Walter said nothing.

For several minutes the two men sat quietly swirling their drinks in that unconscious way men do when thinking. Finally breaking the lengthening silence Walter asked Richard how he was doing.

"Better thanks," Richard told him "but I don't think I've felt so bad in a very long time, but now all I want to do is start working on whatever it is that keeps pulling me down?" Looking at his watch Walter put his hand to his mouth, yawned loudly and told Richard that it had been a long night.

"But," he added "if you want to sit for a while and talk I'm happy to listen." Now it was Richard's turn to struggle "It's a deal." he said "and if ever I can repay your kindness don't hesitate to ask" Richard offered and then with brandy glass in hand he invited Walter to follow him. Side by side the two men sauntered (staggered) down the wide corridor to Richard's office. The room, like all the rooms in Seven Oaks was large. On three sides the walls were lined with high book cases their hardbacked contents ranging from travel to psychology and from Christie to Dickens. On the ash panelled fourth wall were photographs, most of them taken in and around Richard's home in Lancashire. In pride of place hung a winter scene of the hills overlooking Water Grove, the long flat hill backed by a blood red sky.

"What do you think?" Richard asked as he took the picture down and handed it to his friend.

"Are these all yours?" Walter asked as he took the wooden framed photograph and studied it.

"Indeed sir."

"It's beautiful." Walter told him as he handed the work back to its owner and Richard unable to hide his pleasure took the picture, rehung it and then watched as Walter crossed to Gabriella's desk and picking up a glass paper weight rolled it in his hands.

"So does Gabriella have a man in her life?" he asked as he replaced the paper weight and picked up a photograph of Gabriella and her late husband Michael.

"It would seem so my friend," Richard told him "but it didn't sound too serious did it, why do you ask?"

"No reason" Walter lied, "It just that she's such a special person and it would be a waste if she spent the rest of her life alone and lonely don't you think?" Unhappy with the direction of the conversation Richard crossed to his desk. "The boss's chair." he said as he flopped down into the red leather chair "and seat of power in the Emotional Solutions Empire." he added as selfconsciously he began to swivel from side to side. Telling him that he'd done well Walter picked up a photograph of Richard's two small boys.

William and James?" he asked as he turned it towards his friend.

"Good looking lads eh Walter?" he suggested

"Yes like their mother?" Walter smiled as he replaced it.

"Indeed" Richard agreed as he got up from his desk. "Now let me show you the best room in the house." And retracing his steps crossed the corridor and pushed open the door to his 'study.

"Now this is fabulous." Walter told him as he moved into the room and breathing in the manly aromas of old cigar smoke and whiskey selected one of the deep and comfortable wing-backed chairs and sat down.

"And the harassed mans perfect hide a way." Richard added as he settled himself into a seat and taking up his usual 'I don't have a care in the world' stance he placed his hands behind his head and closed his eyes. Then he waited. He knew that Walter would not rush for Walter was a professional and he as such would think about every syllable he uttered.

"Okay Richard." Walter finally said. "We know each other very well, or at least I think we do and that" he added "could make things a lot easier or a lot more difficult. But" he continued "I'm going to try and treat you like anyone else." The nervousness in his voice was clear to both men Richard leaned forward and told Walter that he wouldn't want it any other way.

"Right then," Walter began as he crossed his legs and linked his fingers "before we get into anything heavy can you remind me just how you came to be running a business in Cape Town?"

"It all started," Richard began "on one of my trips to Africa with my second son John. I don't think you've met John have you?" he asked.

"Strange to tell" Walter yawned as he again looked at his watch. "I hadn't met any of your family before today."

"Well," Richard continued Steven my eldest boy was already living here and he asked me about the new developments in the UK practice. You know the Therapy Guest House and the legal and medical services."

"Yes." Walter encourage.

"Well Steven told me that he thought the concepts were, as far as he knew, lacking in the Cape and suggested that I should think about bringing them over here, which I did."

"And were your business plans worked through and all interested parties consulted?" Walter asked his tone to almost sounding accusing.

"They were." Richard confirmed, "And on the whole it was thought of as a positive move."

"On the whole meaning?" Walter asked.

"My number two son, John counselled caution." Richard explained. "He told me that Grace had been more than understanding in letting me visit Steven once a year, he also suggested that it was more than most women would put up with.

"And?" Walter asked.

"Well he told me that if I tried selling Grace the idea of setting up a practice in the Cape and that I would be away for three months of the year I would probably be 'pushing my luck "And? "

"And when I got back to the UK I put the idea to her." Telling Richard that he would probably be with John on this one he asked Richard what Grace had said about the idea.

"Well," Richard told him "Grace had objected for a number of reasons. Her first objection being that we didn't need the money."

"Which I assume," Walter pointed out, "was true?"

"We can always use a little more money Walter Richard told him defensively.

"Okay," Walter conceded "what was her second argument?"

"Well." Richard told him as he got to his feet and walked to the window "her second argument was that I would be stretching myself too thinly and that I would make myself ill.

"And her third argument?"

"Her third argument was that she didn't want me to be away for three months of the year. Then she told me that she'd had been thinking of asking me not to leave her alone with the boys for three weeks every year and that to leave her for three months was ridiculous. It was the 'ridiculous' bit did it for me Walter and my old reaction to criticism kicked in and I stormed off. "

"But that wasn't the end of your expansion plans Richard was it." Walter suggested.

"No," Richard told him as he returned to his seat. "I brought the subject up again a few weeks later using 'the boys would love it' routine. And that they could all come out when school finished for Christmas, that there would be sun, sea and our own swimming pool. We could have a really good time." I told her.

"But I guess she wasn't buying that either?" Walter suggested.

"Not a chance," Richard told him. "She wanted to know what she would do about her own family at Christmas."

"I told that we always saw her family at Christmas and then asked her if it was it too much trouble if we visit my big boy once in a while. But she wasn't having it that either and so the subject was dropped."

"It was?" Walter questioned.

"It was," Richard told him.

"Sure?" Walter asked. Admitting that he had asked Steven to set up meetings with interested parties Richard then informed him that in the December he had faced Grace and the boys with the exciting news that he had booked tickets for Cape Town and that had rented a big house with a swimming pool near the coast."

"You bastard Richard…"

"That's funny Walter," Richard grinned sheepishly "because that's exactly what Grace said when she got me on her own, but the boys were of course thrilled."

"I bet they were." Walter conceded "So then what happened?"

"We all came to the Cape for Christmas and had a pretty good time. Then I saw Grace and the boys off at the airport and got on with building the business." Now it was Walter's turn to get up.

"God Richard I didn't know you could be so callous" he said as he crossed to the bookcase "I've always seen you as laid back and accommodating." and removing a copy of Dombey and Son' flipped it open. "I thought that this guy was calculating but you take the biscuit." Ceding the point Richard admitted that he could be bloody minded, and sadly usually with Grace - Richard joined Walter by the bookcase.

"Shall we get another drink?" he asked.

CHAPTER 27
Thursday 15th January 2010 (Early Hours)

I love her Walter

With glasses re-filled and bladders emptied the two men returned to the study and taking his seat Walter continued his questioning. "So you went home for Easter?" he questioned as Richard, placing his brandy glass on the coffee table resumed his 'I don't have a care in the world' stance.

"Grace was very good about it" he said with some satisfaction gloated "and our relationship seemed to blossom." Swirling the contents of his brandy glass Walter suggested that Grace really must love Richard and then with a more than a hint of venom accused Richard of being a bastard and sniffing his brandy took a leisurely sip.

"She does Walter and I love her, you know I do, that's why we're here isn't it?" Richard told him his heart beginning to race and his breathing growing more laboured.

"Is it now? Walter mocked as again he swirled his drink "That's funny because I thought I was here on holiday and not to sort out your unholy mess." With fists opening and closing as he fought back his feelings of anger and resentment Richard suggested that Walter's words were a bit harsh for a therapist and an unrepentant Walter, informed Richard that he was not his therapist but his friend. "And" he added as he lifted a slightly trembling hand "I think you need you to be clear about that." then taking a calming sip of brandy he advised Richard to do the same. Not yet ready to be mollified Richard got to his feet and stared down at his erstwhile friend.

"It's a good job I know you," he growled "Otherwise my friend I'd be walking by now." to which a back in control and unremorseful Walter told him that 'the door is just there' and suggested that Richard try to redeem himself "And not only with me but with Grace." he directed.

"But I've already told you that Grace had been very good about my…"

"Don't tempt me Richard." Walter told him "Just tell your story." And so the still angry and irate Richard continued.

"Grace and I talked and I agreed to hand over the reins of the Cape Town operation to someone else." he said.

"Good," Walter encouraged "and then?"

"Well she warned me that if I went away again without her blessing I needn't bother coming back."

"Well done to Grace." Walter applauded "but," he continued pointing out the obvious, "I see you standing in front of me now so you must have come back to the Cape."

"Oh how very observant Walter, just how do you do it?" Richard asked sarcastically to which Walter replied that there was no need for derision and that he was only trying to help.

"But I'm feeling threatened." Richard justified.

"And so you should," Walter countered bluntly "now will you please get on with your story. Cowed, for the moment, Richard told Walter that he was sorry and Walter, feeling vindicated told Richard to 'come on pal,' and that they could do this.

"I hope so Walter," Richard told him as heaving a heavy sigh he settled back in his chair "And I really did think that Grace would see sense you know" he said as he sighed again "but I guess that she was hoping for the same thing of me and that I would change my mind. I tried getting the boys on my side by reminding that 'we'd had a good time in Cape Town' but Grace was on to that trick and told them we couldn't afford to go every year. Anyway in June we went away with her family for one of their 'does'. They were always having family 'does' and I tried to talk to her mother and brothers. Tried to get them on my side by selling the idea of growing the business, but they were all negative about the suggestion."

"And you were surprised?" Walter asked.

"I was and things got worse."

"Tell me more."

"Well, John and I used to get together every Thursday for a beer and some Indian food and have a gentle moan about the women in our lives."

"As we men do." Walter suggested.

"But even John was on Grace's side." Richard told him.

"Sides Richard," Walter questioned "it's getting bad when husband and wives are talking about being on different sides. What happened to pulling together?"

"That's not the point …" Richard told him as Walter, pretending to blow his nose, told him to stop or he'd break his heart. Unimpressed Richard told him that he wasn't funny. "John was on Grace's side and then can you believe it, he ups sticks and takes his young wife back to Africa. Okay for him to go to Africa but not me, that can't be right!"

"So he just up and went?" Walter asked.

"Yes, well no." Richard confessed "He did try to mend things with me, but I was still cross…"

"And you still are?" Walter suggested. Finding no argument with the statement Richard asked Walter where all this was taking them.

"You tell me pal." Walter invited.

"Well Grace took me away for a romantic weekend so that we could try and patch things up and make a new start." Richard said smiling at his own joke. Unsmiling Walter told him that it was a good job there was one adult in the family and then added that Richard was here and Grace was there, "so what happened?" he asked.

"Ah," Richard told him "at our last romantic meal I told Grace that I'd booked a ticket for Cape Town, but that it would be my last trip. She just lost the plot and swearing and crying stormed out of the restaurant. I followed her and we argued. I told her she had never been behind me and that she didn't want me to succeed. Then she packed her bags and went home without me and I moved into a boarding house. I was sick of her negativity

Walter." Richard explained weakly "and later that week I phoned the boys to say I was going to Africa but their mother wouldn't let them come with me."

"How many more times am I going to have to say you bastard Richard'?" Walter asked his disappointment and disbelief unhidden.

"Only two or three more times Walter." Richard said sadly as Walter sighing heavily told him to carry on'.

"I was angry," Richard admitted "and so I wrote to her to say telling her I don't need the aggravation and that I certainly don't need her."

"Richard…!" Walter groaned his disbelief continuing.

"I know," Richard sighed. "I told the UK team nothing about the bust up and flew here with Gabriella pretending that nothing had happened and then I just settled into a routine."

"You didn't tell Gabriella?" Walter exclaimed and raising his eyebrows in disbelief told Richard that he was a bloody fool and asked him just what he was thinking. Dejectedly Richard told him that Grace had always been happy to submit to his deranged thinking and was always happy to mend things. "She knows that I'm pig headed." he explained.

"But not this time it would seem." Walter said stating the obvious. "And you really did think that she would just shrug off your stupidity?"

"I love her Walter and I'm sure she loves me." Richard stated candidly.

"But she's not backing down this time Richard is she?" Walter told him truthfully "and it would seem that the ball is well and truly in your court isn't it?" Walter questioned.

"It is Richard" said conceding an obvious truth "and" he added "I don't know what to do about it."

"You do know that you've been a right bastard don't you Richard." Walter said angrily. Emptying his glass Richard again stood up.

"That's a bit harsh." he said as he walked to the window and gazed up at the full moon.

"But true?" Walter asked as he too got to his feet and joined Richard by the window.

"Yes true," Richard acknowledged as placing his hand on his friend's shoulder asked if he could help him.

"I'll try mister." Walter told him and moving to the coffee table he picked up his empty glass. "But," he said "that's enough for one night, I'm off for a swim."

Half an hour later Richard joined Walter by the pool but choosing not to swim looked down at the back-stroking Walter and asked if he could just tell him something.

"If you talk whilst I dry myself?" Walter told him his anger at Richard's stupidity still raw. Coffee made and a glass of whiskey poured Richard returned to the pool and sitting down removed his shoes and socks and dangled his feet in the water.

"Walter I'm in a real mess," he began "I know I've been a bastard and that Grace probably won't want to see me again and yes I know I need to get on with my life, but I'm stuck." Rolling onto his front Walter breast stroked to the side of the pool.

"We both know that life would be a lot easier if we could change the past?" he said as he climbed from the water and picked up his towel.

"Oh how I wish." Richard told him as he sipped his whiskey "and I know" he added "what you're going to say next."

"You do?" Walter asked as he wrapped the towel around his waist.

"Yes," Richard told him.

"And that would be what?"

"That the only way I can go is forward," enlightened.

"Or?" Walter questioned.

"Or I can stay where I am now, both practically and emotionally." Richard added astutely and smiling knowingly Walter picked up his coffee and moved to the patio table.

"How well you knew the script Richard." Walter smiled as he placed his mug on the table and seesawed his towel across the small of his back.

"Well I did write it!" Richard told him as he followed his friend to the table and pulled out a chair and sat down.

"Well Richard," Walter said as he placed his towel on the back of a chair "this is where the script changes. You've told me about Grace but to be honest I'm not sure that your relationship with Grace is the problem. Nor" he added wisely "am I sure how things that happened before you met Grace have impacted on your relationship with her."

"Gee Walter that was quite deep for one o'clock in the morning." Richard admired "so what do I do?" he asked. Thanking Richard for his compliment Walter took another sip of his drink and then with the utmost seriousness told Richard that he thought it would be useful if he shared his past with him.

"Then," he said "I'll be able to see if there is anything else that may have impacted on you and affected you this way."

"That sounds good to me Walter." Richard agreed "and you could be right.

"I know I'm right" Walter told him "You know as well as I do that experience tells us that we may think that we know a person when in fact we don't. Look at you and Grace. Sadly things have gone wrong there even though you had spent an awful lot of time together."

"And" Richard confessed "at this point in my life Walter I'm not even sure how well I knew myself."

"Correct," Walter told him as he took a final sip of his coffee and held up his hand. "Okay pal that's enough for one day" he said "I'm off to bed." and picking up his mug Walter Wilson stood up and walked to the house leaving Richard alone with his thoughts, thoughts that took him back to his childhood. As a boy of ten or eleven Richard could remember winning first prize at school for a poem he had written. The idea for the poem had come to him as he was lying on his back on the hill near Water Grove in his home county of Lancashire. As he had lay there he had watched as a Sky Lark began to rise into the bright afternoon sky. In that magical place a solitary Willow tree had managed to get its roots into the wind blown and rock strewn soil. Now as he sat by the pool six thousand miles away from that magical place the words of his poem came slowly back to him.

'I walked in summer by the steam.' he had written. 'The grass was warm beneath my feet and the sun was warm upon my face. An old Oak stood strong and tall whilst nearby a delicate Willow danced with joy'.

'I walked in autumn by the stream the earth cold beneath my feet and the wind blew hard against my face. The old Oak now battered still stood solid and the delicate Willow still sang and danced her dance of joy'.

'I walked in winter by the stream the ice crunched cold beneath my feet. The snow blew hard against my face and the old Oak lay snapped upon the ground as nearby the battered Willow stood and silently wept'.

Rousing himself from his reminiscing Richard suddenly felt calmer. Death and destruction had come to the mighty oak. 'Bad things happen.' he told himself 'but the Willow although battered and beaten was still alive.' and then, like the willow Richard dropped his head and wept.

CHAPTER 28
Wednesday 14th January 2010 (Morning)

Cape Point

Richard woke with his head banging and the inside of his mouth tasting like the bottom of a Macaw's cage. Dressed and showered he made his way downstairs to the kitchen where he found Gabriella chatting amiably with Walter. He didn't know what about, nor at the moment did Richard care as crossing to the table he pulled out a chair and sat down. Moving to his side Gabriella placed her right hand on his shoulder and with her left felt his brow.

"You'll live." she told him as she removed her hand.

"But I don't want to." the unsmiling and pathetic Richard told her and then whimpering the immortal words 'Never again' Richard dropped his hand into his hands.

"Now where have I heard that before Mr Blackwood?" a smiling Gabriella asked as she threw Walter a knowing look before answering her own question. "Ah yes" she said without sympathy "now I remember. It was in this very room and not more than a week ago." Unable and unwilling to argue the point, any point and with his head still in his hands Richard cursed the bloody wine and closed his eyes.

Half an hour later and despite all his appeals and entreaties, Richard found himself climbing very carefully into the back of the Audi where, closing his aching eyes he pretended to be sleep. Walter on the other hand was more than happy to find himself climbing into the passenger seat next to Gabriella where he immediately began to chatter endlessly and effortlessly.

"Did you know Gabi" he asked as he opened his copy of 'Your South African Holiday' "Cape Point is the most southerly point of the African continent and the place where the Atlantic and the Indian Oceans meet?"

"Mmm sorry Walter," Gabriella told him without pleasure "but technically that meeting place is further up the East coast at a place called Cape Agulhas."

"So why tell us that it's here?" Walter complained reasonably.

"Tourism?" she suggested wisely as Walter, shaking his head, dropped the book on the seat beside him. On they travelled, in the front seat Walter chatting amicably and animatedly to Gabriella, whilst in the rear the motionless Richard snored loudly. The journey to Cape Point took a little less than an hour and on reaching their destination Walter's already pleasant day suddenly became an excellent one.

"Thanks for your kindness Walter." Gabriella told him as she pointed her finger to the back seat. "I don't know what Richard would have done without you." and then leaning across the car she gave him the slightest of pecks on the cheek.

"Or without you Gabriella you're a good friend." Walter added as Richard, rising like a child from the depths of slumber, sat up and bending forward asked 'if they where there yet?'

Climbing from the car the three walked slowly arm in arm up the long causeway towards the lookout point at the Two Oceans Restaurant. "This is quite a place isn't it?" Walter enthused as he moved to the barrier and looked down at the rugged rocks, sheer cliffs and violent ocean below him. "Thanks for bringing me Gabi" he smiled "this has to be the highlight of my trip, it's fabulous."

"All part of the service Walter," she told him as she put her arm around his waist "We aim to please." then turning to Richard and in a tone that left no room for argument suggested that it was his turn to buy lunch.

"No," Walter interjected finding room for argument "please let me treat you and no arguments. This is fantastic and the drinks are on me."

Three hours later Gabriella announced that she was going to powder her nose and pushing back her chair began to move towards the restroom.

"Oh but please don't pay until I come back Walter." she smiled over her shoulder "I'd like to watch the argument when Richard suggests that you split the bill with him." Suggesting that she was very funny Richard asked Walter if that was what they really do.

"Who Richard?" a confused Walter questioned.

"Ladies." Richard explained as he eased chair away from the table and crossing his legs looked around the room. . "Ladies what?" the still unenlightened Walter asked.

"Powder their nose of course?" Richard explained a little impatiently.

"Oh I don't know," Walter conceded "but I have noticed that they always go in pairs. Can you imagine you and me choosing to pee together?" he queried.

"Not unless it was an emergency." Richard told him "But did you know that someone's actually done some research into which urinals men choose when they go to pee?" Richard questioned and then without waiting for an answer supplied the answer. "It seems," he said "that men always leave a space between themselves and the next man and they never, or so the researchers tell us, like to stand next to each other or make eye contact with their neighbour."

"And how much did this researcher get paid for his efforts and how the hell did he carry the research out?" the ever clinical Walter wanted to know. "I can't see him standing there all day watching men pee can you?"

"So you're assuming the researcher was a bloke Walter?" Richard smiled mischievously and Walter, conceding that he had a good argument pointed out that 'life was strange'.

"Which bit of life Walter?" Gabriella asked as she returned to the table and sat down.

"Walter will explain." Richard told her and pronouncing that 'Nature called' got to his feet and set off for the gents.

"Wait, Richard" a laughing Walter called after him "I'll come with you."

"No you won't." Richard told him sternly as he walked briskly away.

"And?" a curious Gabriella questioned.

"Oh don't ask" a grinning Walter told tell her "It's too complicated." Five minutes later Richard returned and once again his he found his friends locked in harmonious conversation.

"You'll never guess who I just saw." he whispered conspiratorially as he slid his chair closer to his friends.

"Was it the Pope?" Walter asked flippantly.

"John Lennon?" an equally playful Gabriella offered.

"No" Richard told them solemnly "It was Charles Ascot Chisholm!"

"What Steven's partner?" Gabriella asked dropping her own voice to a whisper.

"Yes that very man." Richard whispered back.

"So why didn't you ask him to join us?"

"He's with someone." Richard continued his voice still low.

"Who?" Gabriella said her eyes straining as she tried to scan the room without moving her head.

"Over there." Richard nodded "In the corner."

"What with that busty red head?" Walter questioned as he looked in the direction of Richard's nod and then quickly looked away as Ascot Chisholm's eyes caught his own.

"And" Gabriella said in a continued whisper "Whilst we're playing spot the person have you noticed the lady sat over there, the one hiding behind her sun specs?" Once more slowly and nonchalantly the inquisitive Walter turned to his head and looked quickly to his right.

"The blond woman?" he asked "I don't think I know her.".

"Well Mr Wilson if I'm not mistaken." Gabriella told him from behind her hand. "That's our friend sergeant Megan Boyd."

"Mmm now that's interesting." Richard said getting to his feet as Charles Chisholm leaving his companion to study the sweet menu heaved his enormous frame from his chair and with hand outstretched began to move towards him.

"Hello Charles" he welcomed as his own small hand was engulfed in the sweaty flab of Chisholm's "It's good to see you again, won't you join us for a celebratory drink?"

"Celebrate Richard." Chisholm asked as Richard introduced his friends. "You've had some good news?" Charles asked.

"Oh yes," Richard beamed "haven't you heard Steven escaped last night. Two men have been arrested and it looks as though they going to implicate others." In an instant the cheeks of the golf playing Mr Charles Ascot Chisholm turned from a healthy and ruddy tan to a pale and ghostly white.

"Charles are you ...?" were the last words Chisholm heard as his knees buckled under him and failing to grabbing the back of Gabriella's chair fell slowly and very heavily to the floor.

Leaning over Chisholm's fat and sweating body and in a manner that suggested that the action was above and beyond the call of duty, the busty red head clicked his seat belt into place and then walked around to the driver's seat. Lowering her window she waved an unsmiling good bye and then drove swiftly away. Some minutes later the tall slim blond, her dark glasses still in place and her pony tail swishing from side to side, walked briskly across the car park to her unmarked police car and drove off.

"So what the hell was all that about?" Gabriella asked as the three made their way out of the restaurant and into the bright sun shine.

"The result of too much wine and too much sun I guess?" Walter offered.

"That's more than likely Walter." Gabriella agreed "Wine and sun don't always mix, do they Richard?" she questioned.

"Not always." Richard conceded as he linked arms with his friends and began to walk back down the causeway. "Although in this case it maybe the result of too much skulduggery"

"Just what are you talking about Blackwood?" Gabriella asked as smiled across at him.

"Dirty work at the cross roads Gabi," Richard told her but Gabriella, unwilling to embark on another round of murder mystery sighed and turning her attention to Walter asked him what he would like to do next.

"I'm easy Gabi," he told her as he pulled on his floppy hat. "What would you like to do?"

"We could go into town," she suggested "I could ask Adam to join us. He's really looking forward to meeting you." she told him with some excitement.

"That's a great idea Gabriella." Walter agreed with a happy smile.

"What about you Richard?" she asked. Grumpily Richard told her that he was tired.

"And I'm stuffed and it's hot. I think home it the best plan."

"Tired? Walter laughed. "You mean you're afraid of the competition from Adam."

"I don't think so Mister, what could he possibly have that I don't?" Richard challenged and then wished he hadn't as predictably Gabriella told him not to tempt her because she wouldn't know where to start.

"That's not funny and it's very cruel Gabriella." Richard told her without humour as he unlinked his arm and turned to face her. "Walter comes all this way to help me and you just shoot me down at every opportunity."

"But Richard" Walter argued with uncharacteristic exasperation as he too unlinked his arm and turned to face Richard. "What's the point of us doing life changing therapy" he asked "if you're not willing to change your life?" Richard had no answer other than to complain that Gabriella and Walter had become very hard over the last few weeks and turning his back on them both began to walk down the slope.

"No Richard" Walter called after him "we're not hard we're just caring and realistic." and Gabriella, realising that further discussion was futile conceded that home was perhaps the best option but not before she had informed Richard that he was a 'miserable old git' and that wouldn't have been the best of company anyway.

As they travelled home Richard pondered the day's events. His attempts to make sense of his life had not been helped by the arrival on the scene of 'that bloody Adam' and it would seem that and Gabriella and Walter were getting closer all the time.

"I hope you're not sulking back there Mr Blackwood." a forgiving Gabriella asked as she slowed for a traffic light. Richard heard her clearly but still sulking chose not to answer.

"Oh leave him alone Gabi, the poor old man is probably tired let him sleep." Walter suggested good-humouredly but still Richard didn't bother to respond and keeping his eyes firmly shut, continued to sham sleep.

"So tell me about Adam." Walter asked and then waited whilst Gabriella manoeuvred expertly past a slow moving tractor.

"Not much to tell Walter." she told him. "He's forty something, single and from Australia."

"So he doesn't have a great deal going for him eh." Walter joked and then in the age old Australian 'put down' asked how many sheep Adam owned.

"I don't know Walter" Gabriella told him seriously "I didn't ask," and then with her smile broadening asked him how many he had.

"Ah tout shay." Walter told her in a very poor French ascent.

"Tres bon monsieur." Gabriella replied fluently. "Et votre point était?" Realising that he had met his match Walter admitted defeat.

"Okay you win." he said, as Gabriella turned to face him and a mumbled 'Tres bon' drifted quietly from the back seat.

CHAPTER 29
Wednesday 7th January 2010 (Early evening)

Talk to Me

After a light cheese and biscuit supper Richard made his way down to the den and waited for Walter to join him. "You know Walter?" he said as the two men settled themselves once more in the deep arm chairs.

"Know what?" Walter questioned.

"Well about me being happy to listen if ever you wanted someone to talk to." Richard reminded him.

"I've always been happy to talk with you Richard." Walter smiled contentedly, "but I'm fine, really."

"Okay Walter," Richard told him "but don't ever be a fool like I was and leave your worries to take control." For some time the men sat in companionable silence, neither of them wanting to rob the other of the opportunity to talk or share some hidden hope or fear. By now Richard had grown used to sitting on the 'client's side' of the table and in some strange and perverse way he had begun to enjoy the attention he was receiving. In his own practice Richard preferred to use the word 'conversation' rather than therapy, the hope being that if the client could see a session as a deep and meaningful conversation with a good friend then some of their apprehensions and anxieties may start to lift. This was certainly true for Richard who, after waiting for Walter to share any worries he may have, took a sip of his whiskey and began to tell his story. As he spoke he felt a little like the Meryl Streep's character in the movie 'Out of Africa', the film where she had delivered the classic line, 'I had a farm in Africa'.

"I left home for the first time." Richard began "when I was twenty one years old. I had no reason to leave home life was calm, quiet and easy. Back then I shared a terraced house with my parents and my younger brother Robert and my sister Sandra. Robert was seven years my junior and at fourteen spent most of his spare time with his dog and ferrets. I don't ever remember having a conversation with Robert, perhaps our age difference and our interest gap got in the way. Sandra was eleven years younger than me. I do remember holding her as a baby whilst I listened to the 'Archers' on the radio, other than that special moment I have no other memories". Then he stopped. "Am I going too fast?" he asked.

"No you're fine" Walter reassured "I'll stop you if I need to."

"My older brother was married with two children and my younger sisters were living away."

"Where you close to your sisters?"

"Not really Walter, to tell the truth I think their being two and three years younger and girls meant that our lives didn't cross that much. I have few if any memories of those days."

"So you didn't go on holiday together?"

"We did, but only to an Aunties caravan near Blackpool...no I lie," Richard corrected. "We did go to Dundee, my dad was doing a summer session there. My dad was a trumpet player in a dance band. Those trips to Blackpool or Dundee were our only times away from home, come to think of it" he added "the day I left home in December in 1967 was the first time that I had ever slept in a bed other then my own."

"Sorry Richard but can I ask you a delicate question?" Walter asked his eyes searching his friends for any sign of discomfort.

"Of course you can." Richard told him his nervousness clear to both men.

"Well how can I put this?" Walter asked his voice holding an element of surprise. "Are you saying that you had kept yourself pure, if that is the right term, until you were twenty one." Without pause or stutter Richard told him yes.

"The fact is Walter I had never shared my bed or my life with another person, bar" he added "my tiny brothers and sisters. Do you remember that classic line of Stephen Fry's?" he asked. Walter didn't.

"Remind me." he asked.

"Well it's the one where he tells us that 'he failed to penetrate the Arch Bishop's intimate circle." Richard told him.

"A good line," Walter agreed "so your intimate circle consisted of what?"

"Not a lot." Richard admitted.

"You had no friends?"

"You could say that I guess. I did have friends to a limited extent and friends of both sexes. I remember we would meet in a coffee bar on Burnley bus station and one of the girls would invite the boys to her home to play 'hunt the cunt'. I went along but I never found any." Richard joked. "But given all that life was easy. I went to work at eight thirty and returned home at six pm."

"Did you enjoy your work, did you have work mates Richard. I ask because I am getting a picture of a shy loner."

"Oh you may be right about that Walter, but I don't think it was a problem for me. I worked as an office equipment engineer and travelled all across Lancashire visiting various typing pools cleaning keys and rubbing down 'platens'."

"Pardon my ignorance Richard but what's a platen." Walter asked.

"A platen Walter is the round thing that the typewriter keys hit. They used to get shiny and then the paper would slip. Remember?"

"I do my friend." Walter suddenly remembered before adding that it had been a while since he saw one "However" he apologised "I digress, sorry Richard."

"No worries Walter" Richard told him "if you don't ask you won't know, or some other well known saying." He smiled.

"And mates Richard?" Walter continued.

"Well off down memory lane we go. Stan was my mate at work. He was older than me, about thirty five I would guess and although he was married he was a bit of a 'man of the world'. It was Stan that introduced me to pornography" Richard declared "he kept 'dirty books' under his work bench.

"And were you embarrassed by Stan?" Walter asked.

"Oh yes," Richard told him "Stan acted like a predator. On our visits to typing pools he would chat and flirt with, and occasionally 'pull' one of the less fussy girls. I on the other hand spent my time cleaning typewriters and trying not to blush as the typist commented on my rubbing technique. You were right Walter when you said I was shy, I think it's only quite recently that I have been able to talk to women without feeling uncomfortable."

"Gee Richard it's hard for me to see you as a shy loner" Walter confessed "you appear so confident and in control. I wonder when things changed for you." he quipped. Grinning, the effects of whiskey and embarrassment, Richard told Walter that he wasn't sure that he had changed deep down.

"Back in those days Walter I spent my evenings at home with mother. We would watch TV and I would get some relief for my pent up feelings by working on my other rubbing technique, although not whilst watching T.V." he joked in his discomfort.

"You'd pent up feelings Richard, what were they about?"

"Girls I guess." Richard told him "It was certainly wasn't about boys or animals, and never has been. Now" he asked "why did I feel the need to tell you that I wonder?"

"I'm not sure Richard perhaps you are starting to feel uncomfortable, however, I'm not sure we want to go down that road at this moment." Walter told him "But it sounds like you were close to your mother, it's as if she was your main friend and ally."

"Oh yes she was" Richard told him. "I've always been close to mother. I must have been a bit like that 'stupid boy' in Dad's Army. But my mother was my rock and mentor. She was the provider of meals, wisdom and love. What more did I need and in return when I collected my wage packet on Friday I gave her ten shillings. What more did she need?" Richard asked.

"That sounds fair to me." Walter laughed. "And your father," he asked "what about your father?"

"My Father was a trumpet player Walter. He played in a dance band and so worked at night. During the day he wrote music in the front room and we weren't allowed to disturb him, we daren't."

"So you were afraid of your father?"

"I'm not sure if fear is the right word Walter" Richard told him "We knew not to upset him and he was fine if we behave, but six children in one small house, well there was bound to be trouble. Mum would try and keep the peace, but sometimes the noise would reach father and he would react."

"Was he violent?"

"Oh no, we knew where we stood with him. He would make us line up, oldest to youngest and starting with eldest would ask, 'Did you do it?' And then depending on the answer he got he would work his way down the line. If no one owned up he would start again with the eldest, but this time he would prod us with his index finger and prod us very hard in the chest. My sister tells people she has two belly buttons."

"Did you love your dad?"

"Love, that's a good question and I guess my having to think about the answer tells us something about my love for my dad. You know Walter I loved my dad dearly during the final days of his life, for perhaps the last ten years."

"What changed?"

"In the last ten years? Well I was with Grace and William was born. I don't really know what happened, but dad turned from being a kind of grumpy old man into a very caring one. We would walk together by the river and he would say 'You know Richard, if this is earth what must heaven be like?' and he would ruffle my hair, something he had never ever done before, but what changed for him I don't know."

"Did you spend much time with your dad as a child?"

"The answer 'No' comes very quickly to me. I do have memories of being in the park with dad and the other children and I know we travelled to Dundee one 'summer season' with the band. I also remember sitting in a cinema in Southport watching cartoons in the afternoons whilst he played his trumpet at the 'Floral Hall'. It's hard to believe that he thought it was okay to leave a ten year old alone in a cinema, but those were different times."

"They were indeed," Walter agree "so you saw little of your dad?" he asked.

"It would seem so, but did I see less of my dad than any other children? I guess the real difference is that other children's dads were at home in the evenings whilst my dad would don this black dinner jacket, white shirt, black tie and black patent leather shoes and go off to work. He would return after midnight when we children and mother were in bed, in truth I saw little of him."

"Are you like your dad?"

"That's a difficult one Walter. My dad always seemed to be on the edges of the family. His favourite word seemed to be 'shit', which probably meant that things were always going wrong for him. But in fact he had a pretty good life. I know he enjoyed his time in the army and he enjoyed his job. I wonder if it was us children and his responsibilities that brought him down. But to answer your question, 'Am I like my dad?' well, believe it or not, I do enjoy what I do. Grace is a fabulous woman and William and James are delightful boys."

"Which I suppose," Walter added. "Leaves us wondering what the hell is up with you? You've told me about your early days and about your friendships or your lack of them, about your relationship with your parents and siblings."

"And embarrassingly," Richard added "we've talked about my relationships with women or more correctly the fact that I'm crap with women".

"I'm not sure about the crap bit Richard, but you do seem to have been something of an introvert."

"But that doesn't make me strange or abnormal." Richard protested.

"I didn't suggest that it did my friend." Walter reassured. "And I'm not sure of percentages but I would guess that in this big world of ours introverts outnumber extroverts quite heavily." Telling Walter that it was interesting that he should have identified him as introvert Richard then informed Walter that most of the people he saw in therapy tend to be introverted. "You know" Richard explained "the kind, quiet and caring souls. Would you say that I'm kind and caring Walter?" he asked.

"Most definitely" Walter told him "and that's probably why you struggle Richard. Do you feel like you have the cares of the world on your shoulders?" he asked.

"No, I don't think so." Richard told him to which Walter replied that he would like to test the hypothesis.

"But first" he requested "let's take a break and then you can tell me about the next period of your life.

CHAPTER 30
Wednesday 14th January 2010 (Late Evening)

Manchester to Cape Town

"I guess that I had no real reason to leave home." Richard continued without preamble as the two men refreshed and drinks replenished settled themselves once more into the dens comfortable chairs "but my Aunt Nora had a business in South Africa and she wanted someone she could trust to assist her or that's what she told me. Nora was a short, round, red headed woman in her mid fifties. It's hard to think that she was younger then than I am now Walter, but that's bye the bye. Anyway she promised me good money, a flat and a car and so my decision to take her offer was a simple one. I could turn the offer down and regret it for the rest of my life, or I could go, knowing that I could always come home if I didn't like it."

"Fear in the present or regret in the future eh Richard." Walter said wisely as he lifted his drink in salute.

"Correct" Richard told him "and so I chose to face the fear, cheers."

"Was there fear Richard?" Walter asked "or was it just a case of packing up and leaving all you knew behind?"

"I guess it must have been easy Walter," Richard told him as lifting his glass to his lips he emptied its contents in one go "but remember this was my time of innocence. I hadn't a clue where I was going. I now know that South Africa is a very big country, but back then, well I never asked. So I packed my bags, tickets were bought and off to Cape Town I went."

"What about your parents, didn't they have a say in the matter?" Walter queried.

"They must have" Richard told him "because I found out years later that my dad had to sell his car to buy my ticket - two hundred and twenty two pounds one way!"

"So you were beginning a new life on your own Richard. This all seems a bit out of character for the person you have just described to me."

"Naivety Walter," Richard told him his words now beginning to slur "I was naïve, an innocent abroad, a lamb to the slaughter and good old Aunt Nora was soon to be exposed as a predator, and a mean self seeking woman." Lifting his eye brows at the venom in Richard's voice Walter settled back in his chair and wrapped his hands around his empty coffee mug. "So off you went to Africa at twenty one years of age. You sound like one of those white hunters I used to read about, you know with your pith helmet on head and rifle over shoulder, it must have been exciting!"

"No it wasn't quite like that Walter" Richard told him as he leaned forward and re-filled his glass "mother and I were taken to Piccadilly station in Manchester on a cold December night in Nora's shiny black car, another?" he asked

"Gee Richard that's a lot of whiskey and a lot of bitterness." Walter observed, his eyebrow raising working over time.

"Bitterness maybe or anger," Richard told him as he half drained his glass. "I now know that my mother was tearful, but at the time I was oblivious to her distress. I do remember her joking about the 'Not wanted on voyage' labels that were attached to my luggage. Anyway," Richard sighed "my mother helped me onto the train and then waved good bye to me not knowing if or when she would see me again. It must have been like that when she waved my father off as he went to war. What memories that woman must have eh, but as to feeling bitter Walter well, I'm not sure I had any feelings on the night, but now as we talk, now I'm bloody angry, so bloody, bloody angry." Unsure of how to respond Walter did what his father had taught him and with the words 'when in doubt say now't' whispering in his ear he sat silently and waited for the moment.

"Angry?" he finally asked his eyebrow remaining motionless.

"Yes," Richard told him "I'm angry and disappointed with myself. What an unthinking bastard I was. How the hell could I have done that to my mother? I was not going to war, I didn't have to go." And then he was quiet. "Do you think that leaving my mother like that has anything to do with how I am now Walter?" he asked. Again Walter sat quietly contemplating his answer.

"Well Richard" he said at length "It does seem to be having an extreme affect on you now Richard, but to be honest I'm not sure why. Are we talking about your actions or your aunt?" Walter asked. The affect of his words on Richard were both loud immediate.

"Oh that bastard" he yelled "that bastard left my mother on that platform on a cold dark December night having just waved goodbye to her son. That bloody Nora just left her Walter, just left her!" he repeated "Left her to find her own way home." Yet again Walter sat silently, his hand to his mouth and his brain striving to find the right words and actions.

"Okay Richard," Walter managed to say with more calmness and confidence than he felt "we both know that our past experiences can either help or hinder our development. We also know we can't change those experiences and it's clear that on that December night Nora really got to you. So let's pause for a minute whilst I collect my thoughts and have a wee. Then I'll make us some coffee and we'll take a good hard look at the events of that December night in 1967."

"Sorry about that." Richard apologised as Walter placed two coffee mugs next to the newly refilled whiskey glasses and sat "I did seem to get on a roll."

"No worries Richard" Walter told him as lifting his mug he rested it on the chair arm. "Your adventures are interesting. In fact I envy you your chance to see the world. I was married and working in a mill in Colne when I was twenty one, but back to business."

"Okay" Richard told him without relish "but I bet your head's hurting with all this .., just what is this Walter?" he asked "Therapy or a confession?"

"Neither," Walter told him "We are just two blokes having a deep and meaningful conversation. I'm not your priest nor am I a policeman." and then pleased with the fruits of his coffee making 'thinking time' Walter Wilson eased himself slowly backward into his chair and with a self satisfied smile crossed his legs. "So Richard," he advised "I think we need to deal with this anger of yours around this Nora woman, just in case you bump into her again some time." Telling Walter that it was fine with him and that he didn't really didn't know that he was that angry Richard declared that he'd love to go back and deal with it Nora.

"But the old bugger is dead and gone" he grinned and emptying his glass refilled it and declared 'good riddance'.

"Gee!" Walter marvelled at the intensity of Richard's bitterness "such venom even after all these years and the woman laying dead. I'm really not sure I know how we deal with that. Maybe you do need a priest after all. But," he said looking at his watch "it's just coming up to eleven thirty so shall we work for another half hour and then call it a day?" Agreeing that the plan sounded good Richard got to his feet, picked up his glass and crossed to the window.

"But I'm sure we can find better things to talk about than my sad life." he suggested as he pulled back the curtains and stared up into the night sky.

"Maybe," Walter told him "but you're making some real progress so let's try and stay positive eh, what do you say?" Turning from his star gazing Richard eased his backside onto the window ledge and sipped his drink "Sorry." He apologised. "I guess it is just a habit I've got into because I never used to be like this."

"Yes I know," Walter told him with compassion, although if he were honest he really didn't know if negativity had always been a tenant of Richard's life or not. "So," he encouraged "just 'stick with it and you'll get there somehow. Now stop saying sorry and just tell it as you see it. I'll ask you to explain if I need you to, okay?" Telling Walter 'Okay' Richard told him as he moved to his chair and draining the contents of his glass immediately refilled it.

"I began my journey in Manchester" he said as his eyes closing as memories of yesteryear began to filter through the mists of time and alcohol "then I travelled through the beautiful English countryside down to Southampton." As Richard spoke clear and vivid pictures of bare leafless trees and green hills and fields flashed, like a speeding train through his mind and then he was standing on the docks watching the white seagulls dip and weave in the grey winter sky. "The sea trip to Cape Town took me and the rest of the passengers two weeks" he quipped as with a grin of contentment he opened his eyes.

"Gee Richard you're in a good mood all of a sudden, what happened?" Walter asked.

"Well I've had a good day Walter" Richard explained "And you?"

"Yes great." Walter told him as he stifled another yawn "but please, get on with your tale." Joining Walter in a wide and loud yawn Richard confessed that there wasn't a lot more to tell and that if he'd kept a diary it would have included things like 'Left Southampton at six pm, but no band playing like there are in the movies. Spent Friday at sea, Saturday at sea and on Sunday attended a church service. Monday at sea, Tuesday at sea. Was sick in the Bay of Biscay and had the Crossing the Line ceremony where sailors dressed as women were sacrificed to Neptune or vice versa.

"There were deck games where people bet on which wooded frog could be flipped the quickest down the deck and of course Walter " Richard laughed "for the first class passengers there was the captain's cocktail party where large ladies in smart frocks got to shake hands with a ruddy faced sailor."

"Richard," Walter warned as again he stifled a yawn, "I hate to spoil your fun but exactly where is this taking us?"

"It's taking us to Cape Town old man." Richard slurred and then his mood changed. "That bloody James Bond," he cursed, "He's been ruining my life since I was twelve years old. Men, real men Walter are tall and handsome, they wear dinner jackets and have pots of money and they know everything and they never panic. They are suave and sophisticated and" he added angrily. "And they always get the girl."

"Richard?" Walter questioned "are you okay?

"Never better pal" Richard told him "but on that bloody boat I hadn't a clue what I was doing. The menus were leather bound and in some fancy language. I never got what I ordered and I never got the girl, anyway what would I have done with her if I had got one? Send your answer on a post card if you want" he brooded and once more his face broke into broad grin. "Now that reminds me" he said as if coming to a sudden conclusion and draining his glass banged it down on the table.

"Of what?" Walter asked his brain perplexed by yet another change in Richard's mood and then placing his coffee mug on the table put his hands on his knees and stared across as his friend.

"It reminds me Walter" Richard told him as his grin broaden "that I'm in far too a good a mood to be going over this old rubbish."

"So do you want to stop?" Walter asked more in hope than in expectation.

"Yes," Richard told as he moved forward in his seat as if he were about to stand and returning Walter's stare crossing his legs and sat back. "No" he said "just let me tell you this whilst I remember?" Now totally confused Walter sat back in his chair and closed his eyes.

"Penny Swindles." Richard announced.

"Who?" Walter asked from behind his eye lids.

"Penny Swindles, she was my first love. Where are you now?" Richard asked to no one in particular. "Oh Penny how I wanted you, you tall leggy girl, did you know how I felt about you, did you ever guess? She would have had to guess Walter because I never told her." Richard confided "And what if I had told her that I loved her, she would probably have told me to 'piss off' and called me a freak. Her words destroying me just like words have destroyed so many of the young men I work with now. Young men who have built themselves up to tell a girl that they love them, young men have watched and desired the girl from a distance, perhaps from their days at primary school. Yes young men who have longed to tell the girl of their love, young men who have dreamed and rehearsed their lines over and over again. 'I like you, I love you. Will you go out with me?' These young men pour out their souls, pour out their all and are then told to 'Go and get lost you freak'. All their hopes dreams, desires shattered with just six words. Young men who then take to their bedrooms or even take their own lives, their parents worrying about them, but unable to break into the dark lost world of their son's pain. Month's even years pass, the doctors saying 'It's just a stage he is going through', but these young men are unable to tell of or to share their pain. Women and that bloody James Bond. The bastards have so much to answer for." And then for several minutes Richard was quiet. "I'll tell you more about my second wife later Walter, but when I was forty years old my chat up line to her was, *'What would you say if I made a pass at you?'* her reply to me was *'What would you say if I ripped your balls off?'* No harm done Walter, at forty years old I took it all in my stride, but could I have coped with that rejection at seventeen? And what if Penny had known of my love for her and we had married? She would be sixty five now. My Penny a pensioner, so Walter, as that line from Oliver goes, *'I think I'd better think this out again',* what do you say?"

"I say, wow Richard, and I'm not sure how to respond."

"That's alright Walter. Shall I just finish my tale about the boat?"

"You may as well; it may buy me some thinking time."

"Very well then," Richard continued "Back to the ship, what else do I remember of those two weeks afloat? Well Walter you'll be pleased to know that I remember very little that is of any significance or interest to even me and so I won't inflict it on either of us. But what I think I need you know, to understand is that at twenty one years of age I knew very little about a lot of things. I knew nothing of travel or food or people. I was naïve yet I was content and unworried."

"Well that reminds me of the line from Kipling's poem" Walter told him.

"Which is?" Richard asked.

"Well Richard I paraphrase but it goes like this "If you can keep your head whilst all around you people are losing theirs then young man, you just don't understand the situation." Laughing Richard told Walter very good and that was just how he had been.

"I didn't understand and I didn't really care what was going on around me. I could have been at great risk, but I came to no harm. So naive was I that when I was asked by a fellow passenger where I would be staying in South Africa I told him in a little place called Devon Grove. He hadn't heard of Devon Grove. That was because Devon Grove was the name of the house that I would be staying in and not a town or village." Then Richard smiled to himself. "But, it does make one wonder which god has the job of looking after the innocents abroad." he said.

"It certainly does." Walter said as he got to his feet and headed for the bathroom. "It most certainly does."

CHAPTER 31
Thursday 15th January 2010 (Morning)

Desirable or Despicable

When Gabriella came down stairs the following morning she found Richard fast asleep on the lounge sofa. Noting with pleasure and some pride the absence of whiskey bottles or glasses she bent and kissed his forehead. Then, in an attempt to make him more comfortable, she adjusted the cushions beneath his head and set in motion a chain reaction. Rolling as if in slow motion to the floor Richard came to rest face up and with the whiskey bottle (one that friend Walter had missed whilst tidying up) coming to rest beside him. Staring blankly up into the face of his P.A. he muttered 'What?' and pushed himself onto one elbow.

"What?" an angry and disappointed Gabriella echoed back "What? I hope you didn't keep Walter up all night drinking?" Starting to protest his innocence Richard looking up into a Gabriella's face and quickly reviewed his strategy.

"Well maybe, but only 'til eleven." he lied as he leaned his back against the sofa "but Walter was a big boy and it was him asking the questions".

"Big boy or not" Gabriella scolded "you're not to take advantage of his kindness." at which point Richard, recognising the merits of confession told her that he was 'Sorry'. Unconvinced by his assertion of innocence Gabriella told him that he knew what she meant, asked him to be 'Just be a little more thoughtful' and suggested that he take the man out and show him the Cape. Capitulating Richard told 'Okay,' and that he'd talk to him.

"You'll talk to who Richard?" Walter asked as refreshed and wakeful he crossed the lounge and looked down at the dishevelled Richard.

"Oh good morning Walter," Richard smiled up in greeting "Gabriella was just asking if we have anything planned for our day. I was telling her that I have to see Rose at ten thirty and that I'd be away for a couple of hours but then I thought I'd take you out for lunch and we could do a bit of sightseeing. Telling him 'what a good idea' Walter then held out his hand and pulled Richard to his feet.

"Have a bad night?" he smiled as Richard settled himself once more onto the sofa. Grinning mischievously Richard told him 'No thanks I've just had one.' and Gabriella, incensed by Richard's stupidity picked up a cushion and pummelling it into shape. "And as for you, Richard Roger Blackwood," she said waving the whiskey bottle under his nose "after all we've been through in the last few months I would have hoped you'd have learnt your lesson." Knowing that whenever Gabriella's used his first names and surnames together he was in serious trouble Richard repeated his 'I'm sorry'. Unable to hide her disappointment and in language that Richard hadn't heard for some time Gabriella told him that he could be 'such an arse hole' and turning to Walter she smiled sweetly, gently squeezing his hand and wished him a 'good morning'.

"Did you sleep well?" she asked as she put her arm around his waist then turning back to Richard told him that he could be such a thoughtful man when he wanted to be, that his idea to take Walter out was a good one and seeing she hadn't anything planed for her day perhaps she could go with them and then, without waiting for a reply asked "Where are we going"

"Why don't you choose Gabriella?" a happy Walter asked "It'll be my treat." Removing her arm from Walter's waist Gabriella thanked him and moving to the sofa sat down next to Richard "Well why don't we go to Boschendal" she replied her proposal so readily proposed that one could have been excused for thinking it had been pre-arranged. "It's lovely there" she enthused "you sit under the trees and waiters bring baskets filled with the most delicious patties, breads and cheeses."

"It sounds fantastic." Walter told her.

"And maybe a nice glass of wine" Richard urged as, in an attempt to ingratiate himself he placed a cushion behind her back. Unmoved and unimpressed, Gabriella turned to face him.

"You old bugger" she groaned. "We've just had a heated debate about your alcohol consumption and already you're talking about wanting to drink wine. So mister, can I suggest that if you don't think you can cope without alcohol that Walter and I go on our own. And" she added "don't you think for one minute that you can get around me with a cushion." and then, as if to prove her point, she took the newly inserted cushion and threw at him.

"But I suggested a glass." Richard grumbled as he got to his feet and smiling one his best and most insincere smiles bent and pecked her on her cheek. It was an action that received a look of surprise from Walter and a glare of exasperation from Gabriella

"Oh" she told him "you get more..."

"Desirable?" Richard suggested as he moved towards the door.

"Despicable." Gabriella corrected as she launched another cushion in his direction. "Oh and Richard," she called "before you go you need to make contact with Kevin Dorrington. Do you have his number?"

"Indeed I do my dear." Richard told her demurely as he opened the door. 'Will you do it now?" she asked fearful that he would put off making the call."For me she pleaded."

"I'll do it this very minute." he promised as grinning rebelliously he went to shower.

CHAPTER 32
Thursday 15th January 2010 (Mid Morning)

Rose Freeman

Richard's conversation with Kevin Dorrington was short and to the point, he then made quick phone calls to check on Steven's progress and satisfied that all was well went to shower and change for the day ahead. Coming downstairs half an hour later with his head surprisingly clear and his mood decidedly better Richard poured himself a cup of tea and made his way out to the patio where he asked Walter if he like to ride into the city with him. Declining the offer Walter asked if it was okay if he stayed and swam Richard telling him 'Okay' took his car keys from his pocket and telling his guest that he'd see him in an hour or so left for his appointment with Rose.

Taking his usual route into the city Richard parked the Audi and took the lift up to the offices of Rose Freeman's office. Feeling strangely surreal as he got out of the lift a floor earlier than usual he checked the information board in front him and made his way down the corridor. Stopping outside room twelve, where a brass plaque informed him that these were the offices of Rose Freeman M.D. PhD Psychotherapist. Miss Freeman, although in fact a married lady, had specialised for many years in Transactional Analysis; a way of helping people that to Richard's mind was now a little 'old hat', but which he had to concede, still held useful concepts, concepts that he wove into some of his own sessions. Doing as the sign on the door bid him, Richard pushed open the door and walked in.

"Good morning how may I help you?" a smiling receptionist asked as she looked up from her copy of the 'You' magazine. "Good morning." Richard returned as he looked down at the matronly woman who, although probably several years younger than him looked considerably older. As he looked his unwilling eyes were drawn from the back cover of the magazine to the low cut orange, silk blouse that although straining failed miserably in its attempt to encase the women's large and wrinkled breasts. 'Buxom'. The word came unbidden into Richard's mind. 'Buxom', he thought 'like a Yorkshire bar maid's breasts but breasts that on a Yorkshire bar maid would have had him returning to the bar for more beer than was good for him. Breasts that on a younger woman would have had him expressing his approval with a quiet and low 'Wow', but here his thoughts were more of an incredulous 'Whoa' and fearing he had spoken aloud he scanned the woman's face for any signs of anger or disapproval. He saw none and informing her he had come to see Miss Freeman give her his name.

"Ah yes Mr Blackwood." The woman replied in a voice that she probably thought of as high English "Please take a seat. Miss Freeman will be with you shortly."

Doing as he was bid Richard moved to a line of chairs and selecting the middle one he eased himself into its white leather comfort. Suddenly he felt very nervous and getting to his feet he crossed the floor to the magazine rack, conscious as he did so of the eyes of the receptionist following him. Picking up 'House and Home' (not quite his cup of tea) he replaced it and selecting 'What Car' a publication that held little interest for him either, he flicked through its pages and then with a forced air of confidence returned to his seat. On the desk a telephone buzzed and picking up the receiver Miss Buxom listened for a short time, spoke one word "Yes." and returned the instrument it to its cradle. A few moments later the door behind her opened and a woman, probably in her early seventies, crossed the floor smiling.

"Richard, it is so nice to see you." she gushed, her wrinkled but manicured hand held out in front of her.

"And you Rose," Richard told her "how have you been keeping?"

"Fine Richard," she told him, "I seem to feel better with each passing day."

Rose Freeman was a short woman, perhaps no more than five feet tall. The tailored suit she wore was a bright yellow and in her lapel a red rose; the 'trade mark' of her business. Her white hair was collar length with a centre parting, a style that Richard would have described as 'page boy'. Richard always tried to make a point of noticing ladies hair. It was something he had learnt from Grace, along with the wisdom that if a man wants to impress his wife he shouldn't bother bringing her flowers, but instead he should do the washing up. He didn't understand the logic, but then he didn't understand women, none the less he knew the tactic worked and had traded on it many times.

"Well you're certainly looking good Rose and I love the hair." he smiled. Flattered but not fooled Rose thanked him and taking his arm guided him slowly towards her office.

"Would you like coffee?" she asked as she pushed open the door.

"Could I have black tea and no sugar?" Richard requested and Rose, suggesting that 'Alice should be able to manage that' ushered him into her room. The therapy suite unlike Richard's, was of the old style, its fresh flowers and a therapy couch making Richard's already heavy heart heave sighs of dread as he visualised his having to lie on the couch and thus become even more vulnerable.

"Shall we sit over here Richard?" a smiling Rose invited as she moved passed the black leather instrument of emotional surgery and towards the window. "I don't think we are going to need any of the trappings of therapy, but you do know that some of my clients really do feel cheated if they don't get the full 'lie down and tell me your troubles bit'. Moving to the large picture window with its familiar views of the Castle and the docks beyond Richard waited for Rose to sit and then moved his own seat a few degrees to the right and sat down. For a few moments the pair sat in silence as Rose obviously awaiting the arrival of Alice and her tray of drinks, flicked through her note book and Richard, feeling no less vulnerable looking with curiosity around the room.

"Ah" Rose announced as Alice pushed open the door and crossed the room.

"Thank you Alice," Rose told her she placed a rose motif tray with its rose covered tea pot, sugar basin, milk jug and two cups on the low table.

Turning and without making any response Alice walked with slowly and upright dignity from the room.

"I was so sorry to hear about Steven," Rose began as she poured tea into the china cups "is that why you are here?" Telling her that he didn't really know Richard explained that he'd been feeling depressed and drinking. "Gabriella brought a doctor to see me and he threatened to have me sectioned so I asked her to phone you."

"I'm so glad she did, shall we make a start?" A start they made with Richard explaining that on the day that Steven had been kidnapped he had taken to his bed and to drink. "Gabriella tried to help me but I just shouted and swore at her and then Walter came out to visit me." As Richard talked Rose listened, made a few notes but did not comment or interrupt and after twenty minutes talking Richard took a sip of his tea and sat back in the chair.

"Would you like a warm cup Richard?" Rose asked as she lifted the tea pot. Telling her 'No thanks' and this is fine' Richard then asked her what she thought.

"Well Richard" she told him "its early days, but we have loss and we have anger, both are quite normal. I have to say that your drinking is a worry, but again that's quite understandable given the circumstances. To be honest I'm not sure where Walter comes in, but your relationship with Gabriella interests me."

"Interests you Rose, in what way?" he asked, his defences starting to rise.

"Well it interests me because as we both know relationships can be the greatest source of difficulties people encounter. Tell me, Gabriella is what?" she asked as she leant forward.

"That's a bit difficult" Richard told her truthfully "At first Gabriella was a client and then she became my P.A, but I guess she was more than client or P.A."

"Go on."

"Well from the start we got on really well, sort of clicked you know?" Richard explained.

"Perhaps" Rose acknowledged "but please Richard, tell it to me in your own words." For some minutes Richard sat quietly and then getting to his feet he moved to the window.

"Rose" he said as he looked across the green embankment and towards the Castle. "I'm going to put more trust in you than I put in anybody for a long time."

"Go on."

"Well I was going to say can I trust you to keep things secret, but that would be an insult to your professionalism…" Getting to her feet Rose crossed to the window and placed her hand on Richard arm.

"It is fine Richard" she told him "check things out, ask what you want and yes, anything you tell me remains here and between you and me."

"Sorry Rose…" Richard told her without turning. "I didn't mean to be rude, it's just that…"

"Richard" Rose told him as like a master comforting her pet she began to gently pat arm "you've said 'sorry' to me at least twice in the last half hour. Now this is not about me being upset, it is about you feeling better about yourself."

"Okay," Richard told her as he lifted his eyes to the sky and then with a sudden resolve turned and looked down and into the clear blue eyes of his diminutive therapist "I think I need to say this Rose" he said "and maybe I should have said it a long time ago. When I first met Gabriella there was chemistry between us. She's an intelligent woman Rose and I was attracted to her as a human being and I was attracted to her sexually." Pausing in his profound and unwanted embarrassment Richard returned his gaze to the Castle. "Hell Rose that took some saying." he acknowledged and then in his long-awaited relief turned his back on the solid grey symbol of power and strength and returning to his seat sank into its soft white leather and closed his eyes. Remaining by the window Rose allowed her client a few moments to collect his thoughts and dignity and then rejoining Richard by the coffee table she too sat down and crossed her short but shapely legs.

"Did you have sex with her?" she asked. Surprised by the sudden bluntness of the question Richard remained silent.

"Sex Rose?" he finally asked.

"Yes Richard sex, did you and Gabriella have sex?" Again Richard remained silent as he tried to gather the courage to answer truthfully.

Understanding his resistance Rose smiled and looking straight into his face told him that she knew it was hard but that his difficulty in answering give its own message. "I am not however" she added "in the business of guessing, so let me ask you one more time, did you and Gabriella have sex?"

"Yes Rose." Richard finally said. "I had sex with Gabriella." again he paused "but only once" he lied, and immediately feeling silly asked 'why'.

"Because" Rose told him "I was wondering about your need to confess.

"Confess Rose?" Richard asked, his ability to answer a question with a question developing rapidly.

"Yes Richard, confess." Rose told him patiently. "Do you feel the need to confess?"

"Well Rose," Richard pondered as he played for more time and then, deciding that he had nothing to lose told her 'No, he didn't think so'. Unconvinced by his answer Rose pointed out that 'to only think was not particularly convincing' and then asked him to try again.

"To say I'm sorry?" Richard clarified.

"I guess that's what an apology is Richard." Again Richard took his time to answer and so Rose leaning forward lifted the tea pot and placed her hand against its side. Deciding that the contents were still drinkable she removed the lid stirred and replacing lid asked Richard if he'd like another cup. He declined and so, tipping the pot Rose refilled her cup. Being the professional she was Rose knew that there was much more to come and so cup in hand she sat patiently waiting and sipping her tea.

"I had fantasized about having sex with Gabriella from almost the time we first met." Richard finally said. "Are you okay if I tell all Rose?" he asked not really wanting to cause embarrassment to himself or Rose.

"Surely" she told him.

"Well," Richard continued his bullet well and truly bitten. "At first I imagined the sex and enjoyed the view. We did things together, but only in my mind, in real life I had never touched her…and then, well it just happened. No that's silly" he corrected myself "It didn't just happen…Gosh Rose this is difficult."

"Let me help you Richard." Rose offered.

"Please do." Richard smiled as despite his best efforts he remained confused and embarrassed.

"Did you plan to have sex Richard" his therapist asked "did you manipulate Gabriella into having sex with you?" Richard response was immediate.

"Oh God no." he groaned "and I guess in truth it was bound to have happened sooner or later."

"Do you love her Richard?" Rose asked as she leaned forward and placed her tea cup on the tray.

"The answer is yes Rose. Yes and but... "Again Richard stopped in mid sentence.

"But what Richard?"

"But Grace, I love Grace and I don't want to lose her. Grace is well, how do I describe Grace?"

"Don't, not yet..."Rose interrupted. "Tell me about Gabriella. You told me that in the early days you had sexual thoughts and desires about her."

"That's right."

"Do you still have those thoughts Richard?" Rose asked as she tried to hold his eye contact.

"Yes," Richard told her bluntly as he too tried to hold eye contact with his therapist but, unable to cope with the sincerity he saw there had to look away.

"Go on Richard, you're safe here." Rose told him quietly.

"Oh hell Rose."

"Oh hell what Richard?" she asked.

"I don't know Rose. It's Grace..."

"Not yet Richard we'll get to Grace later. Tell me about Gabriella. How long have you known her?"

"It must be five years or more."

"So your relationship now, do you still have sexual thoughts about her?"

"I guess so." Richard confessed and then "You do know that Grace and I have separated?"

"No Richard I didn't, so is it over between you and Grace?" Sighing heavily Richard told her he hoped not.

"Grace remains what I call my soul mate." he said as his eyes began to fill with tears of sadness and regret. Fighting the urge to take Richard's hand in hers Rose pointedly looked at her watch.

"Okay Richard," she said "it would appear that there is a lot to talk about but sadly our time is just about up, so, will you come back and talk to me again. I think we need to investigate these relationships of yours and your feelings about the women in your life. Are you okay with that?" she asked. Telling Rose that she was very good at what she did Richard got to his feet and thanked her. And Rose also standing thanked Richard for his honesty and that she thought that they would work well together. Then with a new appointment card in his hand Richard walked slowly down the corridor to the lift. "Up and to his own office or down to the street and home?" he asked himself and pressing the indicator button he waited for the lift doors to open.

CHAPTER 33
Thursday 15th January 2010 (Noon)

A Right Picnic

Richard returned home without calling at the office, the thought of having to face the staff and their kind questioning filling him with dread. 'Perhaps' he mused as he parked the Audi and walked through to the kitchen 'that's something else I need to talk to Rose or Walter about?'
"Ah Richard there you are, armpit?" Walter questioned as he picked up his coffee cup and cut short Richard ruminating.
 "I beg your pardon?" Richard asked as he crossed to the table and pulling out a chair and sat down.
 "Armpit," Walter repeated as he turned his cross word book for Richard's perusal. "I need another word for armpit, that's how a cross word works, remember?"
 "Ah," Richard told him as straightened the salt and pepper pot set "How many letters?"
 "Five,"
 "Have you tried Oxter?"
 "Oh yes of course Oxter." Walter proclaimed unconvincingly.
 "It fits." Richard told him and then, not wanting to get drawn into a cross word solving session or be late for the Boschendal picnic made his excuses and went to shower. Twenty minutes later showered and dressed he made his way back downstairs where he found Gabriella and Walter waiting for him.

The Boschendal wine farm was a delight. As the three arrived they were immediately escorted to a picnic table that had been placed under one of the many magnificent and ancient oaks. Here they found, as Gabriella has promised, a picnic hamper containing quality hams, salads, patés and to Richard's delight, fine wines, extravagant deserts and cheeses. After taking her fill of the food and drink Gabriella made her excuses and went to the ladies room to freshen up and taking a pair of thick plaid rugs Richard and Walter went to sit under one of the old and shady oaks. The sun was high, warm and bright and when Gabriella returned from her 'freshening' she found both man fast asleep and snoring happily. Not wanting to wake them she dipped her hand into her large and mysterious handbag and taking out her latest Ken Follet novel settled down for a quiet afternoon of reading. Later, very much later and having imbibed more wine than was good for any of them they climbed contentedly into the back of their big and black chauffeur driven car and made their way home. Once there Richard lowered himself onto the soft sanctuary of a lounge sofa and closed his heavy eyes.

"It was a great day Gabriella." he heard Walter say and even though the voice came to him from far away he could still hear the leer of his friend's inebriated grin.

"It was my pleasure." Gabriella grinned back, her own alcohol level way above that recommended by all the medical journals. "It was so lovely to spend some quality time with you." As she spoke her 'lovely' took on a slurred 'r' making the word sound like 'rovely'. Briefly opening one prying eye Richard watched as Gabriella pushed two scatter cushions into the corner of the sofa and pulled her knees to her chin. "It was a pity about the old guy you brought with you though." she laughed wickedly. "Maybe next time we can ditch the pensioner and let our hair down."

"Why not?" he heard Walter mumble as the pair burst into a bout of drunken laughter.

"Richard, Richard, Richard, I'm going to make some supper." With great effort Richard extracted himself from his dream, the contents of which were instantly lost and forcing his eyes open took a bewildered glance across the room.

"Supper, are you mad?" he questioned.

"A man's got to keep body and soul together" Walter told him as he crossed to where Richard lay.

"Oh don't worry Walter." he heard Gabriella say. "If the poor old man's not hungry just leave him."

"Less of the poor," Richard protested as he eased himself onto one elbow "I'm tired not hungry." and then remembering his manners thanked Walter for the offer.

"It's okay old man." Walter laughed as he bent over Richard's prone body, his face distorted by the closeness and his breath smelling like the contents of a three day old bin bag. "But remember" he added "at your age this could be your last supper."

"I certainly hope not," Richard told him in what he hoped was an ironic tone. "but you're right" he added "at my age one learns not to take too much for granted." Behind Richard's irony lay a truth. The events of the last months had hit him hard. The certainties of life had one by one drifted away and he had begun to realise, with more than a little sadness, that there were more years behind him than in front. In therapy with clients Richard would often remind the thirty year olds that they probably had another fifty years ahead of them. He would then ask them if they wanted to live those years as they were living now or did they want to change? How many years were ahead of me Richard wondered? He had often sung along with the Frank Sinatra lyric, *'If you can survive to a hundred and five think of all you'll derive out of being alive, if you're young at heart.'* and he knew that one hundred and five was a dammed good target. On his good and positive days it was a target that he felt he could aim for. At other times, when he was low and depressed, well he would gladly have ended his life there and then. 'Or would I' he asked himself.

Making his way to the kitchen Walter began to prepare a snack supper. In between finding biscuits and cheese he too pondered on life, on the events of the day and of his time in South Africa. Normally a quiet and sober man Walter had found himself drifting into a culture where the drinking of alcohol was an everyday occurrence and the abuse of alcohol rife. Now it seemed alcohol was beginning to take its toll on his own life and on his physical, emotional and mental health. Conscious of a dull ache at his temple he began to massage the side of his head, pushing his index finger in a circular motion round and round with increasing force getting a measure of relief he then opened the fridge door. Taking out a jug of cold water he poured himself a glass, the cold fluid as he drank, striking his already distended stomach and causing him to wince with pain. Moving to the counter he picked up the kettle, shook it to check the water level and pushed the on switch down. Through the window he could see the garden, its lush greens and vibrant colours reminding him of home and his dead his wife. *"Ah Barbara lass I do miss you."* he told himself and then his thoughts moved to Gabriella and Richard. Walter had watched with interest as they had argued and shared warm and intimate moments together. He had talked to Richard about his relationship with Grace and it was clear that Richard was confused and confusion, it would seem, was contagious. Hearing the sound of the kettle clicking off Walter roused himself from his reverie and reaching into the cupboard took down three mugs. Spooning a generous measure of coffee into each he placed them on a tray and recrossed to the fridge. Taking out the remains of a chicken he placed it on the table. Suddenly Walter Wilson felt very alone and in his fear and frustration he began to tear angrily at the flesh of the chicken a tear forming at the corner of his eye. Wiping it away with the back of his hand he looked down at the carnage in front of him and his rage over he began to place the chicken pieces on a plate. Taking a loaf of bread he began to butter the thin slices and then, his task completed made his unsteady way back to the lounge.

"You okay old man." Richard asked as he took a mug from the tray and sat down on the sofa. "Not bad Richard." Walter told him sadly and looking across the room asked where Gabriella was.

"She went for a shower" Richard told him "and then probably fell asleep."

"Oh says you Mister Stamina." Gabriella chided as she stood quietly by the door looking crisp and cool in a black Kimono dressing gown.

"Feeling any better Gabi?" Walter asked as he placed the supper tray on a side table.

"Still a little wobbly," she told him "but otherwise I'm okay and you?"

"A little rough Gabi but I'll live."

"Oh and I'm very pleased to hear it!" she smiled. "And you Richard are you still in the land of the living?"

"Oh never felt better." Richard lied as he pushed himself forward and at the third attempt got to his feet. "Coffee Gabi?" he asked.

"And I've made some chicken sandwiches if you'd like one." Walter offered as he picked up the plate and held it in the air as if to prove the truth of his statement.

"Thanks, but just the coffee for now please." Gabriella told him as she moved to the sofa and easing herself into the corner pulled her legs to her chest and tucked her Kimono under her buttocks.

"Would you like a sandwich Richard?" Walter asked as anticipating another refusal he lowered the plate to the table.

"No not for me thanks Walter," Richard declined "I'm hot, tired and stuffed, so I think I'll go and shower."

"Well good night to you then Mr. Stamina." a knowing Gabriella called from the sofa "I'll see you in the morning." Richard didn't reply.

Picking up the coffee mugs Walter crossed to the sofa and bending handed Gabriella her coffee. As he did so his hand touched hers, touched in that awkward way that hands do when a relationship between two people is unclear or unspoken.

"Sorry." Their words were spoken in unison which seemed to further emphasise the awkwardness of the situation. It was Gabriella, the ever strong one who spoke next.

"It was my pleasure." she smiled as she patted the cushion next to her. "Come sit by me Walter." she invited. It was an invitation that took Walter a little while to process and then placing his own mug on the coffee table he hesitantly moved to sit next to Gabriella, to sit closer to any woman than he had since the death of his wife, so close in fact that he felt decidedly uncomfortable and a little unsafe.

"Walter?" Gabriella spoke his name quietly.

"Yes Gabi?" he asked as his eyes moving unbidden to her silk Kimono and the contours of her breasts beneath it.

"Do you find me attractive Walter?" Gabriella asked as her eyes followed the line of his gaze. Walter's answer should have been a straight forward 'yes'; for that is what he felt and thought, but the sudden boldness of her question threw him.

"Of course." he blurted as if the question had been 'Do you like cheese'.

"And my hair?" she asked as she took his hand in hers and moved it slowly through her luxurious curls.

"Yes." Walter told her as he gently moved his hand to the side of her face "it's very beautiful"

"Do you think so?" she asked as she leant forward to place her cup on the glass top of the coffee table.

"Yes and it suits you Gabi." the emboldened Walter told her as unable and unwilling to stop himself he lowered his hand to the lapel of her gown and began to stroke the soft warmth of her breast. Gabriella's response was immediate. Placing her feet onto Walter's lap she began rubbig her heels against his rapidly rising penis and then Walter, as if following some well known and well rehearsed script, slid his hand under the silken hem of her Kimono and began to caress the bronzed skin of her calf. Mesmerised Gabriella watched as Walter moved his hand ever further upwards, his mind and hand reaching for places that for so long had been denied him. And then it was over and Gabriella's hand was on his.

"Not now Walter, not here." she said softly as she swung her feet to the floor and taking his concerned face into her hands kissed him.

"I'm sorry Gabi" Walter started to say "I don't know what..."

"Oh yes you do young man." Gabriella teased as she got to her feet. "And very nice it was too, but I think we're both out of practice and a little drunk." then picking up their coffee mugs she placed them on the side table and began to inspect the contents of a curled edge sandwich.

"Are you happy in South Africa Walter?" she asked.

"I hadn't thought of my visit in terms of happiness Gabi." Walter told her as moved to her side. "But" he added with a wry smile "I guess I am and the last few minutes where…"

"That's good to know," Gabriella told him "but I was thinking more in terms of your future. Is it here?" she asked. Pausing to inspect and reject his own sandwich Walter placed his hand on her arm.

"This is a beautiful country." he told her "and I'll miss it when I go back."

"Then stay Walter."

'I wish I could Gabi, but…."

"Wish you could what?" Richard questioned from the doorway.

"Stay Richard" Walter told him as his face began to redden like that of a naughty teenager.

"Then why don't you?" Richard suggested as crossing to the wine cupboard he poured himself a large glass of 'Rioja' "Yes why don't you?" he repeated and raising his glass in salute to the idea and pronounced 'cheers'.

"Cheers Richard." Walter replied as he tried to wipe the guilty look from his face and then lifting his empty coffee mug announced "To us."

CHAPTER 34
Thursday 15th January 2010 (Early Evening)

Tea Anyone

Needing some time to gather his thoughts and to read through some the new client referral sheets Richard made his way to his study. At seven o'clock he was joined by Walter who, standing in the door way with two coffee mugs in his hand, asked Richard if he 'Fancied a chat'.

"Great" Richard told him as he closed the file he was reading. "Come in pull up a chair" and lifting the remaining files from Walter's chair dropped them to the floor.

"So what's with the coffee?" he asked as he eased himself up right.

"Oh I've had it with the alcohol" he grinned as he placed the mug on the table and lowered himself into the newly vacated chair.

"Oh me too Walter," Richard agreed as lifted his favourite 'Rioja' to his nose and sniffed. "Well that's until the next time." he joked and bringing the glass to his lips he tipped, sipped and swirling the red liquid around his mouth he swallowed. "You okay pal?" he asked.

"Been better" Walter told him "and you?" he asked.

"Oh I'm still a little delicate." Richard told him as once more he put his glass to his lips. Agreeing that "delicate' was the word brought his hand to his still aching head and with the palm of his hand began to rub.

"So you enjoyed the wine farm?" Richard suggested wryly and Walter, relieved that the question hadn't been about his evenings 'activities told him 'brilliant'.

"What a beautiful part of the world this is." he added as he placed his warm coffee mug against his temple.

"It certainly is" Richard agreed "but I had no idea about its charms when I first came here in '67."

"I just knew that you'd get round to talking about yourself eventually Richard." Walter laughed as in a precurser to another long but interesting session he sat back in his chair and crossed his legs and then, seeing the hurt look on Richard's face added that he was only joking.

"You sure?" Richard asked as suddenly he felt unsure and threatened.

"Sure" Walter told him as he placed his almost empty mug on the coffee table and invited Richard to continue his story. "That's if" he added "you can you remember where you were up to?" Telling Walter that he hadn't a clue where he was up to Richard asked if he'd got off the boat in Cape Town.

"I'm not sure if you actually got off the boat Richard," Walter told him "If I remember rightly you were still chatting to some of the other passengers.

"Right," Richard suggested "let's pretend that the ship had docked and I was walking down the gang plank shall we?"

"That's fine by me Richard but a gang plank" Walter questioned as a vision of a three mast schooner flashed into his mind "just how many masts did this ship of yours have?"

"Okay" Richard conceded "it wasn't actually a plank, but you know what I mean don't you."

"I do" Walter told him "pray continue."

"So Walter down the gang plank I came, oh sorry" he corrected "it was a companionway right?

"Well Richard" Walter interrupted "I hate to stop you again so soon, but I think I prefer the term gang plank. I can't see much the romance or excitement in the word companionway, can you?" Impatiently Richard told Walter to make up his mind and that he had a long and interesting tale to tell. Smirking as he apologised Walter invited Richard to continue and recrossing his legs brought his hand to his chin and closed his eyes.

"So feeling like one of those great white hunters with my trusty black bearers carrying my cases on their heads down the gang plank I walked out into the bright African sunshine. Opening his eyes Walter leant forward and picked up his mug.

"I think I'm going to enjoy this little episode." Walter interrupted to which an unsmiling Richard appended 'do you' and 'I wish I had'. Puzzled by Richard's negative reaction Walter asked him if his statement was based on sadness or sarcasm. Frowning Richard suggested that it had been a bit of both.

"The place was chaotic" he explained. "There were black men everywhere and I remember smelling for the first time that sweet earthy aroma that I now know as the smell of black men's sweat. That's not racist is it Walter?" he asked.

"I don't think that the idea that black men sweat is racist Richard" Walter told him. Agreeing Richard explained that he was still sensitive and maybe a little guilty about what the white man had done to the blacks.

"And what have *you* done to the blacks Richard?" Walter asked pointedly.

"Well I allowed the inequality to continue didn't I?" Richard told him.

"In that case you'd better go into politics, run for government and see if the black people will vote for you and if they do you can set them free. But wait a minute Richard" he smiled mischievously "If they're allowed to vote then perhaps they're free already? So I'm sorry old son but it would seem that there's a slight flaw in your argument. Now" he continued "can I suggest that you stop the guilt trip, change what you can and get on with your life."

For the next hour Richard told Walter about how he had been met by Nora and his other so called family and friends including, he added, "Joan, the woman who was to become his first wife." He also confessed to being embarrassed by the five cent coin his hard working bearers had been given for carrying his cases off the ship and into the customs shed.

"But as I understand it," Walter had explained as he placed his feet on the coffee table "In those days of apartheid tips and wages to black workers were kept low by some kind of unofficial agreement of the white population. Back then black and coloured people had no say in what went on." Arguing that to pay another human being sixpence for carrying his suitcases was wrong Richard told Walter that he had felt embarrassed and ashamed.

"Even in *my* total ignorance of all things worldly I knew it was wrong." he had explained.

"So we're back to equality Richard" Walter had suggested and then he had asked Richard what he'd done about it.

"What could I do Walter" Richard had argued "I had no South African money of my own and I have to say that that situation wouldn't change much in the coming years, despite Aunt Nora's promise of fame and fortune. Come to think of it Walter those tight sods not only gave the black people a pittance but me as well."

"Well,"Walter pointed out wisely "if the powers that be treated black and white the same then perhaps they hadn't been prejudiced after all?" Good naturedly Richard agreed that Walter could be right.

"But," he added "I doubt it. Anyways" he continued "with my suitcase in the boot of the car I was taken to a detached house. The house was hidden behind high walls and solid iron gates. It had large and well kept lawns and" Richard had added excitedly. "In front of the double garage was a brand new Morris Eleven Hundred motor car."

"So you really had fallen on your feet."Walter grinned pleased at Richard's success. "Here was the car you had been promised."

"Yes. Walter." Richard told him before adding. "Well that's what I thought anyway. This was grand and this was posh. This was where rich people lived."

"Or perhaps more correctly," Walter interjected. "This was where the white people lived."

"Gee" Richard had mocked "and I thought that I was cynical? Anyway I was told to get my case. There didn't seem to be any black man around so I had to do the job myself. Out to the car I went, collected my cases and was then led up the garden path and around to the back of the house."

"You were led up the garden path?" Walter smiled.

"I was and more than once." Richard grumbled as even after all the time that had passed his voice still broke in sad disbelief. "The car was not mine Walter" he complained "and the garden path led up to the maid's room." Hearing the sad frustration in Richard's voice Walter leant across and touching his arm asked if his annoyance was born of resentment or anger.

"I'm not sure Walter." Richard told him. "In those days I was much better at going with the flow, with innocence and naivety leading the way."

"So you just went with the flow?"

"Yes I did what else could I do?" Richard asked and Walter, once more hearing the frustration in his voice, asked him not to get defensive and to try and remember that he was there to listen and not to judge.

"Do you feel judged?" he asked. Pausing in his tirade Richard told him that he wasn't sure and Walter, mindful of the time reminded Richard that the hour was getting late and suggested that he just continue with his tale of woe. "That's if you can remember where you where up to." he added with some accuracy and Richard, unable to retrieve the conversation of a few minutes ago challenged Walter to do the remembering for him. "My pleasure." a smug Walter gloated and then with a look of delight on his face informed Richard that listening to him talk was like listening to someone read an audio book. "I just can't wait for the next chapter, but as I remember you were carrying your suitcases up the garden path and around to the back of the house."

"And into the maid's room, in those pre Mandela's release days Walter," Richard continued "most white people had maids, so it was like going back to Victorian times and to maids, butlers, cooks and bottle washers."

"So where was the maid?" a spellbound Walter asked.

"Katie," Richard told him "was a lovely big black mama of a woman who came in every day and so she didn't need the room."

"A big lady Richard" Walter laughed "I guess it's was a good job you didn't have had to share the room with her."

"Not a laughing matter Walter" Richard told him seriously "Katie could have been the one to make a man of me because I needed to be more of a man, be more assertive and stand up for my rights, but we digress. Kate didn't 'live in' and so the maid's room was mine and if I were to be flippant I would have added 'all mine.'"

"And why would you have added 'all mine' Richard?"

"Because Walter it would have been irony. That room was just six foot wide by eight foot long. It had a single bed, but no other creature comforts bar a cold water basin."

"So I guess that's one more reason not to share." Walter suggested cheerfully "But to re-cap," he added seriously "you had no car waiting for you, no flat and only a maid's room at the back of the house. Is that right?"

"That's right" Richard told him "and now only the 'good money' remained to be discussed."

"And was there any discussion?"

"Don't be ridiculous." Richard mocked "of course there no discussion but, we digress again. After unpacking I went back to the house and 'took tea' with the family in the drawing room how posh was that Walter." he asked "Not in the lounge or the sitting room but the drawing room with doilies and fine china cups with saucers!" Agreeing that it was posh Walter suggested that it must have been like visiting his granny in the 1950's.

"Indeed," Richard told him "Anyway," he continued "after tea they told me that I would be having an early start in the morning and that I had better get some sleep. I can tell you they got no argument from me. I was just glad to get off the set of that bizarre period play and so I was in bed by seven thirty. God Walter what had I done?" Richard asked as much to himself as Walter.

"Damn it Richard how am I supposed to know what you had done." Walter questioned. "You tell a good story and yes feel like I was there with you, but I wasn't. So you tell me, what had you done?" Entering into another tirade Richard solemn informed Walter that he had made his mother cry. Had been shocked by the treatment of the black people and had visited the 1930s.

"And" he added "I'm bloody angry about it."

"But I thought you said you were just going with the flow?" Walter challenged.

"I was but now Walter I'm angry, bloody angry."

CHAPTER 35
Friday 16th January 2010 (Morning)

The Waterfront

Richard woke at his usual time feeling much better than he had for some time, his talks with Walter were obviously starting to do him some good. As he started his daily routine he could hear Nellie vacuuming carpets, the gentle hum of the machine taking him back to childhood days and his mother. Conscience pricked Richard moved to the bed side table lifted the telephone and dialled her number. One ring, two and then remembering that the two hour time difference between the two countries making it only be five am in England he replaced the hand set and promising to try again later switched on his iPod. Selecting 'shuffle' his already good mood was lifted further as the voice of Dianna Ross filled the room and told him that 'Nothing will keep me away from you.' and so making his second promise of the day he crossed to the window. Looking out across the wide valley he pondered on the thought that fate may have finally decided to be on his side' and lowering his eyes to the pool watched as Walter made his way effortlessly through the water, the gentleness of the scene taking him back through the years and to his early trips to Southern Africa with his second son John. Those had been good and effortless days for him and now thanks to his sessions with Walter and Rose the good times were hopefully returning. With their help Richard had started, or more correctly had been forced on the road to recovery, a journey that had painfully shown him how he had pushed his luck with Grace. Making his way downstairs he found Walter sitting on the edge of the pool gently splashing his feet in the cool water and cheerfully bidding him a 'good morning, Richard dragged a sun lounger to the pool's side, sat down and asked Walter how he was feeling. Admitting that he was 'alright but not as good as Richard' Walter lifted his legs from the water and rubbing a towel down the back of his legs asked 'what happened'. Smiling broadly Richard told him sunshine, good friends and Dianna Ross. "And did Dianna bring a friend perchance?" Walter asked and Richard, easing himself into the strips of the fabric Richard told him 'regrettably not' and then asked if he'd seen Gabriella that morning.

After a long and sleepless night Walter's early morning conversation with Gabriella had been brief and awkward. His apology about the happenings of the previous night had being shrugged off with a 'don't worry about it we both had had too much to drink and were tired.' It was a statement that had left Walter feeling confused and deflated and when he had tried to protest, to argue, she had just smiled at him and touching his arm had told him that she needed time to think and sort herself out. And then the bombshell as she told him that she was going to spend some time with a friend in Cape Town. "I'll speak to you later." she had told him and then after pecking him gently on his cheek she walked tearfully from the room.

"Did she say anything?" Richard asked.

"No, just goodbye" Walter lied and Richard, taking his answer at face value sank his body lower into the lounger, placed his hands behind his head and asked Walter what he wanted to do with his day. Rousing himself from his melancholy Walter got to his feet and placing his towel on a lounger sat down and told Richard that he'd heard that the Waterfront was a must for us tourists? "And" he added "I need to get some presents for the family so what do you say?" Confirming that the Waterfront was indeed a must for tourists but that they charged tourist prices Richard agreed that it was an experience not to be missed

"And that there are plenty of nice places to eat and drink if you fancy."

"Then I'll get dressed." Walter enthused as he swung his legs to the floor and got to his feet.

"Sorry," Richard said deflating Walter's buoyancy at a stroke "but I have to see detective what's his name at ten so chill for an hour, I shouldn't be long."

Richard's conversation with Kevin Dorrington was indeed short and to the point. "So the news you bring me inspector," he accused "Is no news!" It was a statement that the policeman had great difficulty arguing with and with Richard unable to hide his exasperation the inspector was out of the house in less than ten minutes.

Settling himself behind the wheel of the Audi Richard wound down his window and seethed. "Do you know that bloody inspector still has me on his list of suspects for kidnapping Steven and killing Michael Bennet? The bloody man is just plain incompetent."

"And why does he think you would have kidnapped Steven?" Walter asked calmly as Richard accelerated out of the drive and out into the mid morning traffic.

"I haven't a clue Walter, some shit about Steven having changed his will."

"So who else does he suspect?"

"All of us Blackwoods." Richard told him "The man's a fool. I could do a bloody better job myself."

"So why don't you?"

"Well for one I'm not sure I should be getting involved in a police investigation and two, where would I start?"

"Well you could do worse that use that Socrates and Holmes method of questioning that you're always so fond of using with your clients." Walter joked and then wished he hadn't as unhearing Richard drifted effortlessly into one of his increasingly regular rants.

"But that guy Dorrington is off his head." he snapped angrily. "Fancy putting Steven's mother and Katie in the frame, can you imagine Joan wanting Steven dead? Mothers don't kidnap their own children." Wanting to argue the point but unsure of the wisdom in doing so Walter turned his head away from his irate friend and looked up at the pine covered slopes of Table Mountain.

"Then why not do a little questioning of your own it can't hurt, can it?" he asked his gaze still averted.

"Prick" Richard cursed as a black Mercedes swerved recklessly in front him and then swerved out to pass the next victim. "It's the wives, girlfriends and jealous husbands who commit most murders." Richard continued and then recognising his growing irritation dropped his speed to the one hundred and twenty kilometres an hour limit.

"So that rules out Joan" Walter suggested "but what about Katie the girl friend, could Dorrington have a case against Katie do you think?" "No Walter, not for one moment." Richard said his reply coming too quickly, for deep inside him a little voice had begun to nag and tell him that Katie had been responsible, if not for the murder of Benjamin then the kidnapping of his son. "So," he asked "who do you want to be Walter, Holmes or Dr Watson?" Surprised that Richard had heard his 'Socrates and Holmes suggestion Walter informed him that it was 'elementary my dear friend' and that he'd be Watson. Pedantically Richard pointed out that the phrase 'Elementary my dear Watson' belonged to him as Holmes and then smiled.

"Look Walter if we are going to be serious in this endeavour," he encouraged "then we'd better start as we mean to go on." Smiling back Walter told Richard that he could be annoyingly pedantic at times and then asked if he was sure he wanted to get involved in a police investigation.

"Well someone has to" Richard told him. "And I don't think our detective Dorrington is going to get very far just looking at the Blackwood family."

"Okay Richard if you're sure." Walter told him "So where do we start?"

As they travelled Walter began to scribble into his note book and by the time Richard had parked the car in the coolness of the underground car park his list had reached a solid four.

"Right my friend" Richard enthused as he got out of the car and slid his parking ticket into his wallet "what have we got?"

"We have revenge, jealousy, fear, robbery." Walter reported as he followed Richard towards the exit. "Where do you want to start?"

"How about we start from the top?" Richard suggested.

"Okay so why would anybody want to take revenge on Steven?"

"Perhaps," Richard volunteered as he replaced his wallet in his back pocket and immediately felt to see if it was still there. "Perhaps he repeated "to get back at him for something he'd done in the past?"

"Like what?" Walter asked as he lifted his shoulders in bewilderment and Richard, confessing that he didn't know suggested that they leave revenge until later. "So what's next on the list?" he asked.

"Jealousy," Walter told him "Is anybody jealous of Steven?" Placing his arm around Walter's shoulder Richard admitted that there were many people who had reason to be jealous of his Steven's success "But "he added " I can't see their jealousy being enough for them to want to kidnap or kill him."

"Can you name names?" Walter asked but Richard, his frustration growing told him that they could make a list of who's who later. Unhappy at his friend's tone of voice but mindful of his still delicate state Walter gently asked if Richard wanted to call it a day.

"No." Richard told him and then apologising for his abruptness admitted his frustration. "God Walter this thing is so aggravating and I thought I was getting back on up."

Making reassuring noises Walter began to wonder across the Waterfront's access road "Come on" he encouraged "next on our list is..." and then he stopped as a brightly coloured VW Beetle braked hard in front of him.

"Would it be Fear?" Richard laughed as he watched Walter lift his hand to the pretty female driver and mouth his 'sorry'. Beaming her bright and tanned 'it's okay' smile the pretty young thing slipped the VW into gear and waving into her rear view mirror set off once more for the city.

"What a pretty young thing." Walter smiled appreciatively.

"That pretty young thing near killed you." Richard told as him as side by side the pair continued across the road.

"Yes but what a way to go!" Walter countered as he watched VW disappear in a cloud of smoke and then, returning to the task at hand, asked why anyone would be afraid of Steven.

"Perhaps he knew something that someone didn't want made public," Richard suggested as they sauntered passed Mitchell's Pub and then the bustling Ferryman's. "But this is getting us nowhere, so what else was on the list?"

"Robbery," Walter told him "was it a burglary gone wrong. What did Dorrington say?"

"Well detective Dorrington or should I say defective Dorrington, has not shared that information with me. He's not the chattiest of blokes Walter so what else is on the list?"

"Sorry Richard but that's it." Walter said as Richard turned right and led him between two buildings and into Quay 4. As one of the Waterfront's most popular meeting places the restaurant was already heaving with tourists, most of them in varying degrees of inebriation. Greeted by a smiling and logo shirted waiter they were informed that the restaurant was very busy and then asked if they'd mind sharing. ?"Telling him 'not at all' the two men were then guided expertly through the mêlée to a long picnic style table where a party of loud and drunken German tourists were already ensconced. Stopping their rowdy conversation the red necked visitors looked up and after an initial *good day, may we* and, *thank you,* they happily moved over and made room for their new guests. Brief and laboured Anglo-German conversation followed and ten minutes later and with much back patting and shouts of *'I am hoping you are enjoying your stay',* Richard and Walter were left in peace.

"So" Richard said as he put down his first empty beer glass. "If we go back to our friend Socrates we have revenge, jealousy, fear and robbery none of which seem particularly plausible." Agreeing Walter nodded at a passing waiter and held up two fingers.

"I hope he knows the significance of that gesture Walter." Richard suggested as the waiter lifted his hand and repeated the gesture in their general direction.

"It's a worldwide indication of a man's need for more alcohol." The generally tea total Walter reassured.

"Oh says you," a sceptical Richard told him and then tapping the table suggested they try the Sherlock Holmes method of detection "Let's see if we can come up with a 'who done it Walter, any thoughts?" he asked.

"Well," Walter suggested as his smiling waiter advanced with a tray of beers "Holmes would probably start by looking at the person closest to the victim. Now who would that be?" he asked as two beer glasses were placed in front of him. Taking his turn to thank the waiter Richard unhappily suggested he was probably closest to his son.

"Ah," Walter pointing out "if it was you Richard I'm pretty sure you're not going to admit it are you?" and then without waiting for an answer recommended that they looked at the next person in line. "And who would that be?" he asked.

"Katie?" Richard told him without pleasure.

"So why," Walter asked keeping to the Holmes script "would Katie want to kidnap Steven?"

"Or have him kidnapped." Richard interjected. Conceding the point Walter rephrased his question.

"So why," he asked "would Katie want Steven kidnapped?

"Well our list starts with revenge." Richard told him logically.

"So, Richard" Walter wanted to know, "Do you think Katie had Steven kidnapped for revenge?"

Slowly the pair worked their way through their lunch and their list of suspects at every point stopping to ask what Sherlock Holmes would have done. In the end the only conclusion they came to was that any of the Blackwoods could have kidnapped Steven and try as they may they still struggled to find any real kidnap motives. Finally, his patience at an end Richard suggested that they stop being so nice about it and do something else that the famous Sherlock Holmes always did. With his own head hurting from the combination of sun, beer and thinking Walter asked what it was that Sherlock Holmes always did.

"Tick people off his list." Richard told him. "So let's start with William and James, agreed?" he asked. Agreeing him "Walter added that he thought that they should take Steven's mother off the list.

"And we've already agreed to take me off the list, so what about Grace?" he asked the mention of her name causing him a sudden and unwanted pang of sadness.

"Take her off the list too." Walter told him softly, his words seeming to include more than just removing her from their list of suspects. Not really wanting to go down the path of his loss of Grace Richard asked about John and his wife?" Reminding him that he had never met the couple Walter picked up his beer and asked if John struggled for money.

"John always struggles for money." Richard told him "Does that mean he stays on the list?"

"Well yes if we're being serious about this Richard," Walter told him "Are we being serious?" he asked as he put his glass to his lips.

"Someone has to be Walter" Richard told him "so I guess that leaves us with Katie, John and John's wife Victoria."

"This is good," Walter told him and placing his beer glass on the table throwing yet another spanner of confusion into an already cloudy mix. "And don't forget anyone else who knew Steven." he announced.

"Like who?" Richard asked as he lifted his own pint.

"Friends and work colleagues?" Walter told him.

"How the hell did Sherlock Holmes ever catch anybody." he asked as he drained a quarter of his glass.

"With skill and patience and" he added he added wisely "with the help of his creator Mister Conon Doyle."

CHAPTER 36
Friday 16th January 2010 (Afternoon)

Seeing the Sights

"It's hard to believe," Richard said as led Walter further into the hustle and bustle of the Waterfront, "but this is the very place where I disembarked all those years ago."

"I guess it's changed a bit over the last what, forty years?" Walter asked as the pair moved towards a German themed restaurant.

"It certainly has." Richard told him "There was none of this glitter and shine back then, but I told you all this yesterday didn't I?" he asked to the back of Walter's head.

"Yes you did and what a tale it was." Walter laughed as he dragged his attention away from a scantily clad young black woman at the next table. "So mister, back to Steven's kidnapping, what do we know?"

"Not a lot." Richard told him "I don't want to think that he was taken by a Blackwood even though the inspector seems to think he was. If you thought it was a Blackwood Walter you'd tell me wouldn't you?" he asked.

"Sure," Walter told him, but I'm not even sure we should be trying to guess. We're not policemen and we're probably too close to the situation, but what I do know is that you won't rest until you know who did it, so perhaps" he suggested "we could make it less personal by changing people's names. We could call Katie another name, perhaps Mary and call Steven Joe. It may be easier if we think about why Mary would want to kidnap Joe. So before we go looking for a Blackwood perhaps we should kick around the idea that it was not a Blackwood but someone else, what do you think?"

Admitting that he was more than pleased with the idea of Walter's of the kidnapper not being a Blackwood Richard wanted to know who that someone could be. Walter didn't know.

"But we have to start somewhere Richard," he said "so how about Mr Ascot Chisholm? He's Steven's partner and with Steven out of the way he could take over the business and remember," he added "Steven's other partner Michael Bennet is already dead." Telling Walter that it was an interesting thought Richard asked if Walter really thought that Chisholm would want his boy dead.

"Do we really want to go down that road?" he asked.

"No," Walter told him "but if Chisholm did want Steven dead..." That was enough for Richard.

"Okay" he said "perhaps we should give Mr Ascot Chisholm a visit." Agreeing that it was a good idea Walter suggested that they waste no more time and visit Chisholm the next day. And Richard agreeing that that was a good idea lifted his arm and holding up two fingers prayed that he had ordered two beers.

Placing his black wallet on the table Walter told Richard that he'd get the bill and asked him not to argue and Richard thanked him and told him that if he stayed in the country for much longer he'd have to stop thinking in pounds and start thinking in Rand's.

"If you don't," he explained, his voice beginning to sound like someone's dad "you'll find that you've spent all your hard earned money on what you think of as cheap food and beer. I don't think" he continued "you realise just how much you've spent in the last few weeks. Spending like that is okay if you are here for a short holiday but..."

"But nothing" Walter told him "eat drink and be merry for tomorrow we die that's my motto."

"And tomorrow we die in poverty Walter." Richard corrected.

When the bill came the pair played their little game of 'no let me' and then set off to look round the shopping malls where Walter bought gifts for his family and friends and for some bizarre reason this avid England cricket supporter purchased a South African rugby top.

"And just where and when are you going to wear that?" Richard asked. It was a question that Walter seemed unable to answer.

"Perhaps he finally said." I just want to prove that I have been here?" Shrugging his shoulders knowingly Richard told him 'fair enough' and then asked if Walter wanted to hang around and perhaps have a meal in town or head back home. In Walter's mind there was no contest and thanking the shop assistant followed Richard out of the shop and back to the car. Carefully looking both ways as he crossed the Waterfront's access road Walter turned to Richard and with a slight plea in his voice told him that sometime during his visit he wouldn't mind going up Table Mountain watching the sun go down. Placing his arm around his friend's shoulder, something that of late was becoming a norm Richard promised him anything he wanted.

"Now," he said "let's get the car and go up the coast and have a few beers and head back to the city for night fall." Growing increasingly uncomfortable with Richard's alcohol intake and his propensity to drive whilst inebriated, Walter questioned the wisdom of drinking more beer.

"Don't you think you've had enough?" he asked. Explaining none too convincingly that the local brew was nowhere near as potent as that in England and that it was probably legal to have seven or eight pints and still be fine.

"Now back to the car and Sea Point here we come." Still unsure Walter reminded Richard that if they stayed he would miss a session to which Richard told him 'to hell with the therapy' and that being out and about was better than just talking. Thanking him for the vote of confidence in his skills Walter conceded that he was probably right and that sometimes being out was all we needed to off our melancholy.

"So where are we going?" he asked.

"Sea Point" Richard told him "There'll be a lot of people watching to be done although" he added "I'm not sure if we will be the watchers or the watched"

"What do you mean?" Water asked suddenly suspicious of Richard's intentions.

"Well" Richard told him, his arm still around Walter's shoulder. "What do you think people will say when they see two aging males together?" Still unsure what Richard was talking about Walter disengaged himself from his friend's grasp and asked him to explain.

"That we're a couple of gay guys out for some fun." Richard laughed "and then they'll welcome us with open arms." Telling Richard that he wasn't quite ready to fall into the arms of any gay men yet Walter moved swiftly towards the car and waited for Richard to unlock his door.

"Oh come on you old prune." Richard mocked as Walter slid uneasy into the passenger seat "and don't forget to bring your handbag"

Walter's afternoon in Sea Point afternoon began with Richard leading him down the promenade and at every opportunity trying to embarrass him. At one point holding his hand and then trying to kiss him on his cheek. As evening drew closer the pair returned to their car and took the steep and winding road up to the foot of Table Mountain and from there the cable car to the mountain's craggy summit. Ordering 'sun downers' they moved outside and selecting a table settled to watch the inevitable sinking of the sun. Chatting amicably about their day both men tried to avoid talk of their pasts. It was a task that proved impossible and soon the conversation was drifting back to friends at home. And then the sun began to slide, slowly at first and then with gathering speed, on its preordained path into the deep waters of the Atlantic.

"I wish Barbara could see…" Walter began and then suddenly stopped. "Sorry," he offered as he realised that Richard was probably having his own similarly painful thoughts about Grace. Seeing the look of concern on Walter's face Richard lifted his glass.

"Hey it's okay Walter" he told him "to us and to Barbara and to Grace…" and then hearing the catch in his own voice Richard began to fight back his emotions. "Hell Walter" he sniffed "a perfect day ruined by a sentimental old fool."

"No Richard." Walter told him and getting to his feet walked around the table and rested his hands on his friend's shoulders. "Come walk with me Richard, let the pain out let's miss our women together." As he did so an old couple sitting close to them smiled knowingly at each other. "Mock if you must" Walter told them "but this man is my friend and I love him dearly."

CHAPTER 37
Friday 16th January 2010 (Late Evening)

Budge Up

"Well old friend, it looks like Gabriella is spending another night with her friend." Richard proposed as he watched the garage door slide silently to a close. "Have you heard from her Walter?" he asked as he tapped in the security code and pushed.

"No not a word," the tired and slightly inebriated Walter told him as he as he followed Richard to the front door and waited as he tapped in the security code. "Do you think we should phone her?"

"Phone her where?" Richard questioned as once more his paranoia around the couple's relationship reared its ugly head "do you have her number?" he asked.

"Ring her at the office?" Walter explained somewhat defensively as once more his guilt around his ham fisted attempt as seduction reared its ugly head.

"Ah," Richard suggested as he gently closed the door "if we do ring her she will probably accuse us of prying. "No she'll find us when she needs us." he said with more hope than he felt. "But for now" he added as he led the way to the kitchen "how about a session?" Turning on the cold water tap Walter filled the kettle and replacing it on its base flicked down the switch.

"Perhaps an hour." he negotiated as he reached for two mugs "but coffee first." he demanded and Richard, taking up an exaggerated thinking pose of chin between thumb and forefinger predictably recommended that the coffee be strong and accompanied by a nice glass of cognac.

Coffee and cognac in hand the two men made their way out to the pool where for some minutes they sat in companionable silence. "When I first came to this country I worked a five day week." Richard began as he fought the urge to swirl his brandy. "We started early which meant going to bed early."

"And I bet you were glad to get to your bed if I understood you correctly." Walter interjected his brandy still on the table beside him. Sighing Richard told him yes.

"And were the weekends different?"

"Indeed they were." Richard confirmed "at weekends I would knock around with some of the guys I worked with we would go down to the coast, mostly to Bikini Beach."

"The same Bikini Beach you're going to take me to?" Walter asked, his eye brows rising.

"Yes." Richard confirmed again.

"And were there bikinis?"

"Oh yes my friend." Richard enthused "I used to sit on that soft, warm and golden sand and watch as the soft, warm and golden brown bikini clad girls ran to the sea, their bikinis seeming to defy gravity. In and out of the water they would run and then bending to straighten their beach towels they would lie down and dry their young bodies under the hot summer sun."

"Now I do hope that you're not going to embarrass me with tails of loose behaviour and fornication Richard?" he pleaded with some nervousness as he reached for his brandy.

"Now as if I would." Richard told him, the twinkle in his eye doing little to convince Walter of the truth of his statement "but I used to watch those bikini clad forms, if one can technically be 'clad' in a bikini from behind my sun glasses and as I watched my loins stirred." Pointing out that talk of loins stirring and not embarrassing him seems to be something of a misnomer Walter lifted his glass to his lips and sipped.

"Okay my friend," Richard advised "why don't you do what I did."

"Which was?"

"Close your eyes and think of England." Richard laughed and then suddenly becoming serious told Walter that he had wanted one of those real live, tall, slim, girls.

"Did you get one?"

"Alas no," Richard confessed his tone still subdued "it was not to be. It would be another twenty years before anything leggy came into my life."

"But you had begun to enjoy yourself?"

"No." Richard told him before adding that he didn't think he was happy or even content.

"So what was your state of mind?" Walter asked as Richard got to his feet and moved to the pools side.

"Resigned." he said as he gazed down at the water "yes I think resigned is the word I'd use."

"Resigned to what?"

"Resigned to a life of working from Monday to Friday for very little money and at the weekends going down to the beach with even less money?"

"But you had no one else to think about." Walter questioned "No wife, no kids and no mortgage to worry about and you're telling me that you were still not content or happy? Just what the hell did you want from life Richard?"

"Oh that's an easy one to answer." Richard told him with conviction. "What I wanted was to be loved. I had no one in a six thousand mile radius that I loved or who loved me and more to the point my friend I couldn't see anyone who I was going to give my love to or who was going to give their love to me."

"What about one of those bikini clad young women?" Walter asked perplexed by Richard negatively.

"How the hell was I going to approach such beauties such goddesses?" Richard exploded as he turned to face the hapless Walter. "That bloody James Bond would have wined and dined them. He would have smiled and been witty and the girls would have fallen into his arms and into his bed. And" he continued "you can run the scenario of me as James Bond through your head as many times as you like Walter, but you know as well as I do that it was not going to happen, no bloody chance."

"And whose fault was that?"

"Mine, I know that."

"And what about now?" Walter asked, Richard's angry outbursts no longer causing him to backtrack or shift his ground.

"And what" an irritated Richard demanded "is that supposed to mean?"

"What I mean" Walter told him calmly "is that you appear to be just as insular now as you were then." Somewhat taken aback by Walter's challenge Richard sniffed the contents of his glass, brought it to his lips and smiled.

"Do you think so?" he asked as he lifted the glass to the moon and sipping announced that it was good stuff and not a bad price. Agreeing that the brandy was indeed 'good stuff' Walter got to his feet and moved to stand beside his friend. "So you think I'm insular." Richard repeated and Walter, unsure if he was in the midst of a therapy session or not placed his hand on Richard's shoulder and proposed that it was not for him to tell anyone what to think or feel. "But," Richard persisted "Do you think that you're insular?" Quite willing, for the moment, to play Richard's game Walter again insisted that his question had been about Richard feelings and Richard a little nonplussed by Walter's frankness moved back to his seat and lifting his feet placed them on the table.

"Well he admitted "I know I like my own company and I like your company. I also happen to like Gabriella's company."

"But" Walter prompted "you don't like?"

"Crowds, push and pull, noise" Richard told him.

"And what did Grace like?" Walter asked pointedly and Richard, suddenly understanding the gist of Walter's argument explained that Grace liked to be around people and be busy. Asserting that Richard and Grace sounded like chalk and cheese Walter followed Richard back to the patio table and pulling out a chair sat down.

"Maybe," Richard conceded with a lift of his shoulders and praiseworthy restraint "but I only want to be with her. Is that too much to ask Walter?"

"Yes in a word." Walter told him and then breaking all the rules of therapy told Richard that he'd spell it out for him, "Ready?" he asked.

"Ready." An unready Richard told him.

"Sure?"

"Sure."

Right my man it's time you stopped being so bloody insular." Walter told him "Give a little and perhaps take a little more."

"Okay fine Walter." Richard countered his prickliness beginning to rise. "So we know what I want and that's Grace. I love her and want to be loved by her, but she is not here is she!" Calmly Walter explained that Richard was again missing the point.

"Why are we are looking at your past?" he asked.

"To help me to…?"

"Come on Richard" Walter encouraged.

"To help me…?" Richard repeated

"To help you build your future." Walter told him. "Look" he continued "I know that Grace isn't here today, but she maybe one day so come on, let's continue but learn as we go, okay." Agreeing with Walter's 'okay' Richard apologised and then asked if he should continue with his tale of woe.

"If you can remember where you were you were up to." Walter smirked.

"Of course" Richard declaring as he launched into the next chapter of his adventures.

"So Walter" he began "I was resigned to a life of working from Monday to Friday for very little money and with no one to love and then God."

"Sorry Richard" Walter questioned "what did you say?"

"God Walter," Richard told him "in my little room miles from home I lifted my hand and reached out to God."

"And did he come?" Walter asked as he placed his empty glass on the table and picked up his now cold coffee mug.

"I think so" Richard told him "something touched and comforted me."

"But it wasn't God?"

"Oh who knows?" Richard admitted "but what I do know is that I slept well that night."

"So God had come to you." the not particularly religious Walter offered. "So what happened to your pain and anger?"

"I guess I just buried it and just got on with life." Richard told him.

"As you still do" Walter suggested "No crying or complaining that is until life jumps up and knocks you flat."

Angry at Walter's criticism Richard declared 'unfair' and told Walter that he knew how to sigh and cry.

"And who do you cry for Richard?"

"For me, isn't that why we all cry Walter?" he said and without waiting for a reply Richard recommenced his story. "That night as I lay on my bed no" he corrected himself "it was not my bed it was the maid's bed. So that night as I lay on a borrowed bed in a dark room six thousand miles from home and only for the second time in my life, I cried with unhappiness."

"The second time Richard." Walter asked, "So when was the first?"

"My first tears Walter were shed when my mother's father died. Granddad Howarth was a wonderful man, a kind and gentle man. I had never heard him get cross or raise his voice, subconsciously I think he became my role model. My grandma had developed chronic rheumatoid arthritis and as far as I remember she was bed ridden from the first time I saw her. What a lovely lady she was, unable to move, but she always seemed to find a smile, a beautiful smile. Her hands were bent and gnarled but she would hold my hand and tell me stories. Granddad nursed his wife with such love and patience and at the same time tried to run a grocers shop in Rochdale. His shop I remember had high wooden counters, butter and sugar were weighed out into blue paper bags and bacon was sliced to requirements, but more importantly sweets. There were sweets in glass jars and readily available. We visited my grandparents every Saturday afternoon and watched horse racing and Dickson of Dock Green on a small black and white television."

"Those sound like happy days Richard"

"They were the happiest."

"That's a big statement" Walter suggested "the happiest days."

"Effortless" Richard told him "I hadn't a care in the world and then my granddad died."

"I'm sorry..." Walter started to say but Richard didn't hear him.

"At that time, the time of my granddad's death, we lived in Fardale. My grandma and granddad live two or three doors up from us. The day granddad died I was asked if I wanted to see his body. I'm not sure what words were used, 'Would you like to see your granddad's dead body' seems a little thoughtless.' As Richard spoke a smile began to form at the corners of his mouth. It was a smile of remembering but a smile that flickered for a moment and then was gone. "But to see his dead body I went. How peaceful he looked. I loved my granddad Walter. I wish I could have known him better. I wonder what my sons and my grandson will say of me when I'm gone." Walter made no attempt to reply but instead suggested that Richard had known great happiness followed by heart breaking sadness.

"It was bound to have had a massive affect on you." he said as he picked up his coffee and took a tentative sip.

"And it still does." Richard told him.

"Even after all these years?" Walter wanted to know.

"Yes even after all those years."Richard confirmed and then with a plea in his voice asked Walter to help him. Replacing his undrinkable coffee on the table Walter looked across at his friend and gauging that the moment was right suggested that what Richard needed to do was help himself.

"Have a good cry that's what you need." he advised "Let the sadness out, let it go Richard, let it go." Conceding the cathartic but only theoretical merits of tears Richard promised that he'd give the matter some thought and then in a burst of unfelt bravado told Walter, 'forward and onward'.

"And the tears Richard?" Walter queried.

"No time my friend." he was told.

"And you wonder why you're in a mess?" Walter scoffed in disbelief.

"No comment." Richard told him.

"No comment?" Walter cursed unable hide his mounting anger. "No comment Richard. What's the point of us going through all this pain if you're going to dismiss your emotions with 'No comment'?"

"Perhaps I just need to unburden Walter. Maybe that's all I need to do?" Richard objected his tone flat and dejected. But Walter was having none of it.

"Rubbish Richard." Walter complained angrily "it's plain to anyone that you're suffering, so please don't waste my time and this chance to be ..."

"Be what Walter?" Richard sneered.

"To be free" Walter told him "free to be the person you want to be, to be happy." Again Richard sneered.

"Well seeing that I don't know who I am how the hell I'm supposed to know who I want to be..." For Walter enough was enough and unwilling to travel Richard's road to self pity cut short Richard's rising outburst and with authority growing demanded that he stop feeling sorry for himself and get on with his life and story.

"To more interesting times?" he asked.

"That gets my vote." Walter told him and Richard sighing told him that there was no need for sarcasm and that he was only trying to build up his story. Holding his hands up in defence Walter told him 'sorry' and Richard his tone still heavy said that it was he who should be sorry.

"But sometimes..." Richard began but got no further as Walter tapped his knee and asked him to 'please carry on'.

"Okay if you insist." Richard smiled and closing his eyes as the memories returned told Walter that weeks and months had passed in long days of mediocrity. "And then" he continued "late one night as I lay awake in my bed the door opened. It was too dark to see who was there, but I was sure it wasn't going to be a friend. I lay very still and a voice I know well came through the darkness" Unable to help himself Walter leaned forward and with mounting excitement asked Richard who it was.

"Who do you think it was?" Richard asked suddenly back in control.

"I don't know," Walter pleaded, "James Bond, Batman?"

"No it was the voice of Joan." Now it was Walter's turn to close his eyes and sitting back in his chair crossed his legs and told Richard that he felt a 'oh bloody hell' moment coming.

"Not family member Joan?" he asked as once more he leant forward the better to hear Richard's reply.

"Yes family member Joan," Richard confirmed "and then she whispered 'budge up'. 'Budge up I thought, where is there to budge to in single bed in a six foot wide room?'"

"And was that your only thought?" Walter asked as he suddenly found himself grinning.

"Oh no Walter," Richard told him "and 'Oh no' is what I thought, or as you said, 'oh bloody hell.'"

"So what did you do?"

"I asked her what she wanted" Richard smirked his telling of the story for the first time amusing him.

"And what, I'm loathed to ask did she want?" Walter queried.

"Well Walter," Richard told him "they say actions speak louder than words and in this case it was true. A hand that was not mine found its way to my groin, onto that very loin that had stirred on Bikini Beach. This Walter was the first hand, apart from my own, that I had ever felt on my 'Willie.'"

"Touched your what?"

"My 'Willie,'" Richard verified "as we talk now the very word 'Willie' will tell me of my inexperience. Not a cock or my knob but 'Willie.'" Now openly grinning Walter told Richard that he was not sure if he should ask and then asked 'what did you do'.

"Well Walter you may think me a naughty boy, but my hand moved to explore places that were very new to me, places that I had only seen in dirty books. The 'hunt the cunt' girls had flashed flesh at me, they had made me blush but here was a real live, warm and soft body. Perhaps I should have said 'No.'"

"No can be a good word." Walter agreed.

"I could have said 'No'. Walter, no I don't want pleasure, no this is wrong. I could have said all those things, but I didn't." Feeling somewhere between priest and policeman Walter asked if Richard was okay to carry on and then unable to stop himself asked if they'd had sex.

"No we didn't." Richard told him "but in the morning things felt and were very awkward."

"Was anything said?" Walter asked.

"Not a thing." Richard told him.

"So I guess you felt, well what did you feel Richard?"

"I'm not sure Walter, as you ask the questions I'm having difficulty explaining what my feelings were."

"Does that surprise you?"

"Yes it does, I thought I was pretty much okay talking about feelings."

"Maybe you're better with other peoples feeling?" Walter suggested.

"Maybe," Richard agreed "anyway the next night I lay awake waiting for the door to open and to hear the words 'budge up', but the night passed without event and I slept. Do you think women always mess with men's minds Walter?" Richard asked although he was sure he already knew the answer. "I wanted more Walter, more of being close, more of being…"

"Loved was that the emotion you felt?"

"I don't think so, but then I only had my mother's love to measure against. But if not love what was it?"

"It could have been many things Richard, perhaps you were just in lust?"

"Lust Walter, to my Methodist ears that sounds like a deadly sin. My father had given me three packs of condoms when I left for Africa. At the time I had thought what faith he must have in me if he thought I would ever get to use them."

"A wise man your dad." Walter enthused "But was that really the only sex advice you got?"

"No not exactly. I did receive some words of advice from Prakash, a fellow office equipment engineer. We talked about girls or should I say he talked about girls. It was he who told me that having sex with girls was easy, 'You just play with their 'pussy' until it's wet and the rest is easy.'"

"They didn't teach it like that at my school Richard." Walter grinned.

"Lucky you, I don't remember them teaching us anything about sex at mine."

CHAPTER 38
Saturday 17th January 2010 (Afternoon)

Gordon's Bay

"Well Richard it would seem you make a better Dr Blackwood than a Dr Watson." Walter laughed as he moved to the pool side and sitting down removed his shoes and socks.

"Well I'm glad you think so." Richard told him as he poured and passed Walter a glass of orange juice. "But Mr. Chisholm seemed a little taken aback when we walked into his office and that pretty little black girl well she seemed very keen to be on her way, what did he call her, his business partner? Business partners my foot, if she was his partner I'm a Dutch man."

"And how pray tell Richard did you know that she wasn't his partner?" Walter questioned as he swung his feet into the pool and raised his glass in salute.

"Well she wasn't his PA." Richard told him.

"And how do you work that out?"

"Have you ever seen a PA without a pad and pen? Richard asked a look of mock exasperation on his face. "And she wasn't his wife."

"Okay and how do you know that?"

"Because he didn't introduce her to us, so either he's forgotten his wife's name or he just didn't want us to know who the woman was."

"Hell Richard" Walter suggested splashed his feet in the cool water "you could make the Pope sound guilty."

"And he isn't?" Richard questioned as he pulling a sun lounger to the pool's side and sat down.

"So," Walter grinned as he turned to face his friend "you think Charles Chisholm is guilty of kidnapping your son and by default killing Michael Bennet?"

"No," Richard back tracked "but..."

"But what?"

"Well," Richard told him defensively "he was a bit cagey didn't you think?" Unimpressed Walter suggested that he would have been a bit cagey if someone had walked into his office on a Saturday morning and started asking questions about his relationship with his son.

"Hell Richard" he laughed "at one point I thought you were going to accuse him of being gay and kidnapping Steven for sexual gratification. And what was all that about knowing who did it, you haven't a clue who did it."

"But he doesn't know that," Richard grinned "and I'm sure Chisholm wants Steven's money or his business."

"So you're convinced Chisholm's your man?" Walter pressed as he got to his feet and padded quickly across the hot patio's floor to the table. Smiling at the comedy of the scene Richard craned his neck and followed Walter's painful progress and then with his conviction mounting asked if Walter had any evidence to the contrary.

"I don't know either way" he scowled as he rubbed the soles of his hot feet "and Richard nor do you." Admitting that he was perhaps stretching the point Richard picked up his glass and after draining its contents advised Walter to mark his words.

"Believe me or believe me not Walter but we haven't heard the last of our Mr Chisholm." he pronounced as a Sacred Ibis flew down onto the lawn and began to peck at the grass. "He's a big blighter Walter?" Richard smiled as the bird began hop across the lawn.

"Do you mean the bird or Chisholm?" Walter asked.

"Oh he's a big lad okay but I meant the bird"

"But everything in this country's bigger." Walter told him "Including the people, have you seen the size of some of those Afrikaners!"

"Now that's what meat and brandy can do for you Walter." Richard told him "And you could be that big if you really tried."

"Oh I don't think so." Walter argued "the size of the Afrikaner race is not just a matter of nature or nurture but combination of the two and looking at their history they needed all the nature and nurture they could get."

"And they're not out of the woods yet." Richard added "Hell Walter what a struggle that lot have had."

Finding no argument in Richard's statement Walter smiled across at him. "And you thought you had troubles?" he suggested "but at least if the shit hits the fan you'll have somewhere to run to."

"Correct" Richard told him "and talking about my troubles Walter are you ready for another session?"

"Oh I'm not sure?" Walter told him and then suggested that Richard show him the delights of Bikini Beach?"

Taking the longer, but more scenic route towards Fish Hoek and then on to Muizenberg Richard followed the coast road up towards the N2 highway. "These bloody South Africans are the most competitive and rude drivers I've ever come across, particularly the females." Richard moaned as yet another driver swung past him and settled inches from his front bumper. "They can always find their horn to give a sharp reminder that they own the road but they never seem able to wait their turn the stupid cow." he mouthed as the car in front swerved out to pass one more car. It was then that Richard noticed the white Ford closing fast on his rear end. It was a strange phenomenon but whenever Richard drove he always noticed so much of what went on around him but, once home he remembered so little. In fact there had been times when he found himself sitting outside his home but had no idea how he had got there. "And here comes the next idiot." he called as the white Ford pulled out and overtook. The jolt came before he heard the crash. It was not a loud noise, perhaps a sound like a crystal glass being dropped on a tiled floor, and then they were moving sideways and the beach was moving to meet them. Coming to a halt facing in the wrong direction Richard watched as a steady stream of rude and competitive drivers, horns blaring and angry faces turned towards him, continued to stream passed.

"Don't you think we'd better move?" he heard a stunned Walter asked and looking across as his friend's white face Richard's legs suddenly began to tremble.

The traffic policeman, who arrived ten minutes later, saw little point in processing any paperwork, but to his credit he did his job and after taking Richard's details advised him that the other driver was long gone. Then kicking bits of debris towards the road side gave a half hearted salute and went on his way.

"Not the best of outcomes Walter," Richard suggested "but" he added "this is Africa and we're still alive.

Half an hour later the pair arrived at the small village of Gordon's Bay where stepping out into the bright sun Walter looked out across the green waters of False Bay and to the hazy mountains of the Cape Peninsular.

"That's the back of Table Mountain Walter. To our left is Cape Point and over there is where we just caught one up the rear." Richard explained as he bent to examine the Audi's bumper.

"Never mind the car Richard." Walter told him as he looked first to his right to where golden sands stretched away into the distance and then to his left, where low windblown trees offered welcome shade to visitors. Beyond the trees a rocky ridge proclaimed 'GB' in giant white letters.

"GB Richard?" Walter questioned "It strange that they still have reminders of the empire on show?" Suggesting that 'GB' didn't stand for Great Britain but Gordon's Bay or the General Botha naval college down the road Richard pointed towards the far hills.

"That's the road the Voortrekkers took on the journey north." he explained. Turning his head in all directions Walter took in the varied signs of sea sky and mountains.

"This is a big and interesting country Richard." he said "but it seems to me that most of the history has been written in the last couple of hundred years."

"That's our history Walter," Richard told him "the white man's history and I think that's what Robert Mugabe is all about up in Rhodesia, sorry Zimbabwe. Africa had a history before the white man got here you know."

Telling Richard 'point taken' Walter then suggested that perhaps Mr. Mugabe and Richard could do to learn the same lesson?"

"And what lesson would that be?" Richard asked as he turned and walked across the hot white sand towards the gently rippling waves.

"You need to learn when to fight, who to fight, what to fight for and of course when to let go." Walter told him and Richard sensing that a lecture or a therapy session was imminent turned to his friend and suggested that they eat.

There were a number of cafes facing the sea and choosing the one he usually ate at Richard moved to a table and sat down under a giant umbrella.

"This is great my friend just great." Walter smiled as a young black waitress came out of the cool of the cafe and laid a colourful laminated menu on the table in front of him.

"Good afternoon sir" she smiled in tones warm and gentle and volunteering her name as Joy asked if she could get him something to drink?" Looking up into the girl's dark clear face Walter ordered a glass of red wine and told her that the name suited her. "And you sir?" she asked turning her attention to Richard who feeling a little like a spectator, asked if could have a Windhoek Light and then told Joy that Walter was on holiday form England. With what appeared to genuine interest the girl asked from which part and on being told Yorkshire asked if it was near Scotland.

"Very near." Walter told her. "And you Joy, where is your home?" he asked.

"My home is in Zimbabwe sir."

"Ah Mr. Mugabe?"

"Yes Mr Mugabe." the girl said and smiling a smile of understanding retreated into the darkness of the cafe. Returning a few minutes later carrying a tray of drinks she carefully placed them on the table and asked the men if they would like something to eat. Smiling Walter told her 'No thank you' and as he handed back the menus he noticed for the first time a hint of sadness showing around her eye.

"Are you alright Joy?" Walter asked the note of concern in his voice clear and the girl her tone failing to match her words told him that she was fine and once more departed. Ten minutes later the girl returned to enquired if more drinks were needed, her offer declined she returned almost immediately with the bill. Thanking her Walter again looked up into her eyes but saw no signs of sadness and handing her a hundred Rand note told her to keep that change.

"It was a pleasure to serve a Yorkshire man sir," she told him "you must really love your country and then wished him a good afternoon she turned to welcome new customers.

Waving his farewell to the now engrossed and unseeing Joy, Walter followed Richard across the road towards the beach and turning right walked along the beach towards the windblown trees. For Walter the latter part of the journey to Bikini Beach turned into was something of an anticlimax and disappointment. From Richard's description he had built a picture of long, wide and golden beaches like those he had seen in brochures for San Tropez or Cannes, but instead what he found were just a few hundred yards of sand. Yes the sand was golden, warm and soft sand but sand filled with bikini clad young ladies it was not.

"So what happened to all the young ladies Richard?" Walter questioned his disappointment clear.

"Probably doing their school home work" Richard told him, "do you want to hang around?"

"Now what do you think I am some kind of pervert?" Walter grinned as he turned and followed Richard up the beach and back towards the car park.

"What happens if we go right?" Walter asked as Richard stopped at the road junction and waited for the traffic to clear.

"If we go right" Richard told him "the road will take us up the east coast of Africa and all the way to Morocco."

"Well in that case." Walter smiled. "Let's go left."

Pointing the car towards the Strand Richard took the less direct but prettier coast road. Parking the Audi near the old jetty Richard followed Walter out of the car and was immediately accosted by a gnarled and drunken fisherman.

"Lekker vars vis meneer." the man called in Afrikaans as he grinned toothlessly in Richard's general direction. Understanding a little of the language, but not the man's slurred and rushed version Richard told the man that he was sorry and began to move away. Curious about all things new Walter asked Richard what the man had said.

"I think he said lovely fresh fish." Richard translated.

"Ah English!" The fisherman beamed as he followed, Richard, fish in hand towards the car.

"Yes English." The polite Walter replied as he too began to back away from the stench of fish and the man's boozy bad breath.

"Nice fresh fish sir." The man persisted as he continued to advance on the rapidly retreating couple.

"Yes but fresh when?" Richard muttered under his breath. "By the look of the flies buzzing around their heads Walter those fish have spent most of their day sun bathing and not swimming." then turning to the would be fish monger told him ' no thanks' and taking Walter's elbow ushered him away and suggested that they head home.

"Sounds like a good idea to me." Walter agreed as he moved quickly towards the car and climbed in.

"Now Walter" Richard asked as he slid behind the steering wheel what about our evening meal shall we eat out or in?"

"How about a nice B.B.Q" Walter suggested "but please not fish." he laughed.

CHAPTER 39
Saturday 17th January 2010 (Early Evening)

Babies and BBQ's

The drive back to the house took less than twenty minutes and by the time Walter returned from showering Richard, a glass of red wine in hand was standing in front of a brightly burning BBQ pit. "I thought" he cursed as a fat round sausage rolled off the grill and spiralled to the patio floor "sausages first". Bending to pick up the errant sausage Walter juggled it back onto the grid and licking the warm fat from his fingers pronounced that it was delicious. For the next half hour the men sat, ate and chatted pleasantly about their day and then Richard throwing another log on the fire announced that he and Joan had married in the April of '69'.

"And was she pregnant?" a curious Walter asked as he watch Richard move to the BBQ placed a log on the glowing embers.

"No she was not." he said somewhat indignantly as the dry wood ignited.

"Well, as the Welsh would say" Walter, grinning mischievously 'there's posh' and getting to his feet he moved to stand beside his friend.

"Oh yes posh indeed Walter." Richard agreed "and so we travelled to the UK for a wedding with family and friends and then a brief honeymoon before returning to the Cape to begin our lives together. By the June of that year Joan was pregnant and with medical bills to pay we could no longer afford to live on my meagre wage. Things needed to change and so I made contact with an old friend, Alexandra."

Alexandra?" Walter questioned.

"Yes Alexandra Du Toit had worked for Nora and the family some years before and like me she had been ripped off and so having decided to start her own rival company was willing to take me on as a partner.

"That was lucky." Walter suggested

"Was it luck or fate Walter?" Richard asked but failing to wait for an answer continued. "With the extra money coming we were better able to enjoy Joan's pregnancy and to prepare for our new baby. Steven was born in March1970. Oh Walter he was such a handsome chap and after three days we wrapped him in a blue blanket, a blanket that Joan would cut and hem a hundred times and took him home."

"Home Richard, you had found happiness at last?" Walter suggested.

"Only to a point" Richard told him "Like many people who move from one country to live in another, the ties that bind had started to pull. The lure of England and home grew stronger and stronger and so we decided to move back. Luckily I was able to go back to my old job of office equipment engineer but settling back into life in Lancashire wasn't easy. Joan found the weather, even in summer cold and the life style compared to her life of privilege in the Cape poor."

"So what did you do?"

"What could we do?" Richard told him "Joan was unhappy and I like a willow was able to bend with the wind so we decided to return to South Africa, although" he added with a heavy sigh "with the benefit of hindsight we should have put down roots in England. At least that would have put an end to my whole sad and sorry South African episode and I would have been able to pick up my life and spend more time with my parents."

"There's that bitterness again Richard." Walter warned "At some time in the future I'm going to sit you down and do an emotional profit and loss audit analysis with you. You may find that you made the right choice when you returned to the Cape. Still" he said his short sermon ended "let me get you a drink?" Declining Richard told him 'in a minute'

"Just let me finish my returning to Africa saga Walter because fate hadn't quite finished with me, she still had some more cards to deal." and then turning to his friend Richard asked if he thought that fate was female.

"Well Richard" Walter told him in a bold attempt to lift the mood of the evening, "If we go with the idea that we don't understand women and that we don't understand fate then I think the answer was elementary." Telling Walter that he couldn't argue with his logic Richard smiled and then immediately drifted back into melancholy. "But the cards she dealt me were rubbish, she definitely had the better hand Walter."

"Oh Richard" Walter sighed again "I'm not sure that fate ever has the better hand, perhaps" he added as he tried to restore some balance to the conversation "she's just better at playing the game. Fate isn't vindictive you know?" he said.

"She isn't?" Richard mocked and Walter, his patience now growing thin, suggested that he and Richard do the life profit and loss analysis there and then.

"Not just now thanks." Richard told him defensively "Just let me finish this part of my story."

"Okay off you go." Walter nodded tolerantly and moving to the patio table sat down and picking up the wine bottle refilled his glass.

"Well that's just the point Walter." Richard told him. "Because we didn't go anywhere, before we had a chance to formulate our plans to return to South Africa Joan became pregnant again."

"A mixed blessing?" Walter suggested as he waved the bottle in Richard's general direction. "You ready for another?" he asked.

"Why mixed?" Richard questioned as he moved forward.

"Well" Walter explained "I was thinking that Joan's being pregnant was good news for you, but the thought of returning to Africa was not." Nodding Richard watched as his glass slowly filled and then his mood sliding once more towards happy sipped his wine and sat down.

"You know Mr. Blackwood," Walter told him "there are times when I really can't tell your joy from your pain"

"And there are times when I can't tell my arse from my elbow, Mr Wilson." Richard retorted. "Anyway" he continued "John was born in the June of 1973 at the maternity unit at Birch Hill Hospital, the same unit where I'd been born."

"So that makes him what, thirty six?" Walter calculated as he got to his feet and dropping another log on the fire watched as the sparks flew high into the air. "And the birth went well?" he asked.

"It did," Richard told him "and John James was just as handsome as his brother."

CHAPTER 40
Saturday 17th January 2010 (Late Evening)

Nicholas

"Joan and I did have a kind of settled period in the UK. We stayed with my parents who did their best to make us welcome." Richard said as he placed another log on the already blazing fire "and we were clearly loved but the situation wasn't good enough for Joan and tensions began to mount."
"Not again" Walter groaned "and here was I waiting for a happy ending. So what happened?" he asked the look of exasperation on his face saying more that his words.

"I haven't messed up my life just to annoy you." Richard complained, the look of protest on his face matching that of Walters.

"I know." Walter told him "but you've got to admit..."

"Admit what," Richard asked angrily "that I'm crap at life?"

"No" Walter told him as with some difficulty he pulled a sun lounger to the pools edge and slowly eased himself down onto its stripped cushions. "It's just that..." and then changing tack he told Richard that they'd both had too much to drink and suggested that they start again.

"Okay" Richard agreed as he too pulled a lounger to the edge of the pool "as I was saying my parents did their best to make us welcome but Joan remained unhappy."

"You make Joan sound like a real selfish cow Richard." Walter pointed out "And to be quite honest I don't believe that's true."

"Oh no" Richard corrected "Joan was a lovely person and still is but..."

"But what, do you still see her?"

"Yes, I do now" Richard confirmed "but I didn't for a long time. In fact we probably get on better now than we ever have, but that's another story." Apologising if he'd been tactless and admitting that he'd just been curious Walter watched as a decidedly unsteady Richard lowered himself onto his lounger.

"Well if you don't ask you won't know" he forgave "but old pal on with the tale" he urged. "Now as I was saying we were clearly loved but tensions began to mount then in the late March of 1979 my younger brother died." To Walter the words were said with such calm detachment that at first the significance of the statement failed to register with him.

"Oh Richard I'm sorry, I didn't know." he finally said and then for want of something better to say he asked if the brother had been much younger.

"Our Nicholas" Richard continued, his voice dropping to a whisper "was nineteen when he died. He was a fine outdoor loving young man. He was one of the lads and enjoyed riding his motor bike. Then one night having had too much to drink he decided to leave his motor bike at the pub and got a lift in his best mate's car. On the way home the car skidded and Nick died at the scene. My father went to identify the body but the authorities thought it unwise for my mother to see her son's injuries. Nick's funeral took place at the crematorium at Rawdon in early April. The immediate family gathered at my parent's home where Nick lay in his sealed coffin in the front room. Then it was time. We lifted his coffin from its plinth and walked with him down the front steps and into the waiting hearse. Even after all these years I can still see the rhododendron bushes that lined the road through the crematorium. It was a warm afternoon Walter, and I could smell new mown grass, although I could hear no sound of grass being cut. In the car I sat opposite my mother and father with my older brother next to me. As we travelled we talked to each other in that matter fact way people do when they are trying to make a difficult situation seem normal. 'Don't they keep the ground nice' 'Did you see that squirrel', each person sealed in their own world of pain. When we got to the crematorium courtyard we found it lined by dozens of young people, boys and girls in motorcycle leathers with their crash helmets on the crook of their elbows." At this point Richard's voice broke and the tears so long buried began to run down his cheeks. "We sat on hard wooden pews and listened as a vicar told us about the life that was Nick's. Nicholas's life story had to be told for him Walter, not for him the luxury of being able to edit, distort or delete any of the happenings of the last nineteen years. Then we sang and we prayed and then came the dreaded moment and the coffin began to move away from us. It moved very slowly. I'm not sure if I was the only one who wanted to dash forward to drag it back, to pull the hand of fate away, but I stayed where I was and forward the coffin went, forward ever forward and through the curtains. Last goodbyes were whispered and then the curtains closed and he was gone, a quiet and good boy taken from us, why Walter why?" Silent for so long Walter finally spoke.

"I don't know why the good and the young are taken from us Richard." he whispered "but there's an old adage that goes 'God moves in mysterious ways'. He deals us a hand of cards and we have to play them as best we can Richard. Some hands we win and some we lose. I've also heard it said that whilst some people win and some people lose there are those who don't even get a game." For some reason Walter's words of banality seemed somehow to touch Richard's rationality and smiling he sat up and affirming that Nick had played hard and had been happy got to his feet and moved to the BBQ pit "So Walter" he announced as yet another log found its way onto the fire "I guess I should learn from him and be happy. After all I've had a good number of cards dealt to me in my life time."

"And you've won a fair few hands?" Walter suggested. Agreeing but adding that it didn't always feel that way Richard told Walter that more cards had been dealt to him a few weeks later.

"They were?" Walter asked

"Oh yes," Richard told him "Joan announced that she wanted to return to South Africa."

"And so you left the UK again?"

"No Walter we didn't, for the first and maybe last time in my life I asserted myself."

"You did what? Walter asked in amazement.

"I asserted myself Walter." Richard repeated as Walter rolled himself from his lounger and standing moved to join his friend by the fire.

"Tell me more" he asked as Richard unsure if he was being ironic or not gave him a long hard look and then giving him the benefit of the doubt told him that he and Joan had started to attend church.

"Church?" Walter questioned "I didn't know that you were religious." Telling him that religious was pushing it a bit far Richard admitted that he had always had a deep seated faith that there was a heaven and a God who loves him. "Anyway" he continued "The average age of the congregation at the church was... god!" he said coming to a sudden conclusion. "Those people must have been as old as I am now. Just where has the time gone?"

"On trips back and forth to South Africa I guess." Walter suggested unhelpfully and then asked how the words of the song had gone. "Regrets I've had a few but then again...?"

"But then again" Richard told him wryly, "too bloody many to mention."

"No" Walter reminded him "the words are 'too few to mention' and you know it. Now just cut the poor me stuff and tell me your story." Grinning Richard moved to the table and picking up the wine bottle returned to Walter's side.

"But sixty plus Walter," he said as he began to refill their glasses "the average age of the congregation was sixty plus but bless them they were thrilled to have our young family in their midst and they did everything they could to make us welcome and" he added as he lifted his glass as if in salute to absent friends "the next chapter of my life started at that point."

Lifting his glass Walter told Richard that he hoped that he didn't sound flippant but he said "I just can't wait."

"Three weeks ago" Richard told him "I might have found your words flippant but now...well I'm just glad you're here to listen."

"Oh please Richard," Walter smiled as he clinked his glass against Richards "the pleasure is mine."

"Now Walter" Richard complained as he stirred the coals of the fire back to life "that really was flippant, but I'll let it pass. Anyway" he continued "The people at church helped us to find a house not far from my parent's home and they also got me an interview at a local Children's Home.

"So Lady Fate was back with you Richard" Walter laughed. "Now, I wonder if she still knows where you live" he mused "because as things are I think you could do with a little of her help right now."

"Indeed" Richard dismissed, "however I travelled the ten miles by bus to the job interview. In fact" he added "I travelled on three buses and the journey took me just over forty five minutes."

"Good old public transport." Walter enthused with irony.

"But it was better than walking!" Richard said stating a truth "and I was interviewed in an oak lined office by the head master and his deputy. 'The children here', they told me are assessed as being Educationally Sub Normal (ESN).'"

"Educationally Sub normal," Walter gasped "what a dreadful label to give a child, and it was probably a label that stayed with them for the rest of their lives?"

"Too true" Richard agreed "but there are two pieces of good news for the wearers of those particular labels."

"And they are?" Walter asked in surprise.

"Well for one Walter, a few years earlier these children would have been labelled as 'cretins'."

"And your second piece of good news Richard?"

"Well the 'ESN' label would be changed to 'Children with Special Educational Needs'."

"Mmm well isn't that nice for then?" Walter grinned to which Richard replied that he was getting good at irony and that he was given the job. Impressed by the one interview one job statement Walter slowly applauded his friend.

"I'm not sure if it had anything to do with me Walter." Richard told him "Although my work with the scouts in South Africa and my time as a Methodist Sunday school superintendent may have helped. The nod from my church friends certainly would have helped. So I had a job, the hours were from early morning until ten thirty at night and for five days a week and on a minimum wage." Protesting Walter told Richard that he was doing himself a disservice and Richard thanking him told him that they would have been pleased to appoint anyone who could walk upright and speak English. "Anyway I began my new role of 'residential social worker' on a cold and wet March morning. The children I worked with were challenging, but not half as challenging as some of the staff. The first set of 'seniors' I worked with, a husband and wife team, were an absolute nightmare."

"They were?" Walter question as he unsuccessfully stifled a yawn and then began to move towards the table.

"They were Walter" Richard confirmed as glass in hand he followed in Walter's wake. "It was like being in the army, the children's beds had to be made in a certain way. Their uniforms had to be removed and their shoes polished as soon as they came in from school and then they had to help make tea." Telling Richard that a bit of organisation and discipline never did anyone any harm Walter then suggested that the regime must surely have been good for the children. And Richard, telling Walter that discipline was indeed fine "But Walter it was the way it was done, the children weren't asked to take their uniforms off they were told or 'commanded' and in truth things weren't much better for the staff, 'do this and do that', not 'could you please' or 'when you have a minute'.

"So you didn't like the job Richard?

"Oh I loved the job Walter." "Richard told him "and fate was still with me because after two months I was given a 'House Group' and thirteen children of my own to look after. Joan was offered a job and we all moved into a nice self contained flat."

"And did you see much of Joan and the boys?" Walter asked.

"Yes up to a point," Richard told him "Through the day Joan and I saw each other in passing, but by eleven o'clock at night we were too tired to do anything and so as the years progressed the 'not doing' things together developed into single beds."

"Bloody hell Richard, I wasn't expecting that." Walter said chocking on his drink. "Will you try and warn me when bomb shells are about to be dropped?"

"I'll try." Richard grinned.

"Thank you." told him.

"So Walter, in our attempt to mend our relationship we bought a house and although we had single beds at the school at home we shared a double and more."

"I'm tempted to ask more what Richard but you'd best carry on." Walter suggested.

"And," Richard continued, "I started to drinking whiskey. It seemed to help and our pretence at being a happy family continued for several more years. Staff came and staff went and I went to university to study social work and to learn how to do my job."

"Good move, how did you pull that one off?"

"I was seconded to the course by the school governors Walter. They must have see either my potential as a social worker or perhaps they thought that I still had much to learn. Anyway going to university was one of the best things I have ever done."

"Was this your first time at University?" Walter asked.

"It was Walter." Richard told him. "When I was a boy I went to a junior school and then a 'Secondary Modern'. I don't remember being asked if I wanted to sit the 'eleven plus' and my education ended on my fifteenth birthday."

"Oh not the old I walked out of school on a Friday and was working the following Monday?" Walter grinned.

"The very one" Richard told him "but I'm not complaining, what's the point. But I would have liked to know what happened to other people's aspirations for me. I don't remember anyone saying to me 'come on lad you can do anything if you put your mind to it'. Do you think" Richard said pausing "that this has anything to do with who I am or who I think I am now Walter?" he asked. Pointing out that it was certainly upsetting him now Walter then suggested that it had indeed played a part in his emotional make up.

"Have I told you this before Walter?" Richard asked earnestly as he lifted the nearly empty wine bottle and offered Walter the last drops.

"I won't know until you tell me what it is Richard will I?" Walter said reasonably and lifting his still half full glass declined the dregs.

"True." Richard conceded "Anyway" he said "There was this tutor on my social work course who asked the class how they thought other people saw them and I told him that I thought people saw me as confident and competent."

"And?" Walter asked although he now remembered hearing the story before.

"Well" Richard told him "The tutor said that when I was feeling brave enough I should come and see him and he would tell me the truth."

"And what the hell did that mean?" Walter asked and Richard, his mood a mixture of anger and regret confessed that he didn't know and still didn't know.

"I didn't go back to ask him Walter, but his words are still with me and jump out at me whenever I start to feel 'confident' or 'competent'. The bastard, why did he say that, why burst my balloon, why, why, why?"

"Steady Richard" Walter cautioned "you're beginning to lose it." And Richard was beginning to lose it.

"Fuck 'it' Walter, fuck it" he growled. Calmly draining the last of his wine Walter got to his feet.

"Now Richard, come on take it easy." he calmed as he placed his empty glass on the BBQ side "We've had a good day so let's not spoil it now." and with that he began to move towards the house. Then he turned. "Are you coming?" he asked.

"I'll just have five minutes more Walter." Richard told him his mood already a little calmer. "I'll see you in the morning. And Walter." he added "thanks."

Sitting in the quiet of the garden Richard replayed his conversation with Walter and thought about his life and the mistakes he had made. He thought about his love for Grace and his desire for Gabriella. Then, getting to his feet he returned to the house and made his way down to the office. Picking up the telephone he first dialled Grace's number but hearing the answer machine asking for his name he replaced the hand set and dialled John's number. Again he was asked to leave a message. Cursing his luck Richard poured himself a generous measure of Jack Daniels and made his lonely way to bed.

CHAPTER 41
Sunday 18th January 2010 (Morning)

Adam

Disorientated and lost she was aware that something was not as it should be. Turning slowly in the bed she put out her hand and felt for the comfort of her mobile phone. Lifting the device from the bedside table she pressed the menu button, her action causing the room to be illuminated in it's gentle and reassuring glow. Rolled onto her back she sat up and swinging her legs to the tiled floor wrapped the red cotton sheet around her shoulders and padded slowly across the floor and to the window and pushing the heavy curtains aside she looked out. In front of her the Atlantic Ocean stood still and calm and in the near distance a dozen ships stood at anchor as they awaited their turn to enter Cape Town's harbour. Beyond the ships the infamous Robben Island loomed whilst to her right the tall buildings of Bloubergstrand announced the hope of a new South Africa. Just how long had it been since she and Richard had visited the Blue Peter she asked herself as she lowered her eyes to the promenade below and watched as a lone jogger weaved her way between the mingling crowds. At the sound of the door handle turning the woman quickly made her way back to the bed.
"Morning did you sleep well?" the man asked as he stood at the bedroom door a breakfast tray covering any embarrassment he may have felt. Tall and in his early forties the man, his slimness disguised the obvious strength of his frame. "I thought we'd have our breakfast in bed and then see what the day has to offer. What do you say?" he asked.

"I say great and thanks." the woman smiled as she lifted the bed sheet to hide her nakedness.

"Shy" the man asked as he raised an eyebrow in mock surprise

"No" the woman lied "not shy but cold."

"So I noticed." he told her with a nod towards the round firmness of his lover's protruding nipples.

"Oh Adam please." she pleaded as she tugged the folds of the sheet ever tighter across her breasts

Grinning lecherously Adam placed the breakfast tray in the bedside "Oh please nothing Gabi" he told "you're a good looking woman, and a very sexy lady."

The previous night Adam Western had proved himself to be a caring and attentive lover, his gentleness taking Gabriella to place she had never been before. Her experience of other men had not been unfulfilling, her husband had been caring and yes he had loved her dearly and Richard had been gentle, but with Adam it had been different. The pace of his love making had been special. Adam's obvious willingness to wait for her permission to move on, to move on from the hand holding as he had walked her from the flat to his car, to the stolen kisses at the restaurant. His willingness to wait, to wait for signs that she was ready for him to place his hand on her thigh as he drove her back to her flat. And his skill in knowing when she was ready to move from coffee making in the kitchen to love making in his bedroom. Adam had also been an attentive listener, listening to her as she talked about Michael and Richard and about her sadness, her loneliness and her fears.

"And you sir are beautiful." She said smiling up at him.

"Beautiful! Don't let the guys back in Oz hear you say that or I'll never be able to go in a straight bar again."

"You're beautiful Adam," Gabriella smiled as she pulled back the sheet inviting him to join her. "You're beautiful and I love you."

An hour later a happy Gabriella made her contented way to the bathroom to shower and dress for the day ahead.

CHAPTER 42
Monday 25th January (Morning)

Rose Two

The sun had renewed its journey into a clear blue sky as Richard, climbing out of bed broke for the first time in a long time his morning routine. Mornings had never been a favourite part of his day, his bed always seeming to keep him occupied for longer than it should. With his appointment with Rose Freeman scheduled for ten and having seen Walter and Gabriella in the pool and *enjoying* their morning dips he persuaded himself, against his better judgement, to give it one more try. There was no sign of Walter as he made his way carefully into the water, the coldness reminding him why he didn't like swimming, but telling himself that *'Once you get your shoulders under the water things will get a little more bearable'* he rolled onto his back and headed for deeper water. Deeper water for Richard had always been the place where he could swim, but still be able to touch the bottom of the pool. But today, like most days when he swam he misjudged the point of no return and sank, splashing and panicking beneath the water. Kicking and coughing he made his way to the pool's side and grabbing for the edge looked round him to see if anyone had seen his distress.

"Morning Mr Toad missed our lily pad did we?" a grinning Walter asked. Coughing the water from the back of his throat Richard looked up into his grinning face and wishing him a 'good morning' told him to 'come in the water's dangerous'. Confident in his own abilities Walter dived from the pools edge into its deepest depths and turning expertly popped up beside Richard and told him "I don't mind if I do." Spluttering and coughing Richard slowly breast stroked his way to the steps and vowing that someday he'd 'master this swimming malarkey' climbed from the water. "And then Walter" he tried to convince himself "perhaps I'll start to enjoy the water more. Still," he added self-righteously "I've been in the pool and can enjoy my breakfast tea with pride."

"Really," Walter told him as he watched Richard drip his way towards a lounger "I'd have thought you've swallowed enough liquid for one day." And then laughing said he'd join him in a minute. Picking up his towel Richard rubbed dry his short white hair and with the towel wrapped around his waist lay down in the warm sun to dry.

"Now that's why I like swimming Walter" he called as he closed his eyes and drifted off to a green and pleasant place.

"Richard, Richard?" the voice called for some way off "Richard." the voice called again and opening one eye Richard Blackwood looked around him. "Richard breakfast is served." a smiling Walter told him.

"Already Walter I thought you were swimming?" Richard said as he eased himself onto one elbow.

"And swim I did Richard." Walter told him as he placed a tray on the pool side table "and then made us a full English breakfast whilst you've been..." and then he paused. "Just where do you go to in these dreams of yours?" he asked. "You must have been out for a good half an hour."

"Really, gosh" Richard said in surprise "I must have been tired, I'd better start taking things easy."

"Easy?" Walter laughed mockingly. "An early morning swim and then breakfast served on a tray. Just how easy do you want it my man?"

"Just as easy as I can get it Walter."

"Oh you'll be old before your time if you carry on like this fella" Walter told him as he sat down and took the lid off the oven dish.

"Get old - me!" Richard snorted as he moved to join Walter at the table. "Never, I'm going to live forever."

"Ok Methuselah." Walter humoured. "So what delights have you for me today?"

An hour and a half later Richard found himself sitting once more, eyes closed and hands behind his head as he tried, (in vain) to avoid the gaping cleavage of Rose Freeman's receptionist. Luckily he had only to endure the pain for few minutes before Rose came out of her office and crossing the floor, took his hand and asked him if he would like some tea. Thanking her Richard acknowledged her gesturing hand and followed her into her office.

"Come sit by the window Richard" Rose invited as she ran her hands down the back of her skirt and then sat, feet together and hands on lap in a position that Richard's mother would have called 'lady like'. "So Richard" she asked without preamble "how have you been?"

"Keeping busy Rose" Richard told her as the door opened and Alice came briskly into the room carrying a tea tray.

"Just pop it down there." Rose commanded without looking up and doing as she was bid Alice turned and left the room.

"I heard about the kidnapping Richard" Rose told him as the door quietly closed behind a quiet Alice. "Is Steven alright?" she asked and bend forward she began to pour tea.

"Yes Rose he was shaken up but other than a black eye and some bruising he's remarkably well. Did I tell you that my friend Walter is here from the UK?" Richard continued not really wanting to remember or talk about the events of that particular day. Confirming that Richard had mentioned Walter's visit and that she was pleased to hear about Steven, Rose asked if Richard could remember their last conversation. He told her 'yes' and that it had been about his relationship with Gabriella.

"She's seeing someone at the moment Rose." Richard found himself saying and then feeling silly he picked up his tea cup and sipped.

"And how do you feel about that Richard?" Rose asked in her best therapy voice.

"Upset." Richard told her. When I found out about Gabriella's man I was really upset Rose."

"Upset?" Rose asked her eye brows rising as she spoke.

"Yes Rose I was and a little angry and frightened."

"Fear and anger Richard?" Rose echoed as she leaned forward and spooned sugar into her cup.

"So what did you find frightening?" Quietly Richard sat and stared back at his therapist and wondered why he hadn't asked himself that question before.

"That's a good question Rose." he finally said as he rested the two fingers of his right hand against his temple. "Fear of loss?" he said slowly. "Fear of being alone Rose but that would be a silly wouldn't it?"

"Why do you say silly Richard?" Rose asked.

"Well because we are never alone. There's always someone telephoning me or getting in our way when I'm trying to get somewhere."

"Perhaps the word you wanted was lonely?" Rose questioned.

"Fear of being lonely?" Richard repeated "No I don't think I fear being lonely Rose, in fact I like my own space."

"Now isn't that interesting Richard, if it isn't a fear of being lonely or being alone what else could make you fearful?" Again Richard took his time to answer.

"You know Rose" he finally said "I think it may have something to do with my self esteem, perhaps I take people leaving me as personal."

"And have you been deserted by many people?"

"Deserted Rose" Richard pondered "Now isn't the English language fascinating. I say people leave me and you use the word deserted."

"I guess I could have used the word abandoned Richard. If Gabriella leaves will you feel abandoned?"

"Abandoned Rose, for me that word has connotations of a small child being abandoned by a parent or a pet being abandoned by its owner."

"Go on." Rose told him as she leaned forward and replaced her tea cup.

"Go on where Rose?" Richard asked. "Where are you taking me?"

"Just talk to me Richard, abandoned, do I feel like an abandoned child?" For some seconds Richard didn't answer, couldn't answer as he sought to identify his feelings and thoughts.

"For some reason Rose" he started to say and then stopped.

"Tell me Richard." Rose encouraged quietly.

"Well for some reason I feel suddenly sad, strange eh?" Richard questioned.

"Maybe Richard" Rose answered noncommittally "but pray won't you continue."

"Well when I first came to this country I remember hearing the words from Gershwin's Porgy and Bess.

"Which words Richard?"

"'The words 'sometimes I feel like a motherless child' Rose and come to think of it that song went through my head when I went back home on the day Steven had been kidnapped. I really thought they'd killed him Rose, I really did and I felt so lost and lonely."

"Are we saying?" Rose questioned "That when you heard that Gabriella had met someone you felt abandoned, lost and lonely?"

"Again that would be silly," Richard repeated as he got to his feet and walked to the window "I'm not a child and Gabriella is not my mother is she?"

"I didn't ask you who Gabriella was Richard," Rose told him "what I did ask you was how you feel about Gabriella leaving." Lifting his eyes from his street gazing Richard turned and returned to his chair.

"Oh Rose I don't know what I felt other than frightened and angry." Richard apologised

"Okay Richard I don't want you worry about it and our time is just about up. So I want you to go away and think about what we've discussed?"

"Think about my feelings of being abandoned, lost and lonely" Richard clarified "and if in fact I do feel that way then why? Yes I think I can do that Rose." he added with a grin.

"Ah Richard, the joy of therapy Richard is always leave them wanting more!" Rose smiled as she led him to the door. Unsure of Rose's philosophy of leaving them wanting Richard smiled back and told her that he did want more.

"You know Rose." he said as he loitered in the doorway "I can't believe that I haven't worked this out before." and Rose, unwilling to continue the conversation away from the privacy of her office told Richard that she had other clients to see.

"Alice" she demanded as she moved back into her office "give Mr Blackwood an appointment for early next week please?" and then she was gone.

Walking down the well lit corridor to the lift Richard looked at the console in front of him. "Up to the team or down and home?" he asked himself and then pressed the button.

CHAPTER 43
Monday 25th January (Afternoon)

It Never Occurred to Me

Reaching home Richard found Walter in the kitchen making lunch. "Soup and sandwiches" Walter told him before asking how it had gone with Rose. "Very interesting," Richard said "and it never ceases to amaze me how much we don't know about ourselves."

"So it was a positive session then?" Walter asked as he poured hot tomato soup into two 'willow pattern' bowls and placed them on a tray.

"I think so Walter" Richard claimed as he picked up a bowl and holding it to his nose and sniffed. "But Rose has left me with an awful lot of thinking to do. Is this Heinz?" he asked.

"It is indeed it is my friend" Walter told him "nothing but the best for Mr. B you know." Pleased with the remark Richard following Walter out onto the patio.

"And how was your morning Walter?" he asked as he settled himself at the table.

"It was quiet," Walter replied as he blew across his spoon. "I read a little and swam a little. The usual holiday stuff you know?"

With a note of concern in his voice Richard asked if Walter was getting bored

"A little" Walter told him "but it's nice to have some quiet time. Not that you're noisy Richard." he back tracked and then searched his friend's face for signs of annoyance. Telling him 'steady Walter and that he had only asked how his morning had been Richard laughed.

"I think we're both doing too much thinking" he said before suggesting that they eat their soup before it got cold.

"I popped in to see the team this morning Walter." Richard said as he ran a piece of bread along the edge of his bowl.

"Gee that was brave of you Richard," Walter told him "how were they?"

"Oh pretty much as always." Richard sighed "Still arguing but still getting the job done."

"And how's Gabriella?" Walter asked the interest in his voice clear to both men.

"She was out on business Walter, Scarlet has left to have the baby and Amy and Chris are sharing the team leadership, which means that Gabriella had to spend a lot more of her time acting a referee."

"Well you can't allow that to go on for much longer Richard." Walter said stating the obvious, "And what about your own clients?"

"Being looked after, but it's time I got back to work full time Walter." Laying down his spoon Walter looked across at his friend and asked if Richard thought he was ready to take on other people's problems.

"I think others people's problems might be a dammed sight easier to deal with than our own" Richard grinned. "And I've put off my return for long enough and to be honest if I don't get back soon I never will. Which" he added "reminds me. I've got two appointments next week Walter do you fancy joining me, it may relieve some of your boredom."

When Walter had told Richard that he had spent his morning reading and swimming he had been a little economical with the truth. He had in fact telephoned Gabriella, his first contact for some time. The conversation had been a difficult one and full of awkward silences. Gabriella had talked about her loneliness and about Richard's continued commitment to Grace. Walter had tried to find the right words to help her but on reflection he had been a little too searching and perhaps his questions were more about his needs than hers. Then she had cried, the sound of her tears cutting him deeply, for now Walter realised just how much he loved her.

"So Mr Walter it looks like we're on our own again." Richard laughed and then, as if he had some kind of mind reading skill proclaimed that 'he knew when he wasn't wanted."Anyway" he added "who needs a woman in their life?" and as he spoke the words 'I do' came instantly into both men's mind. Unsmiling and solemn Walter asked if he was sure. "Of course," he lied "Why do you ask?"

"Because" Walter told him "I know so little about women. I met and married Barbara when I was seventeen and I never looked at other women during all the time we were together."

"Never looked or never touched?" Richard asked casually.

"Oh I maybe looked" Walter admitted "but never touched "I loved Barbara so I had no reason to look at or touch other women."

"And since Barbara"

"Since Barbara died?" Walter questioned and suddenly feeling and looking awkward asked if the conversation was turning into a sex therapy session.

"If it is pal" Richard said "then I'm not sure who is client and who the therapist. Do you want to talk?" he asked suddenly aware of Walter's defensiveness and discomfort.

"Talk about what?" Walter asked.

"I don't know, women?" Richard suggested.

"Why would I want to talk about women Richard?"

"I'm not sure old friend and if I've crossed a line I'm sorry. It's just that we've known each other for so long and I thought I sensed..."

"Hell Richard, you and your perceptions." Walter scowled and annoyed and stung by Richard's sudden intrusion into his private life asked him if he was never off duty. Now it was Richard's turn to be defensive.

"Hang on Walter" he blustered "there's no need to be like that. I didn't mean to..."

"Didn't mean to what?" Walter snapped "Delve into my pathetic and desperate attempts at socialising. I've had one woman in my life Richard and would have been loyal and faithful to her for the rest of my life. That's if fate hadn't decided she was too good for me and taken her from me. Shit Richard I miss Barbara so much, sometimes I get so lonely." Getting to his feet Richard moved around the table to where Walter sat head in hands. "Sorry Walter" he repeated "what brought this on, has someone hurt you?"

"No Richard" Walter told him "not someone, people don't hurt me I hurt myself the stupid, stupid man that I am."

"Come on" Richard pleaded" tell me. We both know that holding thing in never helps?"

"Yes" Walter agreed "and we both know that baring ones soul can leave one looking like a right twit."

"Okay my friend enough." Richard told him as he placed his hand on Walter's shoulders. "It's time for honesty. You know you can trust me, just as I trusted you. It's obvious that some woman has messed you about and hurt you."

"No Richard you're wrong." Walter told him and then the name was out of his mouth. "It's not any woman, Richard it's... Gabriella." he said and pushing his chair back from the table Walter got to his feet and walked away.

"Gabriella's the woman who has hurt you," Richard asked in disbelief "I don't believe it, not my Gabriella?"

"No Richard not your Gabriella and not my Gabriella."

"Then whose." Richard asked.

"I don't know whose" Walter told him "and it doesn't matter whose. What I do know is that Gabriella has needs and that she's been on her own for far too long."

"No Walter." Richard argued angrily, "I've always been there for her she only needs to ask..."

"Richard you ass, are you blind?" Walter hissed "Do you expect Gabriella to come to you and say, *'Excuse me Richard but I have needs can you help.*" Slowly, very slowly Richard felt the dawning move over his face

"Needs Walter," he finally said, "those needs?"

"Yes Richard those needs" Walter told him "needs like yours and mine. Surely you haven't got to the age you are without recognising that women have the same needs as men? Tell me I'm wrong Richard, please tell me I'm wrong." Sinking wearily into his empty chair Richard closed his eyes and dropped his head.

"It never occurred to me Walter, not once that women...that Grace that Gabriella, that women ... *wanted* sex, I've always assumed that they were meeting our needs." and then Richard Blackwood drifted off into silence.

CHAPTER 44
Tuesday 26th January (Morning)

Pain Recrimination and Sadness

Today would be Richard's first day back at work since Steven's kidnapping. Rising early he was glad that Walter would be travelling into work with him and hopefully make his return easier. Parking in his reserved bay Richard led the way into the lobby and after introductions to the security guards took Walter up to the Emotional Solution suite. Introducing him to first Rachael and then the rest of the team Richard settled Walter into the work space vacated by Scarlet and went in search of Gabriella. Together they spent an hour getting Richard up the speed, but any attempts by him to elicit information about where Gabriella was staying proved fruitless. At ten thirty he walked down to the team's office where he found Walter deep in animated conversation with Amy. Breaking into their debate, something to do with the merits of same sex interviews, Richard invited Walter to join him for his eleven o'clock appointment with Raymond Taylor. At eleven fifteen Richard picked up the internal telephone and asked Rachael if the Taylors had made contact. They had not and telling Rachael not to worry and he'd ring them himself Richard picked up the still slim client file and led Walter down the corridor to the kitchenette.

"Not the greatest start on my first day back eh Walter." he said as he gave the kettle a shake to assess the water level and assured that there was enough water for at least two cups of coffee flicked the switch downwards.

"So do you get many no shows Richard?" Walter asked as he settled himself at the Formica table and pulling the file toward him began to read.

"No happily not." Richard told him. "But this case in particularly is worrying. The poor lad is being swamped by his mother and I think both he and his mother know it. And sadly" he said and the phone began to ring "there could be some quite serious consequences if the situation isn't sorted soon." Picking up the phoned Richard listened and then uttered a 'yes I understand.' and an okay do you want me to ring her' replaced the instrument.

Raymond Taylor was waiting nervously outside the Sonstraal Mall as Richard and Walter arrived and on seeing them he walked hurriedly towards their car. Thanking them for coming Raymond told them that he didn't know what to do and Richard, telling him that he had done the right thing invited him for coffee.

An hour of excited and intense talk later Richard and Walter were on our way back to the office. "Well." Walter smiled. "If that was only your second meeting with Ray either he or you are exceptional people."

"Or we both are." Richard said as he eased the car onto the N1 highway. Agreeing 'yes or both of you' then Walter suggested that for Raymond to turn his life around in such a short period of time was remarkable. And Richard agreeing that it was indeed cautioned that Raymond wasn't out of the woods yet.

"He isn't?" Walter asked to which Richard replied that he still had Raymond's mother to convince and Walter, his sense of justice as acute as ever told Richard to 'sod the mother' and that Raymond was an adult and was entitled to his own thoughts. "Not to mention his own life." he added "and I think his decision to move out and move on is a good one. And" he continued "I think your offer of a free place in your therapy house is a good and right one. And may I say Mr Blackwood that you're a good man and don't ever let anyone tell you differently." Smiling Richard thanked him and then explained that when he had first met Ray's mother he had thought that she was the one in need of help.

"So Walter" Richard explained as they wound their way through the wine farms of Durbanville Hills "it's a good job you're here because I don't think Mrs. Taylor is going to want to take any advice from me. Now" he said as the tanks of the Caltex oil refinery came into view "have you had a chance to read the Marchant file?"

Twenty minutes later Shirley Marchant was welcoming the two men into her home and garden, the warmth of the welcome making Richard even less confident that she would be willing to engage in any meaningful discussions about changes to her own life. Yet in less than an hour he was back in the Audi and asking how wrong a man could be.

"Do we work with right and wrong?" Walter asked as he made notes in the Marchant file. Telling his friend 'no' Richard then wondered aloud on how Walter had got Shirley to talk about her mother and husband. "And" he added "your selling her the idea of writing a book about her life was well, it was nothing short of genius."

"Genius that's a bit strong." Walter said as he grinned sheepishly across at his friend. "But the session did go well don't you think and I'm quite looking forward to the next session. So who's next?" he asked.

"Next" Richard told him "there will be no next today it's back home for us before we get stuck in the rush hour traffic."

Arriving back at the house Walter went to take his evening dip whilst Richard, feeling the need for music moved to the piano and sitting down began to play. Half an hour later Walter came into the lounge recognising 'The Way We Were' began to whistle tunelessly. No longer able to hear the melody Richard struggled to the end of the piece and then swivelling in his seat moved to the sideboard and poured two glasses of red wine. For the next hour the two men chatted amicably about Walter and his first day at the office and about Amy and her battle with Chris. They then moved on to discuss the Taylors and the best way forward for both mother and son and finally the subject of the intransigent Shirley Marchant came up. "The way you got her to open up Walter was amazing" Richard praised "and your idea about her writing a book was nothing but a master stroke. It's just a pity you can't do the same with Gabriella." he added.

"It is." Walter agreed his earlier conversation with her still painfully fresh in his mind.

"You know I tried to talk to her this morning Walter but she just kept dragging the discussion back to work."

"Ah!" Walter interjected and then wished he hadn't as Richard, reading more into his 'Ah!' than he had intended asked him what 'Ah' meant.

"Ah!" Walter repeated and then knowing that he would be unable to keep his conversation with Gabriella secret any longer told Richard about his telephone call.

"You spoke to her?" Richard asked in surprise.

"Briefly."

"And?"

"Nothing really Richard, I just asked her if she was alright and when she was coming home."

"And?" Richard repeated.

"Well I don't really know, she said something about wanting time to think."

"Think about what?"

""I don't know she said something about wanting to spend time with a friend in Cape Town."

"Did she say which friend?" Richard asked his jealously starting to rise.

"Not directly" Walter told him "but she did mention Adam's name, remember the guy she asked us to meet, the University guy?"

Shit." Richard cursed "I knew that bastard was up to something."

"But you've never met the man Richard." Walter told him reasonably but Richard didn't want to be reasonable and cursing once more told Walter that he had known that Gabriella would leave him at some point. "Women always do." he said and repeating his 'shit' he got to his feet and stalked to the door. "Fucking women." he cursed for the third time. "They screw you and then they leave you, fuck 'um."

"Now Richard let's not go down that road." Walter begged as he moved to Richard's side and placed his hand on his shoulder.

"And which road is that" Richard ranted as he brushed the hands away, "the one that leads me to rejection and loneliness? Damn it Walter what the hell is wrong with me. I've tried to do my best. I thought I was giving

Grace my best too but obviously my best wasn't good enough. Maybe the truth is that *I'm* not good enough eh." Trying to hide his own pain and sadness Walter started to tell Richard that there was nothing wrong with him. "I could list your fine points, you goodness and your decency, but if I did you would just deny them. But you can't have it all ways Richard, either you're a bastard or you're a decent man. Now come on fella help me out here, either we deal with the past, or..."

"Or what Walter," Richard cursed angrily. "You'll abandon me too?"

"Piss off Richard." Walter blasted his patience at an end. "I don't have to take this crap from you Richard. So you've got some pain well here is the news, so have I. Now deal with it, just fucking deal with it." For several minutes the room was quiet

"Okay" Richard finally said "I'm sorry. It seems that I'm going to have to learn to separate the pleasure of conversation from the pain and from therapy. You know that I didn't mean to hurt you or ruin your day or anybody else day for that matter...it's just that."

"No Richard" Walter told him as lowered his now weary frame on to the sofa "my day was ruined when Gabriella told me about her new man. But that's life, so what do you say, shall we start again and get your past sorted?"

"But it's the here and now that I need to sort out" Richard protested as he moved towards the piano "not the past." and sitting down began to play 'Here Comes That Rainy Day'. Hearing the melancholy tones Walter got to his feet and crossing the room lifted the music book from its stand and gently closed it.

"Don't start with the sad stuff Richard," he pleaded and placing the book on the piano top he sat down next to Richard and put his arm around his shoulder. It was a kindness too far and slowly Richard's tears began to roll down his cheeks. His tears of loss, regret and hopelessness all mingling into one all consuming flood of remorse. "They always leave me Walter" he finally said. "Just as Grace left me, you will leave and Gabriella." and then, as quickly as the tears had started they stopped. "My Granddad died Walter, I loved him, but he died and my heart was broken. Heartbroken now what the hell does that mean and what happens to the hearts and minds of the living when a loved one dies, all that emptiness what is it? Oh why oh why do the people we love leave us?"

"Well that's a big one Richard." Walter said after several seconds' silence. "Childlike we would want to say 'it's not fair' but as an adults we already know that life isn't fair, so I guess in reality none of us will ever understand or want to understand death. People leave us and they will continue to leave us, in death, in divorce or just to get on with their 'own' lives." Again the men sat in silence, each of them feeling their own losses. "Are you ok Richard?" Walter finally asked.

"Yes, I'm fine." Richard told him.

"Fine, I doubt it?" Walter smiled.

"You know what I mean." Richard grinned back.

"I do indeed." Walter told him

"When I lost my granddad Walter the tears I cried were the first that I remember crying in grief or loss. And thinking back those tears where silent tears. There was no sobbing or wailing, do you know what I mean?" he asked.

"Oh yes Richard, I've just seen the self same tears. Real tears, but fleeting tears it's as if you fear to cry, why is that do you think? I mean what's wrong with crying?"

"Oh I don't know" Richard confessed, "maybe I see tears as just a waste of time and energy or a perhaps a sign of weakness."

"Or perhaps, "Walter added. "You think that if you start to cry you'll never be able to stop?" Admitting that Walter could be right Richard suggested that in the world there was much to cry about.

"So perhaps you're right and if I hide my tears and I hide my fears and hide my feelings then maybe the world won't get me?"

"Richard, Richard my dear friend." Walter sighed "Don't you know that no matter where you go and no matter what you do the world will always be there. So what we have to do is focus on what this wonderful world has to offer us."

"Sounds like a good idea Walter." Richard acknowledged.

"Good," Walter smiled as he got to his feet and walked towards the door. "So on that happy note sir, I'll wish you good night."

"Walter"

"Yes?" Richard.

"Thank you."

"It was my pleasure sir." Walter told him and then, not wanting to go back down the road of sadness and recrimination added that they had done enough soul searching for one day.

"Oh I think so Walter." Richard smiled "and probably enough for a lifetime or two."

CHAPTER 45
Thursday 26th January 2010 (Morning)

Katie Benjamin

Richard hadn't slept well his sleep disturbed by thoughts, worries and fearful and vivid dreams. Several times in the night he had been woken by his heart beating against his chest and by the morning his pillow was soaked with sweat. At seven thirty, heaving decided to J.F.D.I. (Just Fucking Do It) he picked up the telephone and invited himself to lunch with Katie. Arriving at the security gate the now alert security guard waved him through and steering the Audi up the long drive he parked at the front of the house. Today was no happy banter about wives or loved ones, just a firm hand shake and a meeting of sombre eyes. "Ms Benjamin is by the pool sir," Jacob announced as he closed Richard's door "and she asked me to take you through." Telling Jacob that it was fine and that he could find his own way Richard walked slowly towards the house and out to the pool area. Standing in the shade of the awning he tried to gather his thoughts as he watched the graceful Katie move slowly through the water. Then, suddenly feeling like a peeping Tom, Richard coughed and in a voice that was a little too loud wished Katie a 'good morning'. Startled Katie dived under the water and made her way to the edge of the pool. Asking Richard to pass her towel she reached up and with a manicured hand covering her cleavage took the over sized towel from him. Embarrassed by her action Richard apologised and said that Jacob had asked him to come through. Telling him that it was 'fine' Katie swung her legs out of the pool and wrapping the beach towel around her shoulders asked Richard how his day at Boschendal had gone"

"Dangerous," Richard told her "you know how things can get out of hand when drink is available and the sun is hot?" Smiling her understanding Katie led the way to the kitchen and clicking on the kettle asked Richard if he would make coffee whilst she went to change.

"I wanted to talk to you about Grace." Richard said as Katie returned wearing a long and lose fitting shift, her still damp hair and pulled back from her face.

"I'd love to hear about Grace Richard, Gabriella said she was…"

"What?" Richard asked suddenly feeling defensive.

"That she was one of us." Katie explained.

"So… what did she mean by that?" Richard hesitated.

"Well" Kate explained again "I think she meant that Grace was a strong and kind woman."

"Ah and Gabriella would be right," Richard announced as he placed two coffee cups on the table. "Grace is indeed a fabulous woman. Want one?" he asked. Declining the coffee Kate told Richard that she'd have wine and inviting him to sit outside took a wine bottle from the rack. Settling herself into a sun lounger Katie looked thoughtfully at her glass and then coming to a sudden conclusion took a sip of her wine. "You know Richard," and said quietly I've never been sure about you and …"

"Never been sure about me and what Katie?" Richard asked as he eased himself into an adjacent lounger and adjusted the back rest.

"I've never been sure about you and well..." again Katie hesitated.

"Go on." Richard encouraged.

"Well …about you and women Richard."

"Me and women?" Richard echoed

"Yes" Kate confirmed "I've never been quite sure about you and Gabriella or you and Grace, not to mention you and me?"

"Gosh Katie you make me sound like a beast or mad man." Richard flustered.

"No not a beast or mad man Richard."

"Then what?"

"Well...not exactly a womaniser, but you do seem to like women. And you treat us so well that I think it makes us uncomfortable." Laughing with relief Richard described how he had always been a little scared of women. "I certainly don't understand them." he clarified. "So it seems that we need to get to know each other better." Telling him that that would be great Katie pushed herself upright and getting to her feet invited Richard to walk with her.

"Now tell me about Grace." she said and offering Richard her hand pulled him to his feet. Making their way passed the pool they made their way down garden.

"You must know that I've messed up with Grace." Richard began. "And I thought you may be willing to help mend it." Telling him that Steven had mentioned his father's difficulties Katie asked how Richard thought she could help.

"Well from what I've seen you're a good listener and to be honest I don't think I need therapy but just a good listening to." Richard told her.

"Thank goodness" Katie told him "for minute I thought you were going to do the old 'my wife doesn't understand me' bit, but yes of course Richard I'd be pleased to help if I can, but first I'd like to know how you of all people manage to screw up a relationship in such a big way."

"Oh you and me both Katie "Richard told her "and all I can say is that we both stopped trying."

"Why?" Katie asked.

"I'm not really sure Katie, but I was telling Walter about a college tutor who asked me how I saw myself and how I had told him that I thought I was calm and confident. The tutor had then told me to come back when I was feeling brave and he would tell me the truth. I never went back."

"You didn't Richard, why not?"

"For the same reason that I don't ask women how they see me." Richard told her.

"Okay so are you saying that you have never asked Grace or Gabriella what they thought about you?"

"No I never have" Richard confessed "does that make me strange?"

"No I guess not." Kate smiled "I know that I don't make a habit of going round asking people how they see me."

"So would you feel uncomfortable if I asked you about your relationship with Steven?" he asked.

"I guess that depends on what you ask Richard but before you do, can I just say that perhaps it's us women and not you who mess up? Grace must have seen something special in you, by all accounts she's no fool." As she spoke Katie pointed towards a garden bench. "Shall we sit?" Seeing the bench, one of those that was used so plenteously in the English parks before the advent of vandalism, Richard's mind was immediately transported back to his boyhood days. "Do you remember the 'Parky'?" he asked. One look at Katie's face would have been enough to tell Richard that she had no idea what he was talking about and wasn't really interested. "They were the old men whose job it was to wave their walking stick at anyone who dared ignore the 'keep of the grass' signs." he continued, oblivious to her blank looks. "Those were the days Katie," he smile "long hot summers, band stands, duck ponds and ice cream."

"Shall we?" Katie asked as if Richard hadn't spoken and inching her kimono upwards sat down.

"No Grace is a very clever woman Katie." Richard confirmed as he took his place next to Steven's latest love and wondered when his memories of park keepers and ducks had become so precious? "And she's an absolute joy to be with, have you seen photos of her Katie?" he asked. Telling him 'of course' Katie then gave him permission to ask his questions. "Although," she added anxiously "I'd be happier talking about Grace than myself."

"Oh I understand" Richard told her "but you're the only independent women that I feel able to talk to. I can't talk to the women at work and Grace and Gabriella are just too close. Does that make sense?" he asked.

"I guess so." Katie told him as she crossed one tanned and elegant leg across the other "Now away you go" she grinned nervously "I can always make something up if I get stuck." Crossing his own legs to mirror her stance Richard coughed and with a hint of apprehension in his voice asked Katie if she loved Steven.

"Gee Richard" Katie laughed uneasily "I wasn't expecting that. "You don't hang about do you?" Apologising Richard asked her if the question had been unfair.

"It was both unfair and unexpected." she told him honestly.

"So do you feel the need to make something up?" he questioned playfully. Telling him 'not yet' Katie Benjamin confessed that she love Steven deeply.

"Why?" Richard asked.

"Because," Katie started to say and then stopped. "Hell Richard," she questioned "are you like this with your clients?"

"I can be Katie" Richard told her "It all depends on my reading of the situation, why do you ask?"

"Because Richard it feels more like an interrogation. It's like talking to inspector Dorrington?"

"So do you feel threatened?"

"No, Richard not threatened just uncomfortable."

"Why?" Richard asked as he continued with his Socratic questioning.

"It's well private isn't it? A relationship between a man and woman is private?"

"It is?" Richard challenged "Well I bet that when you and Gabriella get together you talk about your relationship with Steven. I know you and Gabriella have discussed my relationship Grace, haven't you?"

"Yes but...."

"But what?" Richard asked a little brusquely. Unhappy and uncomfortable with the tone of Richard's questioning Katie got to her feet and turning to face her accuser asked him where all the questioning was taking them. Following Katie's example Richard stood and again apologising told her that he had hoped to get a better understanding of his own shortcomings.

"What I wanted to know" he explained "was well..., if you and Steven have a good relationship how did you manage it and if Steven can have a lasting relationship with a woman why can't I?" Gently placing her hand on his Katie sat down and patting the bench invited Richard to join her.

"How long were you and Grace together?" she asked.

"Nineteen years," Richard told her "nineteen wonderful years but ...well, that relationship is now broken, why Katie, why?"

"Life?" she suggested "or Fate, I don't know." she admitted "Perhaps the hand of god?"

"No Katie" Richard told her as his face slid into a wry smile. "Not the hand of god but the hand of me!"

CHAPTER 46
Thursday 26th January 2010 (Afternoon)

Students and Sex

When Richard arrived home he found Walter at the front door waiting for him.

"Hell Richard where have you been I was worried." he nagged as he walked towards him

"You were worried about me Walter," Richard asked in surprise "Whatever for?"

"Well you did end our chat last night a bit abruptly and then this morning when you didn't come down for work..." Telling him that he was sorry and that he had been to talk to Katie Richard led the way to the kitchen and switched on the kettle.

"Okay I see but why the urgency?" Walter asked as he lifted two mugs from the cupboard and spooned in the coffee.

"Because she's a woman Walter..." Richard told him.

"Yes I had noticed and a very attractive one at that, but why the rush?"

"I just needed a female perspective Walter. I miss talking to Gabriella and well you're a man..." Congratulating his friend on his perception Walter then asked what the topic of conversation had been.

"Grace."

"Ah, Grace." Walter said as knowingly he lifted the kettle from its stand and poured boiling water onto the mugs.

"I miss her..." Richard said simply and Walter, pausing in mid task told him to 'whoa' and then reminded him that the whole point of their nightly sessions was to help him understand his relationship with Grace. "Or so I thought!" he added.

"It is," Richard admitted annoyed by Walter's negativity "but I just wanted a female perspective.

"Okay and had Katie manage to enlighten you?"

"Well to be honest Walter I'm more confused now than I was before."

"You're confused." Walter mocked "but be that as it may are you ready to continue with our conversations and before you ask we were up to the point where you were at university and new staff were coming and going.

"How did you do that?" Richard asked amazed at Walter's powers of recall.

"Oh it's elemental Richard" Walter told him as he carried the two mugs to the table and pulling out a chair sat down. "I make notes after every session and then read up before we meet again. Isn't that what you do with you clients?" Selecting the seat next to Walter's Richard adjusted its cushions and sat down.

"Umm it's strange but I don't see myself as your client Walter." he told him. Thanking him Walter suggested that it had in fact been Richard who had taught him to try and make every session feel like a conversation.

"It was, how wise of me" Richard beamed "so" he continued. Staff came and went and then this young student arrived on placement."

"Grace?" Walter speculated.

"Yes Grace." Richard confirmed "She was a tall girl who jelled with the team almost immediately."

"Jelled with just the team?" Walter asked his eye brows rising.

"No Walter she jelled with the children as well." Richard grinned well aware of the direction Walter was leading him."

"And you Richard?"

"Yes and with me, we drink coffee on our own a few times, but nothing happened and then Joan's mother fell ill and Joan flew out to South Africa to look after her."

"And?" Walter asked.

"Well Grace and I continued to have coffee after our shift and then one night I asked her what she would say if I made a pass at her."

"And was that lust or were you in love with her, because if I'm not wrong this is the part where she asked you what you would say if she ripped your balls off?"

"Indeed." Richard confirmed and then Joan returned from South Africa and that sneaky member of staff Barry told her what had been going on."

"The rat" Walter said as he picked up his coffee and sipped. "And how did he know what had been going on between you and Grace?"

"Going on" Richard protested "nothing had been going on Walter in fact Grace had behaved as a mature adult, but that Barry was on a mission."

"What mission?"

"A mission to save our marriage Walter and bizarrely he called a meeting of all interested parties and bizarrely we all attended."

"So then what happened?" Walter asked engrossed by the still unfolding yarn.

"The upshot was that Joan told me that I had to choose between her and Grace and this in turn led me to tell her not to be stupid and to Grace disintegrating into floods of tears."

"Well done Barry." Walter sighed.

"Well done indeed" Richard echoed and then explained that things had been difficult for the next few weeks, but as adults the team had continued to work together." Wanting to be sure of his facts Walter asked Richard if anything had happened between himself and Grace. After confirming that having asked the 'what would you say' question and having received the 'ripping balls' response, consciences were clear, Richard explained that his relationship with Joan had begun to mend. "Grace and I continued to have coffee but not on our own and then fate stepped in."

"Good old fate." Walter almost cheered "I was beginning to wonder where he'd gone."

"Fate is a female Walter?" Richard told him, not for the first time and Walter, not wanting to argue the point asked Richard if he was going to blame all his misdeeds on Fate."

"Blame Walter, have you ever heard me blame anyone but myself?" Unconvinced by the denial but not wanting to break Richard's flow Walter asked him to get on with his story.

"Well" Richard began "Joan's mother became ill again and she went out to be by her side and I was very careful around Grace." Suggesting that that couldn't be the end of the story Richard told him it wasn't and then described how he and Grace were asked to take some children away to the Yorkshire Dales. Pronouncing a 'oh bloody hell' Walter asked who's daft idea that had been.

"Not mine." Richard asserted.

"Are you sure?" a sceptical Walter questioned to which Richard affirming his innocence told Walter that it was on that trip that Grace made a pass at him. Unbelieving Walter expressed his astonishment with a 'she did what' and repeating 'she made a pass at me' Richard described the event.

"The other staff had gone to bed and Grace got up from where she was sitting watching TV and came to sit next to me on the settee. She then began to stroke my hair"

"Is this where the excuses come?" Walter quizzed.

"Excuses perhaps Walter but there I was an unhappily married man in my thirties and here was a young woman at my side showing me affection. That night Grace and I made love, badly, on the rug in front of the TV."

"But there were children and staff asleep upstairs Richard," Walter pointed out. "No wonder the sex was poor." "One likes to think that one can perform in all circumstances." Richard said and thanking his friend for his empathy continued. "Our pretence of normality went on. I guess the structures of a residential establishment have their benefits in hiding most things love affairs included. I guess people must have known or guessed, but nothing was said to me directly. So Grace and I continued to meet whenever we could. We would go out during our afternoon break and on our evening off we would drive to nearby villages. Sometimes we would stop in lay-bys' for what the Americans call 'heavy petting'. On one occasion the arrival of a police car caused panic and the swift putting away of bits and pieces. So we started going back to Grace's room in the staff accommodation block. There was more chance of getting caught, but it was warmer and there were no sex police on patrol. Oh Walter those were good times. We would lie on Grace's single bed and listen to Dianna Ross as she sang 'Touch me in the morning then just walk away, we don't have tomorrow but we had yesterday.'"

"Stop it Richard you're breaking my heart." Walter scoffed as Richard picked up his now cold coffee and sipped.

"And mine" Richard agreed as he placed his mug on the table and then sat silently as the memories came flooding back. "You know even after all those years that song still has the power to touch me and bring back memories of the love I almost lost. Sometimes I hear that song and have to clinch my teeth to hold back the tears. Oh yes these were difficult days Walter but beautiful days. I had never known love like it or felt such contentment and confusion."

"And your boys" a very moral but non judgmental Walter enquired "where were they whilst you were out gallivanting?"

"Gallivanting gee Walter you really do know the way to a guilty man's soul. Where were my boys you ask and to tell the truth I haven't a clue. I can't remember, surely I hadn't just abandoned them. How could a man charged with the care of other people's children leave his own children whilst he philanders about the place? I guess they'd be at school in the afternoon but where were they at night, tucked up in their beds and if so who was watching them? Hell Walter what had I been thinking about?"

"Grace Richard." Walter said simply "That's what you were thinking about Grace." Getting to his feet Richard picked up the empty mugs and placing them in the sink returned to his seat.

"Oh Walter, what I did was wrong, immoral and fabulous."

"So Richard then I think you've have just about answered my question."

"Which was?"

"The question was were you in love with Grace?"

"Yes I was," Richard told him "but what we were doing could not be overlooked or sanctioned by the powers that be."

"So was something said?" Walter enquired his tone now calm and caring.

"No, nothing, but Grace was moved to another flat." Recognising that it was probably a silly question Walter asked Richard if he and Grace had continued to see each other.

"Not such a silly question Walter" Richard told him "because Grace and I had countless conversations about ending the relationship and Grace was being advised by her friends and family to walk away and that I'd never leave Joan."

"But you did!"

"Indeed I did, when Joan returned from Africa we made the decision to part. I handed in my resignation to the deputy head and he seemed more than happy to accept it and so that was the end of my career and the end of an era. I moved into my sister's house and I'll never forget her kindness, because it not only gave me a place to stay but it also meant that I wasn't being rejected by my family."

"And Grace, what happened to Grace?" Walter asked his concern clear.

"Grace continued to work at the school." Richard told him "But she came to see me on her days off and I would drive to the school at night and wait on the lane for her to finish work. There were no mobile phones in those days and Grace was not always able to get away, but being near to her was enough for me."

"How you must have loved that girl Richard!" a sighing Walter whispered.

"And Walter I guess this conversation tells us that I still do."

"And your boys, what happened to your boys, to Steven and young John?"

"I wrote to then and it was one of the hardest things I have ever done. I told them about my sadness and shame and that I would understand if they never wanted to see me again, but bless them Walter. Steven at seventeen years old and his brother John just fifteen wrote back to me and using the words I had used to encourage them in life told me to be happy. Gee Walter even saying those words makes me want to cry. Anyway" Richard said clearing his throat, "I saw my boys at the weekends and we would go to play 'pitch and put' in Harrogate or visit my parents in Leeds.

"And Joan did you miss her?"

"No, to my shame Walter I didn't miss her at all. Twenty years of marriage and I had no feelings about it. How can that be?" Richard asked his surprise suggesting that he hadn't given the subject much thought up to that point. I had no regrets and the only good things to come out of those twenty years of marriage were my boys."

"No regrets, are you sure?" Walter accused.

"Damn it, Walter you've done it again." Richard complained "Yes of course there were regrets. I regretted that I hadn't more time with Steven and John. Steven had kept himself pretty much to himself, although I remember we did make one trip to Paris and I used to go and watch John play rugby but otherwise most of what we had done we had shared with other children and staff. They were good experiences, but not with just my boys."

"And Richard did Grace stay at the school?"

"Only for a short time Walter, we spent her summer break together whilst I looked for work, but it wasn't all a bed of roses. I had split loyalties. During one of the school holidays John joined Grace and I on a day trip to Scarborough. He always enjoyed playing the fruit machines but Grace hated them. As the day wore on tension between Grace and John began to grow and it all culminated in Grace storming out of the arcade whilst John stayed put. Hell Walter what a horrible moment that was as I stood in the middle of the road and pleaded with Grace to come back and not make me choose between her and my boys. But things thing settled down and although we had very little money the sex was terrific."

"Oh I've no doubt Walter smiled as he tried to hide his surprise at the revelation, but I know it's all going to fall apart again... isn't it?" he alleged.

"Maybe" Richard conceded "but not yet, because in October 1989 I got a job in a Children's Home in Cheshire and Grace and I moved into a rented house together. In the November my divorce came through and I married Grace in the Rochdale register office in December."

"Strange how we return to our roots, to a place we know, to a place of safety when we're in distress." Walter pointed out.

"Indeed" Richard agreed "but the next four years were not particularly easy."

"I knew it." Walter mocked glee.

"But" Richard added knocking Walter's gloating on the head "Grace went back to university and gained her degree in Social Work and I got a job as a senior Social worker.

CHAPTER 47
Friday 27th January 2010 (Morning)

Rose Three

As Richard entered the room Alice looked up from her typing and smiled. It was a smile that unnerved his still delicate frame and wishing her a 'good morning' he moved swiftly to his seat where for a long five minutes he tried to avoid eye contact with her ample and gaping breasts. "Richard it so nice to see you again" Rose enthused when ten long minutes later she crossed the red carpet and holding out her hand invited him into her office. Gently closing her door she crossed to the window and taking up her knees together, hands on lap position asked him how he had been keeping. Telling her that he didn't know Richard sat down and crossed his legs. "One minute I'm fine" he said "and then someone says or does something and I just get upset. Like last night when I couldn't get hold of Grace or John and Gabriella is still away staying with friends...well I just had this great feeling of loss."

"So Gabriella still continues to be a big part of your life Richard?" Rose questioned.

"I guess she does Rose."

"And you still fear losing her?"

"I think I have already lost her Rose." Richard asserted "and when Walter goes back to England well I just don't know how I'll cope."

"So will that mean you climbing back into your emotional vault Richard?"

"Probably" he told her.

"So Richard what about using your own Cognitive Behavioural skill to solve the problem, can you think of other options to climbing in that vault?" Rose asked.

"If I start with the right place I can usually solve most problems, but what is my problem Rose?" Richard asked.

"Let's start with loss shall we or is it fear of loss?"

"I think more fear of loss Rose so I guess my need is not to fear loss."

"And does that feel like a problem you can solve?"

"No Rose, because I can't stop people leaving me can I?"

"Name your people."

"Well I can name Gabriella for one?"

"So can you stop Gabriella leaving?"

"No, or could I?" Richard queried.

"Would you want to stop her?"

"Your inference being would I like to stop her living her own happy life?"

"Well would you?" Rose asked.

"No I wouldn't."

"And could you make her happy?"

"I thought I was."

"Meeting 'all' her needs?

"No Rose. I hope that I am a good friend to her, but as to her needs as a woman, her sexual needs no I don't meet those needs."

"So you can't make her happy?"

"No."

"And what about Walter, can you make him happy?"

"No, neither of us is gay." Richard smiled uneasily

"And so" an unsmiling Rose persisted "we come to Grace can you make Grace happy?"

"Not make her," Richard confessed "but help her to be happy Rose."

"So tell me what you're doing in South Africa?"

"Building my business?" Richard told her without thought.

"And is that making Grace happy?"

"No" Richard told her, the light of reason slowly beginning to dawn "and now I know where this is taking me, you're going to ask me if being in South Africa building my business is making even me happy aren't you?"

"And is it Richard?"

"No."

"So your problem is?"

"That I'm not with Grace?"

"And your need is?"

"My need is clearly to be with Grace!"

"And" Rose asked having taken a crash course in CBT "your options for change are?"

"Either I can do nothing or I can to go home Grace." Richard explained and then Rose getting to her feet held out her hand.

"Good bye Richard, I'll send you my bill." she smiled.

CHAPTER 48
Friday 27th January 2010 (Morning)

Sometimes the Truth Doesn't Hurt

Closing his crossword book Walter looked up at Richard and smiling in greeting placed the book on the kitchen table and told him that he looked in a good mood. Grinning Richard told him that he'd just had an awakening. "Now that sounds ominous." Walter groaned and then, being the good friend he was asked Richard to tell him more.

"Later." Richard told him as he lifted his hand to stop further debate "I just want to get cleaned up." and with a comradely pat on Walter's shoulder he moved towards the kitchen door. Twenty minutes later showered and dressed Richard pointed the Audi towards the N2 and Somerset West. The roads being quiet they reached Baden Powell intersection within the hour and turning left continued their journey through the lush green Cape wine lands towards their final destination and the African themed restaurant of 'Mojo'. Parking the car Richard nodded his greeting to the floppy hat wearing car guard. Entering the restaurant they were met by large black lady dressed as one would expect on a visit to a themed Africa eatery, from head to foot in a brightly wrap-around sarong. Behind the lady a group of black men sang happy songs, the meaning of which was unclear but trusting that they were songs of welcome both men applauded loudly and thanked them for their efforts. Stepping forward a white toothed and white gowned waiter announced in perfect Queens English that his name was Albert and then asked if he could get them drink. Replying in broad Lancastrian Richard asked if they could have two beers "and" he added "my friend here would like to know if we are safe here?"

"Safe sir" their waiter queried.

"Yes "Richard repeated, "Are white men welcome and safe here?"

"Oh yes sir," Albert told him "we are pleased to welcome all white men and we like to see them eat well."

"And then you eat them Albert?" Richard asked straight faced. Telling him that he liked white men but couldn't eat a whole one Albert asked Richard if he was the father of Mr Steven Blackwood. Confirming the truth of the statement Richard introduced Walter as a visitor from England and Albert, welcoming Walter to South Africa said that Mister Steven was a regular visitor and a wonderfully kind man. "After the fire in Pilangsburg had taken my job away Mr Steven found me work. Your son is a very fine man sir, you must be very proud of him. I was sorry to hear of his trouble sir, will you give him my best wishes when you see him please?" Agreeing to do just that Richard, with Walter in tow followed Albert across the dirt floor of the open air restaurant towards some deep and colourful settees. Bowing slightly Albert asked Richard about his other son "you were here two years ago I believe?" he questioned

"John yes."Richard verified "you have a good memory Albert." Thanking him Albert suggested that he must be very proud and putting hands together as if in prayer bowed again and asked if he could bring something to drink. Unfastening his top button Walter kicked off his sandals and settled cross legged into the sun warmed fabric of a sofa. "So young man," he began "if I'm to return to England anytime in the near future we'd better get on with your life story."

"Must we?" Richard questioned.

"No we mustn't but if we don't?" Walter frowned as a smiling Albert approached with their beers and grinning Richard waited until Albert had placed the beers on the low cane table and departed and then told Walter that it was an interesting thought."

"And which thought is that?" Walter asked as he lifted his beer and drained a quarter of the glass. Mirroring Walter's action Richard tipped back his own drink and wiping his mouth with the back of his hand asked Walter what would have happen if he didn't complete his life story. "And you know Walter, "he added thoughtfully "there have been times in the last few months when I would have welcomed the end of my life Walter."

"And me!" Walter laughed.

"But," Richard continued "at this very minute all I want to do is to get drunk under the sun with my best friend."

"Ah that's nice." Walter mocked.

"No not 'ah' Walter it's the truth, you've been a good friend and you know what?"

"What?" Walter asked.

"Well my life story seems to me that I have taken longer to talk about my life than live it. I'll bet you'll be glad when it's over."

"Your story or your life" Walter laughed again. Groaning Richard removed his trainer and holding under Walter's nose asked why he always got the punch lines.

"Because Richard, you feed them to me." he said as he dropped the warm trainer to the floor and took another long draught of beer. "However sir, enough of these prevarications just continue with the story and before you asked we had reached 1989."

"Was it as the wine people call 'a good year Walter?" Richard asked.

"Vintage?"

"Ah yes." Richard told him "well 1989 was just the opposite."

"Shit?" Walter suggested.

"Yes shit," Richard told him cheerlessly "the year started with the death of my dad's mother."

"Oh great Richard, I hope it got better." Walter groaned as he drained his glass and then realising what he had said apologised.

"I'm sorry Richard that was thoughtless." He said and as if to emphasis his remorse he leaned forward and placing his glass on the table touched Walter's leg. Smiling weakly Richard told him 'it's fine'.

"I don't want this to be a morbid session Walter" he added "so if it looks like its heading that way please stop me and we can do it some other time, deal?" he asked as Albert approached unbidden with a tray containing two more beers.

"Deal" Walter agreed and lifting his pint from the tray thanked their hovering waiter.

"Grandma left her house in Rochdale to my dad and he let Grace and I buy it at a bargain price and we began to renovate it."

"Were you close to your Gran?" Walter asked as out of character he lifted his second pint to his lips. Telling him that his Grandma been a central point in his young life Richard described how on Sundays he had visited with his dad and brothers and sisters and how the house had always seemed to smell of sprouts.

"That smell has remained with me to this day." he explained with a smile. "My dad's father had died quite young and when dad talked about his early days he always painted a sad picture of a lonely little boy standing at a bedroom window and watching his mother walk into the darkness. My grandmother worked in a cotton mill." Richard explained. "I could see the poor little chap standing there as the rain ran down the window panes and the tears rolled dad's cheeks."

"You're a poet Richard." Walter told him, his face serious for the first time that day and Richard suddenly aware of the change in Walter's mood asked him if he was alright.

"I miss Barbara." he said quietly "and for a moment as you were talking I thought of my children and Barbara." For some time the two men sat silently and then Richard apologising for his selfishness asked Walter if he would like to talk.

"No not now Richard," Walter told him. "But one day and when I feel ready it will be you that I come to." Thanking him Richard again announced that he didn't really want to go down the road to melancholy. "But" he said "if I do have to go that road then there's no one better to travel it with than you Walter."

"Now," Walter smiled "I'm not quite sure how to take that. Are you telling me that you think I'm a miserable sod or that you like my company?" Telling

Walter that whether he was looking for complements or criticism he'd come to the wrong place Richard asked Walter to remind him where he was up to.

"Tears were running down the window and your dad's face Richard, remember the poetry?" Walter asked.

"I do" Richard told him. "So my father was alone in the house from six o 'clock in the morning until my aunt came to give him his breakfast and take him to school."

"Poor little thing." Walter empathised.

"Oh don't start the sad thing again Walter. Please." Richard pleaded.

"But Richard sometimes sadness can be the right emotion, you should know that."

"I do know Walter but somehow when it's my emotions we're talking about, I seem to forget that I'm allowed them."

"Fine, Richard" Walter told him "but do try and learn."

"Ok Gandhi I'll try." Richard smirked and was promptly told that there was no need for sarcasm. "So what happened next?" he asked.

"When the Rochdale house was finished Grace and I moved in and started to settle down."

"A happy married couple at last?"

"We were." Richard smiled at the remembering "We would just sit by the fire together and best of all we would sit without fear of disturbance or guilt. Then in the mid 1990's the residential school where Grace and I had met closed its gates for the last time and Joan lost her job and decided to return to South Africa. I don't know if Steven and John discussed the situation with her but, Steven left his catering course and went out to Africa with his mother and John gave up his job with Volvo and came to live with Grace and me."

"So your carefree nights of sitting in front of the fire without fear of disturbance came to an end?"

"They did and tensions began to grow between the three of us."

"That's understandable." Walter said helpfully.

"Indeed so Walter." Richard told him. "But decisions had to be made and difficult decisions. John was my second born son but Grace was my wife so John was asked to leave."

"You said that in a very matter of fact way." Walter pointed out. "Where did he go?"

"He moved into a flat with his girl friend Walter." Richard explained

"A good decision for all concerned?"

"It was." Richard asserted. "Grace finished her degree and started work as a social worker, but best of all once John was ensconced with his girl friend things between us changed. He was no longer my little boy, a child that I was responsible for. He had become a man and it would seem a far more independent and worldly wise man than I had been at his age."

"Or are now?" Walter laughed. Glumly Richard asked what we call it when you put someone down nicely?" Telling him that he didn't know Walter asked why.

"Because Richard told him "you're so very good at it. You tell the truth and hurt me but somehow I don't take offence."

CHAPTER 49
Friday 27th January 2010 (Afternoon)

Steven and Grace

"So you became what?" Richard asked as he caught Albert attention and raised two fingers.

"The father I hadn't been whilst he was growing up." Richard said as he too caught Albert's attention and nodding his agreement hoping that he had understood Walter's hand movement as meaning that they would like two more beers.

"So you and John found each other?""

"We did Walter, we also found that we both liked Guinness, rugby and fine looking women and we were able to talk freely about what was a happening in our lives, although there seemed to be an unwritten rule that we never discussed the past. We talked about our women and how different they were to us men. Not exactly complaining you understand but, because we both knew how lucky we were to have those particular women in our lives."

"Oh I knew that women wouldn't be far way!" Walter joked as he took his third glass of beer from Albert "and John and Grace?"

"They got on much better. Grace started to relax around John and at one point they seemed to be becoming good friends although they both had feelings about the breakup of my marriage. Grace had been good friends with Joan in the early days and I think that Grace and John would have been very good friends if she had met him before me. They both seemed to laugh a lot, they both enjoyed sport and they were much closer in age than Grace and I."

"You were lucky to find Grace first then?" Walter suggested. Laughing Richard informed him that John had only been thirteen or fourteen when he first met Grace.

"That's just four or five years." Walter calculated "And the age difference between yourself and Grace?" he asked pointedly.

"Twenty Walter and that was under the belt." Richard smiled uneasily. Grinning unrepentantly Walter apologised and then asked Richard to continue.

"Well" Richard said as he pondered the possible implications of Grace having met John first "I guess you're expecting that 'and they lived happily ever after' moment now?"

"Well hope springs eternal" Walter told him "but I'm not the gullible person I was before we started these sessions so no, happy ever after is going to have to wait I think."

"Very wise," Richard told him "Because just as things started to settle down John and his girl friend split up."

"Zoe was becoming demanding and violent towards him." Richard explained "I think she was jealous about the amount of time he was spending with me."

"And all the Guinness, sport and good looking women I would imagine?" Walter suggested.

"Who knows." Richard conceded "What I do know is that John moved in with a friend and then went out to South Africa to join his mother and brother."

"I bet you missed him."

"I did." Richard confessed "but this time I had Grace to help me through the loss."

"Hadn't anyone been there to help you in the past?" Walter asked.

"They had but, this time it was different."

"In what way was it different Richard?"

"Well this time Grace spoke the words that meant the most to me." Telling Richard that he was intrigued Walter asked what Grace had said.

"You are my love" she told me and then held me as I cried for my loss."

"Had no one ever said they loved you before?"

"They must have Walter, but with Grace it was different and the words were more than just words, they were…"

"What were they Richard?"

"They were real Walter, I could feel them. They were warm and wrapped themselves around me. They comforted me and I felt safe and protected you know, 'loved'."

"You're a very lucky man Richard." Walter reminded him.

"And a fool," Richard told him "just look at me now, what a bloody fool!"

"But the good news is that you know you're a fool Richard and you now know what you want."

"I do Walter, but how am I going to get it. How am I going to get Grace back?" Telling him 'all in good time' and that he needed a break Walter got to his feet and walked towards the toilets. Turned his face to the sun Richard closed his eyes and thought about his summers in England and of how the sun had shone through the sycamore in his garden back in England. How he had cursed that sycamore when in the late afternoon its black shadow had pushed him back towards the house? Pushed him back until eventually he was forced to drink his wine sitting at the green cast iron table near the kitchen door. Sometimes Grace would come and sit with him before going to get the boys ready for bed. And then in pyjamas and dressing gowns the boys would come to say their good night and tell him that they loved him and then, as ritual demanded, Richard would tell them that he had loved them first. Those had been good days or had they he mused. Good days for him maybe but for Grace? Just when had the rot set in? Had he been blind? Had the writing been on the wall for all those who wanted to see?

"Richard?" Walter's quiet question rousing him from his reminiscing Richard opened his eyes and feeling the wetness of his tears squeezed then shut. Blinked several time to make was sure no moisture remained opened them again and look up at his concerned friend.

"Sorry were you are sleeping old man?" Walter asked as he placed his hands on Richard's shoulders.

"No not sleeping Walter just thinking. I do all my best thinking with my eyes closed. Smirking, Walter told him that he believed him "But thousands wouldn't." he added "so what were you thinking about."

"About the past and how blind I've been." Richard told him and Walter ever the friend informed him that 'blindness is in the eyes of the beholder'.

"But now I see my blindness," Richard informed him "and what a blind bloody fool I've been." Moving Richard's glass to the centre of the table Walter told him 'no more beer for you mister if it's going to affect you like this." To which Richard informed Walter that he was sorry and Walter told Richard 'enough already' and that he could cope with the listening and empathising but not this self pity. "So for goodness sake just tell the story." Mumbling another

'Sorry' Richard asked where he was up to and Walter telling him that he and Grace were on there our own again asked him to 'get on with it please'.

"Well" Richard began "trouble was brewing and I started to sink into depression. Grace tried to keep me buoyant but down I went. It was the old pattern of being tired, of visits to the doctor, and taking time off work. Only this time Grace bless her, sought professional help for me, help cost me thirty pound for forty five minutes session." Richard added "and day light robbery if you ask me." Raising his eye brow Walter asked how much Richard charged.

"Not enough Walter." Richard told him. "So off I went to Hebden Bridge, the centre for everything arty crafty and therapeutic. Did you know Walter there are more caftans and sandals per square inch in Hebden Bridge than anywhere else in the world. My therapist," Richard continued before Walter could challenge him, "was a serious man in his early fifties. He had converted a downstairs room of his house into a therapy suite and in the middle of the room was a bloody chintzy chaise lounge as the centre piece." Sensing that melancholy, silliness or both were on the horizon Walter suggested that they call it a day and continue tomorrow. Telling Walter that he had almost finished Richard asked that they carry on.

"Okay pal if you're sure." Walter conceded agreed.

"No Walter I'm not sure" Richard told him "but I'll carry on anyway if that's alright."

"Then away you go." Describing how he and Grace had stayed in the Rochdale house for another two years Richard then explained how they had bought a house in Fardale. "That house like all the houses I've ever bought needed a lot of work doing to it, but we were able to borrow some money and do it up pretty much as we wanted. William and James were born there and we had some really good times there, although" he added "my reminiscing can be very different to Grace's when it comes to babies crying in the night. I remember those early hours as being times for holding my beautiful babies and singing 'Goodbye dolly I must leave you' and 'it's a long way to Tipperary' to get them off to sleep. But Grace just remembered being 'knackered' all the time and thinking about it Grace seems to remember more of our 'bad times' than I do."

"Are you saying that Grace is negative?" Walter asked me.

"No not at all," Richard told him "I just have a selective memory and am better able to forget the bad things that happened."

"Like what?"

"Like our stormy falling out and my feeling down. They all seemed to affect Grace more and for longer than they did me."

"Did you two ever talk about it?" Walter questioned.

"I guess not." Richard told him "Well not until things were really bad. But, maybe if I can sort things out thing with you ...?"

"Look Richard." Walter said trying to hold his patience. "You and Grace have been separated for four months right?"

"Right."

"And that can't be good for a relationship, right?"

"Right."

"So what you do need to do is talk to Grace."

"But we did talk a couple of months before we broke up. She told me that she had thought about leaving me before so I asked when that had been. She said some years earlier but I had no recollection of that falling out.

She then told me that she would have regretted going and I told her that she wouldn't have been able to stay away long because she would have had to come back to cut me down."

"A bit insensitive Richard."

"I know that now Walter, but it's too late…"

"Stop!" Walter said holding up his hand "We're only doing positive today, remember?"

"Indeed we are." Richard reminded himself. "So let's have a nice cognac and head home."

Climbing behind Audi's steering wheel Richard rolled down his window and handed the car guard a fifty cent piece. "When we get back Walter will you help me draft a letter to Grace?"

"Maybe," Walter told him "but only if you promise not to embarrass me with mushy love talk."

"Oh no promises," Richard told him. "In fact I could practice on you now. You do know that you're my best friend in the entire world."

"Richard!!" Walter warned.

CHAPTER 50
Monday 30th January 2010 (Morning)

A Crap Life

Would you mind driving Gabi?" Richard asked as he stood blinking into the brightness of the morning. "I think I over did the wine a bit."

"A bit" Gabriella gasped a little too loudly. "A bit you just about emptied the wine cellar." The night before Richard had joined Walter and a few work colleagues to celebrate his return to work. During the evening he had managed to spend some time with Gabriella, but despite his not too gentle questioning he had been unable to get her to discuss anything to do with what she called her 'private life'.

"Please "he pleaded as he followed her to the garage where relenting Gabriella told him she was taking his car and clicked open the Audi's doors and climbed in. "Got your paper work?" she asked as she slid behind the wheel. Richard's 'shit' was heartfelt.

They had travelled for more than half an hour before Richard felt able to broach the subject of Gabriella's 'private life'. "Do you mean Adam?" she questioned innocently as she pulled out to overtake a slow moving bus "would you like to meet him. 'Thinking 'no bloody way' Richard instead he heard himself saying. "Great." Grinning broadly Gabriella told him that she thought the two men would get on well together and suggested that they all went out for a meal. Once more thinking 'no bloody way' Richard again heard himself saying "Great" and then fearing to engage in further conversation sat quietly until they had reached Somerset West. Pulling the Audi to the curb Gabriella turned off the engine. As she did so a smiling Pamela James, watering can in hand came down the brick path to meet them.

Gabriella, Richard, thank you for coming. How was your Christmas?" she beamed and Gabriella, trying to avoid Richard's 'we don't share our private lives with client's' look told Pamela 'the usual rush and bustle' and then asked her "How was yours?"

"Not too bad." Pamela told her "Lee doesn't like all the fuss so I tried to keep it quiet, but come on in, would you like tea or a cool drink?" Five long minutes later, orange juice as his side Richard opened his file and I turning towards his client smiled and asked her if he could take her to the top of his sheet and ask her to score her wellbeing on the scale of one to ten. Telling him 'four maybe five' Richard then asked her if she could remember her score from the last time he was there.

"No I'm afraid I don't remember." Pamela told him apologetically. "We seemed to talk about so much." Agreeing that they had Richard then asked her if she would be surprised if he told her that the last time he asked her to score her wellbeing she had asked him to write a minus. "So," he said "from a minus to plus five is quite a leap, what's changed?" Declaring that she didn't know Pamela informed him that Lee hadn't changed that much.

"And so, what else could it be?" Richard asked. Again Pam told him she didn't know.

"But then I don't seem to know very much today do I?" Telling her that her not knowing was why he was there Richard handed her a copy of his Thoughts- Feelings and Actions hand-out and began to explain how thoughts-feelings and actions are all linked. "If our thinking is wrong Pam then there's a good chance that our feelings will be wrong and as we know, wrong feelings can lead to wrong actions. For example" he clarified "You have just told me that in one session your wellbeing has risen from a minus to plus a five so what changed Pam?" he asked and then sitting back Richard waited for the light of understanding to dawn.

"It's not what changed is it Richard?" Pamela said slowly" but who, that's what you are trying to tell me isn't it?

"I'm not here to tell you anything Pam," Richard told her gently, "but have you changed?"

"If being fed up with Lee's constant negative moods and deciding not to pander to his sulks and his shouting anymore is change then yes I've changed Richard. Do you remember me being surprised last time you were here when I told you it had been hard for a few months and then realised that it had actually been nearly three years? Three years Richard. I've put up with Lee's crap... sorry Gabriella, for three years. And no I'm not going to cry and I'm not going to feel sorry for myself or for Lee." Rising from her chair Gabriella crossed the room and breaking the rules of therapy placed her arms around her client's neck.

"Gee Pam that was quite a speech." he said" Gabriella looked across at her boss told him that she knew it wasn't professional but..." She got no further as Richard getting to his feet put his hands together and began applauding his client.

"Well for a man with a bad head you certainly got stuck into that session." Gabriella said as she steered the Audi towards the Strand. "In just two sessions Pam is already making decisions about her life and the life of her children. So" she asked "what will happen to Lee?"

"Well Gabi get your purse out" Richard told her "because I bet you twenty quid that within the month Lee James will be out looking for a job."

"And are we allowed to bet on the outcome of cases Mr. Blackwood?" Gabriella asked.

"If we're allowed to applaud a client for making changes to her crap life, her words not mine Gabi, then a small wager can't be all that bad can it?"

"Well that would depend on who wins the bet sir but, in this case I'd be more than happy to lose."

CHAPTER 51
Tuesday 31st January 2010 (Afternoon)

Catch

"On a good day I can see Fish Hoek and Simons' Town." Patricia Morgan said as she stood on her balcony a pair of binoculars in small manicured hands. "All places I have yet to visit Patricia." Gabriella told her as she settled under a large brown and gold umbrella and opening her brief case asked Pam to rate her well-being.

"About six." she was told "but Christmas can be such a difficult time don't you think?" Agreeing Gabriella glanced quickly across at her boss, his expression warning her not to go down the 'best of pal's' route. "So Pat," to your problems page and your Grandson, did you manage to see him over the holiday?"

"Oh yes" Patricia told her "he came to stay for a whole week. It's so nice for him here, what with the beach and everything."

"And your son-in-law?"

"Now that's another story my dear, I just want to give him a good slapping."

"And would that help?" Gabriella asked.

"It would certainly help me." Pat smiled the twinkle in her eye telling Gabriella more than words ever could.

"Indeed," Gabriella frown "but I can't recommend it as a way of solving anything."

"Oh I know that dear," Patricia told her "but wouldn't it be nice?" Smiling her understanding Gabriella asked Patricia if she would like to talk about the problem she was having with her son-in-law or perhaps" she suggested "your younger daughter?"

"Oh I think my son-in-law is a more pressing problem, don't you Gabriella but I still worry about Mary." Not wanting to cloud the issues Gabriella confirmed Patricia's choice as her son-in-law and then asked her to define the problem.

At two twenty Richard moved his finger along his watch strap indicating that Gabriella had just ten minutes to draw the session to a close and by two thirty five he was following her to the lift. Walking out into the bright afternoon sun and grateful for the cooling breeze that blew gently off the blue grey water's of False Bay they started to cross the road.

"Would you like me to drive young lady?" Richard asked as Gabriella rummaged into the depths of her hand bag for the car keys.

"Would you mind Richard, I found that a bit hard going. I just wish I had your timing, I always feel as if I'm rushing people. Do you think I rush people?" she asked as she threw him the keys. Lifting his hand Richard watched as the keys flew through the air.

"We all have our own styles and timing Gabriella." he told her "Now get yourself in and I'll treat you to a coff..."

CHAPTER 52
Tuesday 31ˢᵗ January 2010 (Late Afternoon)

A Very Lucky Man

"How's he doing?" Richard heard the voice from far away.

"They say he'll be fine and the bullet went straight through his shoulder but would have hit his heart if he hadn't dropped the car keys.

"Typical Lancastrian couldn't catch to save his..." Walter began.

"And not being able to catch probably saved his life Walter." Gabriella corrected. Conceding a very good point Walter then asked if there was any news on who did it.

"Not yet" Gabriella told him "Inspector Dorrington is interviewing."

"And you Gabi, are you alright Gabi?" Saying that she was a bit shaken Gabriella went on to tell Walter how fantastic Mrs Morgan had been.

"She'd telephoned the ambulance and police before I could get my mobile out and she gave them a description of the car and even part of the registration number."

"But no doubt the plates will be false." Walter suggested. Carefully Richard opening one eye and looked around the darkened room. He was tired and his arm hurt like hell but he was able to make out the two shadowy figures before his heavy eye lids closed again. Putting a comforting arm around Gabriella's shoulder Walter invited her to get some rest. "I'll come and find you as soon as there's any news." he promised. Declining his offer Gabriella asked if he would bring her some coffee and Walter declaring that she had it black with two sugars moved towards the door. Inform him that he was 'close but no cigar' Gabriella told him she preferred 'white and with no sugar' and Walter repeating her words back to her smiled." "Okay," he said as the door began to swing closed behind him. "I'll be right back."

"Gabi" Richard's voice was barely audible above the bleeping and pulsing of the equipment surrounding his bed, but barely audible as his voice may have been it was still loud enough for the anxious Gabriella to hear.

"Richard." she said as she pressed the bed side call button "Oh Richard thank God." She got no further as three medics entered and expertly moving her to one side they began their well practiced routine of patient and monitor checking.

"Looks like we have a strong one here Mrs...?" a medic said as she studied Richard's chart.

"O'Brian," Gabriella volunteered.

"And his next of kin is...?"

"She's in England.... doctor?"

"Blake, Margaret Blake." the medic told her and turning to Richard informed him that he was a very lucky man. "You're going to make a full recovery Mr Blackwood and I can tell you that it's not every day a bullet wound victim walks out of here. Now an Inspector Dorrington wants see you, shall I tell him that you're not well enough?"

"Please doctor," Gabriella interceded "I'll see him Richard, you rest."

"Would anyone like..." Walter asked as he reversed into the room holding two polystyrene cup's in his hands. Seeing the assembled throng stopped. "Sorry." he said as an anxious look began to spread across his face. "Is everything alright?"

"Fine Walter," Gabriella grinned "everything is fine." Cups in hand Walter moved to the bed.

"Richard, gee Richard you're back with us." he beamed as he turned towards the medics. "Is he going to be alright doctor?"

"Fine Mister...?" Dr Blake asked as she reached for a cup of the seaming liquid.

"Wilson." Walter told her as he relinquished the beverage "I'm Richard friend and colleague."

"Well Mister." the doctor began to say as once more the door opened.

"Inspector Dorrington" Kevin Dorrington announced as he walked into the room "can we come in?"

"No inspector you cannot." Margaret Blake told him firmly "This room is already like Cape Town station. If you want to speak to Mrs. O'Brian I'll find you a room, now, all of you out." she demanded and then grinned as Richard made a feeble attempt to rise. "No not you Dr Blackwood I think you should stay a little while longer, don't you?"

"And I'd like to stay with him doctor if that's alright?" Walter pleaded. Telling him 'okay' Dr Blake ushered the rest of the throng to the door and then turned. "But only for a few minutes." and she cautioned as she gently closed the door.

Walter Wilson had grown to be a private and caring man. He was a man who generally kept his emotions under control but now, as he sat in the clinical calm of the recovery room, he reached down and gently began to stroke the back of Richard's hand. The two men had known each other for a little over six years but in that time their respect for each other as friend and colleague had grown.

"Gee Richard I thought I'd lost you." he whispered as a silent tear slid slowly down his face "and then what would I have done?" he asked "Have I ever told you how much I owe you for all you have done, not only for me but for Gabriella and your clients. Just how many lives have you saved, how many lives have you put back together? And then," he continued, "Some sick bastard does this to you. Gee Richard." he repeated as the door opened and a nurse carrying a new drip moved to Richard's bed-side.

As they walked down the corridor Inspector Dorrington handed Gabriella a fresh cup of coffee."Well, Miss O'Brian." he said. "What can you tell us?"

"I afraid no more that I told the officer in the Strand." she told him. "We, Richard and I came out of Mrs Morgan's flat."

"And what time was that?"

"About two thirty, and started to cross the duel carriageway on the coast road when this car."

"Make and model?" Kevin Dorrington asked curtly.

"The make was a Ford I think, one of those big people carrier things. I'm sorry but I don't know about models, but it was quite new."

"And colour?"

"It was white inspector."

"And how many people?"

"I'm afraid I don't know that either inspector, it all happened so quickly."

"Did you perhaps see the driver Gabriella? Can I call you Gabriella?" Sergeant Boyd asked gently.

"No, I mean yes please call me Gabriella and no I don't think I saw the driver."

"Would you have noticed if the driver was black or white, male or female?" Boyd prompted "Please try and think Gabriella it's important."

"We were crossing the road and had almost got to the central reservation. Richard was in front of me and I threw him the car keys."

"A bit of a silly thing to do on a busy road Miss don't you think?" an unsmiling Dorrington asked.

"On the face of it," Gabriella told him "but if I hadn't thrown the keys and if Richard hadn't dropped them he may well have been dead now."

"Please go on Gabriella." the sergeant said as she gave her boss a look of exasperation.

"Yes come to think of it sergeant I did see the car coming. It was on the other side of the carriageway and moving quite slowly. I remember thinking that the driver was probably looking for a parking place. If it had been coming quickly I don't think I would have thrown the keys. Yes inspector," she conceded "if the car had been coming more quickly throwing the keys would have been silly, is that what you called me, silly?" she asked

"I didn't mean to offend Miss I just want to find out what happened." the inspector almost apologised "So the car was coming slowly, travelling which way Miss O'Brian?"

"It was coming away from the town centre and towards Cape Town."

"And do you remember the race of the driver?"

"He was black inspector."

"He?"

"Yes."

"Are you sure, very sure?"

"Yes why? Inspector...?"

"Well," the inspector confided. "A white Ford was stopped at a routine road block on the Stellenbosch road. The traffic department was doing checks on licences and road worthy's. Our Mrs Morgan gave us make, model and colour. She also gave us a partial registration number, false of course, but enough for the officers to give the black driver and his passenger a little extra attention. The men have been arrested and I've just come from talking to them. And in the good old tradition of plea bargaining it seems that they want to give us some information. Does the name Michael Bennet mean anything to you Miss O'Brian?"

"He was one of Steven's partners."

"And Joseph Insignias?"

"Jacob's son, surely you don't think that Joseph is linked to Steven's abduction inspector?" Gabriella asked with surprise.

"We don't know at this time Miss O'Brian. Sadly Mr. Insignias' body was pulled from the sea just before Christmas."

"I'm so sorry."

"That's life Miss O'Brian some people get a second chance and some poor sods don't. Now can I thank you for your time and if you think of anything else please contact me"

"Still sleeping?" Gabriella asked as she put her head around the door.

"Yes Gabi he's out like a light." Walter smiled as he lent back against his chair and put his hands behind his head. "You okay?" he asked.

"Yes I think so Walter. He is going to be alright isn't he?"

"He's tough Gabi." Walter said as he got to his feet. "And he won't want to stay here for very long. I bet we'll be able to take him home tomorrow. Now would you like some time with him before they throw us out?" he asked.

CHAPTER 53
Wednesday 1st February 2010 (Morning)

Adam Western

As Walter had predicted Richard was allowed home the next day, his shoulder heavily bandaged and his movements restricted, but otherwise physically no worse for his ordeal. Refusing Gabriella's order to go to bed or rest he went with Walter to sit by the pool where they talked for sometime about the future of Emotional Solutions. Coming to no concrete conclusions they spent the rest of the day doing crosswords, listening to music and dozing. At five fifteen dirty pots were taken to the kitchen and washed before the men made their way upstairs to prepare for their visit to Steven's and the meeting with Adam Western. At five forty five Gabriella telephoned to check if they had left and Richard telling her that they had but had to run back to answer the phone promised that they'd be with her in twenty minutes. `

"So just what are we supposed to be celebrating?" Richard asked as he sat at his son's kitchen table and opened the evening paper.

"I don't know my friend, but I hope it's not an engagement announcement." Walter said "but please don't look so fed up. This is Gabriella's night so let's not spoil it."

"If you were a woman," Steven asked as he opened the refrigerator door and took out a block of cheese "where would you hide biscuits? I've lived in the house with Katie for six months and I still can't find any logic to where she puts things."

"Please don't ask me to explain the link between women and logic?" Richard pleaded as the newly installed security system buzzed loudly.

Picking up the intercom he listened as the deep baritone voice of a security guard announced that a Mr Western was here "Shall I let him through sir?" he asked.

"Please." Richard said him although he would dearly have loved to have told the voice to keep the bugger out.

"Yes sir." the voice replied and adding a 'thank you' disconnected.

"Gabi Adam's here." Richard called from the bottom of the stairs. Telling him that she was just coming Gabriella took a sip of her Merlot and moving to the bathroom checked her hair in the mirror.

"Beautiful." Katie told her as she stood up from the dressing table "Now" she grinned "go and greet your Romeo whilst I finish my face."

"Come on get a move on there are thirsty people out here." a grating and slightly inebriated Australian voice called from intercom and alerting Gabi to her guest's arrival Richard went to the front door. Looking through the newly installed TV monitor he studied the gaunt face of Gabriella's new man.

"Adam?" he asked.

"Who else are you expecting?" the curt voice replied and feeling his annoyance factor rise a few degrees Richard buzzed the door open and stood back to let the tall slim man enter.

"Adam it's good to see you." he lied. "I'm Richard."

"Ah yes Richard." the Australian grinned as he followed Richard to the kitchen and out into the warm evening.

"Steven this is Adam and Adam this is my son Steven."

"Nice to meet you, Adam" Steven smiled as he held out his hand in welcome "and on your last night." and lifting his arm introduced Walter.

"Ah Walter I've heard so much about you." Adam laughed knowingly.

"You have?" a somewhat nonplussed Walter replied "I hope it was all good?"

"Now that would be telling wouldn't it?" the Australian taunted as he put his hand on the Yorkshire man's shoulder "but never mind eh?" he winked.

"And are you all packed?" Richard asked as he tried to steer the conversation away from a clearly embarrassed Walter.

"No not a sock packed pal" Adam told him "but my flight's not until eleven tomorrow, so there's plenty of time."

"If Richard was flying," Steven suggested as he led his grinning guest towards the long teak patio table. "He would have been ready weeks ago." and indicated the generous selection of wines and spirits asked Adam to choose his poison. Protesting that there was nothing wrong with a bit of planning and that in his book 'failing to plan was planning to fail' Richard followed his son to the table and picking up a bottle of Rioja began to pour.

"That may be true." Adam countered as he too reached for a bottle. "But," he added as he poured three fingers of Steven's twelve year old Cragganmore whiskey into a heavy crystal glass "I've known people who have planned all their lives and never got anywhere. And" he continued "as my dad used to say Walter, 'Faint heart never won fair maiden.'"

"So you like a nice whiskey?" Steven asked as he too, recognising the tension building between the two men, led Adam towards the house "Well just you wait 'til you see what I've been saving."

"You okay Walter." Richard asked as he led the red faced Walter to the pools edge.

"Yes sure." Walter lied as he lifted his glass and sniffed the rich red liquid. "So where are we off to tonight Richard?" he asked.

"The Portswood, Walter," Katie told him as she crossed the patio and stood at his side. "Where's Adam?" she asked.

"Admiring dad's whiskey collection I think." Richard told her. "So where's Gabi?

"She changing," Katie told him "silly thing spilt red wine on her dress, but she'll be down in a minute."

"Never mind the bloody snacks Steven where's that whiskey you promised me?" the already inebriated Adam Western demanded as he began to randomly open cupboard doors. "Ah now that's the stuff," he beamed as he took down a bottle of Dufftown 1984 / 27 Year Old / Signatory.

"Want one Steve?" he asked as he poured himself a generous measure into his now empty glass. Reaching for a clean glass Steven requested 'just a small one please' and then raised his eyebrows at the rapidly deteriorating behaviour of his guest.

"There's trouble brewing Gabriella." Katie warned as she took her friend's arm. "And I think there's about to be a return run of the 'ashes.'"

"Oh god Katie what is it about men and their bloody testosterone?" Gabriella cursed as she followed Katie into the kitchen. "Why can't they be more like us?" she asked as she moved to Adam's side.

"Adam!" she hissed as she watched him pour more of the expensive liquid into his glass. "That's Steven's best whiskey."

"You don't mind, do you Steve?" her man grinned happily.

"But that's not the point Adam." she told him crossly, "And please don't be rude." she added as a laughing Adam Western drained his glass.

"Oh give it a rest woman." he sneered and Katie, feeling the need to intercede and protect her friend confirmed that the whiskey was indeed very expensive.

"It was little lady," the Australian slurred "because my love that's just about the end of it."

"That's a pity Adam," Steven told him calmly "because I've been saving it for a special occasion."

"What special occasion?" Adam asked coldly at which point a very upset Gabriella turned and walked quickly from the kitchen.

"What?" Adam frowned at her retreating back. "Can't she take a joke?" and emptying his glass followed her into the garden.

"So what time's your flight Adam?" Walter asked softly as Adam stood and swayed gently in the breeze.

"Eleven o clock Walt." Adam told him "And it's a direct flight to Sydney."

"I've never been to Australia." Walter offered as he once more he tried to make a connection with the Australian.

"I hope you're not fishing for an invite Walt, because they're fucking fussy about who gets let in." Adam swore dismissively as he crossing the patio and putting his arm around Katie's waist squeezed. "Now here's a good looking woman." he smirked. "Want a drink?" he asked as he waved the empty bottle in the air. "Well too bad old girl," he laughed "because it's all fucking gone." Uncomfortable with his touch and language Katie eased herself away from his grasp.

"I bet Gabriella will miss you when you go Adam." she said as she looked anxiously around for reinforcements.

"She better had Katie." Adam told her as the empty bottle slid from his hand smashed on the patio floor. "Shit." he cursed as he kicked the shards under the table. "I did ask her to fly out with me. They'll let any old Sheila into Oz Walter." he sniggered "Sheila's are more use to us than blokes, but the silly girl she said she was too busy at work and couldn't take time off."

"That's my girl," Richard offered, a wide smile filling his proud face. "I've trained her well." he said as the intercom announced the arrival of their taxis.

"You've trained her too bloody well if you ask me mate." Adam complained. "I think you need to fucking relax a bit. Even Walter here seems to be over doing the fucking caring for others bit, and he's on holiday."

"We do it because we have souls Adam." Walter said calmly.

"Arse souls," Adam retorted angrily. "All I know is that all work and no play makes people ill."

"And no work makes people poor or boring." Walter snapped no longer able to hide his mask of politeness.

"So who are you saying is fucking boring Walt?" Adam snarled as staggered unsteadily against the table.

"Well it's not me." Richard said firmly. "So it must be one of you blokes." emphasising the 'blokes'.

Well I know it's not Steven." Katie asserted "So that just leaves you and Walter. Are you boring Adam?" she asked.

"I've never been told so by a bird." Adam said angrily. "Anyway what is this pick on fucking Adam night?" "No," Gabriella told him as she came out of the kitchen, her eyes showing signs of her tears. "Katie was only joking, weren't you Katie?" she sniffed as she moved to stand at his side.

"Well don't bloody joke about me bitch." he said cursing as he pushed her roughly away. A few seconds silence followed and then Walter moving purposefully placed himself between the Australian and the woman he loved.

"Shit I knew that this was a fucking mistake." Adam swore as he pushed Walter to one side.

"Oh Adam, please don't be like that." Gabriella pleaded as she placed a gentle hand on his. "Come on I'll make some coffee the taxi will be here soon and then..."

"If you fucking think I'm going anywhere with you bloody load of fucking 'Pomes' you can think again." Adam slurred as he staggered towards the pool and moving forward Richard grabbed the Australian's arm.

"Come on now Adam." he began "Don't upset the girl, no harm was meant." Swinging round, his face full of pent up rage Adam Western pulled his arm free.

"And you can fuck off too Blackwood. I know you fancy your chances with her, so just mind your own bloody business you fucking bleeding creep."

"Fair enough Adam," Richard told him with more calmness than he felt "but I'm ready to eat are you coming Gabriella?" he asked.

"Yes," she told him and turning to her man Gabriella asked if he was joining them.

"Fuck off doll and save your breath doll. I'm out of her and don't bother trying to ringing me, you two timing trollop."

Now Steven was on the move and prodding his finger, none to gently into Adam's chest pointed at the door and told him 'out'. There was no argument from the Australian as Steven escorted him to the front door and one of the waiting cabs. "See you around. I don't think." his ex- guest slurred with all the venom he could muster and then Adam Western was gone. For some seconds Steven stood and watched the departing cab and then turning walked back to the patio.

"Has he gone Steven?" Katie asked as she moved to his side.

"Yes" Steven told her as he picked up his whiskey glass and draining the last of its expensive contents placed it on the patio table.

"And good riddance if you ask me" Richard added and then feeling the hot glare of Katie's glare on the back of his neck told Gabriella that he was sorry. "But what a drunken fool he was?" he argued.

"I know Richard," Gabriella wept as she wiped a tear from her cheek "but I really did think that he loved me. He was so gentle..." and then unable to continue she moved to his side and placed her head on his chest" "Oh Richard I miss Michael so much." she sobbed and Richard, happy and embarrassed by her action put his arm around her shoulders.

"He's not worth your tears Gabriella." he told her.

"And," Walter laughed "what about that drunken fool saying that Richard fancied you Gabi? I asked you what red blooded man wouldn't?" he added.

"Well Walter that's not the best chat up line I've ever heard." Katie smiled. "But I guess the sentiment is right."

"And the words were true." Walter confirmed. Thanking her friends Gabriella wiped her eyes and not wanting to spoil the evening told them that there were taxi's waiting.

"So come on lets go eat." she demanded.

Together the five travelled to the Portswood where the service was of its usual high standard. It was during the meal that Walter, aware that he had almost lost Gabriella to another man got the idea and the courage to ask Gabriella to go on safari with him. It was an offer that was without much deliberation and much to his relief, accepted.

"And what about you and Steven, Katie?" the ever thoughtful Gabriella asked much to Walter's displeasure "why don't you come with us? You both need a break." she added.

"No, you two go, we don't want to be wallflowers." Steven said picking up on Walter's obvious distress.

"Oh come on Katie" Gabriella pleaded "and Richard, you come as well it'll be fun, come on what do you say?" After a short lived and half hearted protest from both Steven and Richard Gabriella agreed to book flights to Windhoek after which they all engaged in a heated and excited debate in which a trip to Namibia and a sightseeing trip to Victoria Falls was agreed.

"And perhaps," Gabriella added "We could go in to Botswana to see where 'The Number One Detective Agency' was filmed?"

"Ah yes Gabriella that would be great," Katie chorused "I've read the books, yes lets."

CHAPTER 54
Monday 6th February 2010 (Morning)

It Wasn't Me

The day had not started well for sergeant Megan Boyd. Firstly the early morning telephone call from her often thoughtful, but today *'fucking thoughtless boss'*, had not only cut short her well earned break, but had also spoilt what had promised to be a passionate liaison with a tanned and broad shouldered rugby playing colleague. Secondly inspector Dorrington's demand that she return to Cape Town straight away had been final and her request to be able to have at least one weekend away from the office had fallen on if not deaf than unsympathetic ears. "No Boyd I want you back here now." Dorrington had bellowed, his mood obviously no better than that of his disappointed and sleepy sergeant. Boyd's drive down the west coast had been trouble free until she had reached the seemingly everlasting road works at Somerset West. Here she had joined a long line of slow moving traffic after which she had found herself amongst an unhappy throng of early morning commuters whose sole aim in life seemed to be to get at least one car in front of hers.

"It's so good of you to come." Kevin Dorrington said as his frazzled sergeant dropped her overnight bag onto her desk. "Get some coffee and come down to my office." he told her. From that moment Megan Boyd's day had begun to improve. The two big, black and belligerent men who had spent three weeks on remand had finally agreed to talk and as a consequence the constable's day had progressed into the naming of names of the 'whose who' of dirty deed doers.

"So Mr Potye you wanted to see me." Dorrington said as he sat next to his Sergeant and smiled benignly across the table at his next suspect. "How may I help?"

In less than half an hour Inspector Kevin Dorrington was repeating what was to become his mantra for the day. "So Mr Khamsela what you're telling me is that Priscilla Dwangu paid you twenty thousand rand to kidnap Mister Steven Blackwood is that correct?"

"Yes sir." Khamsela told him, his fear of both the law and of Miss Dwangu written large across his round face.

"Did you have anyone to help you?"

"Yes."

"Who"

"It was Potye sir."

"Did you share the money?"

"Yes."

"And who beat Mr Blackwood?"

"It was Potye."

"Are you sure?"

"Yes sir"

"And who killed Mr Michael Bennet?"

"Who sir"

"Mister Michael Bennet was the man at the farm Mr Khamsela."

"It was Potye sir."

"Why did he kill Mr Bennet?"

"It was an accident sir."

"And tell me about Mr Joseph Insignias?" Dorrington asked.

"I don't know Mr Insignias."

"Mr Insignias worked for Mr Blackwood. You didn't see him at the house?"

"No sir." and with that Dorrington got to his feet.

"Okay sergeant" he smiled "I think we are done here. Give the officer a shout and we'll be off?"

The home of Priscilla Dwangu in the northern suburb of Thornton was surprisingly spacious and comfortable, even so, discretion being the better part of valour, three police vehicles accompanied officers Dorrington and Boyd as they travelled to request the pleasure of Priscilla Dwangu's company at central police station. Dwangu, unlike her two heavies, was at first unhappy to admit to any knowledge of the happenings at 'Kleinkoppie.'

"Why did you send your men to kidnap Mr Steven Blackwood, Miss Dwangu?"

"I don't know anyone called Blackwood"

"Why did you tell your men to beat Mr Blackwood?"

I didn't tell them to beat him." Priscilla said the hatred in her voice causing her face to grow darker.

"But he was beaten wasn't he?"

"I don't know I have never seen him."

"So why have him kidnapped Priscilla?" Megan Boyd asked gentle.

"Because"

"Because is that the best you can do?" Dorrington growled.

"Yes."

"Okay sergeant, I don't have time to waste on little shits like this. Take her to the cells. We'll talk to her again in the morning."

"Wait sir." Megan said turning to her boss. "Priscilla, I can call you Priscilla."

"Call me what you want."

"Priscilla, Mr Khamsela has told us you paid him twenty thousand rand to kidnap Steven Blackwood, is that right."

"No comment."

"Why would Mr Khamsela lie to me Priscilla?"

"I don't know."

"Priscilla if you don't talk to me whoever asked you to kidnap Mr Blackwood will go free and you will spend ten years in prison."

"And don't forget the twenty years for killing Mr Bennet." Dorrington snarled. "Plus another twenty for the murder of Joseph Insignias, that's..."

"I don't know this Insignias person." Dwangu yelled and..."

"Priscilla." The calming voice of Boyd cut in. "How old are you now Priscilla?"

"Twenty four years."

"And in fifty years time when you came out of prison Priscilla, how old will you be then?" Boyd asked her gently.

"I didn't tell Khamsela to kill Mr Bennet or beat Mr Blackwood and I have never heard of Mr Insignias.'"

"Alright Priscilla I believe you. Now just give me the name of the person who paid you to take Steven Blackwood and I'll talk with the judge."

CHAPTER 55
Monday 6th February (Evening)

Now Who Can That Be

"Good evening madam." Dorrington said as he held out his identification card. "May we come in?" Following her boss as he crossed the black marble hallway and turned left into a carpeted lounge Megan Boyd looked around the room and saw nothing but opulence.

"Please sit down inspector" the lady of the house invited "my husband's just gone for a bath. Can I get you a drink, tea coffee?" Telling her that he was fine Dorrington moved to one of the many plush arm chairs and sitting down crossed his legs. "Will your husband be long?" he asked.

"He does tend to loiter, but I'll go and tell him you're here." And with that Mrs Angela Chisholm smiled nervously and left the room. As she left Inspector Kevin Dorrington tapped the keys of his mobile phone and pressed send.

"I'm sorry inspector." a surprised and apologetic looking Mrs Chisholm said when she returned from her fruitless search "but I'm afraid Charles appears to have popped out for something. Will you wait?"

"I don't think he'll be long madam." Dorrington said as the Chisholm's front door bell rang for the second time that evening.

"Now who can that be?" an increasingly bewildered Angela Chisholm asked as she ran a nervous hand through her bottle blond hair.

"Don't worry Mrs Chisholm I think it will be for us." Megan Boyd said as she crossed to the door and disappeared into the hall way. Two minutes later she returned with three uniformed officers and a pink, hurriedly dressed and out of breath Charles Ascot Chisholm. Getting to his feet Dorrington apologised to Mrs Chisholm for the intrusion and then thanking her for her hospitality placed his hand on her husband's shoulder. "Mr Charles Ascot Chisholm, I'm arresting you for the abduction of Mr Steven Blackwood. You don't ..." he got no further as his words were interrupted first by Angela Dorrington's cry of 'Charles!" and secondly by the gentle thud of a fifty four year old woman hitting a shag pile carpet.

CHAPTER 56
Thursday 9th February (Afternoon)

But Only For the Time Being

Richard telephoned Steven to ask if he and Katie would join him for supper. It was an invitation that they were more than happy to accept and so with a contented smile on his face Richard moved to the lounge and sat down at the piano. For several seconds he stared at the front cover of the Marvin Hamish Song Book. Marvin who was pictured sitting at his own piano, smiled reassuringly but sadly he was unable to provide Richard with any inspiration and so found himself replaced by a copy 'Alfie'. Finding the words of the song, 'what's it all about' fitting his mood perfectly. The events of the last few weeks and Gabriella's gentle but persistent 'encouragement' having startled him into action Richard moved outside to join Walter. Several hours later and having failed to progress their plans for the continued running of the South African arm of the business and Richard's return home they were joined by Gabriella.

"Any progress made?" she asked as lifted a jug of freshly made juice and poured.

"Some." Richard claimed although Gabriella's raised eyebrow and knowing smile told him more than words could. Telling him 'great' Gabriella eased herself into onto a patio chair.

"So fill me in," she smiled, the act of smiling transformed her face and causing the tiny lines at the corners eyes to wrinkle and Richard's heart to leap with the old feelings of warmth and respect.

"Well," Richard began as he pulled himself away from the pleasures of her face he then stopped. "Sorry." he faltered "I was miles away, what were you saying?"

""I was about to ask what you wanted to gain from this meeting Richard." Gabriella reminded him as she opened her diary "but you seem to have other things on your mind, like to share?" she asked. Unwilling and fearful of sharing his thoughts Richard told her 'nothing'.

"Nothing Richard" Gabriella told him crossly "aren't you bothered what happens to the business?" Protesting Richard told her that she was being unfair.

"Unfair Richard, you do realise that we have an awful lot of work to do before you leave for Rome, don't you? And" she added "we'll be away from tomorrow night so, that gives us tonight and tomorrow to sort things out?"

"So there's no pressure?" Richard joked feebly.

"But item one remains." Gabriella told him pointedly as she picked up her pen and Richard mirroring her action suggested that step one was to name the problem.

"And" Walter asked joining the rebate for the first time "what is the problem?"

"That I have a business that I don't want." Richard told him.

"Don't want Richard," Walter echoed "is that the truth?"

"It is Walter and I've never been clearer about anything in my life. What I do want, as we all know my friend, is to get back to Grace and come to think about" he added thoughtfully "the last time I so sure about anything was when I first met Grace."

"So the need is Richard?" Gabriella asked.

"For me to get rid of the business" Richard told her and then downcast and slighted by the flow of the conversation Gabriella got to her feet and closing her diary moved to the pool.

"Come on Richard." she demanded with more than a hint of anger "You must have some regrets? What about all the hard work that went into building the business and not only your hard work but the team's and mine?"

"No regrets Gabi" Richard told her casually "do it and move on that's my motto." and then unhappy and dejected by the argument Gabriella moved back to the table and picking up her diary began to move towards the house.

"Okay mister cool guy," she told him over her shoulder, "in that case I suggest that you find his own solution to the problem because to be honest, I have better things to do then watch all I've worked for being tossed aside in a moment's petulance. So," she added "perhaps it's time I moved on as well?"

"Wait Gabi!" The urgent voice called, it was not the voice of Richard but Walter. "I'm sure you didn't mean to be so off hand did you Richard?" he pleaded as he pushed back his chair and getting quickly to his feet took Gabriella's elbow. "Tell her Richard," he said turning. "Tell her you ass." "Well," a rueful Richard conceded "I do recognise your efforts Gabi and the team's, but it's just...well I need to move on, to get my life back on track, you understand don't you Gabi?" he asked.

"Of course I understand you fool, I've understood for the last five years but...oh never mind Richard let's get your life sorted eh and then perhaps we can all move on?"

"In that case" a relieved Walter suggested let's take a break. I'll make some coffee and we'll start again."

Two hours later five options having been suggested, discussed, dissected a decision was arrived at.

"So," Gabriella recapped "You're going to give the Cape Town business to the team."

"I am" Richard confirmed "with you and Walter running it as partners."

"But only until we can train or appoint a regional manager." Walter said as he got to his feet and walked round the table to the now standing Richard. "Congratulations." he said as he took his friend's outstretched hand.

"No, thank you, my friend." Richard said his voice full of emotion and then placing his arm around Walter's shoulder he began to pat rhythmically in the way mothers do when comforting a child. "You've been…" Uncomfortable with the show of emotion Walter took a step backwards and then advanced again as Gabriella, suggesting that the moment called for a group hug pushed back her chair Gabriella walked around the table.

"Thank you chaps she beamed and then the three were together in a warm and joyful hug of celebration and then and unusual for one who tended to like hugs, Richard disengaged myself from the scrum. Embarrassed, joyful but ever the gentleman Walter in his awkwardness tried to pull away but was held in Gabriella's ever tightening grip.

"Not so fast partner." she cautioned and then looking across at Richard as if asking permission kissed Walter gently on his cheek. "Thanks mister," she told him "You've been a brick and a real friend in times of trouble."

"And you Gabriella …" Walter smiled as he took her face between his hands "are fabulous." and then he kissed her gently on her forehead.

"Well I think this meeting is adjourned?" Richard questioned as he picked up his diary.

"For the time being Richard," Gabriella told him, "but only for the time being."

CHAPTER 57
Friday 16th February (Morning)

Without stutter or stumble

"So far, so good Gabi" Richard gloated as he led Gabriella down the narrow corridor and out into a court yard.

"Its early days yet superman," a grinning Gabriella chided "we still have to see Pamela at eleven thirty, Pat at one thirty, then take the files back to the office, get home and catch the nine pm flight to Jo'burg."

"Not a problem," Richard told her as his first client of the day opened the door of his flat and beamed his welcome. Wiping their feet on an obviously new mat the visitors moved to the centre of the room, "This is all very nice Ray," Richard congratulated as he surveyed the gleaming array of new furniture and fittings. "I don't think you've meet Gabriella" he added as his PA stepped forward and offered her hand.

"So how's it going Raymond?" she asked as her hand was engulfed by his the warmth of his smile welcomed them.

"Really great" Raymond told her. "The other place Richard found me was okay but I really love this place and my independence." Nodding her understanding Gabriella moved to the plush sofa her host offered and settling into its red leather comfort prepared to watch her boss at work. "So Ray do you see much of your mother?" Richard asked as if on cue and taking his place next to Gabriella flipped open Raymond's file and prepared to take notes. Without stutter or stumble Raymond explained how his mother had been upset when he moved out.

"But," he volunteered "she's seeing your friend Walter and really seems to like him. But to answer your question Richard, she comes round a couple of times a week. Not too little, not too much and that suits me fine."

"Music to my ears, Ray, so Ray if I asked you to rate your wellbeing, your happiness on a scale of one to ten how would score yourself?"

"A seven or eight I guess, although I do have bad days, you know when my paranoia kicks in and I think people are talking about me."

"Maybe they are talking about you?" Richard suggested "I know people talk about me" he explained as he risked a sideways glance in Gabriella's direction "people just love to gossip."

"But why would people want to gossip about me?"

"Because Ray they have small minds. It's not your problem, it's theirs. So don't think of it as paranoia just gossip."

"Honestly?"

"Honestly!" Richard echoed "Now Ray" he said his voice taking on a serious edge "I'm going back to England for a while, but" he added quickly "don't worry. Walter and Gabriella will be around, won't you Gabi? So if you need to talk just give them a ring okay?"

"Well Gabi" Richard proposed as he steered the Audi towards the R300. "I don't think Ray's out of the woods yet, but he's come a long way."

"And so, thanks to Walter, has his mother." Gabriella suggested.

"Good old Walter." Richard agreed "he's a lovely bloke and you're good together Gabi. I've watched you over the last few days, since Adam...."

"Not now Richard," Gabriella pleaded "save your advice and sympathy for your clients if you don't mind."

CHAPTER 58
Friday 16th tFebruary (Early Afternoon)

There's Nothing We Can Do About The Past...

Pulling the Audi to the curb Richard turned off the ignition. "Now that's interesting." he whispered as eased himself from behind the steering wheel and crossed the pavement.

"Mr Blackwood?" Lee James questioned as he came down the front steps of his home carrying his young daughter. "I'm sorry, but Pamela had to go into work, won't you come in?"

"It was just easier," Lee explain as he poured tea into the already prepared cups "I tried to get a job, but with this black empowerment it's hard for us white guys to find any work. So now Pamela works full time and I'm the chief cook and bottle washer, child minder and gardener. How things have changed" he smiled "but I don't mind it keeps me busy and out of the pubs."

"How is Pam?" Gabriella asked as she turned another page of young Jade's book.

"She's blooming," Lee told her with obvious pride "she enjoys her work and when she comes home we're are a family again. I really love her you know..." and then he paused. "I don't know what she told you, but...."

"Can I ask you a question Lee?" Richard asked as he broke into what he thought may be a long and demeaning speech of recrimination.

"Sure..." Lee told him hesitantly.

"Well," Richard explained "If I were to ask you to rate your happiness on a scale of one to ten what would be your score?"

"Gee is that all you want to know?" Lee sighed with relief. "Well that's easy... I'd say eleven."

"And three weeks ago?" Richard queried.

"Minus twenty Richard, I've been such..."

"Not interested my friend." Richard said as got to his feet. "There's nothing we can do about the past...other than learn from it," he added quickly "But if ever you or Pam want to talk about your future then please give Gabriella a ring. "Now Lee" he said as he held out his hand "thanks for the tea and take care."

The journey from Somerset West to The Strand took less than twenty minutes and with an hour and a half to spare before their next visit Richard was escorting Gabriella across the coast road and towards the Spur Steak House. Richard had often visited the building, first back in the 1970 when his mother had visited from England. Sadly the elegant days of the 'Co op' tea rooms were long gone and now as Richard led the ways up the hollow sounding stairs the unforgettable and slightly sickly aroma of hot meat and BBQ sauce began to permeate the air. Following Gabriella into the still quiet restaurant Richard accepting the mock leather menu from a smiling waiter and nodding his thanks slid into the mock cowhide booth. Ordering fruit juice and coffee Gabriella asked the way to the ladies room and clutching her shoulder bag to her chest excused herself. Left alone Richard let his eyes and then his memory drift across to the now dilapidated and condemned landing stage. In years passed he had walked that jetty with the pregnant Joan and their new son Steven and later with John. Those had been halcyon days, days of evening walks along the beach and then milk shakes at the 'Spur' and fifty years later he had traced the same steps when he had brought Grace, and the young William and James out on holiday.

"So..." a refreshed Gabriella asked as she settled herself into the booth "Who wins the bet?" "Which bet would that be Gabi?" Richard asked as her returned smiling from the pleasures of his reverie.

"The one where you said Lee James would be out getting a job within month." Gabriella reminded him.

"Ah that one" Richard said feigning reflection "Well Gabi to be honest I think I said 'out looking for a job' didn't I?"

"You did." Gabriella admitted.

"And little miss selective memory, I also remember you saying that it would be a bet you wouldn't mind losing, correct?" he asked. Reaching into her hand bag Gabriella pulled out her wallet and clicked it open.

"Okay you win." she scowled "So how much do I owe you?"

"So Richard, how's the shoulder Richard?" Patricia Morgan asked as she led the way onto her balcony and a table set for afternoon tea.

"Fine thanks," Richard told her solemnly "it only hurts when I laugh."

"So he feels no pain at all then Patricia." Gabriella teased and then waited for the rebuke.

"Oh Pat I just can't get the staff!" Richard complained with a winked at his client.

"I'm afraid I'll have to disagree as with you Richard." Patricia told him sternly "Like all men you'd be lost without a woman behind you. Can you imagine managing without the lovely Gabriella?" she challenged.

"I wouldn't even be able to get out of bed in the morning without Gabriella." Richard conceded as he spread fresh butter and then strawberry jam on his newly baked scone.

"Ah that's nice Richard." Patricia beamed not appreciating that the words Richard spoke were more than just nice, they were perfectly true, for without his PA Richard was sure he wouldn't have survived losing Grace or Steven's kidnapping. Somewhat embarrassed but pleased Gabriella opened the Morgan file and removing the top of her pen suggested that they get down to business.

"Thanks for the compliment Richard." Gabriella said as the pair walked out into the bright afternoon sunshine. "It's been one hell of a time for us all. We've both struggled, you with Grace and me with Adam. For me Adam is now history but for you and Grace, Richard well," she told him with a smile that failed to hide her pain "and all I can say is that I wish you well" Placing his arm on hers Richard turned to face his lover.

"Gabi...?" he started to say.

"Richard..." Gabriella echoed.

"So what are your thoughts about Gabriella now that her new man has departed?" Richard asked as sat in the study he raised his whiskey glass in salute.

"Well if you're asking me about Adam Richard," Walter answered before adding a 'gee that name's hard to say'. With a quick smirk Richard agreed the point and then became serious. "But did we give the guy a chance." he asked.

"A chance Richard," Walter queried angrily "did he deserve a chance? The guy was a bully and was well out of order. Anyway he's back in OZ now, so end of story eh."

"But did she love him Walter?" Richard almost whispered, fearful that even at this distance from the lounge Gabriella may hear.

"Hi what is this Richard?" Walter asked his tone equally conspiratorial but questioning.

"I'm not sure Richard told him. "Perhaps being shot in the head opens a man's mind?"

"That bullet damn near opened your brain fella." Walter laughed nervously. Appreciating the joke Richard smiled briefly and before once more became serious.

"But did we chase the man away Walter, did we give him a chance, did we give them a chance?"

"Maybe we did let our feelings for Gabriella get in the way" Walter conceded "but for good reasons Richard."

"And those reasons would be?" Richard asked gently.

"Do you mean our feelings of wanting her to be happy?" Walter questioned.

"Yes... but are they the only feelings you have for her?" Richard pried.

"And what other feeling would I have?" Walter asked defensively.

"I'm not sure." Richard told him meekly "but you two seem to have grown so close and you asking her the go on safari with you, do you love her Walter?" Richard asked bluntly.

"Yes." The answer finally came. "Yes Richard I love her." Walter told him "but I'm not sure I want this conversation now and with you." Nodding his understanding Richard got to his feet and moved to the window.

"Yes I understand Walter but..."

"But what Richard"

"But...well... I'm going back to England to find Grace. Grace is my soul mate Walter, she's my... everything and yet, there have been times when...when I thought that Gabriella and I ..." and then he stopped. "I love Gabriella, Walter hell I'm so confused." Now it was Walter's turn to nod his understanding.

"Yes I know," he said quietly "and I've known for a long time. In some ways that's why I hung back. And then I hung back when she started seeing that bloody Adam. Oh Richard I loved Barbara, I guess like you loved...love Grace." he corrected and then he stopped. "But now Adam's gone and you're leaving so I'm going to try and make her mine.

"And this is the guy who told me we don't own people?" Richard grinned.

"I'm going to try and make her mine Richard," Walter continued ignoring the interruption. "And I'm going to try and make her happy. She's had a rough time but had always been there for us so now it's time she was looked after and cherished."

"Cherish?" Richard questioned.

"Yes Richard cherish," Walter repeated "and it's time I found happiness again, so off you go Richard find Grace, and when you do cherish her."

CHAPTER 59
Tuesday 20th February (Afternoon)

My dear Grace

Grace Blackwood had slowly begun to adjust to a life without her husband. She was, as Gabriella had pointed out to Katie a strong woman, but it was a strength that both Grace and Richard knew to be largely a facade. For Grace Blackwood had learnt to wear one face for the world and to keep the other, her frightened little girl face hidden from everyone bar Richard and her mother.

Grace had grown up in the north of England as the youngest girl in a family of four. Her mother had left the family home after a brief affair when Grace was only four years old. Her father had not found bringing up four children on his own easy. This had left him lacking any measure of tact or diplomacy. He would chastise his off spring with statements like 'if the cap fits wear it' or 'if you don't like it lump it'. These statements had in turn become the motto of his older children and Grace had had to put up with the 'playful bullying' of her siblings who would make her cry and then tease her calling her a 'whingeing baby'. Grace at forty years old now fully understood her mother's reasons for leaving her father and had in fact become her mother's closest ally. Over the years Grace's childhood adversities had moulded her into the woman she was, outwardly strong but inwardly delicate and at times unsure of her place in the world.

Grace and had first met Richard when they worked together at a 'special school', Grace's first job after completing a child care course at college. Richard had been the first kind and caring man she had ever met and she had found his undemanding, non judgmental way of working with the children and staff at first disconcerting and then liberating. Like Richard she was unsure how their relationship had materialized the way it had. His 'what would you say' remark had shocked and disappointed her. She had thought of their relationship as one of mutual respect and for the good of the children. Her only other experience of men had been built around the demands of her father and brothers and the smelly testosterone filled demands of the boys at school and college. Having discussed Richard's 'pass' with her mother she had been advised her to 'walk away' and that Richard would never leave his wife and that she would never find happiness with a married man. Grace had listened carefully to her mother's words but a week later had made her own judgement about him. Her early days with this man, who was twenty one years her senior, had been filled with excitement and doubt, but mostly with a feeling of being loved. Times had been difficult but her love for him, and she had no doubt, his love for her, had pulled them through. The coming of their first child William had added to Grace's feeling of 'belonging' and of having her own role and place in the world. William had not been an easy baby and had cried and demanded her attention but, Richard who at fifty was now a dad for the third time seemed to take his new son's temperament in his stride. This made Grace feel as though she was either unloving or incompetent. The arrival two years later of their second child James helped Grace to see that not all babies were difficult or demanding and although the birth had been 'uncomfortable' as Richard had described it, the early days with her new family had been some of her most fulfilling. Richard had managed to remain well and buoyant for most of those early years, although he did complain of being tired, a state of being that seemed to escalate as the years passed. Grace had understood his fatigue, 'being a dad to young children in your fifties was bound to take it out of you' and so she had allowed him to go off to Africa for three weeks every year to be with his older sons. It was on one of these trips that Richard's eldest son Steven had suggested expanding his practice to Cape Town. Grace had been unhappy about the venture, particularly when Richard had told her he would need to be away for two or three months every year and that he would be taking his PA with him. Grace had only met the PA once and had been surprised to see this women that Richard had described as 'old and foreign' as a tall, well groomed and articulate business woman. Telling herself that she had no doubts about the loyalty of her man, but unsure about his wanting to be away from home for that amount of time, had left her wondering about the strength of their marriage. Richard had gone out to Africa in the early December of 2008 and Grace and the boys had travelled out to spend Christmas with him. The boys had enjoyed the sun, the sand and the swimming pool, but Grace had missed her family, particularly her brothers, who had over the years grown and matured and now had wives and children of their own. On their return home from the Cape Grace had told Richard that she would not be going out to the Cape again and had asked him to sell or delegate the running of his 'African enterprise' to someone else. Richard had promised that he would, but eight months later he had raised the subject again and he and Grace had fallen out and parted, or more correctly Richard had left her. Taking the boys to spend Christmas with her mother in the Lake District she had again been subjected to her mother's 'I told you so' monologue; even though Grace had pointed out she and Richard had lived happily together for almost twenty years. When Richard failed to return home Grace's world had fallen apart. Her mother had then come south to look after the boys allowing Grace to spend more time with her many close friends, drinking rosé wine and pouring out her pain and disbelief that Richard could have done this to her. During the Christmas break Grace had taken the boys to stay with her mother and on returning home had found two messages from Richard on the answer phone. The first was totally incomprehensible, something about kidnapping and sadness. The second simply said, 'Please phone me and I love you'. Grace's initial feelings on hearing his voice was heart quickening joy, a joy that was quickly followed by anger, anger she hadn't felt since her childhood and she cursed him loudly using words she hadn't used since her school days. When her anger had passed she sat on the bottom step of stairs and cried, her words mirroring those of her husband several weeks earlier and six thousand miles away, "Richard my love I'm so sorry" she sobbed and then her crying stopped and her mood changed. "Richard Blackwood" she said cursed, "If you want me back you're going to have to try a lot harder than just leaving me an answer phone message". And with that thought she took herself to bed.

On the Tuesday the 21st of April Grace Blackwood received a registered envelope. Inside were two items, one was a letter which she put to one side, the other was a cardboard file containing flight tickets to Rome. Putting the tickets down on the dining room table she turned her attention to the letter. It was just a single hand written page that she recognised as Richard's.

'My dear Grace' she read, 'please don't tear this letter up just yet. Grace I know that I have caused you much pain, not just over the last few months put probably the last few years'. Tossing the letter onto the dining table she went through to the kitchen and filling the kettle flicked down the 'on' switch. Then returning to the dining room she picked up the letter. 'Grace I want to tell you how sorry I am and well... I don't really want to do it by letter so I'm enclosing flight tickets for Rome. I've book us into a hotel and you are free to decide on single or double rooms. I'll be flying into Rome the day before you and will meet you at the airport. Please come, all my love, Richard'. Putting down the letter Grace Blackwood went to make coffee. In her mind she had no doubt about what she would do, but read the letter again and then telephoned her mother.

CHAPTER 60
Saturday 7th March (Afternoon)

The Willow Weeps

As usual Richard made sure that he was at the airport in good time. With more than an hour to spare he walked the busy concourse and then settled himself close to the arrivals gate. Striking his usual waiting pose of hands behind head and his eyes closed Richard tried to fight off the anxiety and fear. The last four months had been a roller coaster of emotions. His angry and bloody minded attitude to Grace's request that he think again about his South Africa venture had turned into a deep and consuming depression. It was a depression that had led him, with the help of two good friends, to review his life and to try and unlock thoughts that had been long buried. Over the months his thoughts and dreams had held recurring themes, themes that consisted of bereavement and loss, anger, frustration and guilt. Through it all he had tried to hold on to the thought that he was still a decent human being. As he sat and waited for Grace to arrive the words and music of a Sinatra song came into in his head. 'Regrets, I've had a few, but then again too few to mention'. Maybe that had been part of his problem, until Walter and Rose Freeman had so skilfully helped him to replay his life he had always fought the idea that he had regrets. Throughout Richard's early life he had blocked out all things negative and held onto the thought that everything would be alright, that he just needed to weather the storm and then move on, to be like the 'Willow' and dance and sing through the storms of life. But then the unthinkable had happened and he had been unable to cope. Unable to cope with the relentless onslaught of the storm, no longer able to bend like the willow he had snapped and been laid low. In those dark days when all had seemed lost, Walter had been there to remind him that like the willow he had roots and that those roots were deeply grounded in the love of Grace.

Richard's trip to Namibia helped him draw a line under his past. Flying to the Windhoek Country Club the friends had been able to enjoy the privacy and delights of their own private verandas and it was whilst Richard was sitting on his veranda enjoying a 'sun downer' when he received a call from reception informing them that two men from NABTRAV had arrived. Asking the receptionist to send the men his room Richard had then asked his friend's to join him. When they knocked on his door Gabriella had gone to greet their visitors. The first man to enter the room had been a very tall and broad shouldered man who introduced himself as 'Charms Oosthuizen'. The second and much shorter man then introduced himself as John Blackwood. It was a fact that Gabriella, having taken the risk of telephoning John's wife was already well aware of. Trying to keep her excitement and joy under control Gabriella had then led the men through the spacious lounge and out onto the veranda.

"Katie" she announced "this is Mr Oosthuizen, he will be guiding us on our trip and this Richard," she said added after a pause, "Is your son John. Walter could you please get these gentlemen a drink?"

Later that evening Richard went with his boys to the bar where they discussed the events of the last six months and, despite Richard's apprehension it soon became clear that the 'ties that bind' were far stronger than even the combined egos of the Blackwood males. The following day the party left for 'the trip of a life time' where for five nights they slept under the wide African sky, the calls of hyena, lion and leopard filling the darkness. A short detour into Botswana followed giving Richard, for the first time the pleasure of spending time with his first born grandson Samuel. Then north to Zimbabwe and the mighty Victoria Falls where in the less than salubrious bar of the Victoria Falls airport Richard spent the final hours of his adventure. When the time for him to leave came he walked with his companions towards the departure gate. Gingerly taking the giant's hand Richard thanked Charms for a fabulous trip and then he turned to Katie.

"Be happy young woman and look after my boy. Promise?" he demanded with a smile.

"I promise Richard, and you take care." Then he was holding Gabriella. There were no words, just her soft wet tears on his cheek and then she was backing away, letting his hand fall and turning towards Katie for comfort.

"Thank you my friend, I'll…" Richard said as he threw his arms around Walter's shoulders.

"And thank you Richard." Walter told him "thank you for your trust and faith. You know there were times when I…"

"Oh yes me too pal," Richard laughed "but we did it didn't we. Now my friend, look after these ladies for me and I'll see you when I see you?" Then with his sons on either arm Richard walked towards the gate.

"You're a good man Steven Blackwood," he told his first born "now you take care and I'll see you soon." and then he was holding John. "Never never ever let my stupidity get in the way again John." he pleaded. "Life's far too short. Now go and be happy" Richard told him as his tears began to roll unashamedly down his cheeks. For several silent minutes Richard stood with his boys and then he was walking again. Handing his boarding pass to the waiting official Richard turned and looked back. Back to Steven and Katie and to Gabriella who had slipped her hand into Walters and then to John who lifting his arm in silent salute smiled broadly and whispered a silent "I love you dad." Richard's reply when it came was from way back down the years, from a time when he had tucked the tiny John into his little bed. "I loved you first" he said tearfully and then he was gone.

Richard sat in the airport at Rome and shook himself from his reverie and then checking his watch realized that he now had less than ten minutes to wait for Grace's arrival. Also realising that his bladder needed attention he set off hurriedly to find a toilet. His mission complete he returned to arrivals and taking his place as near to the gate as his 'British reserve' and the bloody pushy foreigners would allow he placed his hands 'nonchalantly' behind his back. Two minutes later the double opaque glass door 'swished' open but no Grace emerged. Again he waited his heart leaping every time the doors moved. For the next fifteen minutes Richard continued to wait as close friends were reunited and tired placard holding business men escorted suited colleagues to waiting taxis. Feeling uncomfortable and conspicuous Richard loitered for a further half hour and then moving to the information desk asked if Grace Blackwood had boarded her flight. Informed by an articulate and refined Italian that such information could not be given Richard returned to arrivals gate hall. Settling back into the discomfort of black and chrome seat Richard fears began to take hold. Had she missed her flight or God forbid had she had an accident'. Suddenly he felt tired. The trip to Namibia, the flight back to Johannesburg and the onward flight to Rome had all taken their toll on him. His excitement and anticipation at seeing Grace that had kept his mind and body alert but now he felt drained.

"Come back to me Grace please my love." Richard whispered as his eyelids began to close and then she was there. Running towards him, her ankle length coat billowing behind her like the cloak of a super hero. Getting to his feet Richard began to move forward, slowly at first and then he too was running. Running and running until she was in his arms and he was gently caressing her now long, soft, curls. They began to sway, to sway as they had done so many times before, swaying gently, moving slowly and rhythmically as if to some unheard melody, lost in an overwhelming feeling of love, warmth and belonging.

"Sir si sono ben?" the voice came from far way. "Sir you are well?" the women's voice repeated in English. It was a voice of concern, but it was not Grace's voice and opening his eyes Richard blinked into the bright lights of the terminal building.

"What? Sorry." Richard spoke the words slowly as he tried to make sense of where he was. Then the cold reality struck. Grace was not here. She would not be coming. It was over. Standing Richard wiped a single tear from his cheek.

"Yes fine, yes thank you I'm fine." he lied and then gathering his bag, thoughts and composure he moved slowly towards the exit, the car park, his hotel and an empty bed.

Printed in Great Britain
by Amazon